SHADOWOLF VOLUME 1
THE CELENIC EARTH CHRONICLES

BOOK 2

DRAGONRIDER

An epic fantasy novel
by Shaun M Jooste

NOVELS BY AUTHOR

THE CELENIC EARTH CHRONICLES
1. Windfarer
2. DragonRider
3. *Sadgi*

Silent Hill: Betrayal

CONTENTS

PART THREE: ELDOR'S FOREST

ANNEXURES

This novel is dedicated to my loving wife and wonderful children, who as always have shown great love, patience, support and encouragement while writing my novels

To see the full quality map, please visit
https://celenicearth.wordpress.com/visual-glossary/the-windfarer/ and click
on the map

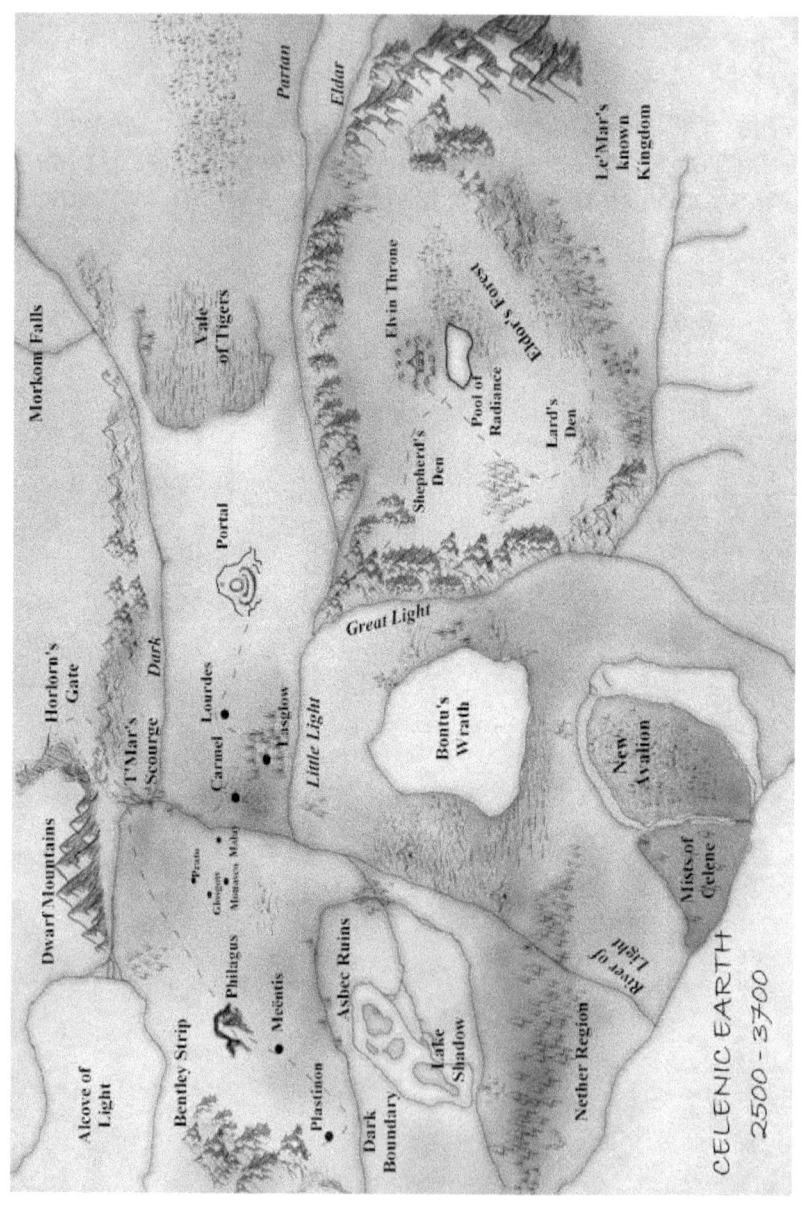

FULFILMENT OF THE WINDFARER PROPHECY PROLOGUE

It has been a year since the fulfilment of the Windfarer Prophecy. I pen this down in the hopes that there will be a generation to read it. It may be that my knowledge of what transpired last year will be essential in the event of my death.

Much has passed since the power node was released, and none of them favourable. Eldor has lost the area that once contained the *Pernonil* forest. The mountains and forest adjoining the area has been taken by Le'Mar, the dark lord. He keeps creatures on watch, waiting for the moment when he obtains the Heart of Tigers.

Asbec Island and the land south of it has been taken and named, "The Dark Boundary." Le'Mar's camps that were once housed in the east of Eldor's Forest have been divided in order to fortify the Boundary.

Ah, I see I forget myself. I have gotten ahead of the story. I need to explain the tale that led up to these dark times. I need to explain how the Windfarer Prophecy started…

Although my son Shadowolf played the essential role in the prophecy, and it indeed started with his birth, I feel I must go back a few years more. It was a time of hardship and the orcs had first showed signs of their existence. They attacked villages, killing humans in order to resurrect them for their army. We did not know where they had come from, or if anyone ruled them, but a man named Mercius led one of these armies of orcs.

Mercius had hoped to catch my Degron tribe off-guard. Although the walls of Avalion were quite secure, the volume of his army would have destroyed us. But our Lord Bontu watched over us, and my friend Malkius Saphin in Costen saw the army creeping along the river on his border. Malkius gathered his army and journeyed to Avalion, arriving just in time to save us. We had victory that night, and captured Mercius. He was imprisoned in Eldor's Dungeons north of Avalion. Unfortunately, Mercius's four elemental leaders, known as the Sandrihelin, escaped.

According to Masara (who brought news of my son's disappearance last year), Mercius had split his soul as they dragged him to the prisons. While his dark half lay enclosed by the magical cell, his better half roamed the world. This better half named himself Farnerd Malerus.

I was blessed with two sons a few years later. One was dropped by my doorstep a few months before Shadowolf's birth. His origin is unknown, but we named him Darcwulf. When we had to travel to Carmel for the Masaran Phenomenon we left Darcwulf in the care of my sister Listren in Costen.

It was during our travel to Carmel that we were attacked by a band of orcs. During the attack, Shadowolf was born. The men of the ship fought valiantly and in the end five of us defended the new-born babe and his mother with wind, fire, water, earth and spirit. Masara commented that he feels this power created the power node beneath Shadowolf's body. We did not realise it was there at that moment, however, having just expelled all of our energy.

But the power node was felt by other elementals. Mercius must have stirred in his cell when it raced through his veins, and I am sure his counterpart Farnerd cringed with excitement too. One other felt it, although he was unknown to me at the time. His name is Le'Mar, and he is the true conductor of the war.

Farnerd was the first to react. He started the construction of a College above the node and when Shadowolf was two it was completed. The node gave the school elemental properties, and because he was an elemental too he decided it best to teach Elementalism as tertiary education to young adults.

The four Sandrihelin heard of the school, and decided it was time to use their elemental abilities as an occupation. I am not sure at what point Farnerd revealed his duel nature to them, but he employed them nevertheless.

The power node distressed many people, as no one knew what its purpose was. Many greedy elementals hungered to obtain the power with the assumption that they would become Sagdi's, an omnipotent elemental who has mastered all five elements. Everyone wanted to know how to release the power and turned to the high elf king Eldor. Eldor was as bewildered as we were and sent some of his elder elves to investigate. Farnerd permitted them entry, but also commissioned three Orion sages in fear that the elves would keep the secret to themselves.

Many writings were jotted by the sages, but the most prominent of note was by the Orion sage, Philgarn Asmuth. Philgarn warned that the power should not be left open and, upon instruction by the Orion, went to the College to conceal the node by lore and passages within the foundation of the College.

The writings of Philgarn became widely accepted and one prophecy, divided into three sub-prophecies, became infamous: The Windfarer, The DragonRider and The *Sadgi* Prophecy. In "A Compendium to the Trichotomic Prophecy," Philgarn mentions the rise of a dark lord to lead the orcs, and that only the Windfarer could claim the power node as his own. But he also said that once the power was claimed it did not mean the end of the war, but only the beginning, leading to the fulfilment of the other two prophecies.

We feared for the worst. Mercius had been called a Windfarer (or *Enodhim* as the elves name it) many times as his skill with the wind was remarkable. Le'Mar must have known this, but for some reason did not react immediately.

When my son was twenty and in his final year at the college, Le'Mar must have realised that the only way to know the truth was to release Mercius from the prison. The prophecy stated that "The Masaran Phenomenon will awaken his power," and he had already missed five in the twenty years of the node's existence to do so.

We have puzzled and debated at length the dark lord's decision not to release the node himself. Masara claims that Le'Mar is an accomplished *Enodhim*, and did not need Mercius at all. We feel that he is up to something that we have not yet deciphered. Either that or he had tried without our knowledge and failed.

It was during this time that my son became involved with the prophecy. Masara says that he had always been a part of it from the conception of the node, but my son was, as all of us were, unaware of it.

The Mer-Kingdom from *Marsandil* tried to warn him, but they were attacked by aVampyere and Lellian became the new mer-king. The city Shenama was then destroyed by Mercius and McCaniban to the north of the college at the same time that Le'Mar attempted to steal the Heart of Tigers from Jin-Tai sanctuary.

This produced two respective results: The College was closed by Farnerd, as he needed to keep the node secure in preparation for the Phenomenon. And Chenesia from the Vale of Tigers decided to journey to Eldor's Forest to seek protection for the Sanctuary.

My son returned home to the War Council with a gift from the Mer-Kindgom. Shedaaij the Merlani took to his heart and I could see that he cared for her deeply. But the war stopped any love developing between them as he took it upon himself to visit Mercius's old prison.

There, he found Dren, Fornoren and Masnen, the gargoyles. They agreed to join him, if only he would help them find the Lapis Pins, magical gems that would stop them from turning into stone in the sun.

Shadowolf accepted, but Masara placed another task on us. Abutja Blue of Iceland was being manipulated into believing that there was no war by Le'Mar through an Amethyst pendant. Iceland's defences remained low. We needed to remove the pendant.

My son succeeded in obtaining the Lapis Pins, but Mercius killed Fornoren and Masnen. Thereafter, Shadowolf failed to meet with Abutja Blue, and so I went to meet with him. I was denied my request, but it was decided that Shedaaij use her mermaid powers to seduce him into taking the Amethyst off.

We did not anticipate that the Amethyst would allow Abutja to withstand her powers. She was taken as prisoner, but Shadowolf intercepted through stealth and removed the pendant. An attendee saw Abutja's generals enter his chamber. There was a cry of death, and the generals, now in their true purorc forms, left.

We lost Iceland. Although Shadowolf and I tried our best, we could not save it. I took as many refugees from as I could, while Shadowolf continued fighting.

The next morning Shadowolf returned to Iceland alone to

search for refugees. In his absence, the War Council decided to move Hasner to Costen, and then both Hasner and Costen to Avalion. It was also in his absence that the Shadow Clan was formed by those loyal to my son.

My son rode into Hasner with one of the enemy's horses and a refugee. There the Hand of the Orion, a special group of warriors, met him and journeyed with him to Costen. The Hand joined the Clan.

Before they could return home, Lellian had sent a message to Shedaaij and Shadowolf about the war occurring in the oceans between the mermaids and the sirens. Shedaaij left to assist the mer-king, and Shadowolf returned home to ask if the Mer-Kindgom could be offered warrens beneath Avalion.

We had two months of peace. Shadowolf grew restless as the Masaran Phenomenon was close, and I am sure Le'Mar and Mercius felt the same. I do not know if Farnerd and Mercius became one again, but Masara assures me it would have been necessary if he wanted the strength to release the node.

Masara also informed me that he had realised that Mercius could not possibly be the correct Windfarer and that he had sent this message to Shadowolf in the Mists of Celene. But, knowing my son, he obviously ignored this information in the event that Masara was wrong.

What happened in the College no one knows. We all felt the power being released. We all feared for the worst. Masara found the remains of two of the Sandrihelin, with no knowledge of where the third and fourth were.

Mercius's body was also gone, and we assume Farnerd's with it too. But Mercius did not join Le'Mar in attacking Eldor's Forest when *Pernonil* fell. He was not there when the dark lord was enraged and captured Chenesia and fled. Something had gone terribly wrong for Le'Mar, and we can only hope that Shadowolf had destroyed Mercius and claimed the node as his own.

But my son is gone. Masara informs me Asgorna the Dragon King had taken him into the mountains. This is the only hope I have, yet I have still heard no further news. Masara resides with Eldor in the forest, but when I ask he simply says that Shadowolf will return when the time is right.

We have seen signs of dragons traversing the skies. It seems that Le'Mar has already chosen his champion for the DragonRider Prophecy. And still, I do not know when my son will return to us…

Nighthale Degron
Degron Core
New Avalion

PART ONE

T'MAR'S SCOURGE

THE EAGLE'S MESSAGE
CHAPTER ONE

You have done what must be done. You have wandered the earth in mist and ignorance, but with your eyes now wide open you cannot escape the truth. You have been hardened and shaped for this purpose. Many will die, but many more will live because of you.

The time of the Sadgi is coming. He who will claim the four elements and the power of the soul to harness them to his will, it is he who will decide the fate of us all. I believe that you are that Sadgi.

My time is almost up, but before I leave this world let me train you in the ways of old. As an Enodhim, the wind will be your sails. As a Merlandsi, you will be emperor of the waters. As a Goudlem, the earth will be your ally. As a KariemsaPh, the fires will rise from the deepest depths. And as a Solem, the soul will be mastered.

You will be the Sadgi. You must be, in order to face him, for he is greater than you. So I leave you with one last warning, Enodhim. Do not face him until you are ready…

***

The eagle descended from the heights of the cold mountains, through the swift air that carried it towards the east and upon the dreams of a forgotten landscape. In the eagle's heart flowed the blood of dragons, but within its mind it held a song of invitation. Its eyes held the words of the prophecy, but its tongue held the tune of potent doom.

For the dragon's prophecy was an invitation to doom. And the dark lord held the prophecy within the chambers of his heart.

The eagle reached the River of Light, and then headed south to New Avalion.

"Hold on… one more!" one of the tavern folk shouted up at him. He was tilting on the table top, the red drink in his hand spilling over onto the wooden surface. The smirk on his face outweighed the shadows on the walls cast by the bracketed torches.

"What tales do you wish told?" he said in his heartiest voice. The folk laughed and cheered. "The orcs may have taken over the lands, the elves may have lost some trees to the dark lord, but I have plenty of song in me left tonight!"

"Oh sit down, Darc!" Amornis the barman exclaimed from his stool at the bar.

"No, no, another song!" the crowd encouraged.

"How can I not entertain my people?" he replied, to which the crowd raised their drinks and shouted. His bald head reflected the shimmering torch flames, and his muscular arms and torso complimented his short height. A black dragon was tattooed on his right arm whilst he had a tiger stretched out down the middle of his back. He raised his drink with hands that held dirty, short fingernails, and his feet were spying out of broken shoes.

"Someone pass me my staff," he called to the crowd, making his way down. The folk of the Hasner Green tavern were not impressed, and made their disappointment well heard. He smiled and tried to make his way to the far wall, but vertigo took over and he fell into someone's arms. Laughing, he looked up at a stone face. An amulet lay on the beast's naked chest, and wings were tucked away neatly behind his back. The gargoyle wore nothing but long briefs.

"Dren!" he shouted and struggled to make his way up. He embraced the gargoyle and then paraded around him, staring him up and down. "I would say you look better than the last time I saw you, but it seems…"

"Some things don't change, Darcwulf," Dren said to him. "Others apparently do."

"Oh give me a break, batty," he replied. "It's my night off. I am just having some fun like the other delightful specimens here." A barely clad woman walked past him and he reached down to pinch her. She exclaimed shortly, but gave him an appraised stare that Dren could tell was nothing but mischievous in nature.

"There is something I must tell you," Dren said.

"Well, it must be something important that it made you come see me after all this time. How long has it been now?"

"I am not sure," Dren answered. "Time does not hold as much value to me as it does to humans."

"Of course," Darcwulf said, staring at another few gorgeous women passing by. "Immortality tends to do that to you."

"Never mind," the gargoyle said, turning to leave.

"Suit yourself," he said, also turning away.

He stopped. An eagle was flapping in front of him. It stared into his drunken eyes as he tried to focus his attention at it.

"This..." he said as he put his drink on the table, "is where a person realises he has had enough."

He tried to dismiss the apparent vision with his hand, when it moved out of the way and returned before his gaze.

"Move!" he shouted and hit at it, but it swiftly dodged him and pecked at his hand.

"Ouch!" he said as he shook his hand. Slowly he raised it and looked at the dripping blood. "An eagle? In a pub...?"

The bird laid out its wings and soared into the air, catching the focus of the drunken crowd. It snatched up Darcwulf's staff from the far wall and rose to the centre of the tavern. Without warning, flames from the staff ran up its feathers and flooded from its eyes, pouring into the damp air and warming it instantly.

The fire was racing around the bird which fed the show constantly. Within moments the eagle turned into a burning phoenix. Flames roared in the air until the people saw dragon wings flapping and a dragon head reared up and spat at the crowd. The crowd ducked, but soon realised that the bar was not up in flames and resumed in anxious mirth and laughter.

The image changed to the fiery dragon returning to a small mountain, with a full sun behind the peaks. It bore something in its claws. Darcwulf shook his head to expel the dizziness and missed the eagle moving from the display, leaving the fires, phoenix and staff to awe the crowd. The eagle flew over to his shoulder and when it realised he wasn't paying attention, it placed its claws hard on his neck and yanked his ear.

The eagle gave one deafening screech into his ear and Darcwulf shouted. The fire burst throughout the tavern and there was no spot in it that was left untouched. Still trying to dislodge the bird from his shoulder, he heard a voice deep within the fire, lost somewhere within the screech too; it was a voice he recognised and sorely missed. It said one thing, and he widened his eyes. His sobriety had returned, and fear filled his heart instead.

The eagle and fires were gone, with the staff falling hard to the polished wooden floor. Darcwulf stared vacantly at his staff while the crowd cheered for more…

The children sat in eager chatter before the three women. Fransiska blew lightly on the flute, yet its tune carried over the delighted faces. Her long black hair was tied back to reveal her deep amber eyes, rich lips and beautiful face. She wore a green dress that split at the hips to reveal a white skirt underneath. Butterfly pins were fastened to her shoulders, and an elvin leaf hung on a necklace.

The sound of the violin carried off from Angelia's shoulders. The court's people beamed gleefully at them, dancing to the music. Her earrings glittered in the torchlight and the fires that the men in the court attended to. Even in the dark times, a little joy could go a long way to alleviate the fears. The open court's air was chill, and so she had chosen to wear a warm jersey over a long shirt, with long leggings to keep her legs from going numb. She shuddered when she looked at Fransiska's clothing, but the girl seemed impervious to the cold.

Skywolf picked the strings of her blue guitar. To complement the shade, she wore a sky blue shirt with white leggings. On the back of the shirt was a design of a wolf's head.

Lord Malkius's people danced before his daughter in the court of Costen Castle. The castle was in the north of Avalion, in the region known as Saphin Vale. It was the first circle outside the core of Avalion, followed by Watre Hills and finally with Lowle Village on the outskirts.

The core of Avalion belonged to the Degron Tribe, hosted by Nighthale Degron. The lords of the various tribes met constantly within the core, always on the lookout for the dark lord's influence, preparing their defences.

Part of the core was the lake known as *Avalendil*, serving as a moat to the Degron Tribe. Its waters ran into the earth beneath the foundations of Avalion, separating the tribe from the other three tribes. Bridges and causeways were constructed as a means of travel to the core.

And *Avalendil* served as another kingdom, a kingdom far separated from the humans within waters that reached through domed tunnels to the River of Light, the Great Light, Mars'Nar River and the southern ocean. The city beneath Avalion held the Mer-Kingdom, governed by the Mer-King Lellian, he who keeps an ever-watchful eye on the sirens and water-demons that have plagued the depths of the ocean ever since the first onslaught of the dark lord.

But the waters have been quiet for many months now. Since the downfall of Mercius, the aVampeyeric warrior of the dark lord, and the loss of the power node, Le'Mar had quietly been taking land to his name, turning the humans in the lands into dreadful creatures.

His most foul creations were the hurorc, a terrible hybrid between human and orc. They served him not in warrior abilities, but in sheer numbers. As humans fell, their bodies were used in his terrible fires to create the beasts. And many had fallen in the conquest.

Skywolf was unsure how much of the land had become his domain. But Avalion still stood strong, a formidable fortress of hope in the form of New Avalion. The tribes were again united as they had been in the time of Masara, a time long forgotten.

Yet the rumours spread that there was one that refused to forget the old days. The tales of the Battle of T'Mar's Scourge were retold in all the homes and taverns, for it seemed that it was the battle where the dark lord had begun his machinacious planning. Could it be, witnessing the death of T'Mar at the falls, that Le'Mar had turned his heart against the world?

But the questions were no longer uttered, and answers no longer searched, for discovering the truth would in no way stop the dark lord from his quest. Yet, what had happened to Masara? Where was the champion that had fallen at the Scourge, and why would the dark lord punish the world for a crime that Masara had done to him?

The music filled Skywolf's heart with chagrin. She felt no pity for Le'Mar, for the loss he had endured at Mercius's death did not affect them at all. Another loss had crawled into their hearts, a loss felt by the whole of Avalion.

She remembered the announcement as clear as day. Her mind travelled back the two years since the fall of Mercius, the day that the Windfarer had obtained the power node. Had it been that long since she had seen the heroic elemental that gave his life to protect the earth?

Although her hands still played true on the guitar strings, a tear fell from the corner of her eye. Shadowolf had failed. The power node had been released, but it seemed as though it had been the wrong time. Mercius's two followers had been found dead in the fields, but Mercius and Shadowolf's body were not to be found. There were so many rumours concerning their disappearance. One tale told of a dragon that claimed Shadowolf's body as its own was the only ray of hope; that ray of hope lay kindled in the ashes of Skywolf's heart.

Her love for him now belonged to another. She looked up at her fiancé Dredwolf's face. He had so much compassion and understanding towards her. He understood her loss for a man that had not loved her in return, and he had been there for her when the announcement from Nighthale had been made. The tears that had rolled down Shadowolf's father's face had been shared by the community.

And still the music played. That loss two years ago no longer stained the people's hearts. They now lived for every little bit of joy they could find. Their music gave them a beat to dance to; although the beat of hope was fading, the beat of faith dwindling with the torches and the beat of love was setting with Creotos the sun.

The prophecy had failed them. The opportunity of the Windfarer had died with the loss of Mercius and Shadowolf. Both despair and hope had faded that day.

The sound of an eagle on the parapet of the court caught her attention. It landed softly and flapped its wings into place on its side, looking down on Fransiska, Angelia and Skywolf. Something about it disturbed Skywolf, and the music fell silent as the girls wondered why she had stopped playing.

Fransiska and Angelia followed her gaze to the eagle that leapt from the parapet and glided down to a raised pond on the west side of the court. The crowd stopped dancing and giggling, and watched as the eagle landed on the bricks that held the water.

There was nothing unusual about the eagle. It had brown wings with a white head and chest, its beak as yellow as Creotos. It looked around at them, but stopped again at the girls.

"What's the matter?" Dredwolf asked when he reached her side.

"That bird..." she started to say when the eagle took flight above the pond.

The water rose from the pond and swirled into the air. Mud splattered on the closest groups until the water was clear from any dirt. It shimmered in the glow of Sothos the moon and an image formed from its centre.

A dragon's head leered over them all, an emerald fury glowing out of its eyes. The eagle left the water and flew down to the girls. The dragon spouted water in the air, leaving the crowd in awe.

There was a glint in the eagle's eye and Skywolf frowned at it, trying to decipher its meaning. The eagle looked back at the dragon, and the girls watched as it roared and flew towards the image of a moon and mountain, something apparently clasped in its claws.

The image exploded and the court was immediately flooded with water. The people screamed and gulped, the stronger men trying to yank the doors to the courtyard open. Fransiska, Dredwolf and Angelia swam for the doors, but Skywolf remained stationery. A calm serenity had fallen over her, the waters soothed her and soon it overlapped her head and she floated under the water.

The eagle dived in and appeared before her. Reaching for her ear, it screeched into it. Skywolf flinched at the sound, but within the scream's primordial depths, she heard a voice. Her heart almost died at the recognition of it. It was clear as the crystal water that swept over her, and it had but one message.

The eagle and the waters had disappeared. The crowd looked at each other and realised they were dry. Dredwolf looked up at Skywolf and feared for her, for she gaped at the ground before her in shock in a manner he had never seen before.

The word passed around New Avalion fast. Watre Hills had received the message of fire concerning him. After Darcwulf had claimed under great duress that he had not caused the fireworks, and the news of the message of water from Saphin Vale had reached them, they were convinced that they were the first to bear the witness of the DragonRider's message.

For who had not heard the prophecy of the DragonRider? The tales of old were again rekindled and a fear rose in their hearts. After the fall of the Windfarer, who would be brave enough to take up the post of the DragonRider? Which mercenary of Le'Mar would ride upon the back of the fiercest dragon and claim the land as his own?

And who would battle the DragonRider and defend their land against their fated doom?

"What do you make of it, Nighthale?" Franklin asked his friend and colleague. Franklin's years showed on his face and his voice carried with it the timber of the years. He was not as young as he used to be, but when it came to the defence of the city, his soul had the morale of an enraged wolf.

Nighthale looked at the faces of Franklin and Nowles beside him. They had been through so many battles and tactics the past few years, and now with the report of the rise of the DragonRider, he was sure they would be in for worse times.

The other tribe lords sat opposite the long table in the North Tower of Degron Castle. The tower afforded them the panoramic view of New Avalion, with the added benefit of being able to see past the outer walls of the city. A large army could be seen approaching from a far enough distance to alert the city, but Nighthale left the scouting to the parapets and towers of the eight pillars of the city.

Malkius of the Saphin Tribe, Sjedwolf of the Watre Tribe, Shadowwe from the Orion Tribe and Jasnon of the Lowle Tribe sat in heavy contemplation. No other minor representatives were present, as Nighthale had requested an informal meeting.

"You know the prophecy as well as I, Nighthale," Malkius said, looking at him through his long white hair. A year-old scar ran from his brow over his right eye onto his cheek from a brief encounter with a Ma-Wreth that had wandered too far into the Avalion region.

The image of the giant with lightning reflexes still plagued his dreams, but his fortitude was encouraging to behold.

"We ignored the signs of the Windfarer two years ago," Shadowwe warned. "We would be ill-advised to do it a second time."

"And the only reason we survived the first prophecy was through the perseverance of my son..." Nighthale said softly, remembering Shadowolf's disappearance.

"Elgoth said there was still hope," Nowles interrupted, referring to Masara's son. Elgoth had left the Council shortly after the fall of the Windfarer, mentioning that he had to attend to his father.

"But he did not say what to hope for, Nowles," Nighthale replied.

"Nevertheless, the prophecy of the DragonRider is upon us," Shadowwe repeated. "We can either prevent the fulfilment of it, as Shado did, or we can await the hand of fate and deal with him in the end."

"We do not know who Le'Mar will use as his champion," Nighthale said. "Until that time, all we can do is wait and prepare."

"Does anyone know what the prophecy says about the DragonRider?" Jasnon asked.

"Not in detail," Sjedwolf replied. "All we know is that he will claim the dragons as his own, and they will participate in the destruction of the war. No man will be able to withstand him."

"So why bother, if the prophecy says he can't be stopped?" Jasnon asked carefully.

"Because my son proved," Nighthale smiled softly, "that even a prophecy can be undone."

There was a scratching at one of the open windows, and the council arose in defence, Jasnon drawing his sword.

"Sorry," the gargoyle said as he landed on the floor of the War Council. His stone-hew skin danced in the moonlight, and the pendant known as the Lapis Pin that kept him from transforming in the sun still hung around his neck. He tucked his wings behind his back as he greeted the Council with a nod. "It is just easier than travelling up your stairs."

"Please, have a seat, Dren," Nighthale offered as the men relaxed in their seats.

"Night," a voice called from the main oak doors.

"Come in, Karla," Nighthale replied. His wife stepped in, wearing a beautiful red dress, her hair tied loosely behind her back.

"Dinner is ready in the banquet hall," she announced. The men noticed her concern, and were awed that she did not send a messenger to deliver the message; another testament of her care for him.

"We will be down shortly, my love," he responded, and the men smiled at the informality. Karla left, and the men faced the gargoyle again.

"I have heard news of the fire and water visions that were received around the city," Dren said.

"We believe it to be the start of the DragonRider's warning," Shadowwe said.

"I have my doubts whether it is about the prophecy," Dren replied.

"How is that?" Nighthale asked, leaning forward.

"I have received a vision too," Dren said, "one that I received before Darcwulf saw the fires."

"Darcwulf was by the fires?" Nighthale frowned. "I am surprised he hasn't said anything."

"Maybe we should summon him to the Council?" Sjedwolf advised.

"You won't find him in New Avalion," Dren smiled.

"Where has he gone to?" Franklin enquired.

"He has left for Bentley Strip," Dren replied, and the men went silent.

"The mountain range of the dragons?" Shadowwe asked. "Why?"

"For the same reason that two girls and Malkius's daughter left," Dren replied.

"Skywolf? What has this to do with her?" Malkius asked.

"She received the message of the water in your court," Dren said. "It is the same reason that I will be leaving for the Strip in the morning, for I have received the message of the wind."

"Explain it to us?" Nighthale asked, intrigued.

"It was the same as the others, perhaps the first, but I don't know who has received the message of earth. Yet it is as the others were: the eagle using the air to reveal its message of the dragon."

"Why has no one told us?" Nowles asked.

"It was sent to me in my home at Eldor's Dungeons," Dren said. "I was alone."

"So, it was meant for specific persons?" Nighthale asked.

"Yes, I do believe it was," Dren replied. "And I heard a voice in the eagle's cry. I do believe your son is still alive."

Nighthale slumped back in his seat, his eyes brimming with tears. It was too much to take in for him, having hoped for two years that Shadowolf still lived.

"Are you sure it is him?" Shadowwe asked.

"It makes sense," Nighthale said. "He called Darcwulf and Skywolf, two of his trusted friends. He has also called you, Dren, and by calling you three he knows others will follow."

"It seems…" Nowles hesitated, "almost too much to hope for."

"Why summon you there when he could have returned home?" Shadowwe continued. "Why wait two years?"

"I don't know, but I intend finding out," Dren replied sternly, standing to leave through the window he had entered.

"Wait," Nighthale stopped him. "I want the Hand of the Orion to join you."

"For what purpose?" the gargoyle asked.

"It does seem strange that he waited this long, and it does seem too good to be true, but the persons he has called are too coincidental. The Hand of the Orion were there when the Shadow Clan was formed. I feel it only fit that the Orion be there again.

"If I know my son well enough he is preparing for another quest, a quest I cannot begin to imagine. I want the Orion to go and assist him."

"Very well," Shadowwe said. "I will request that the Orion send another representative to take my place in the Council while the Hand travels to Bentley's Strip."

"Do you know the way?" Dren asked impatiently.

"Yes, we do," Shadowwe replied. "You may proceed ahead of us."

Dren nodded, unfurled his wings and jumped from the window.

"I wonder what my son is up to," Nighthale whispered, the tension and emptiness of two years finally starting to ease.

***

"You still with me?" the pegasus asked. Her white coat had long ago begun to turn to the black of the dust in the murky dungeon. Her wings were dilapidated, having not been used in years and her tail was in tatters. Yet she had survived the tortures of the dark lord, refusing to reveal the land of the pegasi known as uPendus. Her state of degradation was evidence of her loyalty to the earth.

"I am here, Genewiu," the dull voice croaked from the darkness, her will to live lingering on the last embers of hope. "We need to escape these dungeons…"

"Don't start that again," Genewiu replied forlornly. "You know we can't escape. The dark lord is too strong. He has orcs everywhere."

"Why does he not kill me?" the girl asked no one in particular. "Each day he sends food. For two years he has cared for me as a pet wolf, yet he refuses to let me go."

"We've been through this before, my lady," the pegasus sighed. "Like me he holds you to ransom. He wishes to obtain that which he can obtain through no other means. He wants to enter the elvin kingdom."

"And to do that he needs the Heart of Tigers, I know," the girl interrupted. She spent some moments thinking on the magical gem which was the key to Eldor's Forest. It had been entrusted to her father, Baron Maren-Ti of the Vale of Tigers, knowing that they would be able to protect it from the wrong hands.

But a new evil was in the world, and the new evil would stop at nothing from gaining entrance to the forest. He had almost succeeded two years ago when she had been in the forest, but he had failed against Eldor.

And as the battle came to an end, something happened in the world. A power was released and Le'Mar had grown enraged. Upon leaving, he had captured the only other treasure that was dear to Maren-Ti's heart. It had been an act of despair transformed into a moment of hope for the dark lord. He now had a ransom for the Heart of Tigers. And every day she prayed her father would not sacrifice the Heart for her sake.

"It will work out in the end," Genewiu said. "We are but pawns of death for a greater good, Chenesia."

THE SHADOW CLAN
CHAPTER TWO

Darcwulf looked up from the foot of the mountain and saw a silhouette move on the distant cliff. It was a far way to travel up, and Creotos was starting to set behind the mountain to the west. He was in dire need of sustenance.

"How do you think we're going to get up there?" Shadowwe asked. "The Orion are adept at rock climbing, but the waterfall might exacerbate things."

The fall fell from the lip of the cliff from where the shadow of the man had vanished, running its course from the top of the mountain to the valley at its foot.

"I don't know," Darcwulf replied. "Dren won't have a problem, but the rest of us don't have wings."

"I guess we will all just have to..." Shadowwe stopped when he saw shapes descend from the cliff. Their wings glinted, although the sun cast the east side of the valley in shadow.

When they approached, Darcwulf noted that they looked like baby dragons. The main differences were that they had bald, feline faces and their bodies ended shortly beneath the wings in eagle-like claws. Their back and body were covered in hairless, pink skin and the group felt naked looking at the creatures.

As they got closer, however, it seemed like the colours of their skin were constantly changing, yet semi-transparent at the same time. It was by far the strangest creatures they had ever seen.

Without warning, each creature grabbed one member of the group by the shoulders and hoisted them up into the air. Darcwulf had to fight the instinct to attack, knowing the answer to the messages lay upon the cliff atop the mountain side. The creatures held on to their prey without a sign of difficulty, taking them in the direction of the cliff.

After ten minutes flight they finally reached the cliff, which was a short distance above the mouth of the fall. The ground was rough with sand and stone and a cave's mouth leered over them. From within, a warm light was reflected against the cave's walls, and Darcwulf saw that the tunnel curved towards the source of the light. There was no shadow to reveal the presence of anybody by the fire.

The creatures took flight to the top of the mountain and the group slowly entered. The mouth and tunnel were large enough to allow fifteen men to walk abreast and rock stalactites hung from the ceiling of the cave. It took them another ten minutes to reach the curve of the tunnel that led to the fire.

A solitary figure lay huddled by the fire and finally Darcwulf was relieved. The presence of the wolf confirmed his hopes and his heart leapt for joy. He ran to the wolf, which raised its head at his approach, and the happiness was reflected by the wolf's howl.

"Nelnar!" he shouted as he hugged Shadowolf's faithful wolf. The canine licked his face pleasantly and Darcwulf fell on his back as the wolf pounced on him to the ground. The rest of the group found seats on the eight logs placed around the four bonfires in the centre, two on each side of the fires. Dren flew up into the air and found a perch against the wall against which he could sit.

"I guess you need a lot of wood just to keep warm around here," Skywolf said as she closed the woolen jacket about her upper body.

"Well, these walls aren't exactly insulated," Darcwulf said as he patted Nelnar at his feet. He could not hide the expression of glee on his face.

"Do you think he'll mind us bringing extra people along?" Skywolf asked.

"No," he replied. "I think he intended it that way."

The silence became palpable as they waited for their host.

Suddenly the quiet was broken by the sound of wings, and everyone turned to Dren.

"Wasn't me..." the gargoyle replied from his perch.

Shadows moved from another alcove further down the next tunnel and ten men clad in white with blue-feathered wings appeared in the air. They surreptitiously dove and wove in the dark of the cave ceiling and then dropped down to deliver plates of food and drink to the visitors. Golden tables appeared between them and the fire, and the plates were placed on each table. Soon, they had food and drink in abundance.

"Is this real?" Darcwulf asked as the flying men disappeared back into the darkness of the hidden alcove.

"Well, there is only one way to find out?" Dren said as he dropped to a vacant seat on the closest log. He grabbed a lamb's leg and bit into the meat, murmuring in pleasure. "It's real."

Soon the group joined in the feast, grabbing pieces of meat, pouring some gravy and dishing the salads.

"I meant to ask how you got your invitations," Darcwulf addressed the group, finally comfortable enough to hold a conversation.

"Well, I was trying to tell you in the tavern, but you were too drunk to listen," Dren said disapprovingly.

"Oh, yes, sorry about that," he apologised. "I heard you were summoned from the Dungeons?"

"Yes," Dren replied, "also with the eagle and dragon's vision, but using the elemental wind instead."

"I had the water," Skywolf said between mouthfuls, and then nodding to Fransiska and Angelia beside her. "Angelia knew Shadowolf from college, and I wanted Fransiska to meet the man we kept discussing."

"He sounds intriguing," Fransiska blushed.

"Don't bother," Darcwulf smiled. "He is a hard man to come by. It might take years before he takes a liking to you."

"Didn't take too long for him to like that mermaid," Skywolf commented sourly.

"What about you?" he addressed the Orion warriors.

"Dren informed the council of the messages," Shadowwe answered on behalf of Trevor, Tinonte, Sorceress, Rennick and Scarlette, who were all too busy consuming their food to bother. "So I was asked by his father if the Hand could join the Clan once again. And what about your friends, Darc?"

"Lastgorn, Sny-Ten and Gwyn are friends of Shado," Darcwulf replied, indicating the three. "They were also part of the Clan at the end, if you remember."

"Vaguely," Shadowwe said. "That was two years ago."

"So the Shadow Clan is reunited," Dren said, placing his meat down for a moment. "Hey, whatever happened to that other woman that was with you?"

"Who?" Darcwulf asked.

"I think he is referring to Angelicus," Skywolf sneered.

"Oh," Darcwulf said. "Don't ask."

The sound of footsteps sounded from the cave's mouth and everyone turned to look. The sound grew closer and eventually a silhouette formed against the far wall. A beautiful woman stepped into the light, although her eyes held many sorrows. She wore a sarong around her waist, and a wrap around her breasts, both light blue in colour. A thin, blue veil dangled from the wrap to the sarong, but it was clear enough to reveal her well-shaped belly. On her naval there was a belly ring in the form of a seahorse.

"I don't believe it," Darcwulf said, as he stood to embrace her in greeting. "Shedaaij, it has been years."

"It is nice to see you all again," Shedaaij greeted calmly, apparently striving to contain her anxiety.

"Please, have something to eat," Dren offered her a seat which she gratefully accepted. "Where have you been?"

"In *Avalendil*," she replied.

"The Mer-Kingdom?" Fransiska asked, being the only one of the group that did not know Shedaaij's origins.

"She is a Merlani, Fransiska," Skywolf helped. "She is the only one of human and mermaid conception."

"Oh..." Fransiska replied sharply, remembering Skywolf's earlier reference to a mermaid.

Silence reigned over the crowd again as they continued their feast and their starvations were defeated. No one saw the wind pick up slightly from the sand on the cave's floor, or heard the murmur of the whispers move from the alcove to the fire. The fire stirred uncomfortably and the coals of the wood settled down between the embers.

Darcwulf turned his head at the sound of a set of hooves. A white coat appeared, preceded by a short horn. He dropped his meat and stared at the unicorn in her pristine brilliance. Her eyes shone like a rainbow in an abyss of light, her coat running down in strands from her thighs to her hooves.

"Good evening, guests," the unicorn called, and everyone looked up from their meal. "I am Ursula. I trust you are enjoying your stay?"

"It is rather pleasant," Darcwulf replied in awe.

"I am glad I can be accommodating," she smiled. Nelnar stood from Darcwulf's feet where he had been chewing a bone and ran to join Ursula. "Your host of honour is ready to receive you."

Darcwulf was the first to rise, but waited on the others before proceeding. When the group of fifteen reached Ursula she turned, but not before making one last comment.

"He might not be as you remember him," she warned. "He has changed. But do not fear him, for he is still who he was. The only change is his wisdom and power."

"Oh, is that all?" Darcwulf remarked as they followed the unicorn into the dark alcove.

The alcove led to another wide tunnel, but the ceiling was not as high as the dining hall, nor did it have any stalactites. They passed several doors on the way through, and faint lights shimmered beneath the cracks.

"Ursula," Darcwulf called. "What's behind the doors?'

"Those are the humble dragons of Bentley's Strip," Ursula replied serenely.

"Oh," he said, disappointed. "I thought it would be more daunting."

"Don't let the doors fool you," she smiled, as he walked faster to be beside her. "Those doors conceal many traps and pitfalls before you reach a dragon and its treasure."

"What sort of treasure?" Darcwulf asked without a hint of greed, but only genuine curiosity.

"Your usual gold and gems that they hoard from the many worlds they travel from," she replied. "There are some minerals I won't bother trying to pronounce."

"How long have you known the dragons?" he asked her.

"Longer than you can imagine."

"What has become of Shadowolf since we last saw him?" Darcwulf asked carefully, his anxiety and tension finally getting the better of him. "We all thought he had died?"

"I think it would be better if he told you himself, don't you?"

He nodded and increased his pace. The humidity in the tunnel grew warmer as they seemed to be reaching another bend. On the apex of the bend, a solid red oak door bled from the surrounding cave wall. The Shadow Clan stopped in front of it, waiting for Ursula to say something about the room.

Instead, they all watched as a small hole formed in the centre of the door, and Ursula proceeded to put the horn on her head into the gap. She nudged it slightly and the door creaked open. Removing her horn from the door, she allowed Darcwulf to open the door for her and walked inside.

A triangular room, the point starting at the door with its walls moving outwards, welcomed them with warmth. They walked in single file until they could spread out further. The door closed behind them without aid.

Darcwulf took a moment to observe the door from the inside of the room. On the surface where one hole had been on the outside, there were four holes in line with each other on the inside. As he looked forward, he stepped on a cold surface.

Darcwulf looked down and saw he was standing on a circular disc with a design on it. He was about halfway between the door and the far wall, and the disc was one of four that extended in line between the two sides of the triangle.

He walked towards the left wall and started with the first disc, walking over each disc to the right wall. Each disc had a different design to it, seemingly signifying something that tugged at his mind. When he reached the last disc to the right, he recognised the epitaph of fire and realised the four discs signified the four elements.

The Clan were waiting for him at the far wall and he sheepishly bowed his head, smiled and joined them. Against the wall there were four portholes spread across the expanse of the wall. Darcwulf frowned and looked back. Each of the portholes was in line with a disc that seemed to coincide with a hole in the entry door.

Ursula faced the blank wall between the two central portholes. Without warning, she drove her horn into the wall and a flash of light burst from the new hole. She drew a wide circle with difficulty and then removed her horn. The circle drew in upon itself, forming a similar small hole that the door had. She placed her horn in the hole, and a door that had not been visible before opened up for the travelers.

A very stunned Darcwulf obliged by opening the door for the equally astonished group again. Dren smirked at him as he passed through and Nelnar seemed to be taking it very lightly as it walked on.

Darcwulf closed the door on a very thin, lightless passage. He tried to open the door again, but it was sealed.

"That was bright," someone said, although who it was he could not see.

"Obviously not bright enough," a voice that sounded like Dren's joked in reply.

Ursula's body pulsed with light suddenly, providing respite from the dark. The passage appeared to extend eternally from left to right, but ended before them one step from the door they had entered through.

"Fascinating," Scarlette remarked.

Ursula proceeded to shove her horn into another invisible door in the black wall before them, and with the same procedure, but with a larger circle, created another opening for them. They walked into sunlight.

It was a short open glade surrounded by forest. Darcwulf looked back to see that the door was part of a tree trunk. As the group waded around calmly in the opening, Nelnar urinated on the trunk.

"Good boy," Darcwulf complimented it, glad that the wolf had thought of it before he had. He did not think the group would take too kindly at him marking the tree, and laughed at the thought.

At the edge of the glade on the opposite end of the tree's door there was a stadium. The stadium was meant for an audience, that much was certain, but there was no one to fill the seats. There were four rows of seats rising up from the grass of the glade. Ursula disappeared behind it and waited for them before venturing into the forest.

The forest was beautiful. Tall trees towered into the atmosphere and although the earth was covered in orange autumn leaves, the trees held gorgeous, fresh green leaves upon their branches. A breeze drifted through the air and held a faint smell of spring on it.

Darcwulf turned quickly when he thought he heard little footsteps running over the leaves. Nelnar pricked its ears, but Ursula and the others continued on regardless. As they journeyed further, Darcwulf thought he saw certain areas off in distances where light was concentrated more than the rest. Otherwise the forest was uneventful and they walked into an open field that held a massive monument.

The monument was an aged building where the roof over the entrance door was supported by complimentary columns. Leading up to the doors and pillars was a silver flight of steps. The walls were stone white while the roof, door and window frames were green.

"Amazing," Tinonte whispered in awe, while Darcwulf spied a shimmering lake to the side of the building.

"It is the Temple of Asgorna, the Dragon King," Ursula said, to which no one could utter a comment. It had been too much to take in already. "And his kingdom is larger than what you have seen already."

"In this mountain?" Darcwulf asked incredulously.

"They have the power to place a large enough space in a small area," she replied. "They could fit a planet in the palm of your hand, if they had to."

The revelation ceased as movement on the temple's roof caught their attention. Leathery wings rose up in the air and claws dug into the tiles. The horn-faced dragon peered down at them and gave a hearty roar. Darcwulf defensively dove under his arms in case fire followed the roar, but silence filled the fields in its aftermath.

Asgorna dropped down from his perch and landed on the field, before them. After a moments stare at them he sneered.

"So," Asgorna rumbled his words out, "Are you ready to test your loyalty?"

Not sure what he meant, but not given an opportunity to respond, the Clan watched as the dragon turned to face the Temple, having to duck beneath the trunk of a tail that swung over their heads. Asgorna's eyes lit up and the Temple doors opened. A man, who seemed weak and at the end of his rope, walked past the doors onto the open porch.

"Shado!" Darcwulf shouted and started to run when a barrier knocked him to the floor.

"He cannot see us," Ursula explained, "nor does he know you are here. As a final exam, he must find his way out of the mountains. You will bear witness to this."

"How long has he been in there?" Shedaaij asked, the concern visible on her face. Darcwulf rose to his feet.

"Ever since we found him in the plains," Ursula replied. "We placed him in the temple where he awoke. He has been there since."

"And what have you done to him?" Darcwulf asked with heat in his tone.

"The ways of the dragon are his own," Ursula said. "Suffice it to say, he has received the training he requires to continue his fight against the dark lord."

"Why him?" Shedaaij asked, but Ursula did not respond. Instead, Shadowolf's voice rose in the intermission.

"Have I done everything you require of me, Asgorna?" Shadowolf asked, his voice emphasizing his weakness.

"There is one more task, and at the end a reward," Asgorna replied sternly.

"What reward could be great enough for what I have been through?" Shadowolf countered.

"That which you have loved shall be returned to you," the dragon replied, "but only if you are willing to fight for it.

"This is the only way back to the mountain, but I will leave you to discover the path. At the end of the road you will find the exit to the mountain, and there you will find your reward.

"We have aided each other through this, *Enodhim*," the dragon continued as Shadowolf looked at him through dim eyes. "In the end, do not forget our deal, or you will lose those you love. Remember your vow."

Asgorna kept his silence after that, and rose into the air. The roof of the temple opened up and Asgorna disappeared into its interior. Although it seemed too small, Darcwulf could not imagine how large the inside was.

Shadowolf looked around the field and only saw forest. The

field was empty, yet it felt as if someone was watching him. Turning around, he saw the lake and made his way over to it.

A picket board was stuck in front of the lake that read 'The Lake of Beauty.' It was indeed beautiful, with the sunlight shimmering off it. Yet, something within its depths caught his attention.

He stood on the edge of the lake. There was no beach or walkway into the lake; instead it was a small drop from the edge into the deep of the water. Under its surface, something moved. He stared until he saw a girl's face. He was mesmerised by the face, and soon he fell into the water unwillingly.

The cold surrounded him, but his attention was on the song. The mermaids were swimming to and fro, singing their beautiful songs, entrancing them in their melody of love. He sank deeper and deeper, and although he seemed to have lost his mind, he had learnt enough to know that these were not truly mermaids.

As predicted, his neck burst open into gills and beneath his shirt a tiny light winked upon his chest. If they had thought he would drown, they were wrong. Asgorna had been surprised by this revelation in the Land of Odgjin, but it was one of the many surprises that Shadowolf had in store for him.

He thought back to when he had obtained the ability to breathe under water. He had been in college before the war of the dark lord had disrupted his life, and the mermaids had brought him to their watery city in the college's lake. They had given him a rose pendant that would allow him to grow gills whenever he wore it around his neck.

But the pendant had disappeared, and when he had thought it was lost and he was drowning in the lake surrounded by long-fanged creatures, the pendant revealed itself, fused onto the bones of his sternum.

The pendant shone pleasantly as he swam with the creatures. One of the girls bravely swam up to him, a frown on her face. She rose up to his face, her tail keeping her afloat before his lips. Her eyes seemed lost in the reverie of the moment and their lips drew closer.

As their lips touched, Shadowolf raised his hand to block the strike of the siren's blade. She screamed, but he cut her throat before it could echo in the lake's depths.

The other sirens were upon him. He estimated ten of them and dove done to greet them. The first struck her tail at him, but he drove the blade into the stem of her tail and used it to swing himself into another five, hitting the knife into their bellies and hearts. The water around him started to swirl with power and he swam up to deal with the remaining five.

The one with the bleeding tail screamed into his face, but he used the power of the water to throw the blade through her throat. The last four surrounded him, but the whirlpool grew stronger, and he was the centre of it. Soon the sirens were in the pool's grasp. He pulled the one's hair back and snapped her neck; another's body he bent in half and broke her spine. The last two he knocked into one another, rendering them unconscious and letting them fall to the bed of the lake.

As the pool returned to stagnant water, he detected that there were other sirens around, but they stayed their distance. He was about to leave their waters when a light at the bottom of the lake caught his attention. A metal object glowed and was embedded in the sand.

He swam down the depths and reached the object, an object he had seen once before. It was the same type of object that Lellian had grabbed in the kingdom of the mer-people and became the new Mer-King; it was a trident, its three points ending in spears.

He gripped the handle and shifted the water and sand in order to dislodge it. A wooden post stuck out from the sand, and he read the words 'A light to show you the way.'

When he reached the surface again he crawled a distance from the lake and lay on his back, the trident at his side. He felt so tired and he needed rest. There had been enough food in the lands of the temple, but not enough sleep. Caution had kept him awake most nights.

He was almost there. It had taken so long to get out of the temple, and he had finally made it. Now when he was at the pinnacle of success, he was too drained to attempt it.

He used the wind to lift him to his feet and to place the trident on its butt end so that the prongs pointed to the sky. He looked up to try and locate the source of light, but there was no sun. Yet, the light touched the prongs and was deflected from each one towards the forest. Before it hit the forest, the three unified into one, making it clear where he was meant to enter it.

With trident in hand, he came to the forest wall. A sound of wings made him stop and he stepped back in time as three black dragons dropped between him and his goal.

He didn't stop to think as he let fire erupt around his body and he soared into the air. The dragons rose up to him, taking furious turns to snap at him. One hurled a fire ball, but he caught it in one hand and threw it back. It hit the dragon in the face, but did little to sway it. Instead, it emitted a roar in anger.

The tail of a dragon hit him in the chest and he fell towards the ground. The dragons followed and as he pulled up before hitting the grass the dragons followed suit as in a dance. He rose up again, but the dragons surrounded him and he stopped.

He faced the one dragon, but felt the other two on his sides. They glared at him before their eyes lit up, and they erupted torrents of fire from their mouths on all sides.

Shadowolf flung out his arms to both sides to throw his own fire at theirs, and put up a shield for the one before him. His fire melted within theirs, and reached his hands before he pushed it back to their faces.

With one last shove, he struck at the two at his sides. The fires roared into their mouths and they fell. Dropping his shield, he sliced with his two fire blades at the front dragon's eyes, momentarily blinding it as it joined the other two falling to the earth.

The earth shuddered as they hit the ground. Shadowolf let the fires die down and he floated back to the ground where the three dragons arose to their feet.

"I won't needlessly kill a dragon," Shadowolf told them. "I know the laws of nature and the way of the eternal."

"Valiant effort," one dragon replied, "but in the end you might not have a choice."

"Maybe," he said. "But today won't be that day."

"Very well," another dragon said.

"You may proceed," the last dragon said as the three rose in the air and flew away.

The trident still showed the way into the forest, and so Shadowolf entered. The leaves broke beneath his feet and the trees sang their age old song of nature. It was a short trip before he reached a very small open glade where the light broke through the tree tops. A board on one of the trees read 'Nymphs of Substance.'

The trident's light faded. Shadowolf shook it, but the prongs refused to reflect the light. With nothing else to do, he shoved the butt end into the earth and sat on the floor. Maybe he could finally get some rest before continuing.

As he laid his head on the leaves, objects above his head caught his attention. It seemed like they were fairies or butterflies fluttering in the air, but he remembered the board and wondered what the nymphs would require of him.

They were spectral in appearance. He could have easily have mistaken them for fairy spirits. They drifted down and landed on his chest, not one of them larger than the palm of his hand. Their yellow glow was welcoming and soothing, although he still did not know what they required of him.

Four of them broke from the group and flew above his head. Slowly they laid hands on him and kissed his forehead. His body grew warm and within moments it had received renewed vigour. His mind awoke as if from hours of sleep and well-deserved rest.

The nymphs left him and touched the standing trident. The light broke from the sky and refracted again in the direction he should go. With no need for further rest, he rose, took the trident and walked on the path indicated.

When he entered the glade he was certain he had walked in circles. The trident grew dark again, and he was left with no answers except for the board that hung from the branch of a tree. It read 'Nymphs of Fortune'.

He stuck the trident in the earth again and repeated the first procedure of lying on the floor. This time, however, the nymphs glided down from the tree tops and floated around the board. Shadowolf arose and approached them. Four of the nymphs broke from the group and swam around his head. They were about to kiss him when he broke their dance.

"Do you really think I need luck, after everything I've been through?" he asked sardonically.

"Everybody needs some fortune," one of them replied.

"I think I've managed to survive on Bontu's grace alone, thank you," Shadowolf said sternly.

"Are you denying our gift?" the nymph asked, apparently disgusted.

"Yes, I am," Shadowolf said.

"Then I guess you can go," she smiled and the four nymphs returned to the tree with the board. The trident lit up and shone through the trees to the next destination.

The next glade brought the 'Nymphs of Greed'. The clearing was anything but empty or small. In the large expanse, treasures of many sorts glistened in the light. Shadowolf stuck the dormant trident in the earth as he walked to the riches.

Four nymphs broke off from a group again and spoke with him.

"You may have any treasures you wish," the nymphs said in unison. "It is your reward for making it out of the temple."

There was not only gold, but sapphires, rubies, emeralds and many other assortments of gems. Besides the treasures of the earth, there were weapons of all sorts.

"Where do you get all this?" he marveled.

"We take what we can from the dragons when they go to other worlds," they replied. "Others are gifts from the friendlier, loving dragons."

"You sure have a supply," Shadowolf noted.

"It is only a start," they laughed.

"I can see why they call you nymphs of greed," Shadowolf laughed back, but the nymphs went silent.

"See anything you like?" they asked severely, their mirth lost to the wind.

"Nothing really," Shadowolf sighed, not wanting to disappoint another set of nymphs, but not seeing anything interesting either. "What will I do with the gold and how will I carry it? I've managed…hold on."

He walked towards the weapons he had spied earlier. Past the shields, bows and spears he found a weapon that looked vaguely familiar.

"I haven't seen this weapon in ages," he said, turning to the nymphs. "Where did you get it?"

"That mangy old sword?" they replied. "The dragons dropped it here after they returned from the earth one day some time ago. Is it yours?"

"It was once upon a time," he picked up the sword in its sheath. It still held the rubies on the hilt, and the wood was still immaculate with the dragon design over it. "Ruben-Willow, I called it."

He tied the belt around his waist, and the memories of those days past returned to haunt him.

"Anything else?" they asked, delighted he had chosen a gift.

"One more thing," he said, moving towards the gems. He picked a flower from the ground and held it up to them. "What are the chances you can use your powers to fuse tear drops of every kind of gem you have here onto this rose?"

The nymphs laughed and dust sparkled as they flew over to their treasures. They picked a stone of each gem that lay around, a ruby, a sapphire, an aquamarine, pyrite, gold, a myriad of stones that began to crowd the air above the treasures. Each stone was turned into a gem teardrop smaller than a fingernail and was placed on the petals of the rose. The top of the rose was barely visible beneath the drops, but the colours burnt with the fervour of the sun.

A flash of light ignited and dust scattered around the rose as the drops were fused to it. When the dust cleared, the nymphs tied a cord of leaves on it and carried the rose over to him. They placed the crown on his head with the rose hanging over his right ear.

"For someone special?" they asked.

"If she still has place for me in her heart, yes," Shadowolf said mournfully. "That will be all, thank you."

"Our pleasure," they replied as they touched the trident and disappeared. The path was revealed by the light.

The 'Nymphs of Love' was the next area. These nymphs were red in colour, and Shadowolf laughed as they approached him.

"And what is so funny?" one asked with a smile on his face.

"Nothing," he replied. "Just wondering what gift you wish to bestow on me?"

"I would laugh too if I was dressed like that," the nymph said, nodding at the rose crown.

"Let's get on with it, shall we?" he said quickly.

The nymph flew back and a ghostly woman appeared from a tree. Shadowolf blinked, as he was certain she had been the tree a few seconds before.

She walked up to him and smiled. Slowly, she embraced him. He relaxed moments afterwards as his heart grew warm. It had been a long time since he had felt love for anything. The love he had once held for a woman had begun to dwindle in the lost hope that he would ever return.

But the love returned to fill his heart to its capacity, and tears fell from the corner of his eyes onto the sprite's shoulders. She let go, gave him one kiss and return to her timber form. The tree bristled in the wind, and he stared at it for a moment.

"That was wonderful," he told the nymph.

"After what you have been through, you need some love," the nymph replied. "I think the world out there does too, for love is lost to it."

Shadowolf nodded as the reality of the earth's doom returned to his mind. The warmth was still in his heart as he took the glowing trident and walked its path.

As he struck the trident down in the next glade, he read the next board over three times.

"Uh oh," he finally sighed. "What could this mean?"

The words 'Nymphs of Desire' still rang in his head when a sound behind him caught his attention. Another tree was transforming into a feminine sprite, but this one was not wearing anything to disguise her nudity.

"Uhm," he said bashfully as he reared backwards and found himself caught against the bark of a trunk. "Maybe we could forego…"

He lost his words as her lips touched his neck. Her hands were running over his chest and down to his arms, which she placed on her hips. Her body felt as real as a human, although her appearance was as transparent as a spirit.

She pulled at his shirt with one hand, trying to move it over his head, while the other hand tugged at the rim of his pants. He could feel her toes close over his bare, dirty feet and then she lifted her body onto his hips, her legs twined around his waist. She was kissing him deeply, and he could feel her breasts pushing into his chest.

"Wait," he breathed deeply. "You need…to…stop…"

"Why?" she asked sweetly, still sucking onto his shoulders and neck, and her thighs embracing his body against the tree. Suddenly the tree behind him felt lighter, and he realised there was another sprite touching him from the back, and suckling his ear lobe. He found that he was groaning unwillingly with their bodies entwined with his, but then he gently removed the sprite hinged on his body off him, and turned to face the once behind him.

"I can't," he said, smiling sadly at them.

"Don't you long for it?" they asked.

"Yes," he replied honestly, "but not like this. If my love were present here, I would not do this before her."

"But she is not here now," they said. "And she might have someone new."

"I love her," he said.

"Very well," they sighed, and their naked bodies transformed back into trees. Shadowolf felt bad that he had denied a second gift, but he was not willing to betray her yet. Not until he had found out what had happened to her since he last saw her.

Their bodies still reflected off his memory as he took the glowing trident through the forest and finally out of it.

The back of a stadium stood before him. He moved around it to stand on the grounds that it faced. Looking around carefully, he saw that the wall before him held no way through, but the trident insisted that was the only exit. He thrust the butt of it into the earth and walked around, the warmth of the sprites still on his body.

He found a spot before the wall where the grass was cut in a circle. He leaned down and touched the trimmed weeds, but nothing was revealed. He sighed and stood over the circle, yet it remained dead to his senses.

The wind whistled in his ear and he listened. Although it did not speak, he got the idea. He spread his legs over the circle and focussed on the wind. The wind began to roar and drum around him, and soon the wind became a tornado in the circle. He stepped back to see that the wind remained above the circle, and he smiled.

A noise caught his attention, and he blocked in time as a fist ran for his face. Strange beings made of wind were all around him. They sounded like orcs, but their features were indiscernible.

It became a contest of blows. The wind struck his face and body without mercy and he struggled to keep focus, and soon the wind struck him such a blow that he was sent back towards the wall.

He caught his feet on the grass and after a short distance of sliding he dug in and held his ground. He looked up through his long, ragged hair and growled. The adrenalin was pumping through his veins and the power he had released two years before coursed through his spirit.

He ran for the many children of the wind. The power of the wind erupted on his skin and his soul magnified his aura as he struck at them. Although he could not possibly kill the elementël beings, the wind was accepting the casualties as deaths, permitting him victory over the ones he severely injured. He realised it was just another test, and began to enjoy 'slaying' the wind warriors.

When there was nothing left of the wind but the still air around him, he looked back at the tornado of the disc. It still bellowed out, but there was one difference. The unified light from the prongs of the trident now shone towards the tornado to its left. Where the light hit the tornado, it was deflected towards the wall in line with the trident.

Shadowolf walked to the spot where the light hit the rock wall. He touched it, but the wall was solid. He still had no entry, but he had an entry point. He turned to look at the trident opposite the wall, and then looked to the tornado on his right. He was missing something.

He went towards the tornado, wanting to try something he had in mind, but before he reached it another spot on the ground was revealed. It was another circular clearing in the ground.

Standing over it he called the wind again and, even though the wind stirred, no tornado formed. For moments he remained there, increasing the summoning, but to no avail. He stopped and decided on a different tactic.

He called on the earth. Nature stirred beneath his feet and the trees began to sing with birds, but there was no effect on the disc. He switched to fire, and the clearing erupted with a flaming torch, whirring as fast as the wind tornado.

He reacted too slowly to catch the attack of the fire beings. They were the same shape as the wind warriors, besides the fact they their bodies consisted of a different element. In the same rage and manner that he dealt with the wind, the fire allowed him to defeat the fire fighters to the last flame.

There were now two lights reflected from the unified trident ray of the prongs. One passed through the wind tornado, whilst the second passed through the fire torch. Both were deflected towards the same hole in the wall opposite the trident.

As the two lights were to the left of the trident, he had a feeling two more circles existed to the right of it, as nothing had happened to allow him entry. True to his instincts, he found the two in line with the other two, so he made his way to the furthest one on the right.

"Play time is over," he muttered under his breath, determined not to waste any more time. He called on the earth again, and although the birds sang, nothing happened. Immediately he called on the water and a whirlpool erupted on the circle.

As the water wisps attacked he ran to the last circle and called the earth. The rocks and sand pulled up from the grass and circled the air above the disc with the sound of an earthquake. Earth entities appeared, and Shadowolf was permitted by water and earth to dispense 'death' among the elementël beings.

Soon he was the last one standing. He was dripping sweat mixed with dust. The beings had not been able to cause his blood to fall, but blue marks were starting to form on his skin where the worst contact had been made. He ripped his torn shirt from his chest and turned to see four rays of light deflected from the elements to the same spot on the wall.

The rock wall vanished and was replaced by trees. The lights indicated one tree, and leaving the trident in the ground he approached the tree.

Something caught his attention, an odour that was familiar. He sniffed the air and smelled the base of the tree.

"Wolf urine?" Shadowolf wondered, suddenly feeling more confident that he had found the right tree. "And it is fresh."

He looked around for a sign of wolves in the vicinity, but the forest and clearing was still. Shrugging it out of his mind, he tapped the trunk and a door opened outward. The lights from the elements moved and were deflected to four trees in their range. The lines were parallel to one another.

"Alright," he said. "Pick a tree."

Something occurred to him and he peeped through the open door. It was dark on the inside, but the lights passed through portholes where the four trees had been. It lit the dim room and revealed another wall a step away from the door. On that wall, more portholes allowed the light through to the other side.

He stepped inside the passageway and closed the door behind him. Another door formed before him, and without hesitating he entered, for it felt like he was weightless in the black passage.

The room was triangular in shape. It was bare and held no objects except for the four lights streaming through the portholes and the four discs on the floor. The lights still ran parallel with each other and hit the walls at odd angles, reflecting off the walls and creating a kaleidoscope of colours. Shadowolf knew he had to do something with the discs, but as he approached it, he realised he did not know what that something was.

He tapped one disc that had a strange insignia with his toe. There was no sound, but the metal was cold. He considered using the elements to light them up, when something in the air changed.

There were shadows over him. Not really shadows, as it seemed like the objects behind him did not have solid forms, but something shimmered across the floor before him that could only be described as shadows. He turned to face them.

The elementëls were large and towered over him. The lights no longer hit the walls but seemed to be part of the creatures. The elements were purely puppets on the light's strings. Suddenly Shadowolf regretted not removing the trident from the elementël battleground.

He also realised that he was at the point of the triangular room and they had more space to move on the other end. Not sure what to do or expect, he let his aura explode with power that was non-elemental and charged the fire being.

The fire giant bore its fists down on him, and when Shadowolf intended to run up its arm and use it to as leverage, he fell through the flames and slid under the creature to the other side. The elements were not going to permit him to just 'kill' the beasts. He had to fight them until he found a way to destroy them, and he was unsure how long that would take.

Yet, his dilemma did little to prevent the elements from

attacking. The room shuddered as the fists slammed against wall and floor in an effort to hit the smaller but faster human.

As the fire giant struck at him, he let fire burn at his feet and elevated himself up its back. He was about to draw his sword, the rubies on the hilt now storehouses of power, when he felt water splash on his neck and he rose up in the air and rolled over the arm that just missed him. Water's arm struck Fire, and the room was filled with Fire's roar.

Shadowolf watched as the fire slowly dimmed and Water retracted its arm, now furiously searching for the irritating fighter. Shadowolf smiled as he saw how low Fire's body was emitting its flames.

"Thank you," he said. "That is all I needed to know."

He unsheathed Rubin-Willow and poured his power into it. He ducked under Wind's attack, dived under Earth's legs and transformed his sword into a blade of water. He rose over Fire's hit and slashed at its neck, chest and knees as he fell to the ground and landed on one knee. The roar behind his back echoed into his ears, and the warmth in the room was gone.

The hair over his eyes stirred and he realised Wind was after him. He had no idea how to fight Wind, so he rolled back from the fist that fell down, and turned to face earth. The image of a burning human body entered his mind, and he charged for Earth. He avoided Water's blow but jumped against the wall and ricocheted towards Earth. He transformed his blade into fire, slicing into its legs and then rising into the air to drive the sword with both hands into its heart.

Earth was consumed by fire and the ashes fell to the ground. The roar was horrific and it felt as if the ground beneath him quaked, but he had two more giants to deal with. Without warning, the ground beneath him vanished, but he stayed in the air due to his quick reflexes, using wind to keep him level with the elements.

All that was left was Wind and Water. He could not see any ill-effects from killing Water, but he was afraid what would happen if he defeated Wind. He could imagine the air running out of the room and not being able to breathe. Battling Water while creating air to breathe would become an arduous task.

Wind struck at him, but he quickly changed his sword into a

blade of wind and attacked Water while dodging its arms. The liquid molecules separated, and Water disintegrated into a flowing waterfall down the abyss until nothing remained of it.

Wind watched him carefully. It was alone and it knew it would stand less chance of victory without the others. It saw the human change the blade into earth in the form of its original steel and rubies, not to mention the hidden amethyst within the blade's steel, and gave up of its own accord. The air settled and the room returned to its stable state.

Shadowolf watched as the discs snapped from the concrete of the floor and rose to meet the lights of the trident. The first disc transformed into a ball of wind, the next a ball of fire, then earth and finally water. The first two discs deflected the lights parallel to the left angled wall, and the last two discs deflected parallel to the right angled wall, until the four lines met before the door at the point of the triangle.

The four elements fused and formed one orb of many colours, an aura of power radiating its invitation. Shadowolf had seen this orb before, so many years ago before his disappearance into the dragons' mountains. It was a power orb of the elements, but it had one thing missing: the power of the human soul. And like those years before, he touched the orb and added his power, letting it take him into the air and render him helpless.

This was not, however, the same as the first time. When he had defeated Mercius, the false Windfarer, he had received the power which was his from birth. This time, it was merely a test to verify his power. It had been designed to grant him an exit. He was certain any other person would have had a different test to contend with.

As the orb released him, he fell to the ground and stood. The final door had opened. He wondered why he had gone through such a rigorous trial. He thought maybe it was to see if he was ready for what was to come. But he turned his head at the call of his name and realised the true purpose of it.

Familiar faces stared down at him in awe. One was filled with pride and admiration, a brother he had known his whole life. Others merely applauded him as a sign of congratulations. But one was filled with years of longing, pain and love. He turned and left the room that grew silent, unable to bare the sight any longer.

FORGING THE QUEST
CHAPTER THREE

They were in a different room. It was not the room with the alcove and the bonfires, but a room that was more equipped for comfort. Sofas and mattresses abounded, with a hearth for a source of light and heat. Smaller tables were set out with fruit, biscuits, cheese and bread. All in all, it was a welcome package outside the temple.

A day had passed since the trial and Shadowolf had slept well. His energy had been spent, and he had slept for thirteen hours to recover. His friends were lively and ready to talk to him, but his fears like fire within him.

Nelnar rested near the hearth while Mandy, the dark mare he had obtained during the first war, stood in a corner with straw that had been provided by Ursula.

The unicorn was not around, and he assumed that she was with Asgorna. His friends were stirring from their sleep and one by one greeted him. Words were not easy to find, but when Darcwulf arose, words were not enough.

"I still have to get used to seeing you with me," Darcwulf said. "I thought it was a dream."

"Trust me, it is not," Shadowolf replied, trying to get used to a relaxed conversation. His humour seemed to have vanished in the struggle. Darcwulf, in contrast, laughed and slapped his shoulders, while taking a seat beside him.

"Can I have some of that?" he asked, indicating the food and drink before them.

"Of course," Shadowolf replied. "It is for all of us. Can you imagine me eating all of this?"

"Relax," Darcwulf put his hands up in mock defence, and then helped his stomach to some fruit and meat.

"So," Darcwulf said, "Do you want to talk about what

happened in the temple? Where have you been?"

"Do you mind if I don't discuss that?" he replied. "I don't think I want to recount years of fighting. Let's just say, I don't think I was in this world."

The wakened group raised their eyes, but the sleeping figure remained still on the sofa opposite him. He groaned inwardly, taking in how gorgeous she still looked after so long. But she was different. He recalled a spirited girl, one that did what she wanted when she wanted to. It had been her forced kisses that had caused him to fall for her, besides other winning attributes.

Now, she was very quiet and suppressed. He wondered if maturity had finally taken its toll on her young mind, but he knew it wasn't that. He had left her when she needed him the most, left her behind to fight her own wars without saying goodbye. For two years she had probably thought he was dead.

Did her love die too? What would he find if she awoke?

"Tell me about Avalion?" he interrupted his own thoughts. Darcwulf had told him about the messages, and he had wondered who had sent it for it had not been him. Those questions had brought his mind back to home, a home he knew he might not get a chance to see anytime soon.

"Well, it is called New Avalion now, or NA for short," Skywolf said. He remembered the crush the daughter of Malkius had once had with him, but since the war he could tell it had grown into nothing but friendship and care. "The lands are divided as you remember it, your father's defences have grown stronger and the dream of *Avalendil* has been realised."

"The Mer-Kindgom?" he asked. "They have moved from Sea's Reach?"

"Yes," Shadowwe responded. "It took us several months, due to the constant siren and water-demon threats, but we finally managed to complete the warrens. It is isolated from the ocean beneath NA, but has access to the waters and main rivers via streaming tunnels."

"Fantastic," he said. "One of my dreams has been accomplished."

"While the others are left with nightmares?" Shedaaij suddenly said as she sat up. "Tell me, wolf, were you dreaming of us when you left us behind?"

"You were never a dream," he responded softly. "You were always living in my heart."

He stood up and walked over to her. He removed the gemmed rose from the pocket in his pants, and handed it to her.

"Do you think it changes anything, Shado?!" she said as she rose and walked to the fire, leaving the rose on the sofa. Nelnar came to her and nudged her with its nose, but she ignored it. "Leave me alone, you stupid dog."

Shadowolf whistled for the wolf to join him, and sat back down beside Darcwulf. Silence remained their company for a few moments.

"I suppose she saw the sprites?" Shadowolf attempted a joke.

"Yes," Darcwulf said, "But I don't think she's mad about that."

"One would think it would improve her disposition a little," he said.

"You've been gone so long," Sorceress said, "doing who knows what, who knows where. Allow her to express her anger."

Shadowolf nodded in reply and ate some sausage and salad.

"When can we go home?" Fransiska asked.

"I don't think I've met you," Shadowolf said politely.

"Oh, sorry," Skywolf and Angelia apologised simultaneously, but Angelia allowed Skywolf to answer. "She's from Costen. We went to school together and met up again at New Avalion. She's been a part of our trio ever since Angelicus left."

Shadowolf looked at Darcwulf, but received no reply.

"I won't be going home," Shadowolf said carefully. "There are other things I must do first."

"Can we tag along, then?" Dren asked. He had forgotten the stone-skinned gargoyle was seated at the back.

"Of course," Shadowolf smiled. "You came all this way to welcome me back. I think a journey with you guys would be more than enjoyable."

"Ok," Darcwulf said seriously. "So what are the 'things' we must do?"

"I am not leaving immediately," Shadowolf interrupted his

eagerness. "I need some more rest first. We will leave in the beginning of the next week."

"Fair enough," Darcwulf replied.

"Will you all be coming?" Shadowolf asked. Everyone nodded, and he ignored Shedaaij's silence. "Very well, let's see what kind of team we've got."

Shadowolf stood up and surveyed the crowd. They were well-rested and seemed ready for a fight. He didn't know where to begin, but it was better than sitting with the tension inside.

"I know of four elementals among us," he said, nodding to each in turn, "Darcwulf with fire, Skywolf and Angelia with water, and I have wind."

"I have water too," Fransiska spoke up. "That is why the three of us get along so well."

"Lastgorn, Gwyn and I don't worry with magic," Sny-Ten replied, turning to reveal his double-edged axe behind his broad back. The hilt of the axe had been held by thick rope slung over both shoulders and across his chest. Removing the axe during battle required unstrapping the arms out of the sling, but Shadowolf was sure he was adept at the art already.

His grey fur-coat had hidden the handle well, but Shadowolf could see the blue hilt of Lastogorn's falchion-sword peeping from behind his neck. These men were loyal to their weapons, and he had no doubt their weapons served them well. Gwyn held a green staff in her hand and her bow lay against the wall.

He remembered the effect cold steel had on elementals. His memory surged back to when the war of the dark lord started, and Shenama had been destroyed. He had temporarily gone to the burning city to save a friend that had appeared in his dreams, with an arm that had been injured during a competition at the college.

And once he had found her, he had sent his comrade Lanel back to the college and stayed to observe the destruction. By accidentally becoming involved in a fight, he had obtained Ruben-Willow lying in the grass. It was too neat and clean to have belonged to an orc, but using the blade he felt a strong connection. It enhanced his wind powers and sometimes directed his movements. He was sure there was more to the sword that was obvious at first glance.

Mannius Saphin, the sword-smith and cousin of Skywolf, had said so when he designed the hilt that would allow him to use the sword without the cold burning side-effects against his skin. Eventually it was discovered that one of the dark lord's amethyst pendants that he had taken from an orc had lodged itself in the metal. Later, two Lapis Pins had fused with the sword too. The blade was indeed mysterious.

"I have flight," Dren joked.

"You have more than that, Dren," Shadowolf said. "Your bravery and strength have brought us through more than most men can bear."

"The Orion have always specialised in close-quarter combat," Shadowwe announced. "We use weapons, but we can fight without them if need be. We have developed a very refined fighting style."

"Oh yes, ru-makiry," Shadowolf said softly, and Shadowwe frowned but held his thoughts.

"But to answer your question," Tinonte continued for the Orion, "Rennick and I are strong in the power of the spirit."

"Ok," Shadowolf sighed. "So we have seven elementals, two weapon masters and six makirs."

"And one mermaid," Darcwulf grinned mischievously.

"Darc!" Skywolf scolded.

"What?" he replied, still grinning.

"Nevermind, Sky," Shedaaij said as she left her solitary spot and made for the tunnel that headed back to the alcove. "I am not joining this stupid quest anyway."

"Honestly," Fransiska said, crossing her arms and following Shedaaij.

Shadowolf watched them go and decided to walk to the tunnel in the opposite direction.

"Where are you going?" Darcwulf asked.

"Just for a walk," he replied. "I need to clear my head."

"Don't make us wait two years before we see you again," his brother jibed.

The tunnel was ill-lit, but his eyes were sharp. It turned to his left and continued for a long while on.

He had known it would devastate her when he returned from

the temple and he realised he would not see her again. But Shedaaij had been his goal. She had been the reason that he strove to escape the dragon's world.

He had also thought that obtaining the power orb and killing Mercius would have assisted him in destroying the dark lord, but he now knew that there was more at stake. Another war was brewing, one that the dark lord Le'Mar was aware of and using it to his advantage.

He heard the patter of feet, but did not turn for he knew those paws well. Soon the tunnel came to an end, and he walked out into the open air on a cliff. The cliff stretched out to his right, and water fell from a hole in the mountain above it and rolled over the edge to the rest of the valley below it.

The sickle moon was rising in the east. Nelnar walked before him and jumped up with its paws on his chest. He bent down and snuggled with his neck into its neck. It nipped softly at his ear, and he laughed. He stood up and wrestled with the wolf, pulling at the mane at its neck and dodging its teeth.

"You missed me too, didn't you?" he said, sitting cross-legged on the cold stone floor and allowing the wolf to lay with its head on his right leg. They both looked at Sothos, absorbing the music of the water and the calm complacence of the venue.

"Shado!" a voice echoed from inside the mountain. It sounded urgent and he could tell from the second summons that the caller was not getting any closer. He sighed deeply and arose.

When he returned to the resting place, an odd site greeted him. He could not believe who he was seeing.

"We found him in the tunnel," Shedaaij said while she and Fransiska helped the man to a seat at the fire. Everyone was cautious with him, standing in a wide circle.

"Did Le'Mar send you?" Darcwulf demanded. Lastgorn and Sny-Ten drew their weapons.

"Wait," Shadowwe forestalled them. "I don't think he is here to spy on us. How could he know we were here, and why is he is so weak?"

"Besides," Shadowolf added, "Le'Mar thinks I am dead and I haven't done anything to tick him off lately. Wait a minute..."

"Exactly, Shado," Darcwulf said as Shadowolf approached to

get a better look. "He is a Saneth. Remember them, Lister's buddies?"

He remembered too well. When he and Darcwulf had gone to Eldor's Dungeons to find Mercius's cell, a Saneth by the name of Lister had found and attacked them. They had escaped the four-armed beasts and found the three gargoyles Dren, Fornoren and Masnen.

Later in the war, they discovered there were a group of four of them, including Lister. This man before him had been one of them. Shadowolf recognised the face.

The man looked up at him. Although he was weak and pale, his face was still intimidating. It had scales of a reptile instead of skin, and the lips were tightly tucked in. His mouth was human enough with the same type of denture structure and tongue, but his eyes and ears were by far different. It sunk into sockets like a dead man's skull. And deep in the depths of the eyes' abyss, a feint pulsing red light represented his pupils.

The other noticeable characteristic was the horns on his head. They were close-cropped, short horns that began above his brow and ran in a circlet around the top of his head. The centre of the circlet revealed the top of his bald skull.

He could tell the man was healing. The near-human skull started looking more human. The scales faded slowly to be replaced by skin with a green hue. The gaping eyes and ears remained hollow though. Shadowolf looked through the tattered shirt and saw his body had hardened scales, green on the sides but yellow on the stomach and chest.

Each scale looked like a small but strong coloured ball, and they all fit snugly together to form the natural armour of his body. But it took a moment to realise he had no nose. All that was visible were two tiny slits above his mouth that had been hidden by the scales before.

"I know you," the man said. "I saw you kill a Froth Hun a few years ago in Mercius's camp. In Iceland, if I remember correctly."

"That's right," Shadowolf replied. He had forgotten about that, and it seemed he had forgotten to tell his friends. They all looked at him and gaped.

"And then you rode off with his horse," the man pointed to

the black mare in the corner.

"Her name is Mandy," he said tersely.

"She never had a name before," the man said, his red eyes growing stronger. The man was getting better. When he moved his eyes back to Shadowolf, it left a small trail of light that faded in its wake. The pupils stopped pulsing and appeared to be at optimum strength.

"The Huns never cared for such pleasantries," the man continued as he straightened his back and then rose from his seat. Everyone tensed a little, but Shadowolf smiled.

"I must have made some kind of impression on you for you to remember me that well," he said.

"Are you kidding?" the man said. "It was you that caused so many problems for Le'Mar and Mercius. After seeing you that night, I changed. And Le'Mar felt that change."

"Which is why you are here," Shadowolf finished.

"Yes," the man said. "He had me banished from his castle and sent his army after me. I barely escaped before dropping off a cliff."

"Hold on," Dren said, dropping from his perch. "You know where the dark lord's castle is?"

"It's in the east, just off the elvin forest, everyone knows that," Skywolf said.

"No it isn't," Dren said, and Shadowolf could see in the man's eyes that Dren was right. "I have travelled on the outskirts of the foul lands of the east. He enters a red portal to his castle. I don't know where he truly abides."

"His castle is in the north," the man informed them. "It is above the Alcove of Light, west of the Dwarf Mountains."

The Clan were silent. Shadowolf sat down as he absorbed the news. The man nodded to the food and Shadowolf nodded in reply. He took a plate and dished some meat and salads.

"How did you get here?" he asked the man. "How long did it take you to come to the mountains?"

"I don't know," the man said. "I was knocked out by the fall, and I awoke in a sunny land. There, a dragon by the name of Mynisna led me through his villages and helped me find the way out. It's been a while since I have been on earth."

"How long?" Shadowolf pursued.

"About two years," the man confirmed his suspicions. "The trial at the end almost killed me."

"What was it?"

"I don't really want to think about that right now," the man said, and went back to his meal. He still had so many questions, but it could wait. Shadowolf stood and walked back to the tunnel that led to the waterfall.

"What is your name by the way?" he asked before he left the hall.

"Trimistus," he replied. "My name is Trimistus."

***

The assassin awoke from his dreary sleep. Something stirred his mind awake, and it wasn't the usual hunger and thirst. He got up from the bed and walked to the open window where the breeze greeted him with a joy he could not afford.

He had been hired by this earth for murder. Nolraldun had almost failed his test to be graded as a master assassin, but they had granted him one last test: to search out the man by the name of Trimistus and kill him.

As he looked out on the earthly city known as Carmel by the humans, the city where he had spent his two years on earth, he remembered how he had lost his quarry.

He had entered the portal to earth and immediately his job had begun. He had been in a castle that belonged to a man known as Le'Mar. He had jumped through the window and scaled the building's wall in pursuit of his prey.

But Le'Mar's army had caused some problems. In an attempt to stop Trimistus they had only succeeded in obstructing him in killing the man. And when he finally had his hands around the man's throat, they had dropped off a cliff to a deep chasm.

When he had awoken from the fall, Trimistus was already gone. Without any evidence of what had happened to him, Nolraldun was forced to seek refuge in Carmel until his assignment was complete, for the Semhum Kateth, the Guild of Dark Assassins, would surely kill him for failure.

He sent his black crow out again for the hundredth time.

***

Lucian Par'Mal sat on the dusty knoll overlooking the Harhonsa Village in the desert known as Bontu's Wrath. Ever since he and his wife Kailan had arrived in the village, he had wondered when the attack of the Windfarer would begin, but the winds were still and the only sign of destruction was from the dark lord Le'Mar.

Mercius was nowhere to be seen, and the mysterious power of the *Enodhim* had gone silent from the world. Yet, someone had to have claimed it. Was it possible that Le'Mar had betrayed Mercius and taken the power for himself? Why then had he not used it against the earth? Le'Mar still only used his fierce armies to conquer the lands.

While the Orion grew stronger in the sands of the Village, and Almos prepared the Sand Scorpions, Lucian was building a plan of his own. He was once a servant of the dark lord too, in a school that had trained children in the power of the elements, but thanks to his wife's love, he had turned to assist the earth.

He would not forsake them; he would not forsake her...

***

As Creotos was near rising, Ursula trotted to the only figure still awake. His wolf lay asleep at his side, but he watched the green world beneath the waterfall as if he were its master and could call forth giants and dragons at his will. Yet, his mind was lost to her observations, and she called him forth from his distractions.

"What are your plans, my boy?" she asked. "Will you go home?"

"Ursula," Shadowolf replied to the Unicorn. "Why did you request that I meet the dragons?"

"Excuse me?" she asked politely as she stood at his side looking out at the orange horizon to the east.

"Those many years ago, when I was on my way to stop Mercius from obtaining the power of the Windfarer, why did you ask me to forget the node and consult the dragons?"

"To give us time," she replied calmly, as a mother reassuring her child. "I knew that Mercius would not be able to unleash the power, for so it was foretold in the prophecy of the *Enodhim*."

"What if you were wrong and he managed to?"

"Was I wrong?"

"You know what I mean, but I guess the question doesn't make a difference now," he sighed. "Was it not better that I had defeated Mercius then instead waiting for another time to do it?"

"Yes, there was some fortune with you obtaining the power, although I wondered if the time for its release was right. But by fulfilling the prophecy of the Windfarer, you have begun a chain of events that must progress to its end.

"You know of what I speak," she continued in his silence. "Already, the dragons are rebuilding their opposition to Asgorna. It is a war that is unavoidable. Even in their worlds, it is a war that has been long anticipated."

"I have been to his world," Shadowolf finally uttered, "And I know what is expected of me at the end of all this."

"There is one thing that I would request of you too," Ursula said.

"Another? I might consider charging a fee," Shadowolf smiled softly.

"I am glad to see your humour has returned. I always liked that about you. It concerns an artefact that was lost many years ago. Do you know the importance of the horn on a unicorn's head?"

"Besides stabbing someone to death?"

"Contrary to popular believe, we unicorns try to keep our coats clean from such mess. Rather, it homes the sack that contains our power.

"You see, when we are born, the unicorn starts to form a sack under the cranial skin of its head. As its power grows, the sack pushes the mound of skin and plate outward, and the horn forms to create a tower of release.

"In such a way, the power can be concentrated at a central source, creating a larger exponential release."

"Ok, I understand the theory," he replied.

"How much do you know about the Battle of T'Mar's Scourge?" Ursula asked.

"Thanks to my acquaintance with Masara and the search for the Lapis Pins, quite a bit. Something to do with Masara and T'Mar having a great fight over the river, and causing horrific earth tumults from their battles until Masara defeated T'Mar. My history is a bit clouded after the past years with the dragons."

"I will not go into too much detail, but the important thing to note is upon what they were mounted when they fought. T'Mar was on the back of a pegasus, while Masara rode a unicorn."

"I see," Shadowolf said.

"During the last moments of the battle, T'Mar called dark forces from the bottoms of the darkest places. These forces are known as demons on several other worlds and I hope you never have to encounter them."

"What do they look like?" he asked, something tugging on his memory.

"They are effervescent beings, made only of spirit, but with the power to overcome weak minds and enslave bodies to their doing. They consist of pure evil, and I trust that you will know them when you meet them."

"I think I already have," he said. "I once helped mermen fight a score of sirens at Sea's Reach, and one of them was horribly deranged with a trident. It had an evil aura to it, and I think Lellian, the Mer-King, referred to her as a demon-queen."

"Then you know of what I speak," she continued. "When Masara and T'Mar finally clashed their last powers, their rides were submerged in the dark waters of the newly created fall, and in that battle for power, the unicorn won the fight, but lost her horn."

"What happened to the sack?" he asked.

"The sacks power is fused to the horn, so although the sap ran out into the water, the power was not lost."

Shadowolf looked up at Ursula's forehead.

"Your horn was longer then, wasn't it Ursula?" he assumed.

"Yes," she confirmed. "It was twice this size. With my powers gone, I struggled to bring Masara's unconscious form to the surface. If it were not for the elves…"

Shadowolf allowed the silence to reign for a moment as the sun breached the horizon.

"You want me to reclaim your horn?" he asked.

"Only if you plan to travel that way," she replied. "I have regrown some of my power, yet if I could get the old one back, there is a chance I could return to my former state. Otherwise I would have to wait another three thousand years before ever reaching that dream."

"Another three thousand?" he looked up at her in shock. "Have you never tried to reclaim it?"

"The waters are dark and unfit for a creature of light such as I," she said sadly. "I do not have the power for such a quest."

"And I do?"

"You are an *Enodhim*, are you not?" she smiled.

"I have released the power, but I have yet to be fully trained in its means. I don't know what I am completely capable of yet."

"Will you go?"

"Yes," he accepted. "I planned to have a look at the devastation that Le'Mar has caused in my absence. I will make it part of my trip up north."

"How do you plan to travel?"

"I want to take it slow. No teleportation, no flying, no hunting. I want to travel on Mandy's back and get used to horse riding again. It will give me time to talk to the others and see what the dark lord is up to."

"There is a chance," Ursula cautioned, "that, just like the prophecy of the Windfarer, the time of the DragonRider is upon us."

"I know," he replied. "Asgorna has spoken to me of the prophecy, and the chance that Le'Mar will use this war to fulfil it. And his words are still a counsel to my mind."

VILLAGE OF THE BEWITCHED
CHAPTER 4

A week later the Shadow Clan were three days into their journey south. Although Shadowolf's plans were for the north, he felt the need to visit the island where his college used to stand.

The days at the Asbec College of Elements were still fresh in his memory. He smiled as the images of Lanel, Harmony and Mourna flashed in his mind. They were his best friends at the school and he missed them dearly now. They could be anywhere and he wouldn't even now where to start looking for them.

His journey south upon Mandy's back to Lake Shadow would probably take another week, but he had time. He saw no signs of Le'Mar's army, no evidence that the dark lord knew he had returned. Surely Le'Mar knew of Mercius's failure and the death of the two Sandrihelin, Malfius and Kelsey.

And surely he knew that, with the failure, Shadowolf had released the power of the *Enodhim*. The Shadow Clan now knew what had happened and that the power resided in him, and it made them more apprehensive towards him. How much more apprehensive would that make the dark lord, and how much more prepared?

Shedaaij and Gwyn rode near the front of the troop. Shedaaij had decided upon joining them, but he was still unsure as to where he stood with her. Now and again he caught her smile and it gave him joy to see it. Fransiska, Angelia and Skywolf were good company for her, and he left her in their hands.

Darcwulf rode at his side, and Sny-Ten and Lastgorn on his other. The three spoke past him, but he didn't mind their chatter. It was good to hear these long dead voices return to his mind and echo off his brain. It made him feel alive again.

Dren walked mountless behind him and kept his silence, albeit he laughed at some of their uncanny humour. Nelnar trotted beside him, with the gargoyle's laughter reflected on its face. Beside the two, Trimistus rode upon a mount provided by Ursula, and next to him the unicorn trotted in silence.

The six Orion brought up the rear, each with their own mounts. They discussed nothing, and when they did it was in near silence. Shadowolf wondered how he would manage in a group that didn't talk.

Shadowolf looked down to see his sword dangling at his side. He had missed and sorely needed it in the Temple of Asgorna, but he was glad to have it back.

"What is that?" Lastgorn pointed at Shadowolf's chest.

"Oh this?" he smiled, pulling the chain out from under his shirt. "This is the Amulet of Larna Thorn."

"What does it do?" Sny-Ten asked eagerly.

"I can summon Asgorna when in need," he replied.

"Will he come?" Darcwulf asked.

"Only if he is free to do so," he said and the three friends laughed at the irony.

They marveled at the amulet of two dragons entwined around one another for a moment longer before moving on to another conversation.

"So here we are," Lastgorn raised an arm, "Finally on one of Shado and Darc's infamous quests." Shadowolf barked a short laugh.

"I told them about the quest for the Lapis Pins," Darcwulf smiled.

"Dren can tell you that it didn't end as well as we had hoped," Shadowolf told them. He briefly thought back on how they had obtained the pins that would allow Dren to walk in sunlight without turning to stone, but they had lost the two other gargoyles, Fornoren and Masnen, in the attempt.

"You know, for a world riddled with war, I must say it seems quite peaceful today," Shadowolf commented.

"Le'Mar has lain quietly for the last few months," Darcwulf said. "I am not sure if he is content with his conquest, but he hasn't invaded any lands recently."

"He builds his army in the east," Dren said behind them. "I have been to the wastelands of Eldor's Forest, and looked off its cliffs.

His army is in the thousands now."

"Wastelands?" Shadowolf almost stopped riding. "What happened to the elves?"

"They are still there," Dren reassured him, "although I do not know what their plans are. Since your disappearance, Eldor has been losing ground on the eastern border of his forest. The eastern mountains have been taken, and Eldor finally has a new defence set in place. As Darcwulf has said, Le'Mar has held back his attack these last few months for that very reason; to build an army for the final assault once he gains entrance."

"What is stopping him?" Shadowolf asked.

"Eldor has used a gem known as the Heart of Tigers to recreate the defence of the city. *Pernonil*, once the only gateway to the forest, has fallen, and I believe he has now chosen a new site for the gateway, yet none but the elves know the way."

"Maybe we should visit Eldor after our trip to the Scourge," Darcwulf suggested.

"Yes," Shadowolf agreed. "If the dark lord intends to strike there with his main force, we should be there to confront him and frustrate his plans."

"You love doing that, don't you?" Sny-Ten jibed.

"With all my heart," he smiled.

"Village!" Fransiska shouted up ahead, and the men looked up at her. A mist had rolled over the hills during their conversation, and was floating through the legs of their mounts already. Mandy remained calm as the mist touched her dark coat and frayed mane, but the other mounts became uncomfortable and stamped the earth lightly.

Shadowolf rode to the front of the group and led them to the apex of the rising hill. He looked over a small village barricaded by fence and rocks. The village was hugged by the hill on all sides, forming a bowl for its home.

But it was less a home than an empty wilderness. The timbers of the houses were rotten. Once two storey houses now had the wood of the top storey laying in the yards and forsaken stone roads. Even the roads were nothing but rubble.

"This is the work of Le'Mar," Shadowwe murmured.

He was right. Crude orc swords lay scattered over what used to be grassland, and the arrows of the Dra-hu'Mar stuck up from the hard soil and tattered tree trunks.

"There is one odd thing, though," Sorceress said. "There are no bodies."

Shadowolf noted that her usually pale blue face had darkened in the mist and her eyes were glowing like blue lights in the growing fog. Hers were not the only, as he saw Trimistus's eyes burning red. Mandy remained strong beneath him and it seemed that she became darker with the thickness of the fog. Her mane rustled in the wind like the broken leaves of the dying trees before him and her steamy breath had a hint of blood in it.

He turned back to look at the village and saw that Sorceress was right. No bodies littered the streets. It was as if the city had fallen in upon itself.

"You look like a soldier of death on that thing," Darcwulf commented as they viewed the ruins. Shadowolf smiled as he patted Mandy's neck. "Are you sure she's a mare? She stands as upright and strong as the best stallion in Avalion."

"You could check if you want, but I doubt she will afford you the opportunity."

"Shado," a voice called from the murky depths of the fog. It was Ursula. "I can't enter this city."

"I wasn't planning to," he replied, knowing her purity would not permit her entry into such desecration. "There is nothing to find here."

"Where to then?" Rennick asked.

"Around the village," he said. "I still plan to go south a bit longer."

"Very well," Shadowwe said in a nonchalant manner and the Clan rode east along the rim of the hill, leaving Shadowolf and Darcwulf still brooding over the village. Shadowolf closed his eyes and Darcwulf kept his silence for a moment.

"What do you feel?" Darcwulf whispered as the group left them behind in the mist.

"Besides the obvious evil in this place," he answered, "it feels like there is still someone in the village."

They watched until he caught a movement from the window of an abandoned warehouse.

"There!" he shouted and kicked Mandy to ride into the village.

"Shado! Wait!" Darcwulf tried to pursue, but the horse wouldn't budge. Instead it watched the mare ride away.

In frustration, Darcwulf started to dismount, reaching for his staff and cross-bow, when the stallion moved and rode into the village.

"Why didn't you just do that the first time round?" he asked it. The horse grumbled in response and continued on its way.

As they rode further in, the stallion's coat changed. The mist rolled over them and its brown hairs turned red. The stallion was still calm and unaffected by the change, but Darcwulf's eyes widened. Not only did the colour change, but in the chill of the fog the body of the horse became warm to the touch. Soft steam arose from its pelt.

"How did you do that?" Shadowolf asked him when they met in the centre of the bowl of the valley.

"I don't know," Darcwulf replied in astonishment. "There is some kind of evil in this village."

"You don't say?" Shadowolf said smugly and they looked around them.

They could hear the clatter of their group's hooves in the east along the outer rim. It echoed off the fallen houses and scattered dust, along the broken rocks and unsettled debris.

"Well, at least they're not worried about us," Shadowolf commented.

"I'm not so comforted by that," Darcwulf replied.

A little girl ran into their view with inhuman speed. Both horses trotted back from it and the two men had to hold them down. The ghost smiled at them maliciously and stuck her tongue out at them.

The tongue lengthened and snapped at Mandy's legs. The horses reared and they fell to the ground. Stallion and mare removed themselves from the ghost's presence, leaving their masters to deal with it.

"What did you say about Mandy's stallion-like nature?" Shadowolf asked as they stood up.

"Me?" Darcwulf said teasingly. "I don't recall saying anything about that."

The girl was gone. She had looked horrific. Not only had her glow intensified with the density of the mist, but she looked like she was a mature woman trapped in a small girl's body. Her face had been pockmarked with rabid rings of accentual ash and burnt blood.

"What seek ye in Plastinon?" a woman's voice called from behind a hedge in a yard off to their left.

"Oh, this place has a name," Shadowolf noted to Darcwulf.

"Never heard of it," he replied before addressing the woman in a mockingly formal manner. "We be in Plastinon seeking the wisdom of its spirits."

Shadowolf tried not to laugh, but Darcwulf's tone was intentionally imperious.

"There are no spirits here to consort with, traveller, so be on thy way," a second voice uttered. The two men looked at each other.

"How many are there of you?" Shadowolf called.

"Oh no, here they come," the little girl whispered behind the hedge.

"Ooh, trouble," Darcwulf said excitedly, running to his stallion to grab his staff and returning.

"Looking for a fight?" Shadowolf asked, drawing Ruben-Willow from its sheath.

"With you around, always," was the reply.

Three people emerged from behind a building to the right of the hedge. Shadowolf strained his eyes to view them, and could hardly make them out in the fog. He could sense their power, could almost see it radiating around their silhouettes.

"They are saying something," Darcwulf said.

Shadowolf listened carefully, and heard their voices travelling on the low breeze. Suddenly, Darcwulf's staff flared with fire and roared into the mist with ferocity, but still could not dissipate it.

"What are you doing?" he asked him.

"It's not me," Darcwulf replied. "But if it is fire they want, I can give them that."

Darcwulf rammed the end of the rod into the ground before him and an arc of fire spread around him. It then met at the rod's end again and flew along the ground towards the women with instant speed.

The woman on the left flung her hand outwards and the fireball went surging into the sky and hit one of the buildings, causing it to catch alight. Still, the mist held its cold and the fire died. Darcwulf commanded his staff to be still, and the staff went cold.

"She didn't even touch the ball, Shado," he said. "She just moved her hand and it followed."

"What are you?" Shadowolf asked them.

"We are the three witches of Plastinon," the centre woman responded in an aged voice. "We are not here of our own accord, but serve lord Le'Mar nevertheless."

"By declaring yourselves servants of Le'Mar is to declare yourselves my enemies," Shadowolf said.

"And who are you that we should be swayed by your voice?" the left woman asked.

"I am the *Enodhim*. Perhaps you've heard of me?"

The witches went still and then conferred between themselves.

"I am not sure you should be advertising your status just yet," Darcwulf commented.

"I know what I am doing," he replied, but Darcwulf looked upon an uncertain face.

"The Windfarer," the centre woman said before laughing a horrendously evil laugh. "Of course, who else would dare to enter such a desolate village but the Windfarer? My, my, where have you been all this time?"

"Relaxing on the beach," Shadowolf joked, "A little swimming with the mermaids and drinking some juice. You know, some retirement."

"Well, you have spunk, I'll give you that," the woman replied.

"What's spunk?" Darcwulf asked.

"Don't know?" he whispered in reply. "What are the chances we could just walk out of the village quietly?"

"Sure," the woman replied. "But first, I would like you to introduce you to some of my ... friends."

"I have a bad feeling about this," Darcwulf said.

"As you should, my dear boys," the right woman said eagerly. The left woman said nothing.

The centre woman started humming and speaking at the same time. She raised her hands to the earth and made some circling motion with them. The air shimmered before her and two pairs of eyes appeared. They were not physical eyes.

"Demons," Shadowolf informed Darcwulf.

"What is that?" he asked.

"You'll find out," Shadowolf replied.

The two supernatural demons flew at them. They swirled around them and struck at their bodies and souls.

The men rose up in the air with screams and wails that were lost in the fog. Darcwulf dropped his staff, but Shadowolf held on to his sword. He could feel the demon driving through his mind and out his eyes, into his veins and out of his aorta, back into his neck and out his mouth, all in one second.

Shadowolf clenched his teeth and summoned his spirit through his sword. The sword flared blue and he struck, looking through the blood on his eyes and dirty long hair into the ethereal eyes of the demon. The demon was motionless on his sword, and then disappeared. Shadowolf dropped to the earth.

As he was about to free Darcwulf, a wave of fire caught his attention and he turned to greet it. The fire was consumed by his body the moment it hit him. He opened his eyes after the fire dissolved into his soul, and then he ran to kill the fire witch on the right.

She continued to throw fire at him, but he allowed his body to consume them. This ability had come in handy with the dragons on Asgorna's world, and he knew it would come in handy on a world abundant with elementals too.

As he struck, time stopped. He was not aware of it. No one, except the three witches and an exceptional few, were. The witches of Plastinon walked around him and surveyed him.

"He still has the fire in his veins, yet it has diminished," the centre lady said.

"Amazing," the fire lady marveled. "He is moving past the age of the *Enodhim*, and it seems he is moving on to something much stronger. What do you make of it?"

"He is unique," the quiet lady said. "He is very strong, but not strong enough to face either Sonersaat or Le'Mar."

"Should we leave him to die at the hands of those merciless morons?" the time witch asked. "Or should we finish them now?"

"I say we finish them," the fire witch responded. "I am sure we will be rewarded greatly by our lord."

"I agree," the time witch said, but the third witch remained silent. The time witch touched Shadowolf's face and toyed with his shoulder-long hair. "Though he is such a handsome specimen."

The time witch opened her palm and an orb of darkness was born in it. It swirled with grey clouds and red lights, absorbed and released constantly by the core of black. She pulled back her arm for the attack, and then a bright light broke their concentration.

Hooves hit the earth and the unicorn reared up on her hind legs, her white coat reflecting the sunlight that had earlier been hidden by the mist. She dropped to all fours, but her horn still shone with the light of purity.

The time witch stepped back and tripped over a root of a nearby tree. She hit the earth with her back and looked up through the soft mist. The black orb was falling down on her and she lifted her arms to stop the blow.

The orb hit her, and her scream died. Black veins and vines tugged at her from her body and the earth, pulling her in upon herself. Her skin turned black, and then the grey of ash, before she became part of the soil of the earth.

Shadowolf's sword thrust continued to slice through the mist and he fell upon the earth confused. He was on his hands and knees staring into the ash that should have been the witch. Only moments before she had been standing before him, and he was sure she was about to defend herself. Now her dust lay before his eyes, a mere shadow of her former self.

He heard footsteps on the plain behind him, and although he was struggling to see through the sweat on his face, he was certain it was the Clan.

One of the two remaining witches moved from him and started chanting at the top of her voice. Soon, fire rose from the sands of the earth, and several creatures made of fire stood around the village. He estimated about a hundred of them. The fire witch left the area, but the third witch stayed behind.

Shadowolf arose with sword in hand and surveyed the village. He could sense they were more demons, yet their essences were pure fire. They were elementël demons of the strongest form, and he had no idea how he was going to stop them.

The Clan had drawn their weapons too, and Darcwulf, now freed of his demon, picked up his staff. He was weak, but Shadowolf knew he would fight.

"This is beyond you," the last witch muttered. "To vanquish a demon requires a power that you do not yet possess. Only a *Sadgi* can destroy one, and you are only an *Enodhim*."

"Thanks for the prophecy of doom," Shadowolf said, sword still dangling from his hands. "But I managed earlier with the other demon."

"He was a demon of the twelfth class," she said, and the fire demons were now closing them in. "These will kill you."

"Let them try!" he cried, and three of the demons were upon him.

He used the wind to thrust one aside, and dodged the second's attack while striking the third with his sword. The sword went through the demon and it landed on the earth unscathed.

"Oh," he said, as the hordes of demons attacked the Clan.

"I can help you!" the witch shouted. Shadowolf got struck in the face by fire and he fell to the ground. Without a moment for thought, fire erupted from his body and sword, and he returned the strike at the demon.

With absolute arrogance, the demon accepted the blow to its chest. It breathed brimstone into his face and roared as it pushed the blade further in. Shadowolf smiled at it.

He forced more fire into his sword, but also used his spirit to change its essence. He closed his eyes as his head burned with pain, but he thrust as much power through his arms as he could afford. The fire was concentrated mainly in his arms to the sword now, and the demon started howling. Its eyes burnt red and its mouth opened to the sky. Light from within stormed out its cavities and it exploded, throwing Shadowolf to the floor.

He rose from the ground again to face all the demons looking at him. The Clan were hitting them, but they were unmoved.

"Damn," the witch said, and she held out her arms to the demons, but whatever she was planning took too long. All the demons grunted aloud and flew into Shadowolf.

He exclaimed for a second, but then went silent. The Clan watched as he opened his pitch black eyes and grinned maliciously at them, a purple fire blazing around him. Darcwulf dropped his staff in defeat. He was not prepared to fight his brother.

More hooves clambered into the village and Shadowolf was knocked off his feet by a centaur. Another centaur stormed into the area, and stood over the unconscious body. The centaur that had hit Shadowolf slammed his open palm over Shadowolf's sternum, and the purple light erupted from his chest. Shadowolf's body rose up into the air and the demons fled into the open plains, surrounding the clan again.

The witch was still chanting with her arms held out wide. The demons cried and their light diminished. Their fire turned to soil and rock.

"I can't vanquish them, but they are now mortal," she told them. "You may now kill them."

Shadowolf's levitated body fell to the ground, and he slept as the Clan and two centaurs chopped away at the army of demons.

He awoke to the warmth of the fire. They were still in the bewitched village, but the mist was gone. It was night with the moon overhead, so he guessed that it was midnight.

His body was in pain, but it was nothing compared to the confusion in his mind. It was twice in one battle that he had been rendered unconscious and events had unfolded without him present. Even in his weak state, he vowed that he would not permit it to happen again. The Clan would not always be there to save him.

He sat up, but not without a sharp pain shooting through his head. His movement caused Darcwulf to run to his side. He was talking, but Shadowolf could not hear him for a few seconds. Soon, however, his voice entered his head.

"...over there. They say they come from the north, and are willing to journey with us for company until Philagis."

"The witch..." he muttered as Darcwulf brought warm ale to his lips. "Where did you get ale?"

"Millon and Kentaur," he smiled. "The centaurs, the ones I just told you about. They had some sacks of ale with them. They said it would bring you to your senses more readily than water."

He drank more of the brew and sat up steadily as it travelled through his veins. Blood moved to the parts of his body that required it most, and the ale moved to his head where he really didn't need it at all, but he welcomed it. It soothed the headache, but heightened his senses. He was worried about the after-effects, but ignored it. All that mattered was that he was alive.

"Shedaaij?" he asked.

"One matter at a time," Darcwulf said. "We killed them all with no casualties, thanks to the centaurs and the witch. She is still with us, sleeping over there by the tree awaiting your forgiveness.

"Shedaaij is over there by the girls. She is tired from worry over you, and has passed out finally, so I wouldn't wake her."

Shadowolf looked at the sleeping form of the witch. She was pale compared to the others in the Clan, with the exception of the pale blue of Sorceress. Her hair was as black as her tatty robe, and she held her beauty well.

"Her name is Heula," Darcwulf told him. "She is from Philagis too, which I believe is one of Le'Mar's hives of activity. And get this; she is thirty five years old."

"What?" Shadowolf exclaimed softly. "That's thirteen years older than I am. She doesn't look a day older than twenty."

"I know," he agreed. "But I suppose witches can do that."

"You could almost look past that," Shadowolf smiled.

"Hey, you've got the mermaid," Darcwulf joked.

"Oh, right," Shadowolf said somberly. "I am still not sure where I stand with her. She won't talk to me."

"I think she's over that, Shado," he told him. "She was really concerned about you. She still loves you."

Shadowolf stared at the sleeping back of Shedaaij and sighed.

"But do I still love her?" he asked his brother.

"That is something you will have to confront," Darcwulf replied. "So, where are we heading tomorrow?"

"Still south," he said. "I don't know why, but I need to see Shadow Island again. I need to find closure. I want to make sure it really is over."

DESERT'S WRATH
CHAPTER FIVE

Creotos broke upon the soft sands of Bontu's Wrath. The Harhonsa Village was bustling with activity and the children were playing their sand games. Lucian sat in his living room with his wife Kailan, their two year old toddler playing on the blanket before them.

"Growing up in the desert," Kailan said. "I was hoping something better for him."

"Dreams of our past," Lucian replied.

"I knew we should have left Asbec long time ago," she said, referring to the college that they had both taught at before its destruction by the Windfarer. "Or at least, you should have resigned from the Sandrihelin."

"You know I only remained with Farnerd to better learn of their plans."

"And yet, we are here in the desert," she replied snidely.

"Almos is strengthening the Sand Scorpions," he said impatiently. "He is the only man that would overlook my allegiance with the dark lord. No other tribe would have accepted me."

"And how long do you think the dark lord would overlook your treachery to him? How long before the desert feels the wrath of his vengeance?"

"We will fight," Lucian promised sternly. "You are right; he will not rest until he has me, and no matter where I make my abode, he will destroy their homes too."

"Is there no where we can go where death will not follow?"

"I have a place in mind," Lucian said. "But it is but a shadow of hope."

"And where, pray tell, is that?"

"uPendus," he said.

"uPendus?" she said. "Does that place even exist, Lucian? Now

I know you've gone mad."

"I have studied the scrolls," Lucian said. "I know I can find it. And once there, not even Le'Mar would dare its lands."

Kailan replied with her silence. He understood that she thought him absurd. After all, only the philosophers and prophets spoke of the fabled land of uPendus. For him to suggest...

The ground shook. Lucian caught a vase before it fell on his son, and waited. The ground shook again. Something was wrong. The Horn of Harhonsa sounded, and Lucian turned to his wife in alarm.

"Take Philanus and go to the barracks," Lucian ordered. "Go now, woman!"

He ran for the circular stairwell and made for the top of the tower that was attached to his home. He broke the surface and looked out over the desert. He couldn't see the danger, but he could still hear the catapults being fired.

Then he saw it in the northeast. They were small because they were still a distance away, but their forms were distinguishable. The dragons were carrying men on their backs, and he counted eleven of them.

The Sand Scorpions would be enough. He trusted that they would be able to handle the situation. Looking down on the village, he saw his family running with other families to the barracks. They would be safe there.

The armies of Bontu's Wrath marched in groups of hundreds over the dunes towards the approaching dragons. The nets were pulled up from under the sand to create a makeshift barrier. It would force the dragons to fly higher than planned and give the catapults and archers a better distance to their targets.

They were ready. The dragons were almost upon them. Lucian tightened his grip on the tower wall. And then the battle began.

The dragons dropped on the men standing outside the net wall. Flames belched down on them and their claws raked at the men. One dragon did enough damage with one strike that a garrison of a hundred fell to naught.

Sand Scorpions caught the claws of the dragons and started to clamber up their legs. The men astride the dragons struck down with their arced blades and the Scorpions fell, their blood mingling with the sand.

One of the catapults hit a dragon on its head, and the dragon fell from the sky. The man on its back pulled the rein, but the dragon still plummeted and hit the nets. Like a fly in a spider's web, it hung there. The archers turned their arrows towards it and a catapult was ready to fire when the dragon opened its eyes and immediately tore at the net.

The net broke and the dragon landed inside the village. Fire flew at the catapults and the wood went up in the flames. The dragon ran and stomped at the archers, but not before the man on his back was struck in the heart by an arrow and fell to the earth.

There were still many Scorpions, but this would not last. Lucian ran down his tower and into his living room. Suddenly the timber of the houses imploded with the force of the dragon's power and Lucian was hurtled to the floor.

His head throbbed intensely. He could see blood dripping from his head to the floor. His family's faces appeared in the blood and, with anger growing inside, he rose.

He ran for the opening that the dragon had created and summoned the wind as he jumped. The wind carried him up and he landed on the back of the dragon. The dragon thrashed and jumped about, but he yanked the rein and it rose up into the air.

With force, he directed it towards the closest dragon. If he knew how, he would have commanded the dragons to spew fire, but as such he could only direct its course. The other rider had no such problems, and the dragon Lucian rode on turned its back to allow the other dragon to burn him.

Lucian leapt from its back and the wind carried it to the other dragon. The wing almost clipped him, but he twisted in mid-air and recovered to dodge the thrust of the rider's blade. He extended his legs to simultaneously knock the rider off and saddle the dragon's back.

The largest dragon reared up before him, his scales magnificently red and green, with a yellow belly shimmering in the sunlight. Its black wings spanned across his vision, but before it could attack he leapt for its neck.

He called the wind to push him onto its neck. He sat on it facing its rider.

"Sonersaat," Lucian remembered. "It has been a few years."

"Too many, old friend," Sonersaat replied. "Or should I call you traitor?"

"Call me what you like," he replied.

"Very well," Sonersaat said. "But you shall call me DragonRider."

"DragonRider?" Lucian repeated. "You deign to carry that title? You know what happened to Le'Mar's Windfarer?"

"Mercius was pathetic," Sonersaat said. Lucian could hear that the dragons had entered the village. He feared for his family's life, and turned to see the families riding on camels out of the city. They were heading south to New Avalion, as Almos had planned should things go wrong. Why was Almos giving up so early?

"At least they understand when they are defeated," the DragonRider said. "If I remember, your stubbornness would never allow such surrender."

"You will never fulfil the prophecy," Lucian warned.

"And who will stop me?" Sonersaat asked haughtily. "You know my command of the wind is better than yours. The dragons have pledged their allegiance to me, as the prophecy foretold. I will claim this land as my own."

"Then I will ensure that the prophecy falls at my feet!" Lucian leapt for Sonersaat, but the wind recoiled against him and buffeted him over the dragon's head. The dragon struck at him with its claws, lashing his back and stomach. The riderless dragon burnt his wounds with fire, and he struck the sands with a loud crack, rolling down the dune to his resting place beside a burning catapult.

"And so my reign begins!" Sonersaat shouted. The remaining Scorpions watched as the DragonRider called his men away, and the dragons left.

Almos rose from behind a burning pyre, his face covered in sand and blood. He groaned as he crawled over to Lucian's body, and used it as his pillow.

"Our families will be safe," Almos sighed. "That is all that matters. Bontu bless them, and us."

Over the dunes above him orcs stormed into the village after the caravans and remaining Scorpions heading south. Almos, not having the strength to protect the families, closed his eyes to the desert sun, and gave up his spirit.

***

It was another wasteland. They had reached a large iron wall, but he had scaled it to the top and looked over it. Dark towers stood everywhere south of the boundary, and fires erupted spasmodically from the earth in lakes that should have held water. To the southeast, where Asbec College once had been, was the corrupted Shadow Island. The rocks were strewn over the barren land and crumbling into the lake. Lava pits boiled over from the centre, and the magma flowed into the waters.

It was truly gone. The iron walls surrounded the vast perimeter to the south.

"It is known as the Dark Boundary," Kentaur informed Shadowolf. "As I said, everything in these walls belongs to Le'Mar."

The land was vast, larger than Avalion even with its new defences. It would take an army ten times the number of the earth's men to destroy this stronghold.

"The two closest cities are Marnak and Lister," Millon said. "The three you see running in line south are Larnal, Tristah and McCanibal. The tower area you see along the lake is the part they call Tal."

"I recognise at least one of those names," Shadowolf said, frowning hard.

"Something bothering you?" Darcwulf asked.

"I'll discuss it tonight at camp," he replied. He called the wind and let it carry him down to the earth again. He enjoyed the cool breeze whipping up his hair from his face and rustling is clothes. When he landed, his long hair fell on his cheeks again.

"We head north," Shadowolf told the Clan as he mounted. Nelnar stood beside him regally, "To T'Mar's Scourge."

***

"Almost," Chenesia whispered. She could see the shadow of the guard against the wall, but her heart beat so loudly in her head it distorted her vision.

"Are you ready?" Genewiu asked, with her frail body about to give out on her.

"As ready as I have ever been," she replied to the pegasus. She held in her hand a fragment of rock that had fallen loose from the cell wall the night before during a mild shake in the earth. She had never felt such a quake before, and she had lost her balance. Soon after, a rock fell onto her arm, the rock she now hid behind her back.

"What is this noise? You should be strapped for waking me," the guard muttered as he neared Genewiu's cell.

"Aren't there extra rations of food?" the pegasus asked.

"Do you think this castle was built to serve you, fair one of light?!" he mocked her. "Should I lay out the golden trestles and silver chandeliers?"

"We're hungry," Chenesia leaned towards the bars, her dirty body pressed against it. She had become accustomed to the reek of her body and the black soot that accumulated on her skin. Without sunlight, she had become a specter of her former life. Yet, the guard stared at her body in longing. Never in her life did she think she would sell herself for freedom. She felt violated by his stare.

"Then you shall wait for your supper," the guard turned to leave.

"How about some water?" she sang, as she grasped a bar with her free hand. Her face caressed the bar. "Maybe some pineapple suine?"

"Oh, you are pushing your luck," the guard said. His face was rippled with scars and dried blood. The clothes on his body were filthier than she judged her own body to be, and she felt revolted when he approached her cell. "But mayhap it is time that we taught you a different type of lesson."

She could feel the fear rising in her. She had anticipated his lust, knew that he would be drawn to it. It happened exactly as she had hoped. Yet, as he pulled his keys out to open the cell, she retreated to the back wall, her eyes open.

"Leave her alone!" Genewiu stamped the ground and rammed her body against the bars between their prisons.

"Oh, shut up. Or I shall deal with you as kindly," he sneered.

The cell opened, and he grinned malevolently at Chenesia. He looked down at her smooth, dirty neck and then at her plump breasts that her torn and shriveled purple dress found hard to conceal.

She leaned against the wall and let her body sink to the ground, huddling her knees against her breasts. The dress was torn on the side, and her left leg and thigh opened up before she caught his eyes looking down at it. She closed her leg, tears starting to fall down her cheeks.

"That's it," the guard said in a dark voice. "Cry for me. Let me hear you whimper."

"STOP IT!" Genewiu renewed her attacks in the bars. With one swift move he drew his sword and slammed it against the bars.

"I told you to stop, or I will gut you, I promise!"

Chenesia's fear forced her to rise and slam the rock against the side of his head. It wasn't hard enough to cause him to fall, but it gave her time to steal the heavy short sword and drive it into his heart. After a stagger and a snort, he fell on his face.

"Chenesia, the keys," Genewiu called, but Chenesia dropped the sword and fell to her knees in tears. She had never killed a man before. She had always been pursued and chased, and had defended herself in *Pernonil*, but she had never drawn blood. This truth stung like an arrow in her head, and she watched as her arms and legs shook with the shock.

"Chenesia, please…" Genewiu pleaded. "We must leave before it's too late."

With frustration, she pulled the keys from the guard and flung it through the bars to Genewiu. She didn't have the strength to do it.

"Do you want us to die here?" Genewiu shouted. "I don't have hands!"

Chenesia knew time was running out, and she found it hard to rise. But the promptings from Genewiu were making her mad, so she reached for the keys which the pegasus kicked back, and opened her cell.

With no more strength remaining, she mounted Genewiu without permission. The last thing she remembered was the cold coat of Genewiu's neck hitting her face as she collapsed into darkness.

"I urge you to be strong, Maren-Ti," Eldor, lord of the elves and keeper of the elvin forest, said. "I know the desire that claims your heart."

"Two years, Eldor," the baron of the Vale of Tigers replied from the dark recess of the study. His closed fist glowed red. Within it he held the key to the elvin kingdom. "Two years since he captured my daughter from your forest, the safest place on the earth."

"I am sorry that I did not do everything in my power to protect her," Eldor said sadly. "With the power of the *Enodhim* released, the protection of the forest also fell. I lost *Pernonil*."

"And I lost my daughter," Maren-Ti reminded him again.

"If I could find her, I would," the elvin Lord said.

"Then why don't we attack the eastern camps?"

"I have surveyed the lands with the eye of Bontu, but I can find no trace of her in the camps or in Iceland. If she is on this planet, I cannot find her."

"I thought you were above any power?"

"I never claimed such talent," Eldor retorted. "Will you put the life of the elves in danger for the sake of your daughter?"

"No, I didn't..."

"I have trusted men before and they have betrayed me," Eldor warned. "The only reason I stay from my home is for your sake, remember that."

The lord of the elves stormed from the room, his last remaining grace gone.

***

Kailan held Philanus in her arms at the rear of the wagon. The orcs were plenty, but the Orion and Sand Scorpions had done the best they could to hold off the fittest orcs.

Now they needed to do no more. Although a hundred orcs still raced across the desert after them, the desert was doing the killing. One after the other, the orcs fell to the ground, dehydration and sunburn getting the better of them.

And they were almost there. The grasslands lured them further south and the high bastioned walls of New Avalion rose upon the horizon like the morning sun. Soon, they would have Degron warriors to bring them to safety.

The horses raced off the desert sun and onto the welcome lush grasses. Someone called for the Harhonsa Tribes to halt once they were far enough inland. They watched the final approach of the orcs.

There were ten remaining. It must have been an hour ago that Kailan had counted a hundred, but the desert sands had brought them down to a tenth. Yet they continued in subservience to their master. Rather death by humans than the cruel punishment of their lord.

Only one made it to the grassland, and the orc dropped on its face. A few men hurried to the orc and lifted its face. It was still alive.

She had been a woman once, before the dark lord had fused orc blood with hers and transformed her into a hurorc. Her long black hair hung cruelly on her bloody cheeks, but she had beautiful blue eyes that squinted out at them.

At the command from a Scorpion general, they gave her water and tied her up, placing her on the back of a wagon. Then they continued south to New Avalion.

The wind rose upon the sands and rolled over the dunes. It was unusual for the sands to feel its embrace this far north, yet it had been summoned and searched for the requester.

His body lay limp under a dead body, and he was unconscious, yet the summons was clear. The wind thrust the body aside and gently lifted Lucian up into the air.

Lucian grumbled as he opened his eyes to the vast vista beneath him that was covered in smoke and fire. He wouldn't waste his energy on regret or anger. He turned over on his stomach and transformed into an eagle. He headed south.

VILLAGE OF THE DAMNED
CHAPTER 6

The Shadow Clan trudged north in the fading sunlight. Shadowolf had many questions in his head, but he held his peace for camp. Since he had left the world it had turned into a nightmare, but protected within the confined walls of New Avalion, the Clan would not have been able to provide the answers, with the possible exception of Dren.

Nelnar ran at his side, and he could see the wolf was exhausted.

"Break for camp!" he shouted, raising his arm at the front of the group.

The horses were groomed and led to fresh grass in the plains. It was looking to be a clear sky in the open fields, and he feared to light a fire still so close to the Dark Boundary, but they would need warmth and food.

Soon, blankets were laid out where their centre of commune would be, and Shadowolf and Darcwulf started the bonfire from the wood Dren provided. The centaurs arrived with a deer and an antelope and stepped off to a near shallow lake to skin and clean the meat.

"Strange that they would kill their own kind," Skywolf said to Shadowolf by the fire.

"I think it more a case of them offering their lives to the centaurs," he replied.

"Shado," Shedaaij called from behind him. He turned his head around to her and saw the difficulty in her eyes. She needed him.

"Excuse me," he told Skywolf.

"Of course."

He stepped over the log he had been sitting on and made his way to her. Her back was towards him now as she walked away from the group, but soon she waited for him to reach her.

He marveled again at her beauty. Her black hair still fell upon her shoulders, probably trimmed to keep it that length, ending in curls. The white buttoned shirt revealed the armoured coral breast straps she still wore, although it seemed a different hue than he remembered. On her legs she wore tight purple leggings with black straps that twirled about her legs. At various places, the straps had sheaths that he assumed were meant to hold throwing knives, although none were present.

He noticed she had a dagger on her hip with an ornate coral hilt. Another glance to the other side of the hip, and he realised there was a twin dagger on the other side. Each one was the length of her forearm.

"I am sorry that I didn't say goodbye," he started.

"It has taken..." she began to say, and swallowed hard. "It has been a hard two years, but the mermaids were there for me. I guess the construction of *Avalendil* kept my mind occupied."

"There was nothing I could do."

"I've slowly come to accept that", she nodded, more to herself than to him. He caught a twinkle of a tear in the rising moonlight.

"But now seeing you again after all this time, I am conflicted inside," she cried openly now. "I am not sure whether to feel relieved or hate you."

He grabbed her and held her in his embrace. Her eyes flooded open onto his chest and the rivers flowed from his onto her hair.

"I missed you so much, Shedaaij," he confessed. "When I saw you again, I had forgotten our time apart and had wanted to embrace you with my soul."

"I know," she said and then pulled away from his chest to look into his eyes. "I am still yours."

"As am I yours, Shedaaij," he said as he leaned down to kiss her. They were lost in each other's love before holding each other again.

"We had better return to the group," Shedaaij said, finally with a smile on her face. She cleared her eyes and then kissed the tears on his cheeks.

They returned to the fire and Shadowolf sat down between Skywolf and Shedaaij on the log. Darcwulf, Fransiska and the Orion were seated across blankets opposite them, laughing and getting to know each other better. He had no idea where Dren and Nelnar had disappeared to.

Then he realised that Heula and Trimistus were also gone. That disturbed him. Had they returned to Le'Mar? He feared that the dark lord would learn of his return and start trouble before he could reach the Scourge. But there was nothing he could do if that was the case. He knew what was expected of him, whatever the outcome.

The others on the blankets broke his reverie by moving the blankets around the fire. Shadowolf looked at the horses to ensure that Mandy was alright, and saw that Ursula stood at her side, apparently asleep.

"So, Shado," Darcwulf addressed him. He suddenly felt hot. Why did it always seem like he was under interrogation? "I think it's time you explained something to us."

"I'm listening," he replied tensely.

"We want to know," Scarlette said, "if there is something about the dragons that we should know about."

"What makes you think that?"

"Well let's see," Fransiska said. "You arrive from a dragon temple with the Trimistus fella. Then we hear about this DragonRider prophecy. It all seems very strange."

He had never heard an accent like Fransiska's, but he liked it. It amused him, and she frowned as he smiled. Darcwulf smiled too, and looked deeply into her eyes without her noticing.

"Sorry," Shadowolf apologised. "I should have told you sooner. At the moment a war between the dragons is brewing. It is a war that has been expected for centuries in their world. There is a split amongst their loyalties."

"Asgorna is the king of the dragons. He governs them all and lords over them whether good or evil. However, a dragon by the name of Maneto caused dissent among the dragons in Asgorna's kingdom, and many followed him into the darkness."

The group stared at him entranced, and he saw that Ursula had joined them.

"When did this all happen?" Darcwulf asked.

"Ten years ago," he replied. "But when I arrived, Maneto and some of his followers had disappeared from the kingdom, leaving us to deal with the followers of the dark that had stayed behind."

"Is that why Asgorna called you?" Shadowwe asked. "To fight in his war?"

"No, not initially. Ursula had spoken to him of the Windfarer prophecy, and they had realised that only a pure *Enodhim* could unlock the node of power. Their search brought them to me.

"He requested Ursula to urge me to meet him that he may speak with me about the dark lord. But I didn't listen. After I destroyed Mercius and the Sandrihelin, I had no power left and passed out. Asgorna then took me to his world, which is when a battle began.

"I asked to be returned, but we were under attack and I had no choice but to fight. We were on guard for two years when we had a short victory over them. Asgorna then asked me to join him on a journey to another world, but I told him that I had to return."

"So the war of the dragons is over?" Skywolf asked beside him.

"No, unfortunately Maneto is still out there," he replied. "As a matter of fact, when Asgorna and I returned here, he told me he felt Maneto's power, and he is here on Celenic Earth."

"You speak of your home as if you are a visitor," Darcwulf commented.

"I still feel like a stranger here," he confirmed. "Everything has changed."

"Will they be waging their battle here?" Shadowwe asked.

"Not unless Asgorna can help it," Shadowolf replied. "But I think it will happen anyway. I believe that Le'Mar will use the war of the dragons to his advantage."

"He will use it to fulfil the DragonRider prophecy," Shadowwe guessed.

"Exactly my thoughts."

Dren, Nelnar, Trimistus and Heula arrived just as the centaurs brought the meat for the fire. Millon had a roughly crafted grill made of steel mesh and two wooden pylons for support in his hands. He drove the pylons into the earth a small distance from the fire and placed the mesh across them. Kentaur hung the skinned meat from a nearby tree while Millon stared into the fire.

"I need something to carry coals over," he said.

"Hold on," Darcwulf said as he rose. Fire blazed from his hands and he reached in for burning logs. He carried it over to the mesh and pylons and tossed it underneath. Shadowolf smiled as the girls' worried screams subsided.

"That was amazing," Fransiska said as he sat down.

"It was nothing," Darcwulf said, smiling back at Shadowolf.

"Now I have some questions for our fellow travelers," Shadowolf said.

"We will answer what we can," Millon said as he burnt the grill in the fire to sanitise it.

"Where do you come from?" he asked politely.

"We are from the north," Kentaur replied. "We are from a town called Philagis."

"How is it that you know so much about the dark lord?" he asked.

"We work for him," Millon replied. Shadowolf stared in shock at the centaur and the group was similarly stunned. They were not sure whether to attack or not.

"Excuse me?" Shadowolf finally asked. "You work for Le'Mar?"

"Yes, we do," Kentaur confirmed.

"I don't understand," he said. "You helped us in Plastinon."

"What you don't understand is your good fortune," Millon replied. "We were sent to Plastinon by Kraakis, lord of the centaurs."

"The Butcher of Philagis?" Shadowwe asked.

"Yes, he is known as such by many," Millon continued. "He asked us to bring the three witches to him, and when we arrived we thought we saw you, Shadowolf, preparing to kill the last of the witches. Little did we know you were possessed by a demon."

"However," Kentaur interrupted, "You did kill the one, and we tried to stop you from killing Heula, but Heula confused us when she converted the demons."

"Why did you help us, Heula?" Shadowolf asked, the suspicion clear in his voice.

"You are the *Enodhim*," Heula replied. "That is the reason why I have asked the centaurs not to attack you. They are not merely journeying along as your companions. They are taking you to Kraakis."

"What business..." Darcwulf rose.

"Very well," Shadowolf stalled him, and he stared dumbfounded and angry in return. "We will meet this Butcher of Philagis."

Dren nodded in agreement, and Ursula smiled, but the others were not so accommodating. Yet, they held their silence for the time being.

The rest of the evening went on without further discussion of the topic, and Shadowolf went to sleep early.

***

"Shadowolf?" he said, staring out the large window that faced south over the land.

"The *Enodhim*," she added.

"You're sure?" he asked.

"Nestef looked into his spirit," Maerlesa replied.

"She had time to do that?"

"Nestef stopped time," she said, and then hung her head in shame.

"And yet, he killed her and probably Heula too?" he asked.

"There was a unicorn with them that countered the spell," she replied.

"Interesting," he said.

"Isn't it, Sonersaat?" a voice said as the door opened.

"Lord Le'Mar," Sonersaat replied as he bowed his head.

Le'Mar walked with a black staff in his hands. He wore simple, red clothes with a dark purple cape, the hood dangling on his back. His long black hair reached down to his shoulder blades and his eyes shone blue. His face was free of any marks; in a sense, Le'Mar reminded Sonersaat of grace of the elves, but he knew Le'Mar bore no kin to them.

"Is this why you summoned me from the desert?" Sonersaat asked.

"It is a mere matter," Le'Mar replied. "My crows inform me that the tribes of Bontu's Wrath have reached Avalion. That is good."

"Why is that?"

"I can now use the desert for my own purposes," the dark lord replied. "A lot of history and power lies in those sands, Soner."

"And what of this Shadowolf? What is he to me?"

"I had forgotten about him," Le'Mar said as he took his seat at the window and turned to face them. "Two years ago I sent an *Enodhim* by the name of Mercius to claim the power of the *Sadgi*. Mercius had neglected to inform me that Shadowolf was interfering with business in Iceland, but the Saneths told me about him once Mercius had been defeated."

"Why did you not send me? I am an *Enodhim*."

"You only claimed mastery of the wind a year later," Le'Mar replied. "Because of Mercius's experience I was sure he was chosen to claim the power.

"One of my Saneths, namely Lister, mentioned that he met Shadowolf and his brother in Eldor's Dungeons. According to him, the boy did not hold significant power. I could not understand how he could release the node.

"But I have pondered on it, and remembered when the power node had been made. Judging by Shadowolf's approximate age, I could say that the power was made at his birth, but I can't be sure. If that is true, then the power was rightfully his from the start, waiting to be released when he was ready to receive such power."

"And what of the DragonRider prophecy?" Sonersaat asked.

"That is what concerns me and why I have summoned you," the dark lord brushed his goatee with his fingertips. "Maneto has informed me that Asgorna has returned to earth after his victory in SumonsVale. Now Maerlesa tells me Shadowolf is back."

"But what of the prophecy?!" Sonersaat said, trying to quell his impatience. Le'Mar glared at him calmly.

"I must consult Philgarn's scrolls again. It mentioned that the DragonRider would have to find the power of the dragon within him, but the philosophers always considered a theory that the position would have to be contested for. I still have to determine whether he holds that power or not."

"So, it could either be him or I," Sonersaat realised. "Should I find him and kill him for you?"

"He isn't strong enough to defeat Sonersaat, my lord," Maerlesa said. "I have seen his low power."

"And unless he grows very strong, very quickly, he won't be a problem for a while," Le'Mar pondered.

"But I can take him now!"

"No," Le'Mar said. "Then the war of the dragons will be upon us, for Asgorna and Maneto will be as much part of the prophecy as you and he are.

"No. You will wait until I have what I want. Maerlesa, I need you to meet them in Meëntis. I want you to call on the dead."

"Where will I find the bodies to do this?" she asked.

"Trust me," Le'Mar grinned. "The bodies have already been provided for."

"Why so much effort for such a weak fool" Sonersaat asked.

"Because Ursula is with them," he replied. "That is my greatest concern."

***

"Shado," Shedaaij rode to his side. "It's been a day since we've spoken about Philagis. How long do you want us to believe you are agreeing to this because we are passing through?"

"Well, we are passing through," he smiled, but kept his head facing forward. Creotos was warm and gentle on his neck. There was no wind or clouds and he soaked in the warmth. Nelnar trotted at his side while the group rode behind him.

"It's me you are talking to," Shedaaij said. "What's the real reason? Please don't lie to me."

He looked at her and realised she was right. She did not deserve to be lied to.

"Darcwulf!" he shouted, and after a moment, he rode up laughing at something Fransiska had said.

"Hey, what's up?" he asked.

"Nothing much," Shadowolf said calmly. "Look, I feel bad about not letting you know about my intentions."

"No hard feelings," he said. "But it would be nice to know what's going on in that estranged head of yours."

"I just didn't want to confront them too much about the issue," he told them truthfully. "If they want us to meet Kraakis, then let's meet Kraakis. When we left on this journey I told you I intend finding out what the dark lord is up to. This is part of that plan."

"So you thought you'd just find out, seeing as how it is on the way?" Darcwulf finished. "I got ya. Now, can I go?"

"Sure," Shadowolf and Shedaaij laughed. Darcwulf left to join Fransiska again.

"Hey, look," Shadowolf nodded ahead of them.

In the distance, huts and shacks were portrayed on the northern horizon. Trees that extended from the east bordered the village on the right, but the village itself was situated in the open grasslands.

Trimistus rode up on Shadowolf's right.

"The centaurs informed us that the village is called Meëntis," he told them. "We should make our way around the town, they say."

Shadowolf looked at Trimistus. His green face was pale in the sunlight, but his strength had returned. His silver sword glistened in the rays, dangling on his hip with no sheath, with the insignia of the dragon Mynisna etched on the blade.

"I don't trust them either," Trimistus stated.

"We ride through," he said. Trimistus returned to the others.

"Your quest to study Le'Mar?" Shedaaij asked, and he nodded.

It was dark again when they finally reached the village. The moment that they entered the border of the village, he knew he had made a mistake.

"I think I am going to be sick," Darcwulf said. Ursula trotted ahead of them, her coat glowing slightly. They rode in deeper, staring at the hundreds of bodies littering the muddy sands.

"This, Shado," Millon said, "is the work of our lord."

"The Butcher?" he asked, which Millon confirmed.

There were men, women and children. In some instances there were dead centaurs, but Kentaur said they were a worthy tribute to their lord. Gashes, cuts and open abdomens were written all over their bodies. The smell of the dead permeated the village, and their open, vacant eyes pleaded that they leave.

Something caught Shadowolf's eye, and he dropped down to inspect a dead woman. He turned her head and felt the large holes on her neck. He had seen it before, at Asbec College.

"What's wrong, Darcwulf asked. The Clan dismounted and joined them. Nelnar growled and stared at the forest next to them.

"Remember the aVampyere that I told you about?" he asked Darcwulf.

"Oh no," Angelia muttered, removing her staff and bow from her mount.

She had been there when Shadowolf had battled an aVampeyer on the school grounds. She had listened when he had explained how they killed, and how they could be killed. The memories rushed back, and fear grew in her heart.

"There are aVampyere here," Shadowolf said, drawing Ruben-Willow. The Clan drew their weapons too. "Aim for the heart, and be wary of their bite."

"Hold thy sword!" the aVampeyer said. He had travelled from the trees to Shadowolf within a second. It had seemed to Shadowolf that he hadn't travelled at all, but moved as if there were no distance between them. There were three of them. They were dressed in black coats, white shirts and black pants. Their feet were bare and skin pale.

"Wait!" Shadowolf shouted to the Clan. "I know you. Where do I know you from?"

"Think back to Iceland, *Enodhim*," he replied.

"Of course!" he remembered. "When Mercius was taking Slmet, you were the aVampeyer that had killed that Saneth."

"My name is Nellice," he told him. "This is Danto and Malice. We defy the dark lord and have denied the ways of the aVampeyer Cult."

"Are there more like you?" he asked.

"No, unfortunately we could not turn the others," he said. "The ones that have turned have since died. Only the three of us remain."

"Why have you confronted me, then?" Shadowolf asked.

"Did you not claim the power?" Danto asked in return. "And now you are back."

"Just give me a moment," Shadowolf said, walking around to try and grasp what was happening.

"How many more of the dark lord's men can we trust Shado?" Darcwulf asked.

"I know," he replied. "But I saw him kill a Saneth."

"You refer naturally to Ma'Kanak," Nellice replied. "He was an abomination. He was a cannibal, a man eater."

"So are you," Shadowolf countered.

"We are cursed," he said. "We need blood to survive. He lusted for flesh, hungered for it."

"Does that make you different?" Shadowolf asked.

"We can live off animals," Malice said, "though the blood is cold. He chooses to feast off men."

"We will burden you no longer," Nellice bowed. "We only wished to meet."

"How can you say that, when you cause such desecration in the name of evil?" Shadowolf called as they turned to leave.

"We did not kill these people," Nellice said in disgust.

"Then what is this?" he said, pulling the head of the dead woman to reveal the teeth marks.

"That isn't…" but Nellice couldn't finish. A woman was shouting. Or rather, canting.

"Oh no," Shadowolf said as he recognised the fire witch's voice.

Evil stirred in the village. It crept like a cold wind up his skin and onto his spine. Murmurs of the spell called from the leaves of the forest and a deep groan resounded from the bowels of the earth.

The dead moved. The dead woman in his hands groaned and he dropped her head to the floor. Even the dead centaurs rose unsteadily to their feet. When Shadowolf thought that was all he would deal with, the earth shook and the leaves rustled. Skeletons were rising from the ground. One skeleton walked to an abandoned hut and broke a sharp wedge from the door. Soon the other skeletons followed and they were armed.

"Heula!" Shadowolf shouted, kicking the groaning woman on the head. "What's happening?"

"I can't counter this, Shado!" she shouted over the rumble of the earth. "Maerlesa is calling the dead back from their resting place. They have no souls and will stop at nothing to feed off you. They are the undead."

"Can they be killed?!" Shadowwe asked.

"Yes!" she said. "Remove their heads! It severs communication of the undead brain through the spinal column with the rest of the body. It kills their urge to feed."

"The skeletons?!" Sorceress asked.

"Make sure there is no part of their body left to fight against," she replied. "Destroy their bones. Those with the power of the spirit can remove the evil afterwards."

"Right!" Tinonte shouted as he concentrated on his spirit and his body exploded with ethereal flames. Soon Rennick was also a ball of white ethereal flames.

The earth stopped shaking and Maerlesa seemed to be gone. The undead stood around them groaning and the skeletons held their spikes before them.

"Let's go!" Shadowolf shouted and the Clan attacked.

Shadowolf hacked at the first undead and watched as its head lobbed off to the ground, its body following afterwards. The undead ran and gnashed their teeth at him. Soon he was surrounded by twenty of them.

He reached within and drew the wind. With one blow the wind threw them in all directions, but did not kill them. They steadily rose to be greeted by Angelia's arrows and Darcwulf's staff. The arrows stuck, but had no harmful effect. No blood dripped from their bodies. The staff bounced off.

"This isn't working!" Darcwulf called as Sny-Ten and Lastgorn beheaded a few more undead. Darcwulf struck with his staff again and fire ignited on the body of the undead. The creature writhed and groaned and walked into Shadowwe's sword.

"Ooh, that could work," Shadowolf said excitedly. "Everyone, get behind Darcwulf and I!"

The centaurs just watched in fascination, but the rest heeded his call. When they were in place, Darcwulf held his staff tight, flames licking the surface and teasing the ground. The power thrummed around them and Shadowolf's hands held flames that rose in the air above him.

"Now!" he shouted and they released their powers.

The fire arced around them, hitting the abundant undead in the village. Unfortunately, it also struck the huts and forest.

The undead writhed under the fire and ran around in a crazed frenzy. The members of the Clan with swords went to work slicing their heads off.

"Skywolf, can you do something about the forest?!" Shadowolf shouted.

Skywolf, Angelia and Fransiska looked at the burning trees and held out their hand while closing their eyes. Water from the earth slowly rose around the burning trees and flowed up their barks, extinguishing the flames. Shadowolf beheaded a giant of the undead and then looked straight into the skull of a skeleton.

"Uh, Rennick, Tinonte," he called, "your turn."

The skeleton moved with such flexibility that Shadowolf didn't see the blow coming. It struck him across the cheek and then the chest before his sword moved and blocked the third thrust.

Behind the skeleton Shadowolf saw the aVampyere breaking the skeletons with their bare hands. Their strength was astonishing. In one move, Malice snapped one's neck and then removed its arm from the shoulder.

The skeleton struck Shadowolf's shoulder and thrust for his abdomen, but he blocked and then hit its ribs and pelvis. The sword clanged off the bones as if it were made of steel.

"Great," he said as he sheathed his sword. Now there were two before him. He could see that Sny-Ten's axe was making good work of the skeletons. Tinonte struck the skull, chest and ribs before grabbing the skull with his bare hand and thrusting the power of his spirit at it. The bones exploded around the area.

Shadowolf was relieved of his two skeletons by Rennick. The man grabbed the two spines and, as the power flowed through it, he released the final blow and they shattered. Two bones struck Shadowolf on his forehead and stomach before he raised his forearm. Then a skull hit his forearm and he sunk to the ground in pain.

There were several more skeletons, but they would win.

"Just one," Shadowolf whispered. "I just want to kill one. Otherwise I will always fear them."

He ran for the closest one and hit the back of its head with his fist. It turned to him and glared down on him. Shadowolf summoned the wind and the two of them rose into the air above the rest.

It hit his face and chest and then growled. When it struck again, he caught its fist in his palm. It struck with the other, and he caught it in his other palm. He pushed his spirit with the wind into the marrow of its bones, driving it into every crevasse until it was pouring out its sockets. And then it exploded into white flames, its remaining parts falling to the ground.

Shadowolf returned to the quiet earth. The battle was over. The undead were dead again and now bones and burning bodies littered the plains. The fire of the forest was extinguished.

He was in pain. The bones had not pierced his skin, but he could feel the bruises on his body. They would be blue in the morning.

"Can we go?" Darcwulf pleaded.

"Yes, let's get into one of the large houses and camp," he said. "One of us will have to stand guard tonight."

"I'll do it," Dren offered.

"Very well," Shadowolf accepted. He looked around. Heula was still with them, but the centaurs and aVampyere were gone.

***

Another two hours of trudging and she fell to her knees again.

"I can't go on like this, Genewiu," Chenesia said. She was not sure if it was sweat, tears or both falling down her face. "One rocky passageway looks exactly like the other. I am starting to feel like I am in the Fairiwell again, just a darker version of it."

Her dress was tearing by the knees, and it felt like it would come loose any second. She could feel the wetness of the blood clinging against her, and the knots in her hair tugged at her skull.

"We'll rest again," Genewiu replied. "Get some sleep. We are so lost; I don't think anyone would be able to find us."

Chenesia's head sank to the floor. She had no dignity left, no self-regard. The dirt was her brother and the silt her sister. There was no area of the mountainous pathway that was not part of her.

A sound rang softly in her ear and she held her breath. She thought someone was coming and she lifted her head in fear, but the sound vanished. Lowering her ear to the floor again, brushing her hair aside, she listened intently. It was definitely a sound, maybe a thrumming sound of power.

She swept her head along the floor and reached a nook where it joined the wall. She tapped slightly against the wall and it did not sound entirely solid.

"Can you kick this out?" she asked.

"I can try," the pegasus replied. "But if I break my ankle, we're stuck here."

She reared around, Chenesia moving out of the way. With her back legs, she lashed out and the wall caved outwards into a haven of golden light. It was not the light of the sun, but rather something else.

The room was the largest vacant space she had seen since the prisons. The thrumming was louder now. In the centre of the hall, taking up all the space up to the roof, was an ornate cage with runes written on the steel bars. The bars were spaced very narrowly apart, and between the bars a blue power surged. The protective barrier was there to prevent anyone small enough from entering the cage. The bars were for the larger creatures on the inside.

They were strange creatures, and she was sure she had never seen the like before. Their ears were sharper than the elves and their naked skins were red. They were her height, and there were approximately fifty of them. The same amount lay dead at the bottom of the cage. On their backs, leathery wings as frail as Genewiu's feathered wings hung limply.

Chenesia and Genewiu stepped onto the ledge leading to the bottom of the cage and made their way down. The creatures closest to them eyed their progress, but made no motion to approach them. At the bottom, the frailest of them lay panting with his arm near the barrier, his skin scorched.

"Hello," she greeted.

The creature closed its eyes and died. One from the top dropped down and landed without subtlety. It flared its broken wings outwards, revealing that the total span was three times its height, and then closed it again.

"What are you?" she asked without thought.

"Fretlings," it groaned with a deep voice. "We be F..F..F..Fretlings."

"How did you come to be here?" Genewiu asked.

"We be...be..." it replied with difficulty, "we be the blood...of the vampires."

"Blood of the what?" Chenesia asked, pulling her tattered dress's strap back onto her shoulder.

"Vampires," it repeated. "Dark creatures brought here from another world. Here known as aVam...aVam...aVampyere."

"Never heard of it," Chenesia said. "But what do you mean you are their blood?"

"Lord take blood, use arcane p…p…power to create Fretlings," it said sadly. "But Fretlings die. Not serve master as should."

"Why are you dying?" she asked.

"The light," it said. "He try to make us immune to the light. But not working."

"How can I help?" Chenesia asked.

"Shouldn't we be trying to find a way out of here?" Genewiu retorted.

"Fret know way out! Fret know way out! If you help Fret, Fret show way."

"Fine," Chenesia shrugged. "How do I help?"

"Lever," he pointed. "Against wall."

Chenesia looked in the direction and saw three levers.

"Which one?" she asked.

"All of them," it said enthusiastically.

She walked over to the large levers at least half the length of her body. She pulled the first one on the left down. The blue barrier and lights went off.

The Fretlings screamed and scurried around the cage, finally free of their torment. Chenesia dropped the second lever, and the cage door opened.

The Fretlings flew out of the cage and made for the roof. There they clung to the rocks of the ceiling. Chenesia pulled the last lever down and high above the wall, opposite the ledge Genewiu and Chenesia had used to descend, a door opened.

The Fretlings wasted no time making for the opening. To the last, they escaped the tomb, including the one that had told Chenesia about the levers.

"Alright," she said. "So maybe I am at fault for trusting him."

"Not necessarily," Genewiu said. "I am assuming that door leads to the exit, otherwise they would not have made for it so quickly."

"Even so," Chenesia continued, "the door is far above our reach, and there is no ledge leading up to it. It was not made for wingless access."

"I might not be able to fly up, but you can make it by scaling the cage and jumping the distance."

Chenesia looked up at the side bars closest to the door and

saw that she could very well make the distance, but an uncomfortable pit formed in her stomach as she looked back at the pegasus.

"I am not leaving without you," she replied.

"And you are very honourable, but your freedom means more than mine."

"I will come back for you," Chenesia started to cry. She hugged Genewiu's neck and kissed her forehead.

"Do what you can," she replied. "Now go before it is too late."

She nudged Chenesia and the girl stood there looking at her forlornly. Genewiu was about to shout and vent her impatience when Chenesia climbed the bars.

She clung to the warm steel, worming up the post to bring herself level to the door in the cave wall. She braced her body for the jump, but the failing dress was giving her a hard time.

She suddenly realised she wouldn't be able to make it. It was too far and even if she made it, her fingers were too tired to grasp the rocky ledge of the door. She sank back against the bars, her feet on a horizontal bar beneath her, despair creeping into her mind.

"I can't make it," she informed Genewiu sullenly.

"You haven't even tried!" she replied.

"But the try will kill me," Chenesia said.

"You have to get out of here, Chenesia!"

She looked at the ledge again. It seemed so far and so unattainable. Yet Genewiu was right. She had to try.

She pressed against the vertical bars and jumped. The moment seemed to pass by slowly until she grabbed for the ledge. The sand and stones shifted and her fingers failed. She fell from the ledge.

The gravity pulled her down fast and she dug her short, dirty nails into the ascending wall. When she was about to give up and admit defeat, something hit the side of her head and she reflexively grabbed for it with both arms. A loud snap erupted into the chamber as her shoulders cracked against the sudden jerk and she yelped in pain. She could feel the blood running down her left cheek from the side of her head.

Opening her eyes, she saw that she had caught a bronze lever that her body weight was pulling down. Once it had reached the apex of its descent, she kicked against the wall and caught one of the horizontal bars of the cage. She dropped down to another bar two meters down, and then to the next and finally to the floor.

Genewiu made her way over to Chenesia. The girl could not stand anymore and fell to her cracked, bleeding knees. Welts and bruises ran along her once fine legs.

Before the pegasus could find the words to apologise, Chenesia looked up. Genewiu was speaking, but her hearing had gone. Then she looked up at the wall and saw the lever six meters up.

"I have an idea," she murmured. "Go stand by the wall directly under the door."

Genewiu was protesting, but the look on Chenesia's face contested her and she obeyed. Once the pegasus was where Chenesia wanted her, she stood up from the wet ground and went to the three levers. She pulled the first lever on the left again, and the lights and power returned to the chamber.

As she had hoped, a platform broke the surface of the floor upon which Genewiu stood and began ascending towards the door. With her last strength she ran for the platform and jumped onto it, and then lay sprawled across its length by Genewiu's hooves.

They passed the platform's lever on the way up and after a few seconds reached the open archway of the door. Chenesia struggled to her feet and they looked into the tunnel lit only by the chamber.

Although they saw no end to the tunnel, the smell of distant moisture and fresh air promised escape.

"After you," Genewiu's voice slowly streamed into Chenesia's as she led the way out.

BUTCHER OF PHILAGIS
CHAPTER SEVEN

"Shado," Dren called softly from the one of the windows of the house. Shadowolf had been lying with his eyes open since the sunrise waiting for the others to stir, when Dren's voice broke his daydream.

He walked over to the opening between the wooden logs that were the substance of the house and looked out onto the grim village. A solitary man with a staff was walking over to the entrance of the house.

His robe was mottled with dirt, creating a grey image of him, and his beard and long hair down to his chest were silver-grey. It added to the atmosphere of the damned city. Yet, his eyes were green and his aged face held wisdom. He did not appear evil in the least.

Shadowolf pulled the shredded pine double doors slightly ajar, walking out into the misty sunlight.

"Good day, old man," he jibed, hoping the man's humour was not as grey as his robe.

"Go'd day, laddie," he replied. "Go'd day for a stroll, say yur?"

"Excellent day, although not in such a black city as this," Shadowolf replied, somehow not able to hide his smile.

"Mer name is Malanite Osgrown," the old man introduced. "And mer wonders what's a go'd feller, namely yurself, doing in a village as this?"

"Well, the feeling is mutual, but the journey requires it," Shadowolf said.

"There are many jerneys men can take that will be a safer route than this I assure you, Shado," Malanite said, winking at him.

"You are wiser than I thought, old man," he replied, frowning.

"Names are easy, young feller," Malanite said as he sat on the rock. "Knowing ther motives and spirit is another."

"You have not told me your purpose here," Shadowolf said rather than asked.

"Ah, laddie, yur do me wrong. This fer village was used to be my home, it was. I do not know whur it is I can go, but mayhap I may jerney with yur and find me a new home?"

"I won't be heading to a haven for a while," Shadowolf replied, "for I have many things to do first. I can point you to New Avalion..."

"No, no," Malanite protested. "I be not travelling alone. Anywhur with go'd company is go'd enough for me, if yur'll have me."

"Of course!" Shadowolf said, slapping him on the shoulder. "I will enjoy the company, and maybe your wisdom will be a fortune to our travels."

"Ai, I have much knowledge of prophecy and poems," Malanite agreed. "Camp fires please the telling of them."

"Very well," Shadowolf laughingly said, showing him into the house where the Clan waited to be introduced.

It was noon when the enlarged Clan, with the final acceptance of Heula by all, left the house. Their weapons and Ursula's rations were all packed to the horses and they rode north. Nelnar trotted beside Shedaaij and Shadowolf in the front, the old man conversing with Darcwulf and Dren in the centre.

"So, what can you tell us of the DragonRider prophecy?" Darcwulf asked enthusiastically. Shadowwe left the rear Orion and joined the group.

"Ai, me matey," Malanite answered his audience, "yur asks when no fire is lit, and no hand holds a go'd ale, but the storey is a go'd one, and needs be told at this time.

"It is a mysterious prophecy; the complete words escape me now, but are as portentous as the dark lord's conquerings, if such a word may be used by me."

"Does it involve the dragon war?" Shadowwe asked.

"Maybe, maybe not," Malanite replied strangely. "Philgarn was not explicit in the mention of a dragon war. But dragons must meet at the end, and when meet be completed, thur the DragonRider will face his enemy, and the power of the dragons will be his to ordain."

"You speak in riddles, man!" Darcwulf exclaimed, frustration knitting his brow.

"Mer only speak of what I know," he replied, hurt. "But the rank of DragonRider might have to be contested for, for the prophets are uncertain as to whom the power will go to: a servant of evil, or a servant of good. The significant part is this," he continued, and Dren, Darcwulf and Shadowwe huddled closer to the old man. "It states that the *Enodhim*, a master Windfarer, shall claim the right of the dragons."

They looked before them at Shadowolf, who was laughing at something Shedaaij had said.

"We did think it was the DragonRider who sent us those messages by eagle, Shadowwe," Darcwulf said.

"If indeed he is the one," Malanite said, "then he will have to contest for the position."

"Who will oppose him?" Dren asked.

"It could be Le'Mar," Malanite shrugged. "He is well versed in all the elements of late and may be seen as an *Enodhim* himself. But, no, likely he will send someone to do his bidding."

"Sonersaat," Ursula said, and the others jumped at her voice. "When I broke the time spell cast by the witch in Plastinon, I heard one of them say that he was not strong enough to face Le'Mar or Sonersaat. My guess is that Sonersaat could be his chosen."

"Be that as it may," Malanite said, now profusely in thought, "if Shadowolf is the challenger, I don't know if he is strong enough to face the DragonRider."

"Shado can defeat any man," Darcwulf said proudly.

"That remains to be seen, young lad," Malanite said. "That remains to be seen."

The sun hung over the solitary plains at approximately two hours before sunset. Shadowolf slowed Mandy down to a halt and stared at the mountainous cave ahead of them. It rose from the plains like a bulwark upon the natural earth. Its ruddy construction broke the peaceful cloudy sky with snags and tears, ripping at the cloth of serenity that had been soothing moments before.

It bit into Shadowolf's calm soul. He bore the aggravation and noted that the cave, although high, was too tapered at the top to house a large arena on the inside. If there was a dark king within its walls, it appeared that only he could abode in the rocky sanctuary. Its diameter was too small at the base.

"What a crude design," Shedaaij commented.

"I agree," Shadowolf said.

The Clan halted on either side of him and looked at the monstrosity, each adding insults of their own. It took a moment before Shadowolf realised that there were ten centaurs guarding the cave. They did not look as friendly as Millon or Kentaur who were now standing to the west side of the guards.

"I am surprised no one has stumbled upon this cave before," Shadowolf said. "The plains are open and you could see this cave from the River of Light, I am sure."

"Much have tried, lad," Malanite informed. "Much had died entering the cave, others by the hands of the guards. No more try."

"Very well," Shadowolf replied and trotted towards the centaur guards, followed shortly by the Clan. Millon and Kentaur awoke from their thoughts and rode over to meet them.

"So you made it passed the dead," Millon said, his voice shaky.

"Yes," Sorceress said. "Thanks for your help."

"It was not our business to interfere," Kentaur replied. "We only wanted our king to meet you and decide your fate."

Shadowolf ignored them and rode on towards the entrance of the cave.

"Halt!" The central centaur shouted. "Who goes there and what purpose has thee with Kraakis?"

"I believe that he would indeed be pleased to see me," Shadowolf answered. The centaur moved closer and smelled his face, before moving back and leering at him.

"You're a useless mortal," the guard said, laughing. The other guards joined.

"Useless indeed," Darcwulf said, mockingly laughing with them. Shadowolf smiled, but the guards stopped.

"What do you have to offer that thousands of other mortals, and a few undead, haven't offered already?"

"I am Shadowolf, *Enodhim* of recent note, Froth Hun-killer, Mercius-slayer..." Shadowolf said, counting them off on his fingers.

"Hold on," a guard on the left said. "You killed Mercius?"

"Anyone can hold that claim," the central guard pushed the

other one back. "Mercius was a dolt."

"Show them, Shado," Darcwulf said.

"Very well," Shadowolf sighed.

Suddenly the wind picked up. It fell from the dark, wet coat of Mandy's legs and strolled along the grass and sand. With instantaneous velocity, the gale thrummed against the guards. The centaurs were almost lifted from the ground, but their weights and muscular four-legged bodies kept them down. They raised their arms as sand blasted their faces. When the wind died, they saw that the Clan was untouched by the weathered attack.

"You are indeed he," the central guard said. "You may enter at your own peril, but please leave your horses behind. They cannot enter the cave."

"Who will care for them while we are gone?" Rennick asked suspiciously.

"We will," Millon said, indicating Kentaur next to him. "We serve our kin well."

"Oh," Skywolf whispered. "Guess I was wrong about the deer."

Shadowolf grinned as he dismounted. He patted Mandy and let her and the other mounts be taken aside. The guards moved away from the entrance, looking at the Clan's weapons.

"Don't even think of trying to disarm me," Shadowolf warned.

"Never," the central guard replied with a grin. "As a matter of fact, it might provide more sport."

Not knowing what he meant, Shadowolf looked into the cave. Steps descended into the earth through a well-dug square hole. The Clan were going underground.

They had to walk single file, as the path was too narrow to allow for more. Thin torches lit the way down, but through cracks in the rock and earth, they could see a red light glowing. The steam from the apertures was hot and at some points they had to duck when jets of stream erupted.

They reached an opening into a square room. In the centre of the room was an oddly shaped net running the breadth of the hall and waist high. On the other end of the room another archway led further underground.

By the dim light of the torches, they saw a centaur enter from the archway. He was broader in the chest than the guards, and his four legs and two arms were more muscular. His head had been shaved clean like Darcwulf's, but he wore a goatee that was braided beneath his chin.

In his hands he held two oddly shaped wooden tools. He threw the one over the net to Shadowolf and waited for him to pick it up.

"First one to three wins," the centaur announced. "If the ball hits your wall, I gain a point. You cannot pass if you lose."

"What is this?" Shadowolf studied the tool in his hands.

"It is called a racket," the centaur answered, and tossed a ball up and down in his free hand. "Ready?"

"Sure," he replied.

"Do we have time for this?" Trevor asked. Shadowolf was surprised to hear him speak for a change.

"What's a little sport?" he smiled.

"But you can just thrust him aside," Sorceress said.

"Now what would be the fun in that?" Darcwulf replied, sitting on a rock to watch the game.

"What's the game called?" Dren asked, joining Darcwulf.

"Racket," the centaur answered, ready to start the game.

Before Shadowolf could get into place, the centaur launched the ball in the air and hit it over the net. The ball hit the ground with a thud and struck the wall.

"Aaah," the centaur jibed. "I guess that's one."

Shadowolf walked over to the ball and picked it up. It was green and furry, with a white line running along its surface. He could fit the ball in the palm of his hand and close his fingers around it.

He tossed the ball up and down, letting it fall on the racket, getting the feel of the ball in contact with the instrument.

"Uh, uhm," the centaur called impatiently, "your turn to serve."

Shadowolf lifted the ball in the air and struck, but the ball landed on the ground beside him. The centaur laughed at him.

He launched it in the air and struck, this time hitting a hard volley. The centaur stretched across and returned the ball, sending it to the opposite end of where Shadowolf was standing. He raced to get to it and hit it before it touched his wall. It ricocheted off the side of the room and hit the centaur's wall.

"Not bad," the centaur said. He took the ball and launched it again, driving it hard into Shadowolf's area. He in turn hit it up in the air, and the centaur ran forward and slammed the ball into the wall.

"What happens if I lose?" Shadowolf asked with a smile. "Do I get a rematch?"

"Unfortunately not," the centaur replied. "Serve the ball."

Shadowolf picked up the ball and served. He was getting the hang of it, returning the ball seven times when the centaur hit the floor by mistake and the ball bounced against the wall.

"Deuce," the centaur proclaimed.

"Deuce? What is that?"

"That means you have to get two points above mine before you can win," the centaur replied.

"Very well," Shadowolf said, taking the handle of the racket in both hands.

The centaur served, and without warning two balls flew towards him. Reflexively he hit one then the other, sending them in two opposite directions. The centaur hit the one with the racket, and kicked the other with his rear hoof.

The balls bounced off the side walls. Shadowolf knew he couldn't hit one and reach the other, but he didn't want to lose. Instinctively, still holding the racket, he aimed his hands towards the balls and the wind caught them, turning them slowly in the air. The wind brought the balls to his racket and he bashed them against the ceiling.

The balls ricocheted onto the wall. The centaur stared hopelessly at the balls and then turned his anger on the human.

"How dare you!?" he screamed.

A purple portal opened on the wall behind him, and a voice boomed into the racket hall.

"Where are the guests, Sandeur?" it asked.

"I was just bringing them to you," Sandeur replied, then indicated the portal to the Clan. "This way."

Sandeur leapt through the portal. The Clan joined Shadowolf and stared at the portal.

"Very good game, if I must say," Darcwulf said. "We should try it at home some time."

They walked to the wall and entered the portal. Shadowolf walked onto a cliff edge and immediately brought his hands to his face. The underground cave was a cavern of lava and rock. Magma flowed like rivers underneath bridges and between walkways. The stench of brimstone permeated the area. Now and again a splash of fire and liquid sprang from the lava lake at the head of the cave. On the landings, centaurs stood and worked on various timber and metal devices. Some devices were circular and others cubes. None of it made sense to him.

A long brick bridge ran over the lake to an island. On the rock and sand island was a single item. It was made of rough bronze and stood on four legs. It was a table or similar surface, concaved in the centre towards the ground.

Two centaurs stood by it. One of them was like all the other centaurs in appearance; four legs, half-horse and abdomen of human, spiky ears attached to its head, a nice long tail at the rear.

The other moved to place its belly over the concave altar, the table supporting his body. Shadowolf realised this was his throne. From his shoulders he wore a regal cape that flowed from his neck onto his long, hairy back. Gold armour plates sprung up from his muscular shoulders and biceps. His chest and stomach muscles stood out as a bane against any weapon. It would take an axe twice the strength of Sny-Ten's to pierce that skin.

The most peculiar characteristic was his head. Unlike the other centaurs, this one had horns protruding from the sides of his head. They twirled up like a majestic antelope's antlers, at least as long as Shadowolf's forearm.

His eyes were pitch-black. It was not the black of an abyss, nor the black of sunken sockets like Trimistus. Rather, the membranes bulged out like a human's eyes, but the white and pupils were replaced with liquids pool of black. His teeth were fangs that could tear the skin of any creature in the cave. With sudden fear and apprehension, Shadowolf realised that this creature was an aVampeyer.

We did not kill these people, Shadowolf remembered Nellice's words at Meëntis.

With further anxiety, as the Clan moved down to a lower platform, he saw that it had been Millon that had spoken to the Butcher. The centaur now walked astride Kentaur to the Clan. They had to miss and dodge a few balls of flame that jumped ashore before they met up with the two creatures.

"No matter what happens next, Shado," Kentaur announced, "know that Millon and I are with you." Resentment burned on his face as he turned to face Kraakis. That ire was reflected on Millon's face, but without further questioning the Clan moved forward. Before they reached the bridge to the Butcher, Millon stopped them.

"For your safety, let Shado go alone," he warned. The Clan looked at Shadowolf and he nodded.

"I trust them," he replied to the Clan, "even though they deserted us before."

"We are yours," the centaurs kneeled before him and bowed their heads.

"I accept your allegiance," Shadowolf replied, turning and walking onto the bridge alone.

"What happened to our mounts?" Darcwulf asked. He could see Ursula was getting edgy in the cave.

"They are in a forestral sanctuary to the west of here, not many hooves off," Kentaur replied. "They are in the safe hands of two allies of ours."

Shadowolf made his way to the Butcher's throne. He was definitely a vile creature of the dark, and he stared back at him with a complacent expression. The other centaurs started to mumble and laugh as Shadowolf stood before him, the giant that was two and a half heads above him.

"You are the *Enodhim*?" Kraakis asked.

"Yes," Shadowolf sighed, tired of answering that question. He couldn't even come up with a sarcastic retort anymore.

"Huh," Kraakis laughed. "I expected someone tougher."

"Sorry to disappoint you, but it is I."

"And why do you lend yourself to me? Do you not know that I am of the dark lord?"

"That is exactly why I am here, oh evil one" Shadowolf replied. "I wondered what your purpose is here. Why would Le'Mar want an underground tunnel filled with vermin that play in their own urine?"

The demeanour of the Butcher changed, and Shadowolf was satisfied that he was angering the beast.

"We will serve his purpose when the time is ripe," he said.

"And until then, you will feed off the land. Tell me, what will he do when all his prospective servants are eaten? Do you think he will reward you?"

"I can sate my hunger," Kraakis replied.

"How? Do you eat your fellow centaurs in the meanwhile?" Shadowolf could see he was pushing the right buttons.

"Get ready," Millon whispered to the Clan. They looked around and saw the other centaurs preparing to attack. The Clan drew their weapons. Ursula's horn glowed softly, and Nelnar left the group to run across the bridge to Shadowolf's side.

"Ah, an extra little treat," the Butcher said, to which Nelnar growled. "You will make a fine desert."

"I fear," Shadowolf said, drawing Rubin-Willow, "that it is you that I shall dine on tonight."

"Another carnivore!" Kraakis exclaimed, drawing his own sword from beneath the altar. Shadowolf's eyes gaped; he could have sworn it had not been there before. "Pity. We could have made a good team."

The Butcher's sword was massive. It reached above the centaur's head and gleamed in the lava's fire. The steel was pure silver, and he could tell it was built to be handled with both hands.

"Kill them," he groaned. "Kill them all."

Shadowolf poured his spirit and wind into Ruben and met the strong blow. The block hurt his wrist and drove his arms to the ground. The beast glared over him and breathed brimstone into his face. Shadowolf removed his sword and prepared for the next attack.

Darcwulf and Dren were side by side, dodging legs and striking hooves and bone. The staff flared with fire drawn from the lava, and Dren's fists pounded into their chests. He flew up and dropped on a centaur's back, snapping its neck.

Darcwulf continued to cripple the centaurs as he struck at their knees. This left a good opportunity for Sorceress to lodge arrows into their muscular bodies. Yet, although blood flowed into the rivers, it didn't slow them down. Darcwulf hit a centaur in the face with his staff and let the fire race into his face and out the back of its head. Its body fell to the floor. Another centaur kicked outward and threw Darcwulf over to a distant island. His head banged against the floor and he was rendered unconscious.

Sny-Ten hefted his heavy axe into a centaur's chest, but it got stuck when the beast fell on it. Lastgorn drove his blade side to side, swinging it to attack the hooves trampling on top of him. One of them rammed their bodies sidelong into him and he fell to the floor. Sny-Ten raced to help him, but a centaur threw a fist into his face and he fell over.

Ursula drove her horn into a beast and kicked another with her rear. With the power of the horn, she killed the centaur dangling over her and pulled out. A centaur that Shadowwe killed fell over her. The weight was greater than she could manage, but she eventually shifted out in time to kill another beast. She butted a centaur into Gwyn's waiting staff.

Rennick and Trevor were decapitating and killing most of them, the beasts trying to overwhelm them, but their blades were accurate. Rennick exchanged blows between his double-edged axe and one of his sickles, while Trevor used his shoulder-braces to ram them aside and then drive his two-handed sword into their bellies.

Rennick's green torn cape was falling apart and his scarred right cheek was revealed. The lava lit the strain in his muscles as he killed centaur after centaur.

Sorceress put away her bow, and unsheathed her one-handed, two-edged sword. With a style that much resembled a dance more than an attack, she calmly dodged hooves and fist, striking the beasts in the face and on their arms. One centaur rushed at her, his long arm flying in a flurry of attacks, but she dodged, moved aside, turned the arms away and hit the beast on the heart.

The wolf-head on Skywolf's back was muddied with blood. She struck with her rough short sword into the beasts, slicing into their legs. Soon Angelia and Fransiska were by her side, and their staves added weight to the battle. Five centaurs ran at them, but Darcwulf suddenly emerged riding a wave of lava and hit two of them. Two of the remaining three turned on him, and the other was killed by Rennick.

Trimistus used his dragon sword to its best, although it seemed as if the sword was doing the work and his arm followed. His training with the dragons served him well, for his muscles bulged as he sliced and hit every fist and leg that flew his way. His eyes were burning sockets of fire now as he extended his energy.

Heula merely tried to stay out of the way, but often she had to lift her hands to shove a centaur aside with a softly whispered spell. A centaur stood in still animation as his throat turned red from within and exploded. When three turned on her, a shield of power surrounded her and then hurtled them into the air away from her.

Shedaaij was the most athletic. She twisted and swirled her twin daggers as she jumped off a centaur's back, into another's neck and sliding to cut open a centaur's belly. The daggers were strong enough to pierce bone and sternum, but most of her attacks were used to defend Clan members that were caught unawares by a centaur attack. A centaur attacked her, but she kicked his knees in and drove the daggers into either side of his neck.

Millon and Kentaur held their promise by hitting their fists into former allies. Their powers were unmistakably held in their biceps and rear legs as they forced centaurs to fall back into waiting swords and axes. Kentaur hit a centaur's face so hard that it spun around to greet an arrow from Gwyn.

Scarlette and Tinonte used their thick, single-edged swords to kill the centaurs. When Tinonte was confronted by two centaurs, he decapitated the one and as the head was still falling over him, pulled a short sword from his back and struck the second centaur's legs. Scarlette's red cape swirled and blinded centaurs as she turned in the air to perform kicks, hits and slices resembling a storm of death.

Shadowolf hit the ground for the seventh time. Nelnar jumped for the Butcher's neck, but the beast dodged and hit the wolf to the floor. He then reared up and landed with his front hooves atop Shadowolf, who rolled out of the way in time.

Ruben met the giant sword again and Shadowolf's arm ached from the impact. He rushed forward, but with demonic speed the centaur turned and kicked with his rear legs. Shadowolf soared backwards and landed by the lava. His sword fell to the fire, but he called up wind to save it and it returned to his hand.

An idea struck him. He rushed forward again. The centaur's sword cruised over his head, and Shadowolf dodged and slashed at the wrist. After a deafening scream from Kraakis, the hefty silver sword dropped, but before it hit the ground, Shadowolf used the wind to send it into the lava. The metal sank into the boiling pit, eventually submitting to its heat and melting.

When Shadowolf returned his attention to the Butcher, the beast's uninjured fist hit his cheek and he fell to the floor. Fangs the size of his hand fell to his neck, but the beast roared up before he could pierce the skin. Nelnar had bitten his back leg.

"You damn wolf!" Kraakis screamed, and kicked Nelnar off into a distant wall. The wolf sank like a doll onto the island's ground. Shadowolf plunged Ruben into the centaur's sternum and forced as much wind into the veins and muscles as he could. Soon, the centaur's body could no longer hold the power, and meat, flesh and bones exploded onto the throne island and into the lava. Shadowolf sank to the ground again, the relief not good enough to soothe the pain running through his body.

The Clan had finished with the centaurs. The cave was silent except for the rivers of fire that coursed through it.

Shadowolf looked around and saw a solitary grey tree standing in a dark corner. He stood up and eyed it. It had no leaves, but only dead branches that reached to the high ceiling of the cave.

"Malanite!" he called, and when the old man made his way over the bridge, he indicated the tree. "What is a tree doing here?"

"It is called the Tree of Life," he replied. "I will tell yer about it another day."

***

The red mirror opened. Le'Mar waited patiently for the occupants of the planet to answer. Soon, the president of the Semhum Kateth appeared, surprise written on his face.

"Well, well," the alien face said. "It has been a while."

"I only call," Le'Mar replied, "to report a failure on your behalf."

"Failure?" the president asked. "The Guild of Assassins does not fail."

"Two years ago I employed an assassin by the name of Nolraldun to terminate one of my traitors, Trimistus. Recent events have brought to light that the quarry is still alive, and no sign of your assassin."

"That is troubling," the assassin remarked. "What will you have us do?"

"Nothing," the dark lord said. "I only wish to warn you that your failure will not go unmarked. I will dispose of him myself."

The portal closed on the assassin.

"Guilmark," the president called.

"Yes, my lord," Guilmark answered.

"Where is Jutbacca now?"

"Your master assassin? He is returning from Planet Fornicka as we speak with another success."

"I have another job for him," the president said, "on Celenic Earth."

Sonersaat and Maneto soared over Meëntis and saw the dead littering the plains. Smoke arose from the wastes and the foul stench infiltrated their senses.

"I don't see their bodies," Sonersaat remarked.

"Neither do I," Maneto grumbled, his dragon wings ripping the air. "Do you think we missed them further north?"

"I didn't see any movement, except for the centaur guards at Philagis, and everything seemed normal enough to me there."

"Should we go further south, or swing east?"

"Let's go east," Sonersaat replied. "Maybe they are heading for the Avalion mercenaries by the River of Light.

"Either way, I don't care what Le'Mar says. I want that boy dead."

***

"You've returned?" the guards said as the Clan exited the tunnel into the starlight on the plains. "Kraakis set you free?"

"He had no further need for us," Shadowolf replied, the marks still etched on his face. Heula had opened a portal for them back to the racket room and they had made their way up into the open air.

"Gave you a fair hiding by the looks of things," the guard said, receiving laughter and applause from the others. When the Clan had moved away, Heula whispered into her palms.

"Guards! Guards!" Kraakis's voice boomed from the tunnel.

The guards looked back. Without hesitation, they ran into the tunnel. When the last one was through, Shadowolf turned to the cave and raised his right hand, palm open to the tunnel.

"Farewell, guardians of Philagis," he said.

He closed his eyes and concentrated. The horrid rock enclosure collapsed upon itself, killing the remaining centaurs within it.

Suddenly, the wind picked up of its own accord and swirled around Shadowolf. His eyes burned, and he raised his palms to watch the wind pass through his fingers into his face. He couldn't control the power that surged from his body.

He was lifted up into the air, and then he fainted…

TRIAL OF THE *ENODHIM*
CHAPTER EIGHT

Shadowolf lifted his head to alien surroundings. All around him there was a landscape of clouds, sketching strange runic symbols in the sky.

He didn't feel weak or tired. It appeared that those physical attributes had been stripped from his body completely. He felt neither hunger nor thirst as he levitated within the barren sky. Yet to call it 'sky' was a guess, for there was no sky to speak of. The world was covered by a darkness he could not name. It was an absence of light, be it the stars, moon or sun.

His acute eyes could see no land though. It was almost as if the clouds emitted their own phosphorescent light, just enough to enable him to see the curls and wisps.

He frowned as he whirled in circles. He had no idea how he had come to this place. He had not teleported, at least not consciously. Even if he had meant to do it, he had never seen the place before.

Movement shook the clouds slightly and there was a change in the humidity. He turned when he sensed a shift in the vapour of the clouds, and a woman walked out from within it. Her body was composed of water, rivers of skin running through her naked form.

"Where am I?" he asked the water elementël, but it did not answer. Instead she ran into a sprint and suddenly water flew at him from an upraised palm.

Shadowolf hit at the water stupidly, but he fell back as the onslaught continued. Soon, the elementël was hitting him with watery fists. He reached for Ruben, but the sword was gone.

He was gargling for air. The water was rapidly drowning him as he tried to fight the creature. Calling up wind, he thrust it at the being, and finally the water subsided. He summoned more wind from the sky, and then struck back at the being with fists of torrential air.

Fire broke from another cloud, and a man approached. He was now buffeted by two elementëls, their power striking his face and chest.

The pain was ultimate, and he was sure it would be fatal. He coughed as the brimstone and water filled his lungs. His eyes bulged as he weakened, and finally in desperation he plunged wind at them from all directions. Gasping for air, he saw that the beings had been joined by a man made of earth.

He tried to call fire, but none arose. Trying earth and water, the powers seemed to be dead within him. The three elementëls laughed and rushed to the attack again. Fire, Water and Earth hit his face, chest, legs, back and groin, causing him to do a ceaseless dance of agony.

His veins coursed with death, his skin was charred as he used his waning energy to call the wind one last time. Only a whisper of air rose for he was too spent. The beings stopped, surrounding him calmly. They raised their palms to him and thrashed their powers at him.

His back arced and his muscles pulled into a spasm. His spirit burned with supernatural pain. Soon he was grinding his teeth in agony, blood flowed from his lips. With an outcry, he tore into each of them with spirit and wind, reaching into their individual elements and ripped them apart.

The air went still in the aftermath. He coughed again, spitting out blood and gum flesh. His chest was wracked with torture, the brimstone still surging unfiltered through his lungs. He tried to think of Philagis, tried to return to Celenic Earth, when a new sound caught his attention.

The wind arose from its own volition. A hurricane broke through the still of the clouds. To his left and right, wind bearing water twirled in a tornado at him. All three typhoons struck him, and he was caught in its embrace.

The winds ripped at his skin. His clothes were pulled off his body and his hair torn. The charred remains of his face were eaten at by stone in the wind, licked at by an ever-present fire.

Yet he knew he was wind. Had he not received the power of the wind? Had he not fulfilled the prophecy of the *Enodhim*?

He tugged at the wind when it struck again, and it shifted away. Another blow hit him, but the third attempt was cast aside. Shadowolf focused on the core element of the wind, straining to call it to his command. When his spirit had reins on it and he could pull at the strings of its existence, he calmed the wind. The fire died and water fell as rain from clouds. The stone turned to dust. And the wind calmly returned to its subtle tranquility. The serenity of the cold breeze was soothing to his defeated, naked body. He smiled, hoping it was over.

He opened his eyes and gaped when he realised he wasn't breathing. The air no longer held him in suspension and he fell headlong towards whichever direction the source of gravity was pulling from.

But the fall was the least of his worries. He tugged at his neck and beat at his chest, trying to force the air to return. His vision blurred and his mind went numb as he fell. No longer sure of what to do, he released himself to the fall. What was the sense in fighting if there was no way to combat it?

Yet it was not that simple. When he knew it was his last breath, he thrashed about, gasping at nothing. He wanted to scream, but with no air in his lungs, nothing was happening. He called his spirit, focused his mind on his lungs and the air around him, his head thrumming with the ebbing flow of blood, when he gulped a breath of fresh air created from within.

He allowed his body to continue falling. He was too weak to consider halting the drop. Let death come, let the impact arrive.

But it didn't. It was a ceaseless fall, and soon Shadowolf resigned to the fact that it would not end. He pulled the wind around him and levitated in the air. The clouds around him looked the same; it was as if he had never left.

The elementëls were back. They stood before him like a nemesis to his life. He could feel their power; feel how they were increasing it every second. He considered increasing the power state of his soul too, when another idea came to mind.

As soon as the idea came, the beings disappeared. Shadowolf looked around but they were nowhere to be seen. It was almost as if they had meant for him to arrive at a conclusion.

A winged beast broke the cloud cover this time and made to

attack him. Its claws hit his chest and it kicked him down, but Shadowolf used the wind to rise up again and hit its belly with fist, wind and spirit. The beast roared, but no harm was done. It circled around to attack again, and again the idea came to him.

He had thought about the air that had been removed from him. An element, a significant piece of nature and part of the law of the world, had been stripped from him and he had to create it within his soul.

But each of the elementëls was made of components too as significant as air. What if their elements could be removed? The same notion returned to him as he faced the beast. He stretched his right palm, making a circular hold with his fingers as if he were strangling the air, and the beast stopped.

In the distance, Shadowolf could see it was working. He increased his power and the beast dashed from side to side as the air was moving out of its lungs. The wind removed all components of its essence from the beast, every iota of air molecule. Soon, the beast stopped struggling as it died of asphyxiation, and its body fell.

The elementëls returned. They stood by their clouds and faced him, but did not attack. There was an air of expectancy about them. Their heads were lowered almost in a bow, but their eyes faced him intensely, and grins crossed their faces.

Shadowolf closed his eyes and focused on the air. He breathed in as much of it as he can and let it suffuse into his soul. The power hummed from his body and his aura burned white from his tarnished skin. His body began to repair as the wind became one with him, and soon there was no body.

His skin was replaced with effervescent rivers of wind that swirled in organized chaos as the hurricanes had. He opened his spiritual eyes and received a nod of approval from each elementël. He was the wind, and the wind was one with him.

The Earth moved to his cloud and soon stone and rock fell down. Trees and plants, animals and birds were born in a second. Water moved to her cloud and rained down upon the earth, creating the rivers and oceans, fish and predators of the waters. Fire spread across earth and water and provided warmth and life to the fauna and flora. The earth was still, and no movement took place.

Shadowolf moved to a cloud behind him and meditated into his spirit. He separated his element across the sky, letting it fall to the earth. He filled them with life and love. Soon, animals were running across plains and grasslands, rivers were flowing to the oceans. Celenic Earth was alive…

Shadowolf awoke, lying on his back. He lifted his head and looked through groggy eyes at the Clan. His aura was still pulsing white, although it was fading. A strong wind was subsiding, and his friends were releasing the trees and rocks they were clinging to. He felt relieved that he was clothed and his sword was at his side.

"The *Enodhim*," Malanite said in wonder, and Shadowolf let his mind submit to sleep.

NEW AVALION
CHAPTER NINE

They were making their way steadily north after a day's rest. Shadowolf had to repeat his experience for the hundredth time to Darcwulf and Shedaaij, the others lingering in the back with Millon and Kentaur.

Nelnar still hurt as much as he did, but the wolf was running better. Its appetite was picking up, and that pleased Shadowolf. He wanted to make sure his loyal friend was strong for the road ahead.

"Listen," Shadowolf addressed the two, "I am sorry for getting us in so much trouble. I know I could have avoided all these battles we've had just by going north in the first place."

"That's ok," Darcwulf said. "I've really enjoyed the training, although I thought that Butcher really had us."

"We are heading straight for the Scourge now," he promised. "No more detours and side battles. If I can help it, we won't be fighting for a long time now."

"Good," Shedaaij said, riding closer to him. "I was wondering when I was going to get some attention."

"Ooh," Darcwulf said, slowing his mount and retreating to the back. "I guess that's my cue to leave."

Shadowolf and Shedaaij laughed. He was growing fond of the Merlani again, more than before. He was glad that they could laugh and spend time together, satisfied with the promise that he would not fight again until needed. The battle with the elements and the claim of his power had strained him, and he needed the rest.

It was a beautiful day. The sky was cloudless, much to his personal relief, and there was a warm wind in the air. They were still in open plains. They had passed the end of the eastern forest of the River of Light that they had encountered at Meëntis. The river was still too far east to be seen, but the heat wave above the water was visible on the horizon. Bentley's Strip still loomed as a departure point to the west, with the Dwarf Mountains slowly rising in the north.

Night fell on them and they made camp. To the east the lights of human villages could be seen. It made Shadowolf's heart warm with the knowledge that there were still men and women who might be willing to stand up against the dark lord.

They sat in a circle around the fire that the centaurs constructed. All the girls except Shedaaij sat together, talking about their homes and families. The Merlani sat beside Shadowolf, and Darcwulf between Fransiska and Dren. Nelnar was spread across Shadowolf's lap and Ursula stood talking to Malanite. Gwyn was the last girl in the line, with Lastgorn and Sny-Ten beside her.

The three men of the Orion completed the circle with Trimistus on the left side of Shadowolf. The centaurs found it hard to sit, so they stood behind the Orion. Heula looked at home between Skywolf and Angelia.

"You won't believe the difference your last battle has made to you, Shado," Fransiska said.

"How?" he asked, frowning.

"She's right," Shedaaij agreed. "You radiate an energy that we could barely discern before."

"It's like..." Fransiska thought for a moment, "...it's like we feel warm if we walk beside you."

"Oh, so that's why you're leaning your head on my shoulder," he teased Shedaaij.

"I can take it off," she smiled, and he kissed her on her forehead.

"Do you plan on heading home after you have the horn?" Skywolf asked.

"Maybe," Shadowolf replied. "It is a good possibility. I haven't really thought about it."

"You could teleport," Angelia offered, "if you remember how, of course."

"Yes, I do," he smiled. "But what about you guys?"

"We'll be fine here," Shadowwe said. "You haven't greeted them since your return."

Shadowolf sat in thought for a moment and then arose from the grass. He went over to Ursula and Malanite and waited for their discussion to end.

"Come, Shado," the unicorn invited kindly. "It will be a pleasure to speak to you."

"Interesting little battle, yer had," Malanite said.

"Do you know what it was about?" Shadowolf asked.

"We were just discussing it," she replied. "Malanite seems to think that it is a result from the power that you released at the node."

"That was so long ago," Shadowolf said.

"True," Malanite answered. "However, I feel that you have not truly mastered the power. It could be that, due to your battles over the years and your increasing use of the wind, that you were somehow challenged for the power."

"It did appear to be some sort of test," he said. "In the end, they accepted me."

"Have you ever met Masara?" Ursula asked.

"Only in spirit form," he replied. "But that was in the Masaran Ruins. Why do you ask?"

"Centuries ago, before the Battle of T'Mar's Scourge," Malanite said, "he was training to become the ultimate *Sadgi*. Mayhap he may have some answers for yer."

"But you didn't come here to discuss that, did you?" Ursula asked. "You must be tired of the topic."

"I am," he agreed. "I came to ask for a favour."

"I am listening," she said.

"I want to travel to my home," Shadowolf said. "I was thinking I could teleport, but I would like to take Shedaaij with me. I don't think I can visualize the new Avalion either."

"Are you asking me to take you?" she smiled.

"Humbly," he replied. "I understand if you feel offended at being asked to carry us."

"Surely you could fly there? You've just staked your claim as *Enodhim*."

"I know, but I still feel weak. And…"

"…she would feel impressed at how romantic you are?" she finished for him.

"Something like that," he blushed.

"Usually I would say no," she said, looking at Malanite, but Shadowolf missed a movement he made. "But in this case I will make an exception."

"Great," he said, making his way back to the group.

"Like a little kid, he is," Malanite said.

"When are you going to tell him?" Ursula said.

"Once I've convinced him to go with us to Eldor," Malanite replied, his false accent gone.

"You still feel it necessary?" Ursula asked.

"Le'Mar is close to finding the new entrance to the forest," Malanite answered. "I want Eldor to examine Shado's power before that happens."

Shadowolf returned with Shedaaij in arm, her expression filled with confusion. Ursula bowed her knee and Shadowolf helped Shedaaij mount before he jumped on.

"Yer better hold on tight," Malanite said. "It will be one fast ride."

"Where to?" Ursula asked.

"Where you and I met," Shadowolf said.

"Why there?" she asked.

"I want to see the extent of my father's kingdom," he replied. "And the mists refresh me."

Ursula trod the ground and then she ran. The plains started opening up to them as they headed south. Soon they could not tell one speck of stone from the next as they traveled at a speed he had not thought possible. Trees passed by them and they ran over the River of Light to the eastern embankment. They entered into a forest Shadowolf did not remember, and he sensed more than saw men living in cabins built in the trees' branches.

The desert was on their left as New Avalion came into view. Ursula turned right along the river's shore and stopped in the Mists of Celene.

The forest was as he recalled it. It glowed in the night with a green mist, keeping all evil from its presence. The trees whispered soft songs in the air. Little fire-light bugs danced between the trunks to the melody of serenity, and Shadowolf could feel that his spirit was instantly refreshed.

"This place is beautiful," Shedaaij sighed.

"This is where Ursula and I first met," Shadowolf said. "It was just after you and I said our farewell at Sea's Reach."

Shedaaij bowed her head in sadness, remembering the last time she had seen her beloved man. She leaned her head back against his chest.

"I love you, Shado," she said.

"I love you too, Shedaaij," he replied as they headed out of the forest at a slow canter.

When they exited the forest, they were greeted by a towering, wooden wall. It was one and a half times higher than the tallest tree bordering it and upon closer inspection he saw that it was emerald in colour. Shadowolf squinted as he stared up at the dark, foreboding structure.

"What happened to the old gates?" he asked.

"There is only one gate now," Shedaaij replied. "It is located at the north of the city."

"The Welcome Gate?" he asked.

"That was what you used to call it, yes," she replied sadly. "It is now the Messenger's Gate, for it is often the scouts and messengers that travel through it."

"It is huge," he gaped.

"It is small compared to the north and east," Shedaaij forewarned. "If we had time I would take you through the Outer Defense, but it would take three days to survey it all."

"Incredible," Shadowolf marveled. "Is it elvin work?"

"Some of it, yes. There is also some dwarven skill added to it, where bits of stone and rock were infused with the timber. But the bulk is from the elemental men and women of the city. Their lore and wood-work holds it all together."

They traveled along the wall until the forest broke away and they rode on open fields. The defensive wall ran northeast after that, and it appeared as if it would never end. Shadowolf could see no change on the horizon and wondered if it reached Eldor's Crest.

Casting his thoughts aside, he held onto Shedaaij as Ursula picked up her pace. With lightning speed she broke the distance and they stood before large, iron double-gates as high as the wall. Behind each corner of the gates, stood a tower made of a black metal he did not recognize.

"I see the people have overcome their fear of steel and iron,"

Shadowolf said.

"It serves as a warning to the dark lord that steel alone will not conquer this city," she replied. "The darker side of dwarven-lore was used, and after a year the stones are still immaculate. Its substance is unknown to us as they would not reveal their secret."

"Where did they get all this wood?" he asked.

"A lot of it was supplied by Eldor from his forest," she told him. "When it was decided that their own lore had to be used to sustain it and to ensure future repair and maintenance by your own people, the elementals duplicated the wood of the elves using earth and spirit. They were assisted by Prince Lesan and the High Elvin Circle until they could manage on their own."

"Prince Lesan is Eldor's son, if I remember?" he asked.

"Correct."

A shout sounded from the right tower and a wheel turned on its gears. The gate opened inwards. The city was hidden in the dark of the night, but he could see another wall half the height of the outer wall not far inside. Gates made of a different substance opened to an unknown area, but a hill rose behind it and he spied the topmost parts of his father's castle.

"Avalion has really changed," Shadowolf replied. "I don't remember the hill, but I am guessing that it is more elemental work."

Shedaaij nodded in response. A sentry rode out to greet them. He was dressed in black uniform and carried a staff tied to his back. His mount was a strong brown stallion, and he could tell by the scars on its muscles that it had survived a battle or two.

"Shedaaij, Ursula," the unknown guard greeted, his eyes mingled with awe and peace.

"You know me?" Ursula asked.

"Who does not know the mother of all unicorns," he smiled. "I am Jinsin of the Watre Tribe, but instated as a guard of New Avalion. So the rumours of your journeying the earth are true."

"How did rumours of our travels reach you?" Shadowolf asked skeptically.

"We have mercenaries hidden in the forest on the eastern shores of the River of Light," Jinsin said, and Shadowolf recalled sensing a habitation there on their path to the Mists. "There was word of a unicorn passing with an Avalion group called the Shadow Clan.

"There is another rumour," he continued, "that the son of Nighthale walks among them."

Shadowolf smiled and suddenly the sentry's eyes widened.

"I am sorry, my lord," he said, his voice shaking slightly. "I did not recognize you after so long."

"No harm done," Shadowolf replied. "Although the sooner I see my family the better I will feel."

"Of course," Jinsin said turning his mount. "Please, follow me."

He led them into the inner walls and signaled for the gates to close. Shadowolf was amazed at how silent the hinges were, and the gears emitted only the slightest creak.

"Its fine, Jinsin," Shedaaij said. "Don't leave your post. I will show him the way."

"Shall I send word of your arrival?" he asked.

"No," Shadowolf said quickly. "I want to surprise them."

"Good, then," Jinsin said and resumed patrolling the grounds.

"Ursula," Shadowolf said. "Do you mind if enter slowly? I want to take in as much of the new land while I can."

While Ursula trotted to the second gate before them, which Shedaaij said was called the Lowle Gate, Shadowolf looked at the valley around him.

The wall that supported the Lowle Gate stretched to the left and right and disappeared around bends that he could not see past. The wood was the same emerald as the outer wall.

"What's with all the green?" he asked.

"It is the colour that Jasnen Lowle, the tribe lord, chose for his clan," Shedaaij explained. "The timber has emerald gems infused with it."

The Lowle Gate was made of the same black substance as the towers. He waited as the double-doors swung inward and he faced walls on the other side again, except that these were purple in colour.

"Let me guess," he said. "Someone chose purple for their colour?"

"It's the amethyst in the wall that gives it the hue," she replied. They rode into the area and Lowle Gate closed. "Welcome to Watre

Hills."

"Oh, the Watre Clan," he remembered. "They are from Hasner if I recall. Remind me where Lowle fits in again?"

"Lowle became the tribe lord after Abutja was killed in Iceland," she said, and he sighed as it came back to him. Abutja had been wearing an Amethyst-pendant that belonged to Le'Mar, and it had taken his mind and convinced him there was no real threat. Nighthale had to intervene, with a little help from his son.

"I am surprised that anyone would choose amethyst after that, but it is a powerful crystal," he muttered.

They turned left after the Watre Gate closed. Shadowolf saw that both walls were purple as they headed south.

"How come the wall is green on the Lowle side, but purple on the Watre side?" he said, feeling stupid with all the questions.

"They managed to fuse emerald on the one half, and amethyst on the other. You will see that is so throughout all the villages."

Ursula picked up her pace into a slow run. Soon, village huts and buildings surrounded their path as the habitable area widened between the walls. The material used for the houses were purple in colour. Shadowolf sighed in relief when he realised that the villagers were not also dressed in purple. It was only the occasional guard that wore a purple uniform.

"Shado!" a voice called behind him. Ursula stopped and turned.

"I don't believe it," Shadowolf said as he dismounted. "Professor Par'Mal?"

"Please, call me Lucian," his former Wind tutor replied. "My, how you've grown in power. It's so palpable."

"So I hear," he replied as they embraced in greeting. Yet, Shadowolf frowned when they pulled away.

"What's wrong?" Lucian asked. "I swear you were delighted to see me a moment ago."

"I don't know," Shadowolf said, trying unsuccessfully to return his smile. "Something tugs at my memory, something I wanted to ask you, but I can't remember."

"Then it was probably not important," he said. "It's so good to see you. To think, one of my pupils would make me proud and become an *Enodhim*."

"Trust me," Shadowolf grinned, "I am attempting to forsake that name. The fame is just not worth it, what with the undead and demons trying to kill me for it and all."

"Undead and demons? You seem to be as troubled as I am. Where are you headed; to your father's?"

"Yes, indeed I am," Shadowolf replied.

"I will join you," Lucian informed rather than asked. "I need to meet with you both, for I am sure Nighthale will want me to relate my happenings with you."

Lucian disappeared and Shadowolf mounted while he waited. After a few minutes Lucian finally emerged from a small stall with a mount that Shadowolf recognized instantly.

"This night gets better and better," he said. "Lancenat, my old steed! How many years is he now? He must be about five."

"Yes, you hit it right," Lucian said. "I hope you don't mind me riding him. When the Orion and Harhonsa tribe migrated here last week I…"

"The Orion moved here?" Shadowolf frowned. "Ok, let's make haste to my father. There is too much to tell and hear."

They rode south past the others huts and homes. Lancenat held good pace, but he only kept up because Ursula slowed her speed to match his. A half hour later, they approached the Saphin Gate on their right.

"Pity Skywolf isn't here now," Shadowolf said as the gates opened silently. When they entered, he saw that the tribe had chosen the mottled brown of timber as their colour.

"This does not seem to be just natural timber," Shadowolf sensed.

"No," Shedaaij informed him. "There is a gem called pyrite infused with it. Because of its attributes and iron sulphate compounds, it is hardly discernable."

"Yet, the brown does seem richer in colour than normal timber, even by the wan light of the torches."

He saw that there were huts to the left and right, but they turned left, heading further south. Shadowolf thought they were almost certainly heading for the ocean. When he peeped over Shedaaij's head, he could see over some of the lower walls due to the soft descent of the hill. Purple and green roofs peeked out at some places, and sure enough the ocean was on the outskirts of Lowle

Hills.

"I don't understand," Shadowolf said. "Do the villages run in circles?"

"Sort of," Shedaaij said. "You were here when they started construction, weren't you?"

"Yes, but I don't remember it reaching the ocean."

"Avalion has been extended all the way to the southern ocean, which might be better understood in the next village."

It took another hour before they reached the southern apex of the village before it turned northwest. The half-Sothos shimmered down on them when Shadowolf realised it was midnight. He wondered if the Clan were asleep already.

On his right the *Avalendil* Gate appeared. On the left of the black iron gate was the insignia of a wolf howling and on the right was a picture of a mermaid on a rock singing.

"So you named it *Avalendil* after all?" Shadowolf laughed.

"It was what we agreed in Sea's Reach," Shedaaij smiled back, but she shifted closer into his arms. He could feel that she wanted to be alone with him, but he kept calm. He imagined for a moment his old friend Lellian holding the trident and ruling over the mer-people.

Before they could enter the fields, two people ran up behind them. They took a gasp of air before the man and woman were ready to speak.

"Shado," the man he recognized as Darna Saphin called. The gorgeous woman next to him, claimed to have been the fairest maiden of the Saphin tribe, was Claire, Darna's sister. He knew them well, for they were Skywolf's kin.

"Hello Darna, Claire," he greeted. "How is Tacent?"

"My son is well." Darna replied. He was apparently glad that Shadowolf remembered. "But word of my sister would be better."

"I go to my father to bring such news to his table," Shadowolf said. "Will you join us?"

"With pleasure. Give us a moment to mount."

"Does everyone always talk with such regal air?" Shedaaij asked as they disappeared into Saphin Vale.

"Darna holds his house in high esteem," he replied. "They always speak with cumbersome tones, and I always oblige in return. It irritates me though to do so."

After a moment of waiting, hooves pounded through the gate and the Saphin siblings joined their entourage.

They entered the open fields. At the distant top of the hill were his father's castle and the village of Avalion as he remembered it. It had shrunken a little, but it was Avalion nonetheless.

But between them and Avalion was a river, or rather it was a moat, Shadowolf realised. Bridges ran over from their side of the land to Avalion at regular intervals east and west of their position until the river turned north at both ends.

"Avalion really has become amazing," Shadowolf marveled.

"The land up ahead is known as the Degron Core by some," Lucian told him.

"If you descend these waters twenty minutes down, you will enter the vast warren of the Mer-Kingdom, as large as New Avalion," Shedaaij said, giving Shadowolf a moment to recover from the news. "It opens at the south into the ocean, and through many watery tunnels we can reach any of the great rivers."

"And you are protected from siren attacks," Shadowolf assumed. Ursula rode on with Lancenat and the Saphin mounts at her side and they made their way over a bridge into Avalion.

"The crops are promising good harvest this spring," Malkius Saphin said. "If the world really is in the grasp of the dark lord, it does not show in your land, Night."

"Our land, Malkius my good friend," Nighthale smiled. He was tired and his wife Karla had already gone to bed. Sleep did not come as easy as it used to. The four lords sat in the study, where the fire crackled in the furnace and fine wine and finger snacks lay on the common table.

"You can't deny that our fortunes are prosperous and that New Avalion provides a reprieve from the doom of the world," Jasnon Lowle added. "The people are still in good spirits."

"No one can take this city," Sjedwolf Watre confirmed. "It was built against his dark forces."

"I have no doubt my friends," Nighthale said, "that we have a good defense. Yet, while we linger here, the dark lord will build his forces and grow stronger. Where will we get such arms?"

"Help will come from above," a voice called from the door.

"Elgoth, come in," Nighthale invited Masara's son. Elgoth had been part of their council and circle since the start of the war, and had never left the village except to attend to Masara. He was as much part of the group of lords as any one of them.

"Any word on your father?" Jasnon asked.

"None at the moment," he replied. "Eldor says that my father's health leaves much to be desired."

"Strange, that your father has left the Far Isles to return to the continent," Sjedwolf said, and not for the first time. "His health will deteriorate here."

"His health is still preserved by the forest," Elgoth replied, finally sitting down and filling a glass with red wine. "Yet, he is not as strong as he used to be. He says that, in some ways, it seems as if the Battle of T'Mar's Scourge remains a deep wound in his soul."

"I don't envy him," Malkius said, "to be chosen by Bontu to be His greatest disciple, and then to be afflicted by its responsibilities."

"He was close to becoming *Sadgi* before the Battle," Elgoth said. "He just doesn't have the strength to pursue it anymore."

"We still have to decide who will represent the Orion in the council," Nighthale said. "I know I said we wouldn't be working tonight, but they need someone to lead them."

"Will be difficult," Jasnon said. "We can't build any land for them, and so we have provided land within various circles."

"We still need a leader," Malkius said. "The only noticeable lord among them was Amon from the Harhonsa Village in the desert, but as you heard Lucian say, he was killed."

"The most likely choice would be Lucian," Nighthale said. "Yet, if I know Shadowolf's teacher well, it is a post he will decline."

"I heard my name," another voice called from the door. Everyone turned in astonishment.

"And mine," Lucian said behind him. Ursula walked in behind the two men followed shortly by Shedaaij, Darna and Claire.

Nighthale rose slowly from his seat. In the flickering torch lights, Shadowolf spied wetness in his father's eyes. The man's hair was brushed down, obviously tended by his mother before she retired to bed.

Shadowolf's hair was a mess and dirty, which matched his

soiled face. His clothes were torn in some places, his sleeve almost falling from his right shoulder. Suddenly, among such finely dressed men, Shadowolf felt ashamed.

"Shado," his father sighed. "It is so good to see you."

He went to embrace him and the room held its breath in silence. The reunion went swiftly after that as everyone was greeted and reintroduced to Shadowolf. Ursula appeared to know everyone without introduction.

"Where are Nowles and Franklin?" Shadowolf asked when he took a seat, Ursula standing behind him and Shedaaij, Lucian, Claire and Darna sitting beside him.

"They have retired for the evening," Nighthale replied.

"I am afraid to say that I can't stay long," Shadowolf said. "So much has happened, and my friends wait for me in the north."

"Surely you can stay long enough to tell us where you've been and what has happened?" Malkius asked.

"Yes," Shadowolf laughed, forgetting himself. "I have recently returned from Bentley…"

"No, no," Jasnon asked excitedly, a hint of awe in his voice. "Start from the beginning. We want to know about the node."

"Oh, that!" he said. In truth, he had forgotten about the node. "To keep it brief, I went to the school at the turn of the Masaran Phenomenon. Mercius was there as expected, but so was my previous Headmaster Farnerd." Lucian narrowed his eyes at the mention of the name. Shadowolf again thought he should be remembering something, but ignored it.

"Apparently, when the tribes had captured Mercius, he had split his being into two, and the one known as Farnerd had built his school above the place where I was born."

"Of course," Nighthale said. "That was where we had protected you with the five powers."

"In that protection," Shadowolf continued, "you created a power that was my birth-right. Only I could release it at the time of the Windfarer. Mercius had mistakenly been taken as the Windfarer because that had been his nickname for so many decades."

"So you fulfilled the prophecy?" Jasnon asked.

"Maybe, maybe not," he said.

"What do you mean?" Elgoth asked, and he acknowledged

Elgoth's presence for the first time. He had a way of becoming inconspicuous.

"I fulfilled my birth-right," Shadowolf said. "It might have nothing to do with the prophecy."

"We think it does," Lucian said.

"We fear that the age of the DragonRider is upon us," Sjedwolf said.

"You see, Shadowolf," Elgoth said, "the triple prophecy is said to be fulfilled in succession to one another. First is the Windfarer, and then the DragonRider and finally the *Sadgi*."

"If you have fulfilled the Windfarer prophecy," Jasnon said, "then the DragonRider is next."

"And we could be there already," Shadowolf said. "But it seems like you already assume that. May I ask why?"

"Lucian?" Nighthale said.

"Shado, the Orion tribe was nearly wiped out in the desert."

"What?!"

"We were confronted by many dragons," Lucian continued. "They were merciless and destroyed many homes.

"Riding the lead dragon was an old friend of mine from the days when I once served Le'Mar. His name is Sonersaat."

"I know that name," Ursula said. "It is the name I heard when we fought the witches in Plastinon."

"Witches?" Jasnon and Sjedwolf asked.

"I guess I better tell you everything," Shadowolf said.

He proceeded to inform them of everything that had happened since he had left Bentley's Strip, leaving out only the trial that he had endured as the *Enodhim*. They all sat in mesmerized silence as the tale unfolded. After almost an hour, his story finished.

"To think, my sister in battle," Darna laughed.

Shadowolf sat down and thought about what Lucian had said, "When I once served Le'Mar". It now came to mind what had bothered him. Lanel, his former school friend, had mentioned at the school that Lucian had been seen meeting with the Sandrihelin. How had it come to pass that his father trusted this man?

"I wish we knew the full prophecy," Jasnon said.

"Eldor keeps it in his library," Elgoth said. "I will request that a copy be scripted and sent to us."

"I will ask around New Avalion," Sjedwolf said. "Someone must know."

"It is sad that ancient words have left us," Nighthale said. "But once again you seem to be in the middle of it all, Shado."

"My quest is almost complete," Shadowolf replied. "We are a few days travel from the Scourge. Once we have the horn, I will return here before making any further plans."

"Very well," Nighthale said, sitting deeper in his seat as his body relaxed.

"I still wonder why Le'Mar doesn't start the Dragon War," Sjedwolf said.

"Well, Asgorna isn't here to be challenged," Shadowolf said. "I can summon him, but he has returned to his world for now."

"There are other things that are happening in this world," Elgoth said.

"The Heart of Tigers," Ursula interrupted, and Elgoth nodded.

"It is a sacred gem," Elgoth informed the group, "that Baron Maren-Ti and his ancestors have held in his sacred Vale for centuries. The secret to the forest is held in that gem."

"If he gains the gem," Ursula said, "he will have at least two months to work out its secret doors and passes before the way is open to him."

"And he may use the dragons to fight in the forest," Jasnon concluded. "I see where this is going."

"Once the dragons fight in the Dragon War, the new leader will dictate what part they will play on Celenic Earth," Elgoth said. "It could go either Le'Mar's way or our way. And that is why he probably doesn't want to risk the battle just yet. He doesn't care who becomes the Dragon King, as long as it assists him in gaining the elvin forest."

"But why does Eldor not keep the gem in the forest?" Sjedwolf asked.

"It is part of the lore," Elgoth replied. "Returning the gem to the forest will break the Gate and clear the lore. It must be kept by something other than elvin hands. Yet, one cannot enter the forest with the gem, without first unveiling the secret within the gem."

"So we can rest assured until Le'Mar has the gem?" Nighthale asked, pretending not to be confused.

"I wouldn't bet on it," Elgoth replied.

"I should go," Shadowolf said. "The Clan waits."

"It was good seeing you again," Nighthale said. "Take care."

"Oh, one last thing," Lucian said as he rose. "You were correct when you said I would refuse the post of lordship over the Harhonsa."

"Tell my sister we send our love," Darna said. Claire smiled as Shadowolf greeted them. His mother had provided him and Shedaaij with fresh clothes and food, not allowing them to leave before Ursula's back was well provisioned.

Ursula turned away, and Shadowolf and Shedaaij held tight as she ran back to the north. Shadowolf hoped that Lellian would receive the message he had sent earlier and understand its significance.

The trees of the River of Light came into view and they passed through the inhabited area. Without blinking Ursula raced over the river and crossed on the western embankment.

Fire rose in the north. If Shadowolf's estimates were right, it was in the area where the Clan had camped. Horrendous roars erupted from the glade.

When they reached the camp, Shadowolf and Shedaaij dismounted and unsheathed their weapons. The three aVampyere were jumping from the trees and launching into the air, but they were not attacking any humans. They were attacking six dragons. The largest of the dragons, red scales with a yellow belly, had the only human mounted on his back. The man was bald, with a thin moustache on his lip and a scruffy beard. A red scar burned on top of his naked head.

Dren was flying up high with the dragons, wrestling with their huge bodies where he could. Nelnar was barking, but the others of the Clan were dodging claws and walls of fire, striking with their weapons where they could.

"Great," Shedaaij said with her twin daggers at hand. "We were just talking about them. How do we fight dragons?"

"I have been doing that for two years," Shadowolf said, raising his voice over the rising wind and roaring flames. "Just stay alive and leave the rest to me."

He clutched at the dragon amulet on his sternum and ran for the closest beast. Ursula called to Shedaaij to assist her with the provisions.

A tail swept the ground and Shadowolf jumped onto it. The scales were gray and murky. He struggled to stay on, and then used the wind to drive him higher into the sky. Ruben-Willow glowed in the moonlight as he twisted mid-air to miss the dragon forearm and stab its chest.

The dragon howled and struck at him again. Shadowolf took the blow to his right shoulder, but he turned to minimize the injury and grab the beast around the neck. As he was hurtled to and fro, he drove the sword in deep, letting fire coil the blade into its blood. The neck erupted and the body fell to the earth. Trevor and Skywolf were beneath it and they held out their hands in preparation for the blow.

The dragon was gone. Somewhere to the west, near Bentley's Strip, they heard a dull thud. Where the dragon had been falling Shadowolf appeared, teleporting back to the camp.

"Did he just teleport a whole dragon?" Trevor asked in astonishment. A sound exploded next to him and he turned to see Tinonte and Rennick stretching their arms into arcs of lightning. A black dragon was held in their web of power, although they were losing their grip.

The aVampyere Nellice and Malice dropped from the air and bit into the dragon's side and spine. The dragon tried to rear, but the lightning held it and it couldn't move. Soon its life left its body and the two warriors carried the animal lightly to the ground.

Fire burnt onto the dead dragon from another. Malice didn't make it and his ashes drifted to the earth. Nellice barely rolled away and ran for cover. Danto hit the dragon in the chest and it recoiled, but not before clawing into the aVampeyer's chest and ripping it open. It blasted the long-dead flesh and organs, making sure there was nothing left of the aVampeyer to strike back.

When it closed its mouth and nasal passages, the fire still continued. Its claws raked the vacant air, but it couldn't see where the fire was coming from. Steel entered its left eye, and it died as power rushed into its body from the blade, crimson as blood and wild as wind.

Shadowolf watched as the dragon slipped from his sword. He flew down to the earth beneath the falling body and held his arms high. With a hurricane he threw the beast over the top trees away from the Clan members around him.

"Why didn't you teleport him again?" Sorceress asked.

"I don't have that much strength," Shadowolf replied. "It takes a lot out of me. Watch out!"

Flames ripped towards her. She held up her palm and chanted unknown words. A shield appeared around her body and the flames fell to the ground.

"Just three to go," Shadowolf shouted. "Keep it up!"

Dren was still wrestling with a dragon when he leapt to the only mounted dragon. The man swung down from the spine and lobbed him away with a calculated kick. The gargoyle's unconscious form fell to the ground where Darcwulf caught him.

"Now I've had enough," Shadowolf whispered. "Nelnar!"

The wolf ran towards him, but Shadowolf had already started running in its direction. As they met, he grabbed Nelnar by the scruff of its neck and leapt into the air. He flew towards the mounted dragon and flung Nelnar onto its neck.

The dragon thrashed around, trying to dislodge the biting wolf. Shadowolf landed on its side and as he faced the man, balls of wind and fire escaped the stranger's palms and hit Shadowolf in his chest.

Shadowolf twirled over in the air and clutched both his palms by his thighs before thrusting them forward, a shower of wind and water hitting the dragon and his mount. They held fast, the dragon still trying to fling the wolf away, until the man almost slipped off the dragon's back.

Suddenly Shadowolf couldn't breathe. He clutched his throat as the asphyxiation increased, and he coughed trying to force his lungs to breathe.

He remembered his trial and called wind from the depths of his soul. If he couldn't get air into his lungs from the outside, then he would create it from the inside. Fresh air rushed into his body, through his blood and into his heart.

Nelnar was finally thrown aside and fell to the ground, but Shadowolf didn't see it as he flew to the attack. He also did not have time to see that the grass rose to catch Nelnar and let the wolf roll to safety. Darcwulf stared in astonishment as Shedaaij relaxed her power.

"I didn't know..." Darcwulf started.

"Leave it!" Shedaaij said and ran from another rain of flame.

Shadowolf stood on the dragon's back. Although he was losing his balance, the stranger seemed to be glued to the dragon. The dragon still continued to fly around and burn the surroundings while they fought each other.

Shadowolf decided to use the art of the Orion known as *rumakir*. If this man was as skilled in the elements as Shadowolf thought he might be, then maybe close-quarter combat would be the better option.

He sheathed his sword as the man lunged forward with his. Shadowolf used the wind to draw it aside and the man fell over his feet. The man stood up and sheathed his sword into straps behind his back.

As the man hit with a large left fist, Shadowolf grasped his wrist and pulled it towards himself. The man's shoulder approached, and he twisted the arm and struck with his palm into the man's chest, a ball of fire blasting him backwards. But the man was fast; as he fell he turned on the axis of descent and hit Shadowolf with a streak of lightning.

Shadowolf's skin felt singed, yet he rose up on the wind and ran to the man. When he was upon him, the dragon twisted and Shadowolf fell. The dragon's tail swung and hit him into the air. Shadowolf stopped mid-air and faced the dragon and man. He was exhausted, but he knew their attack would not stop until he was dead. Without warning, Sonersaat's body flared with ethereal dragon wings. Ethereal claws bit at Shadowolf's chest and heart, and he screamed as it tore at flesh.

They flew towards him, the dragon's nasal passages warming up for the attack, when it reared up and its wings braked in the air. The supernatural claws disappeared and all was silent.

Behind him, Shadowolf could feel the cold draft of air slapping against him. He relaxed his muscles. The pain of the claws still coursed through his body, but he stared defiantly at the enemy.

"About time," he said, his eyes not leaving the three stagnant dragons and the single man.

"I had to make preparations before I could leave," Asgorna replied. "How long has this been going on?"

"I arrived when I touched the amulet," Shadowolf said, feeling for the amulet on his chest to make sure he hadn't lost it.

"Maneto," Asgorna greeted.

"Asgorna," the dragon replied.

"Then you must be Sonersaat," Shadowolf said to the man.

"One and the same," Sonersaat replied.

"Then let's finish this stupid prophecy now," Shadowolf clenched his palms into fists.

"Unfortunately, I can't," Maneto said. Shadowolf thought he saw a smile on the dragon's face.

"Afraid?" Asgorna asked tartly.

"Of you?" the dragon roared in laughter. "That will be the day. Your time will come, lord of dragons. Until then, may your days be dark with fear."

The three remaining dragons turned and flew northeast.

"I don't understand," Shadowolf said. "We could have ended this now."

"And he would have killed you," Asgorna said, and Shadowolf turned to him. "I do not doubt your skill and luck of evading death, but his power is greater than yours. He has displayed that he indeed possesses the power of the dragon. I am afraid that he is the DragonRider."

"Alright," Shadowolf said, a little aggravated. "Well, I guess you can go back if you want."

Asgorna narrowed his eyes slightly, but forgave him his anger and flew back towards the Strip.

"What's the point of a dragon if he doesn't arrive in time?" he said to the recovering Clan when he landed on the earth. "That's probably why Maneto has the DragonRider, because he makes the effort to actually be here for the war."

"Shado," Ursula said. "Asgorna cares as much about…"

"Forget it!" Shado shouted, looking for his mare. "I don't want to hear it. I was taken without question to defend his world. The least he can do is spend some time here and help us instead of waiting for this damned Dragon War."

"You would have died if the war befell us now," Ursula replied calmly.

"I DON'T CARE!" he shouted as he mounted his horse, heading north with Nelnar at his side. "Let's go get your stupid horn, the good it will do us…"

SHENAMA RECLAIMED
CHAPTER TEN

"Why do you insist on doing this?" Kailan asked.

Lucian stopped packing and stared out the window at the rising sun. The sigh escaped unbidden from his mouth. Lancenat was being prepared and saddled in the small stable joined to the small hut.

"I could sit here and wait for Le'Mar, but something inside me says that I must move."

"But uPendus..."

"I know, it is a mythical land," Lucian turned and grasped her shoulders. "Kailan, I will be safe. The dark lord won't be looking for me in a land that possibly doesn't exist."

"How will you know where to go?" she asked, getting desperate.

"I have the notes I copied from Asbec," Lucian said, referring to the school he once taught at. "Nighthale let me script some pages from his library. I am certain that, if uPendus does exist, these notes will suffice."

"And if it does exist? What guarantee do you have they will join our cause?"

"I don't," he replied sincerely, "but I won't know unless I try. Their powers will be a great aid against the dark lord."

"Is there something else bothering you?" she asked. She could tell there was something on his mind. "Give me a better reason for this rash behavior."

"During the Battle of T'Mar's Scourge, T'Mar rode a pegasus while fighting Masara," Lucian replied while returning to his pack. "I want to make sure we gain their service before he does."

***

The sunlight hit her as hard as a stone against her eye. dead Fretlings lay across the rocks; their corpses were red and emitted a foul stench into the immediate air.

Chenesia vaguely saw that the red was not from blood, but rather another substance. It resembled rusted bronze hinges that were left too long in the rain. Their insides were spilled out onto the warm stones and the ants and buzzards were wasting no time in collecting their share.

At first she did not recognize the area they had entered. The vast grasslands stretched towards the north and east. When she turned to look west, she only saw the heights of mountains. The mountain range ran along the south towards the east. After giving it some thought, she realised where she must be.

"There are only three mountain ranges that are known to us," she said to Genewiu. "Bentley's Strip, which runs from north to south, is one. The other is Eldor's Forest, but that is on all sides and the innards are made of forest."

"Then this must be the northern valley of the Dwarf Mountains," the pegasus said.

"Is there a quicker way to pass the mountains without having to go through them?" Chenesia asked.

"That depends," Genewiu replied. "I could take you to uPendus, but then it would lengthen the trip to your Vale. The only other way is to travel west to the Alcove of Light's beach, head south past the range, and then head east again along the southern valley of the mountains."

"I would rather we take the second route then," Chenesia said. "How far do you think until we reach the range?"

"We could reach it by nightfall if we ride a good pace," Genewiu said.

The air shimmered in the study. Baron Maren-Ti awoke from his unsteady sleep and slipped off his chair, knocking his head against the table. He rose and rubbed the side of his jaw, feeling the humidity change and watched as the bookcase morphed horridly.

The air stilled and the bookcase returned to normality. Maren-Ti's eyes searched the room, but the source of the disturbance remained silent. The sunlight lit the room terribly, throwing obscure shadows over the carpets. Maren-Ti reassured himself that the elvin lore had prevailed, when a blast of wind erupted in the room and he was thrown off his feet.

A red portal glowed in the centre of the bookcase. A tall figure cloaked in black walked into the study very calmly, and the head tilted down at his sprawled figure. The portal was making a noise of rushing wind, yet the man's voice overcame it.

"Did you really think that elvin magic would keep me away for long?" Le'Mar said. "You, like everyone else in this miserable world, underestimate me."

"What do you want?" the baron asked.

"Please don't offend your own intelligence," the dark lord laughed. "You know why I am here. I have your daughter and you have my gem."

"It seems like I am not the only one whose intelligence needs questioning, for you know that the gem is not mine to give."

"Baron," Le'Mar approached the crouching figure, "do not make this more difficult than it should be. It is quite simple, I assure you. You hand me the gem, and I release your daughter. Or I can take the gem for myself and kill your daughter."

Maren-Ti held his silence at this, his heart beating faster and perspiration raining down his brow.

"If you are able to take it for yourself," Maren-Ti frowned, "then why do you still offer an ultimatum?"

Le'Mar raised his arm in fury and the baron was flung against the far wall. He strode under the darkness of his cloak out of the study into the west wing. Closing his eyes, he teleported to the courtyard outside the Jin Tai Sanctuary.

He remembered it being kept here the last time he had attempted to take it. Two dwarven guards raced across the courtyard to hit their axes into him, but he drew a dark sword with a midnight-blue wooden hilt and sliced the one's neck and cut the other's belly.

The large oak door opened and three more dwarves exited. He teleported behind them and slammed the door shut with one wave of his palm. The dwarves banged on the outside and he walked through a corridor into a second passage lit by the sunlight through open portals.

Five dwarves charged down the passage and, something he had not expected, two elvin archers were situated on the inner courtyard's trees. He laughed as the dwarves approached and the elves notched their arrows. Darkness drew about him and the sunlight dimmed. Soon, the sanctuary was drawn in nightfall.

The arrows ricocheted against the wall behind Le'Mar, and the dwarves stopped their approach. Coughing rose from the trees, and the screams of the dwarves traversed the halls. Two throwing axes swung in the chill night, and two bodies hit the dry earth.

When the darkness dissipated, an evil sight was revealed on the stone walls. The walls had seen many centuries and survived many wars. But the ghastly entrails sprawled across the walls and upon the sacred grass of the temple showed an evil they had not witnessed before.

The elves' heads were on the ground, the axes lodged in the foreheads between their eyes. Their heads were angled against the ground, facing the blood-shed walls, as their bodies were raised against gravity. Their feet hung in the air by some unknown force, the body pulled up towards it as if hung by a rope. The blood was draining out of the pupils of their eyes.

Their mouths were murmuring the words on the walls. It was an ancient language, bred from the days of lore.

The oak door blew inwards, splinters flying into the corridors. Eldor ran with his white staff down the passage with Maren-Ti close behind him. As they turned the corner, Maren-Ti gasped and threw up while Eldor leaned heavily on his staff.

The dwarves were hanging with their backs upon the edge of the axes lodged into the stone walls of five pillars. Eldor walked into the passageway of the inner courtyard and saw the elves staring at the single wall of the passageway. The dwarves, each on his own pillar, faced the same wall and repeated the same words:

"*Ser him nec torna, ser him Sadgi nit a ni, ent ser him na nom ni him ser. Nacta him ta norpa, fer ser him na bontu.*"

The words were written in the blood and innards of the dwarves upon the wall. Eldor risked looking into the open guts of the dwarves and saw that their hearts were still beating. It was not the usual double-beat of a heart, but a single beat that danced at a sickly tempo.

Eldor faced the doors at the end of the passage. Upon whispering the baron's name, he received from Maren-Ti the Heart of Tigers, and placed it in the top nook of the staff. His staff flared red momentarily before returning to its snowy state.

The elf lord's ear twitched as Le'Mar entered the courtyard. The dark lord's black cloak swayed in the wind, hiding his face, but the ancient elf knew he was smiling beneath the darkness.

"We meet again, Eldor," he smirked. "Rest assured, the next time we meet, I will have your kingdom, and you will leave this world to my ruination."

"My lord, Bontu, would not allow such a travesty," Eldor said.

"Did you not read the writing, or have you forgotten the old ways? Living among such weaklings will do that to you."

Le'Mar charged for the attack and Eldor rushed to defend, but the dark lord vanished in the returning light.

"Where…where is he?" Maren-Ti asked in fear and sickness.

"He is gone for now," Eldor said forlornly. "Come."

He touched the baron's shoulder and the staff lit up. As they vanished, a pale, green mist crept up into the courtyard and covered the bodies. The moist vapour next rose into the air, and the bodies were taken into the heavens.

The baron and the elf lord stood in the circular tower room, facing the confused, gaping assembly.

"Lord Eldor," Elgoth smiled, and bowed.

"Where are we?" Maren-Ti asked.

"We are in New Avalion," Eldor replied.

"I take it all is not well?" Elgoth asked while the others remained in silence.

"No," Eldor replied. "Le'Mar has attempted the gem, and left us a message."

"The writing on the wall?" Maren-Ti asked, getting more agitated.

"It said, *'I am the dark lord, I am the Sadgi foretold, and I am your ceaseless night; it is I. Kneel before me, for I am your god.'*"

"What are we doing this far south?" Maren-Ti asked, worried about his Vale.

"I am here to ask a favour of Nighthale," Eldor faced him, "to bear the burden of Keeper of the Heart of Tigers."

Le'Mar sat in his throne chair, the restless crow staring out the large, domed window towards the southern lands of Celenic Earth upon his shoulder. The door to his chamber opened and a voice called weakly towards him.

"Please, take a seat," Le'Mar offered his servant. The man crossed the distance and took the proffered seat. "My bird tells me that you took matters into your own hands."

"I did not engage with Asgorna," Sonersaat replied.

"Did I not instruct you not to attack Shadowolf?" the dark lord asked.

"Yes, but..."

"Yet, you deliberately disobeyed me?"

"Yes, but..."

He was hushed into silence as Le'Mar rose from his seat, the black cloak around his body, but his hood down to reveal his serene face. He thanked the crow for its allegiance, and let it fly from the castle.

"I cannot allow you to disobey me again," Le'Mar said and raised his hands. Sonersaat grabbed at his throat as his body lifted from the chair. He was levitated to the rear wall, and his arms were forcibly removed to his sides. The stone of the wall reached out over him and covered him in a thick veil. His body turned to granite and his vacant eyes stared out the window.

"You will remain there until it pleases me to release you," Le'Mar said and left the chamber.

It took half an hour to get to his dungeons below. The gates were worn and rusted, but he spared no energy to renew them. He walked into the chamber he sought, and the sight caught him off-guard.

The sentry he had placed there lay dead on the floor of the open cells, his short sword lying carelessly at his side. Genewiu and Chenesia's cells were empty.

"NOOOOOO!!!!!!!" he shouted and slammed his fist into the closest wall. The concrete shimmered and then crumbled to the floor as he left the dungeons.

***

"I am sorry," Shadowolf said as they rode north. "I guess losing to Sonersaat was a defeat I had not anticipated."

"I understand," Ursula replied, although her tone held a stubbornness that bit into his heart.

"I have never felt such fear before," he told her. "I am not sure what I am more afraid of: fighting Sonersaat, or starting the War of the Dragons."

"It is not easy when one is faced with such troubles," she said, sounding more tolerant. "We've established that he is indeed the DragonRider, or *Wisoum*, as is known in the elder tongue."

"Ursula, why is so much of the ancient lore not taught today?" Darcwulf asked, relieved that the tension was finally over.

"Many felt that its relevance had fallen with time," Ursula replied uncomfortably. "I suppose saying 'DragonRider' or '*Wisoum*' does not really matter, but the ancient prophecies are written with such words. It is essential that someone in each generation is taught to read the elder tongue, or the mysteries of the future told in the past will be forgotten in the present."

"We are doing quite well without the prophecy," Skywolf said. "We don't even know what is going to happen, but it doesn't stop us from doing what we do."

"We have a chance to stop the prophecy from being fulfilled," Ursula said. "That is why we are on this quest."

"And here I thought I was doing you a favour," Shadowolf said to the amusement of the others. Even Ursula smiled.

"I still can't believe you're an earth elemental," he said to Shedaaij. Darcwulf had mentioned to him earlier that morning about Nelnar's rescue and the rise of the earth, and he hadn't had the mood to discuss it.

"When the elementals built the Avalion walls, I asked some of them to tutor me," Shedaaij responded. "I found that the earth was easier to work with. It came more naturally, I guess you could say."

"I would have thought you'd do better with water," Fransiska said, referring to her mermarian nature.

"Me too, yet, the earth appealed to me more."

Shadowolf stopped his mount and squinted into the distance.

"Malanite," he called. The old man, mounted behind Rennick,

rode up to him.

"Yes," he replied.

"Was this city always here?" Shadowolf asked.

The ruins stretched before them. The walls were still strong in certain areas, but others were weakened by gaping holes that revealed charred buildings and long dead lands.

To the east he could see the cities called Prato, Glosgow, Malay and Monisco that bordered on the west of the River of Light. They would not enter those villages, but he had been assured by Dren that they were still inhabited by humans.

"Yes, although not as frail as yer see before yer," he replied. "You might remember this land once called Shenama."

Suddenly Shadowolf's heart filled with emotions he could not contain. All at once he wanted to scream and cry, ride and fight. He remembered Shenama all too well.

He had still been at the college, when the first outbreak of war had been announced. He had been injured in the hospital of the school, and warned by his friends Lanel, Mourna and Harmony.

Against their will, he had teleported to a close friend of his whose home was in Shenama. Nashela had been hiding from the orcs, and through the help of Lanel he had ensured that she returned safely to the college. After a battle with a few orcs and a Dra-hu'Mar, the mystical warrior that changed his bow into a sword and back at will, he had found Ruben-Willow on the battle field. Mercius had left a general by the name of McCaniban in charge.

And now they had returned to the sword's home. The barren wasteland seemed silent, but something evil lurked behind the walls. He could feel it in the wind.

"You said we would avoid any further battles," Darcwulf reminded.

"I have something to reclaim for an old friend of mine," he said, turning to his brother. "I owe it to her. You don't have to come."

"Says who?" he smiled, drawing his staff and igniting it with fire.

Those with weapons similarly drew it, and the weapons sang a cry for war.

"Alright," Shadowolf smiled and faced Shenama. "In we go."

He kicked Mandy forward and the dark mare leapt in a lust for battle. Her eyes flared red and her dismantled main flew back from the rush of air. He raised Ruben-Willow when they neared the walls, and hit an arrow away as several flew into the air and fell upon them.

Three arrows headed his way, when the centaurs moved to the fore and grabbed them before their target. Millon and Kentaur smashed through the broken areas of the wall with their front legs and pulled two of the archers down. Heula chimed under her breath and a large expanse of the top wall crumbled and the goblin archers fell to their bloody deaths.

The Clan was in Shenama, and realised too late they had just started a battle with an army. Shadowolf appeared unperturbed as he raced through to the newly-formed frontline orcs. One man led the army.

"McCaniban!" Shadowolf recognized him, although it had been two years since he had had the one opportunity of seeing him. The general's silhouette burned red on his iris and his spirit grew in power.

"Who the hell are you?" McCaniban asked, but raised his sword as the young man fell upon him. The Clan broke into the front line as Shadowolf and Nelnar engaged with McCaniban and his mount. The horse was distracted by the wolf's bites and the general fell to the ground, receiving an instant blow to the heart. He died with the dark mare snorting above him and the sword was removed from his body.

In all their time together, Shadowolf had never seen such fast work made on an army. The Clan was ruthless, mowing down the orcs relentlessly. Shadowolf, however, turned his attention on the rear Dra-hu'Mar.

He felt as if the evil, dark side of Mandy was seeping through her black fur into his blood. Something powerful was building inside of him, and he could feel the essence of the *Enodhim* reborn within his soul.

He bore his teeth at them in a grin and pushed past the orcs to the Dra-archers. The wind picked up the gathering orcs and flung them sideways into a waiting Clan member. Millon and Kentaur added their weight in getting the orcs out of his way as he turned the gale into the wave of arrows and thrust them aside. This in itself astonished the Dra-archers, as the elements had never had any effect on steel-shafted arrows.

They morphed into Dra-infantry, their bows instantly becoming swords. They all looked alike with shoulder-length blond hair and green eyes. And they had one other thing in common; Shadowolf was going to kill them all.

He stood on Mandy's back and leapt off, allowing her to fall away from the battle. Nelnar caught the attention of one warriors, who swung and then received a fatal blow from Shadowolf.

The Dra-hu'Mar turned to him, and all at once found themselves attacked by the Clan. Shadowolf drove his sword into the closest warrior and then kicked another's sword aside and lobbed his head off.

Shedaaij appeared beside him swinging her daggers. Even in the midst of battle, he couldn't help but stare at her attractiveness. Her body appealed to him, but then almost as suddenly an enemy's sword appealed to his more urgent attention. He ducked, rolled and cut the warrior's back and then lower legs.

The earth shook and trembled. Shadowolf held his balance, lifting off the ground slightly so that he would not fall. While the Clan continued to fight the warriors around him, he turned to face a beast he had not seen since the Battle of Iceland.

It was gigantic relative to Shadowolf's body, at least twice his height. Its arms were as huge as rocky boulders, but this time he was not fazed by its immensity. He knew those arms could move at lightning speed. He was just glad there was only one of them.

The attack began, and Shadowolf dodged flailing arms. It struck him once in the abdomen, and he had to move reflexively to avoid another blow to the skull. The *Enodhim* awoke within him, and he dissolved into a mist, rolling around the Ma-Wreth's waist. Dren attacked its front as Shadowolf drove his sword through the back into what he hoped was its heart. A horn broke through its lumbar vertebrae, and Ursula pulled back as the beast fell forward to its deathbed.

Shenama was reclaimed. Shadowolf looked back. The previously barren landscape was now strewn with bodies.

"I am so glad I am on the right side this time," Trimistus said as he joined Shadowolf's survey.

"Do you think your buddies will come to the same conclusion?"

Shadowolf asked.

"Lister and Ru-Maak, if they are still alive, will come to their senses at the edge of my sword," the former Saneth replied.

"I meant to ask you before," Shadowolf smiled as Ursula joined them. "I thought the horn wasn't meant for killing?" He was also wondering if they should clean up the mess.

"I said it was contrary to popular belief," she replied. "I didn't say it wasn't done."

"We will remain here a day or two," he said to the Clan's satisfaction. "And then, the Scourge."

***

Chenesia and Genewiu reached the western range on the eastern beach of the Alcove of Light by nightfall as predicted. Half way to the range, Genewiu had consented to allow Chenesia to mount her, as the pegasus's strength was renewing the further they left the dark lord's dungeons behind. Her wings were still dilapidated, but showed signs of healing.

Chenesia was still in a sad state however. Her body was bruised and she struggled to keep her dress straps on her ailing shoulders. She was sure one or more joints were out of place as the ride emphasized the dislocations.

When they made the range she dismounted and they found a soft spot under a cave to rest. To their surprise, they were not the only ones to use the reprieve of the mountains.

"No, no, don't hurt me!" the little man hurtled from his small fire and made for the southern sloping hills.

"Wait!" Chenesia called. Genewiu charged forward and stopped him with a stomp of her front hooves.

"We mean you no harm," the pegasus informed him.

"How...how can I trust you?" the man snorted, trying to evade the hooved animal. "Fer all I know, you's be belonging to him."

"Who?" Chenesia asked. "Le'Mar?"

"The dark lord indeed," the man whimpered. "But by your state, it seems like you are a victim as I."

"We are free of his tyranny," Genewiu answered.

"As am I," he smiled softly. "I am Nucial. Where be you traveling to?"

"We're heading east," Chenesia said, "to Carmel."

Genewiu frowned at the lie, but held her silence.

"May I join you?" Nucial asked. "I have been in his prisons for four years and I have no where's to go."

"Of course you may," Chenesia smiled and they returned to the fire. Both she and Genewiu had many questions to ask him, but they held their silence for the night. They needed rest. They would ask the battered and bruised man along the journey.

URSULA'S HORN
CHAPTER ELEVEN

Shadowolf opened his eyes to the morning. The air was filled with a fresh wind that blew from the north-east. They had stayed a day at Shenama, choosing among various broken buildings to sleep in. Millon and Kentaur had provided constant meals for them, while Fransiska, Angelia and Skywolf ensured that there was clean water available. The girls had to use some of their power to bring up the water from the deep trenches of the earth, but eventually a small stream flowed from a rocky bed over the wasted plains.

Shadowolf watched from his second-storey abode down on the others. The sun would rise in the next hour, but he wasn't able to fall back into sleep. He had gone to bed early the previous night and now his body was restless.

They had camped closest to the northern walls. Judging by their average pace over the days since they had left Bentley's Strip, he guessed that they would reach the Scourge by mid-afternoon if they left two hours after sunrise.

Darcwulf was cuddled down with Fransiska in an open-roof building on the ground below him. Angelia, Skywolf and Heula had found a home in a building adjacent to them. In a separate room from the same building, were Lastgorn, Sny-Ten and Gwyn.

The six Orion of Shadowwe, Scarlette, Sorceress, Trevor, Tinonte and Rennick were lying in a straw attic that had somehow managed to survive the orcs' destructive hands. Trimistus, Malanite and Dren were in the bottom of a circular tower that was broken mid-way up its stairwell.

The horses had been placed in three separate stables. In one of them, Ursula, Millon and Kentaur slept. Although Shadowolf said they could use the houses, they felt the most secure and warm in the stables.

Shadowolf could feel the winter approaching. The air was nippier and clouds were starting to cast against the sky. Nelnar was snoring softly beside him and Shedaaij was curled on his chest, her one leg wedged between his legs. He sat with his back against the only wall of the upper room he was in. The other three walls were scattered on the foundation of the building. The roof was suspended over him, still attached to the rest of the second floor and the pillars in the former corners of the room.

She stirred and looked up dreamily into his blue eyes. His long, dark brown hair hung over his ears onto his shoulders, his goatee was thick and black and he was growing a scruffy beard along his jaw due to lack of self-maintenance. She leaned up to kiss his lips.

His fever for her burned in his body as he returned the kiss. His hands ran along her sides and back, pulling her closer and kissing her harder.

"I love you," he said, and she returned the gesture. He decided they could stay a little bit longer if need be…

As Shadowolf had judged, they could see the waterfall in the distance by mid-afternoon. The troop was jubilant, having finally reached their goal. Creotos shone brilliantly in the sky, but the chill of the wind still broke through its false promise of heat.

The remainder of the journey was ridden in silence. Shedaaij had already informed him that she would stay with the girls while he and Darcwulf went searching for the horn. They would camp on the west embankment.

The water stormed into the Scourge from the high cliffs of Dwarf Mountains. It flowed from a deep and vast canyon on the other side of the mountains to fall down the landscape into Dark River.

They stopped at the junction where Dark River and River of Light met. This was where the waterfall was the deadliest. No rocks broke the surface, and Shadowolf was sure that if there had ever been any rocks, the waterfall had eroded it with its force ages ago.

It felt like a wonderful day. Shadowolf's heart was singing within as the chill wind danced upon his skin. He repeatedly turned his head to look and smile at Shedaaij. She returned his look with longing and he could almost forget that the world was under the tyranny of war.

But then he remembered that she was in as much danger as the earth, and it would encourage him to do everything he could to stop the dark lord. Yet, even that did not steal the comfort he felt that she was his love. As soon as they had the horn he planned to take her back to Avalion and spend all his time loving her.

Why should he spend so much effort being the saviour of the world? Who had put this task upon him, but himself? He had no reason not to return home, assist his father at the council and love the woman beside him for all time.

The words of Asgorna returned to him, and he remembered their bargain. He knew he could not sweep aside his promise, unless he wished the wrath of the dragons to be visited upon his family and loved friends.

The bargain would only take place after the final war with Le'Mar however. Until then, Shedaaij would be his top priority. That was a promise he made to himself.

When he would tell her and the Clan about the silent bargain, he did not know. He only knew that the time was not yet ripe. The time would come for the revealing of the horrible truth, but not now…not when Shedaaij loved him so much!

The Clan came to the edge of the frothing bank and dismounted. Some went to nearby trees to find shade for their horses, and then returned to bid farewell.

Shadowolf heard a voice from the water and turned with a smile to see Lellian swimming in the centre of the River of Light's stream.

"Glad you could make it!" he shouted over the breaking water.

"Got your message from your father," Lellian said. "I wouldn't miss this for the world."

"I sort of expected something more regal," he replied. "Like a crown or something."

"I thought it might attract too much attention," Lellian smiled. "Besides, I never got the hang of royalty."

"Ahhhh," Shadowolf said, and then laughed. "Did you bring it?"

Lellian swung his hand over the water and a thin rope hurtled over the distance to him. Shadowolf inspected the rose pendant. Its design had not changed. The chain was thin, but strong, and dangling from it was a red stone in the shape of a rose.

"You sure you don't need one?" Darcwulf asked skeptically.

"Yeah," Fransiska smiled, peering over Darcwulf's right shoulder and folding her arms around his stomach. "You don't need him, do you?"

"I would like it if he came," Shadowolf replied, embarrassed. Darcwulf had turned to plant a gentle kiss on her cheek. "But I under…"

"No, no," Darcwulf said. "I want to go. I just wanted to make sure I wouldn't have to come up and ask Shedaaij to give you mouth to mouth if you start drowning."

Shadowolf laughed, but could see the rest of the Clan were getting restless and staring awkwardly at this open display of their affections. Although the Clan were close and strong, he knew that no one would get as close to him as Darcwulf and Nelnar. Shedaaij would get there, but it would take time.

I am only twenty-two, he thought as he reached for his pack-bag and pulled out two objects before handing the bag to Shedaaij, *yet I have the weight of the world on my shoulders.*

Darcwulf apparently picked up on the vibe too. They handed their weapons to the girls and then he placed the chain around his neck. The pendant fell silently to his sternum.

"Cute," Fransiska said, and then Darcwulf and Shadowolf bid the Clan farewell and made for the water.

"What should I expect?" Darcwulf asked him.

"The skin beneath your ears will break open after a while," he replied, remembering his first experience. "Don't touch it, just let it happen."

Darcwulf nodded. They stared back at their girls for a second. Nelnar groaned, and then ran to Shedaaij's side.

The two boys walked to the bank. The land rolled down to the beach of the river, so they were comfortably hidden from the view of the Clan. Shadowolf handed the light red swimming material, known as joggens in Avalion, to Darcwulf.

It was a lengthy pair of pants which reached down to the ankles. It was not transparent, but the flimsiness of it indicated that it should be. Shadowolf had made sure that he had taken these from his room before he had left Avalion.

Then he stared at the waterfall. The River of Light was pure and crystal clear. Yet in contrast, where the water split at the waterfall, it became the red tint of the soil that was known as Dark River.

They discarded their clothes and hopped into the joggens, Shadowolf taking the white one. They braced their bare torsos for impact as they ran for an overhanging rock far from the destructive waterfall and dived in.

The water hit him like an ice block against his head. He had underestimated the current that the waterfall produced. When his sight cleared, he could make out the green scaly tail of Lellian. He turned to Darcwulf and awaited the transformation.

It took a minute before it happened and the pendant glowed. Darcwulf started thrashing and twisting in the water, trying his utmost not to touch the tearing skin of his new gills.

He looked at his hands, half expecting them to turn into fishy pads, but then looked past them at Shadowolf's chest. A light burned from his sternum, and then he also twisted as the forgotten sensation of the gills broke his skin.

When their bodies were at rest, the two smiled at each other before swimming to Lellian.

Just you and I on another adventure, brother, Shadowolf spoke to Darcwulf's mind. Darcwulf almost choked from fright before he realised what was happening.

Like...d old..ays..., Darcwulf struggled to reply with his thoughts *...Just like the good old days, I mean.*

Lellian pointed with his trident to the gushing foam of the waterfall. Its power was tremendous, the falling water descending a distance along the mountain side before settling in with the rest of the Scourge's dark water.

Swim into the froth, Lellian advised. *It will make it easier on your legs and take us where we need to go.*

The three swam to the froth and without warning they were ricocheted into the dark depths of the Scourge.

Shadowolf straightened his legs and allowed the push to take him down. He did not think they would travel long, as he could not imagine a river being too deep.

Yet, after a minute, he had to start kicking on his own and he could not see anything in the darkness. As if reading his thoughts, Lellian's trident ignited with a yellow light and the bed could be seen below them surrounded by the northern and southern banks.

Shadowolf studied Lellian for a moment as they descended. Where he had been a scrawny, short-haired merman before becoming king in *Marsandil*, he was now stock built with blazing blond hair down to his mid-back. Somehow, his eyes revealed his gained wisdom and experience and Shadowolf felt awed by his exudiant power.

In the light of the trident, the green tail and red and white joggens sailed down to the bed. When they were close enough, they could see that the bed sank down at the centre through a small hole and the sand slowly seeped into an unknown area below.

Lellian swam idly above the hole and studied it. Shadowolf wanted to question him, but at the same time he didn't want to disturb his examination. Alarming the other two, Lellian rolled over and placed his head in the hole. Squirming, he broke the sand with his shoulders and then was gone.

The light vanished as the aperture closed again. A thin ray shone from below through to them, and Shadowolf followed Lellian's example. He pushed his head through and closed his eyes as the light hit his face.

Sorry, Lellian apologized and promptly moved the trident away from the hole. Shadowolf squirmed through and waited for Darcwulf to follow before proceeding.

***

Lucian opened the door to the Blue Periwinkle. The tavern was jostling with activity, and the crowd's voices broke the serene music of the violinist on the stage; although, Lucian mused, she was there more for the looks than for the music.

He made his way to the bar where he paid the landlady for stabling Lancenat and the room he would be renting. Telgar was a good friend of his, and the discount was for more than just a favour. He had helped her through many hard times, the hardest of which was losing her husband to an orc. Her husband had also been his brother.

"It is good to see you in Carmel again, Lucian," she smiled happily, although a dim shadow of her widowhood crept behind the pupils of her eyes.

"It has been too long," Lucian replied.

"Busy with the war, I take it?" she asked uncomfortably.

"I see business in the Periwinkle is at an all-time high," he commented, ignoring her politely. They could get to more serious discussions later.

"It's the war," she said. "People are trying to find other things to think about besides impending doom."

"Carmel is well protected," Lucian replied.

"By the elves, yes. But if the elves leave?"

"They won't," Lucian reassured her.

Suddenly a skinny man with a pale face raced past them to the door and forced it open. He looked to the left and right before dashing away from the closing door.

"That's strange," Lucian murmured.

"He has been like that since he arrived," she said. "He's one of the more permanent tenants. Been here almost two years now, being constant with the rent. Don't know where he gets the gems though."

"Where's he going?"

"Don't know," she shrugged, pulling a mug over and cleaning it with her rag and some water from the basin. "Keeps asking the customers for something he calls "Saneth". Talks about a reptile-like man. Needs help, that guy."

"A Saneth?" he said. "There are three currently on this earth that I know of, and one of them is in Shado's Clan."

"Is that good?"

"All the Saneths worked for Le'Mar until this one, Trimistus, turned to our side."

"Then I guess that makes more sense," Telgar said, taking more mugs and plates to be cleaned. "Maybe the dark lord wants him dead."

"Shado mentioned something about Le'Mar's army trying to kill Trimistus, so it's a possibility." Lucian looked at Telgar's lithe back struggling over the basin. "Let me handle the dishes while you deal with the customers."

"Thanks," she replied gratefully. "Adel is at home with her sick mother and Jonan is out to the Vale. The few colleagues I have left are on the floor serving the taverners."

"Not a problem," he smiled, digging his hands into the warm water.

***

What is this? Darcwulf asked. *Looks like some sort of chamber.*

The wall descended around the three of them to a second bed below. The wall formed a cylinder around them and tapered down before opening up to the sand again.

At the top from where they studied the chamber, ten men could stand with their arms outstretched beside each other to form the diameter of the cylinder. But at the bottom, Shadowolf would be surprised if the three of them would be able to squeeze down to the bed.

What amazed him was that the wall was smooth in the sense that there were no plant or root protrusions jutting out of it. The only distinctive objects that identified the wall's nature were the stones and sand.

Looking up, Shadowolf saw that the roof of the chamber that they had just broken through was made from an amalgamation of seaweed and coral. If fifteen men were to stand upon each other's shoulders, they could cover the distance from the bed to the roof. Yet, for all its space, they felt claustrophobic, as if the walls were closing in on them.

I don't see the horn, Darcwulf thought.

Well, we better have a look around, Lellian suggested.

Shadowolf swam over to the wall for a start. At first there was nothing unusual. He passed his hands over the surface to find that it was as seamless as it had appeared. He could find nothing odd about it, but a gargled sound below him indicated someone had.

Dammit! I almost choked that time, Darcwulf told them in frustration. *I keep forgetting to think my words and not speak them! Anyway, I think I found something.*

Lellian and Shadowolf joined him. By his fingers there was a small intrusion. It was a hole the size of an acorn, and they took turns to look into its depths. The shaft ran to an unknown area behind the wall, but the water around the entrance was warm.

Shadowolf placed his palm over it, and winced at the extreme heat.

I am surprised the water isn't boiling, he remarked.

Hey, here's another one! Lellian called. Sure enough, in line with the hole but a certain distance from it was another one. The second hole was larger in size and did not produce warmth as the first. Upon further investigation they discovered that these were but two of five holes in line with each other, in varying sizes and with an equal distance between them.

Guys, there is another one below, Shadowolf informed them, descending to the hole he spotted. This hole was directly below the last they had found in the row above, and so spurred by this realization they checked the other holes in the second row and found that there were again five holes beneath the first five.

Let's go down and see how many rows there are, Lellian suggested. They swam down and found an additional three rows with five holes each. The further down the tapered chamber they went, the closer the distance between the holes, but still maintaining their slanted line to the holes above them.

Five holes in each of the five rows, so that makes twenty-five, Darcwulf calculated. *Excuse my frankness, but I don't see any connection between twenty-five and the horn.*

Maybe we are looking in the wrong place, Shadowolf said, but he too was puzzled.

Lellian went down to the only access to the secondary bed. They could only see his tail as he examined the sand.

There is a crawl space between the rock and the sand, Lellian said. The other took turns inspecting the bed and saw that he was correct. Not only was there an opening to the bed, but the sand continued beyond their sight beneath the chamber and was not confined to the opening.

Do you care to journey with me? Lellian asked with a smirk.

How? We can't fit in there, Darcwulf asked.

I can help with that, but you might not like it. I can turn us into sirens, which will allow us to travel as a spirit upon the sand.

Shadowolf had gaped at the word "siren", and still stared unbelievingly at Lellian. Was he offering to turn them into his enemies?

I know it is odd, but at the moment it is the best I can offer,

Lellian said helplessly.

We'll do it, Shadowolf replied. Darcwulf still looked shocked for a second, but then bravely accepted his fate.

Lellian planted the base of his trident in the centre of the bed's opening where it proceeded to glow warmly. Without being asked, the brothers grasped the shaft of the trident. A sizzle ran through their veins and Shadowolf and Lellian's hair rose in the water.

The power of the trident was unmistakable. Shadowolf looked up at Darcwulf's burning eyes, and then they were all gone.

Without understanding how he did it, he had already traveled onto the sand and flashed under the rocks. It was dark, but somehow he managed to see everything through an ethereal sight. Waves of blue light lit the sand and rocks in sharp contrast, but the light was not natural. And he knew this with a knowledge that was not his.

Some objects caught his eye. They did not belong to the river and it disturbed him that it was there. With hands he did not possess, he picked up the rough objects. He managed three before deciding, with wisdom that did not originate from his mind, to return to the trident. Once back, he saw two sirens carrying strange gems in their ethereal bodies.

The trident dimmed and their bodies returned. No longer did they share the same thoughts and sight. Shadowolf shook his head to clear the numbness, and then watched as Lellian and Darcwulf dropped their gems to the bed.

What was that? Darcwulf asked.

That is how the demon-queen controls her sirens, Lellian said. *You were under the trident's spell.*

Hang on, Shadowolf said. *You mean everything I felt and did was through the trident? But it is just a pole…?*

I don't think this is the time to explain it, Lellian warned. *We can spend the whole day discussing the personality and power of this wonderful weapon.*

Ok, Shadowolf said, still confused, but turning his attention to the gems instead.

They had each collected three gems, and the nine lay upon the sand that was starting to cover them. They were varying in size and colour, but it was easy to identify the gems.

But there were still sixteen gems to go. He could easily see that the gems' sizes corresponded to the different holes they had seen along the walls, which meant there would be a hole for every gem.

So I guess it means another journey, Darcwulf said once he had reached the same realization.

No, Lellian said. *I wouldn't advise that. Spending too much time as a siren can become depressing. Your soul starts corrupting as the nature of the siren becomes one with yours, and you will soon feel despondent. That is why the trident pulled us out early.*

There is another way, he continued and swam to the trident. Grasping it, he closed his eyes and it flared with power again. It was hardly a minute before the remaining gems appeared from their hiding places and floated onto the bed. *It's easier when I know what I'm looking for.*

The sight was an anomaly, but they could see a certain connection. There were twenty-five in total consisting of five sets of five different gems: rubies, sapphires, emeralds, amethysts and quartzes.

Slowly, Shadowolf took a ruby and made his way up to the first row at the top. He searched for the hole that had burnt his palm. When he finally located it, he propped the ruby into the shaft.

It was definitely the right size. The head of the gem stuck out, but the neck was slotted against the hole. To further confirm his suspicion, the heat of the shaft lit the gem to a bright red glow.

With delight in their hearts, they proceeded to claim the four remaining rubies. They traveled to all the holes and slotted them in where warmth was felt. The pattern was unclear, but Shadowolf saw that there was one glowing ruby per row.

I will handle the quartz, Shadowolf said. The other two nodded. Darcwulf proceeded to take the emeralds and Lellian the sapphires.

Shadowolf investigated the bottom row while they went to the top. He checked each hole individually for their unique characteristic.

The first to the left of the ruby had a slow current pushing from the hole. He looked into the shaft, but could not find anything unusual within. However, he noticed something etched above the hole, and wiped the sand and grime aside to reveal an insignia.

It was three lines parallel to each other. The lines were not straight, but curved. It resembled waves, and Shadowolf guessed that the insignia must represent the water element, hence the current.

The quartzes were too thin and narrow to fit the hole, so he moved to the next one on the left. He could not feel any draft or current, and peeped into the shaft.

Along the edges on the inside, vines and corals lived. Their green shade was luminous in the dark tunnel. He rubbed his fingers over the top of the hole and found another insignia representing what he assumed was the earth element. It looked like the trunk of a tree with a branch on either side hanging lazily down.

He moved on to the left and knew immediately that he had found the right hole. He had specialised in wind long enough to know its presence, and the quartzes in his palms thrummed softly with the calling.

When he looked through the hole, there was a vacuum of air in the small tunnel. He thrust one of the quartzes in, and it shone a brilliant grey shade of white.

He swam one row up and found the same insignia two holes to the left of the first wind shaft. Another row up and two holes to the left was another. This pattern continued until he had inserted all five gems into their sockets.

Lellian had completed his water sapphires and Darcwulf placed his last earth emerald. While Lellian waited, observing the glowing gems, Darcwulf volunteered the task of collecting the amethysts.

The symbol of the final holes was a circle within a circle. Shadowolf learnt in college that this represented the spirit, the core and habitation of all power, and he informed them of this while Darcwulf placed the spirit amethysts.

All the gems were burning with light, but nothing else happened. Every gem had its partner one row up and two holes to the left. It was an odd pattern and neither of them could work out what the answer to the riddle was.

Suddenly, they realised that the top row had begun to shimmer. It was barely discernable, but there truly was an unknown force spread between the gems of the top row. Soon, the once dim force became a sky-blue disc.

Shadowolf swam up and placed his head level with the gems.

An onslaught of images washed into his mind while the current broke against his skull. He could see two men and felt hatred before he was pulled down.

Are you ok? Darcwulf said with concern in his eyes.

Yes, Shadowolf said uncertainly. *The water is strong there, not just in form but in power too.*

We must have activated it somehow, Lellian surmised.

Would it be foolish of me to suggest that maybe we should align the gems? Darcwulf asked.

Shadowolf realised that he could be correct. Yet, he did not know how they were going to do it. His head reeled with confusion.

He lined up with the second row while the other two swam below to the others. Stretching his hands outwards, he tried to force the gems to move somehow, but no luck. It took him three minutes before he decided to look where the symbol for water was in the first row.

Going back to the second row, he studied the symbol beneath the water element of the first row. The symbol had three straight lines parallel to each other with arrow-heads on the end. The quartz still glowed, and he swam to the centre of the second row again.

Using the power of wind, he threw his element to the circle around him. With a satisfactory grind, the circle of gems broke through the earth and moved two holes to the left. He let the wind turn him too as he circled around until the quartz was below the quartz of the first row.

Before he could release his power, an earth-shattering hurricane drove the water out of the way and a disc of fury battered his head. Images of a unicorn and a pegasus drove unbidden into his mind, and a feeling of warm love betrayed cracked through the walls of his heart.

He was pulled down again, but it was almost too late. His mind was very fragile, and he tried to mentally speak but the words were incoherent. It was only when Darcwulf hit his head from the back that he came right.

Find the symbol aligned with the water symbol of the first two rows, he told them. *Use that power to move the disc.*

Darcwulf nodded and moved to the third row. In line with the two water symbols above was a ruby. Above the hole were three parallel flame-like lines.

He called fire and as the flames stretched in a circle along the wall, the gems moved once to the right in order to align it with the two rubies above. Learning from Shadowolf's mistake, he dropped down as a disc of fire roared into the chamber. The heat was nearly unbearable, but they were thankful that the fire did not boil the water in the rest of the chamber.

Deciding to work together, Shadowolf moved to the fourth row and Lellian to the last. They found their symbols in line with the water elements. Shadowolf called earth and moved the circle once to the left, whilst Lellian used the spirit of the trident to move it two to the right.

Nothing could have prepared them for what happened next. Shadowolf had swum to get out of the earth disc's way when they were all thrown to the bed of the chamber. A bright light blinded them all, and when it cleared they looked out onto a land they did not altogether recognize.

Eldor's Forest was to the south and Bentley's Strip to the west, but where T'Mar's Scourge should have been was a flat landscape with the River of Light flowing from the north to the southern ocean.

There was no break in the river. Dark River was gone and there was no canyon. Even Dwarf Mountains was replaced by steep grassland.

They were taken into the sky by an unknown force until they were placed before two men. One, which they recognised as Masara, was mounted upon Ursula. The other unknown man was seated upon a pegasus. They were both exhausted, the sweat falling upon their brows.

"T'Mar," Masara muttered, "this madness must stop."

"I cannot lay it to rest, Masara," T'Mar replied. "These are my ways."

"Have you not learnt anything from me?" Masara asked.

"Your ways are old," T'Mar said, panting. "I cannot let it be so unadapted. We must have recourse to better powers."

"These powers that you seek are dark. Let it be, for the sake of our world and under the grace of Bontu."

"I cannot lay it to rest," T'Mar repeated. "I have found my way, and I will teach it to all, including my son."

"Firewolf, please…" Masara said more calmly.

"Do not utter that name!" T'Mar screamed. "I am no longer Firewolf. My name is T'Mar!"

T'Mar charged and the three could no longer keep track of the battle as power was summoned at lightning speed. The sky grew dark and the earth rumbled from the massive forces. The audience groaned as the power escaped through time to afflict them.

Shadowolf knew it was an arcane power, for its age spoke through his soul. Words and runes were thrown into the air. While some were warded against, others struck their intended target.

The earth was transforming. Below, mountains broke from the earthquake and rose up to greet the sky. Behind the mountains, the earth split to form a large canyon that ran north. The River of Light broke off at the mountain and split to run to the east and west.

After half an hour of battle, after all rage was spent, the two appeared before them again. They were exhausted and blood dripped from their heads onto their shoulders. In one final attempt to kill Masara, T'Mar rode his pegasus straight into Ursula. The two men clung to each other, but their mounts spiraled down to the new waterfall.

Masara slammed his fist into T'Mar's face, but they landed into the water and fell beneath its fresh depths. The three on-lookers were taken below the surface and they saw the struggle come to an end as Masara dealt a death blow with his white staff. He broke free of the drowned body, but the pegasus gave one large kick and snapped Ursula's horn off her head. Blood encircled them, and it felt as if they would never surface.

Masara and Ursula made the surface, but Masara struggled to keep his head up. Ursula bit into his neck and dragged him to the beach. Elvin hands reached for him and lifted him onto Ursula's back. As Masara lay numb on her back, his eyes closed, he found the strength to move his palms over her head, spoke softly and the skin was healed, although remained hornless.

Shadowolf thought the scene was over as the troop traveled south, but when they turned their attention to Dwarf Mountains, a man was standing at the top. Something told him that this was Le'Mar. He did not know how he knew, but the vision seemed to instill the knowledge into him.

The man he knew as Le'Mar jumped and dived from the mountain cliff and after a few seconds hit the water. Once again, arcane words filled the area, and the water turned a tainted red. The once clear water became the water that everyone would refer to as Dark River in time to come.

Le'Mar emerged with T'Mar draped in his arms. He rose in the air with the power of the wind, his eyes closed and his lips murmuring strange words. Spirits that Shadowolf had come to know as demons circled around the dead body. Before the three could see what happened to the corpse, the scene vanished.

On the bed beneath them lay Ursula's old horn. It was three times the length of her current horn, and twirled sinuously into a corkscrew. The chamber was gone, and all that remained was the waterfall's murky depths.

Were we in the horn all this time? Darcwulf asked.

I guess so, Lellian replied, perplexed.

Let's not waste any more time, Shadowolf said and picked up the horn. They raced to the surface, wanting to be rid of the waters as much as share the knowledge with the Clan.

When they reached the beach, Darcwulf and Shadowolf bid Lellian farewell and made for the Clan. Darcwulf hissed as the gills hurt on his neck and he removed the rose pendant and placed it in his pocket. They were in intense discussion when they stopped on top of the hill.

Clothes and equipment lay scattered on the fields. Not one member of their Clan was anywhere to be seen. Shadowolf grasped the horn tighter as he almost let it go in shock.

"Where are they?" Darcwulf asked.

Shadowolf scanned the land, but try as hard as he could, there was no one. The wind blew listlessly into his face, but carried no hint of blood or battle. Leaving his dry clothes on the grass, he grabbed his sword lying by one of the single trees. Darcwulf grabbed his staff.

Shadowolf climbed the bark of a high tree and made for one of the many branches. He tucked the horn neatly into the saddle of a branch and its trunk. Finally he moved branches and leaves in place, breaking some off for the purpose of covering the horn as best he could.

"There!" Darcwulf pointed. Shadowolf made his way down and looked at the base of Dwarf Mountains, just over the Dark River. The man was too distant to be fully described, but he was very scrawny. Compared to the rocks that he was clambering into, his face was pale.

"Let's go," Shadowolf said, and they ran for the stranger that was climbing into the darkness of Dwarf Mountains.

oooooo***ooo***ooo***ooo***ooo

PART TWO

DWARF MOUNTAINS

DARK WARRENS
CHAPTER ONE

The darkness encroached around them. Any sound or sight of the man they had been following was gone and the loneliness accompanied the dark they traversed through. The only comfort was that there was only one path. No tunnels branched off from the main passageway, and their fingers traced a long wall on either side of the passage.

"Talk to me," Shadowolf said. "This silence is killing me."

"Don't you think we should be listening for danger?"

"If there is danger, it is bound to find us anyway," Shadowolf replied.

"Let me put on some light then," Darcwulf said.

Darcwulf's staff flared at the top with a small flame, just enough that they could see what lay ahead of them on the path. Their backs were still laced with the dark, but Shadowolf kept his ears to the air for any sign of trouble.

The wall rebuffed the light instead of enhancing it. As they continued, it felt almost as if certain morbidity crept into Shadowolf's mind. It was a hand that he could not remove from his throat or a poison he could not bleed from his veins.

A scuffle further ahead reached their ears and they ducked to each side of the tunnel, the staff flame dying instantly. Shadowolf held his breath to better assess the noise, but relaxed when a familiar aroma drifted to him.

"Come here, boy," he knelt to the approaching wolf. He could feel blood under the front right paw, but more disconcerting was the smell of blood in its panting. "There's a fight somewhere."

"Can Nelnar take us there?" Darcwulf asked, and Nelnar's

panting ceased as it looked up at him, clearly insulted.

The wolf turned and trotted away from them. The boys jogged behind Nelnar, both trying to tread softly on the loose gravel floor. Shadowolf's bare feet alternated between hard and soft rocks, some pushing between his toes and gashing the skin.

They entered a small cave barely lit by embers on the ends of two torches. The earth in the centre of the cave was disturbed.

"Various footprints," Shadowolf said, kneeling to observe it better. "Maybe an hour or two ahead of us."

"Were we that long in the Scourge?" Darcwulf asked.

"It seems so," he replied and looked up at Nelnar's bark at the other end of the cave. An opening split into two tunnels, and the wolf waited at the right tunnel.

The tunnel was also dark, but Darcwulf's staff relit with new flames. They walked for five minutes before another passage broke off to the left. Nelnar stayed in their current tunnel though, ignoring the opening.

The tunnel was bending to the right and almost seemed to be returning to the cave. Darcwulf was getting edgy next to him, but continued on the path. He knew from youth experience, although he sometimes forgot, not to question Nelnar's integrity.

Without introduction, foyer or welcome, the tunnel split into three. One tunnel broke off to the right, leading into the unknown mountain range. The one they were in continued forward. Nelnar turned its body to the passage that broke to the left and the boys followed.

Two minutes later, Nelnar stopped. It turned to look at Darcwulf and then his staff, and he promptly calmed the fires burning through his spirit. The tunnel went dark and they proceeded slowly into the next area.

Two ledges, one on each side of the tunnel, overlooked the path. Large openings as wide as the ledges led into unknown places, but their destinations was irrelevant compared to the Dra-hu'Mar that were stationed there.

There were two of them, one on each platform. They were very aware of their surroundings, which told Shadowolf that the Clan must have passed through the area recently. Otherwise, why would they be bothered with being so alert? He could think of no soldier so committed to his general; then again, he had underestimated Le'Mar's army before.

"Shado," Darcwulf whispered as loudly as he could without being overheard. "Are those dwarven axes lying at the base of the platforms?"

Shadowolf followed the ledges to where they met the walls that supported them. This in itself was a feat, as the darkness did not present any light, but even in the absence of light he could see the few axes scattered on the floor of their path.

He did not know how good the Hu'Mar eye-sight was. He remembered seeing the green vastness of their eyes that were as amazing as the lawns of Eldor. Surely that beauty would not be wasted on sub-supernatural sight?

"We need to move fast," Shadowolf said. Darcwulf nodded in agreement and then indicated the right. He returned acknowledgement and moved along the left wall.

The Dra-hu'Mar on the left platform looked down the passage. He had sworn he had seen movement. His sudden alertness caused the other Dra-hu'Mar to join his gaze.

Nelnar walked patiently down the centre of the tunnel. The Hu'Mar discussed something in a foreign language, but it was obvious from their body gestures that they had seen the wolf earlier.

They grabbed their bows and unloaded arrows at it. The wolf charged, dodged the arrows and moved underneath the ledges. They continued to fire as it passed, turning down the other side of the tunnel.

They notched two more arrows, but their bodies dropped as Ruben-Willow and the staff killed them. Shadowolf and Darcwulf looked into the passages that led downwards from their ledges into the openings behind them, but Nelnar insisted that the path continued down the tunnel into the mountain. As tempted as they were to go into the holes, they decided against it and jumped down.

It took them a while before they reached the next juncture. Here at least was a foyer with flaring torches set along the walls. They were presented with four tunnels, excluding the one they had just left behind.

Without stopping, Nelnar entered the second from the right.

"I really am glad he is with us," Darcwulf said as they continued. "Do you know how long it would have taken for us to figure this out?"

"We could have become sirens again," Shadowolf said jovially.

"No ways!" Darcwulf said just a little too loud and left an echo traveling before them. "Sorry..."

The path twisted like a snake from left to right in wide arcs. What might have taken them only moments to cross in a straight line took them thrice as long to complete.

A wider cave opened up ahead of them and once again Nelnar cautioned them. Where the tunnel became the cave, the walls narrowed before widening into the court. This presented them with a wall-bulwark on either side from which they could peer into the area for enemies.

Four Dra-hu'Mar were stationed in the hall, two on each ledge that hung on opposite sides. They were well-positioned to face any uninvited visitors, but as disturbing as that was, it was not as bad as the sight that made all three of them groan with helplessness. Even Nelnar seemed more dismayed than it should have, and that did not help the situation.

Shadowolf realised that this was where the Clan should have been. From the torch lights surrounding the cylindrical cavern he could see marks on the sand where the Clan had tried to break free. Dust was settling at the far end of the hall on rocks that had collapsed to form a barrier from the rest of the mountain.

Whoever held the Clan captive was making sure no one could find them. It bothered Shadowolf that Le'Mar might have decided to take personal steps to ensure that they would no longer pose a problem to him, and that he might be too late to save them.

But why would he take such an arduous trip, cover all tracks and entrances if he planned to kill them?

An arrow hit the wall he was watching from and he dived back. Two thick vines broke the tunnel wall behind Darcwulf and chained his wrists to the wall, his staff falling to the floor.

Shadowolf looked into the cavern and saw a Hu'Mar on the right ledge holding his arms horizontal and his eyes flaring with emerald light. His arms stretched into vines that had broken into the wall of the ledge and was obviously the one choking Darcwulf.

Shadowolf ran to assist him when an arrow from the left nipped his calf muscle. He dropped to one knee and looked to see another arrow approaching his thigh. He summoned wind and tried to push the arrow up, but although he had succeeded in Shenama, the steel shaft wouldn't budge. He jumped towards his brother and the arrow skimmed over his leg causing a thin line of blood to form.

He unsheathed his sword and waited for the next arrow. As three arrows raced to meet him, the sword glowed silver and the gems flared upon the hilt. He called the wind optimistically, and two of the three shafts crashed into the wall before him. The third he caught and struck into the vine holding Darcwulf's right arm.

The Hu'Mar screamed in the hall, and removed the damaged vine. The remaining vine he wrapped tightly around Darcwulf's neck.

"Great!" he gasped.

He plunged his sword into the vine, just missing his brother's ear, and the vine vanished into the mountain.

When they recovered and Darcwulf reclaimed his staff, they turned to see the Dra-hu'Mar jumping from the ledges and transforming their bows into swords.

"What else can Ruben-Willow do?" Darcwulf said as he walked to the two on the right, coughing from the strain on his neck.

"They're about to find out," Shadowolf replied, facing the two on the left. Nelnar sat quietly by the crumbled rocks that should have been their path to the Clan. Shadowolf barely saw the staff flare with fire as the Hu'Mar attacked.

He blocked the left sword so vigorously that the Hu'Mar stumbled. He blocked the right sword outward instantly and kicked the Hu'Mar's sternum so that he flew backwards to the floor.

The left Hu'Mar recovered and offered two attacks which Shadowolf dodged and blocked. He heard an arrow notch to the right, and kicked the left Hu'Mar's leg up, followed by a lunge kick to its abdomen. As his leg thrust forward, he bent his supporting injured leg and laid his head back. The arrow passed over his throat, barely missing his skin.

With the left Hu'Mar down against the wall, the right transformed his bow to a sword again and approached. It opted for a vertical attack, but Shadowolf danced to the side, used the wind to push the opponent into him and bent its sword arm down.

He kicked into the Hu'Mar's knee, struck with his elbow into its face and turned to deliver a smashing kick to its jaw. Before he landed again, something grabbed his injured leg and he crashed to the ground. He looked back to see the left Hu'Mar pulling him along by its arm that had become a thorny vine.

The blood from his spiked leg was rolling onto his shirt and face. He tasted sand and rock. He twisted onto his back as the viney Hu'Mar stood up for the attack. In its left free hand appeared a sword.

Before he was below the Hu'Mar he hopped onto the vine-entrapped leg and lifted into the air. His injured leg kicked the sword hand away while his right leg delivered a devastating kick to its face. When Shadowolf landed, he placed his palm around the vine and fire coursed over its green, slimy surface.

The Hu'Mar wailed and retracted its vine. Its scream was silenced as Ruben-Willow found a lovely spot on the right side of its sternum and the Hu'Mar died.

Shadowolf whirled up and caught the arrow that he had heard whistling towards him. The steel shaft burnt softly against his elemental skin, its evil power fighting against the will of good. His remaining opponent charged towards him. In the background he saw that Darcwulf had also killed one of the Hu'Mar.

The Dra-hu'Mar kicked at him, which Shadowolf deftly kicked down at its ankle, and it drew a horizontal slash, which he merely swept carelessly up into the air with Ruben-Willow. The Hu'Mar was losing control and precision as Shadowolf smiled at it with up-curled lips.

Before it could strike again, Shadowolf sheathed his sword and delivered a flurry of blows to its chest and lastly its face. It stumbled backwards and he shifted his injured leg forward, anchored it into the floor and planted his right leg sideways into its abdomen. He arced the angle in order to lift the Hu'Mar into the air and used the wind to carry it backwards.

He threw the arrow he had caught into its left eye and it went through to meet the cave wall that its head banged against. When Darcwulf joined his side, the Hu'Mar's suspended body broke into flames.

"This is really getting messy," Darcwulf said.

"Thanks for the help," Shadowolf said sarcastically to Nelnar. The wolf merely got up and trotted to the left ledge. It rose up on hind legs and pawed the wall. A hidden panel turned on a central axis and opened a way for them. Shadowolf looked at the hand that had borne the arrow and saw a purple bruise across it.

The boys followed Nelnar into the dark tunnel. Another passage broke off from the main tunnel and turned back, and Shadowolf saw that it led to the ledge.

"I guess we go forward then."

Something in Shadowolf's face changed suddenly and even the darkness of the tunnel was no match for his expression.

"If they've harmed one hair on her head..."

***

"Eldor," the aged man entered, leaning lightly on his knotted grey staff.

"Masara?" the elvin king rose from his contemplation. "Should you be up from your bed?"

"I am well enough, my dear friend," he smiled wanly. "My dreams warn me, and the trees of the forest whisper dire omens."

"You expend your remaining life by extending your senses so," Eldor offered him a seat that he heartily accepted.

"Whether you come to terms with it or not, I will be part of this war."

"T'Mar nearly killed you," Eldor sat down. "Your journeys around Le'Mar's encampments and secret groves these past years have not done you well, Masara."

"He is preparing his army, Eldor," he replied in a serious tone, gazing at the elf through crystal eyes that still held power. "He might not have the stone, but there are other ways of entering the new gate."

"It will take more than his power to gain this fortress," Eldor replied. "And as long as I remain, the earth is safe."

"How long before he proves you wrong?" Masara murmured.

"My elves tell me that, although you are present in body, you stare out your window and it seems as though you are not really there. What are you up to, Masara?"

"Resting, of course," he countered. "Reminiscing of younger, more peaceful days."

Masara rose, and limped to the door. Eldor knew Masara better than that, but did not know wish to question his stubborn will any further.

Masara turned at the door for one last omen.

"Prepare your elves, Eldor. Le'Mar is almost ready. Prepare your elves."

DWARVEN RUINS
CHAPTER TWO

The fresh air coursed through her lungs. Even Nucial, the battered little man that had joined them in their escape, seemed to walk easier. Genewiu's wings no longer looked so tattered, but were still in need of healing.

Chenesia wished that she had better clothes than the torn dress to cover her filthy body. Ash and grime covered every part she could think of, and although the Dark River lay to the north, she had no wish to swim in the murky waters.

Genewiu had informed her that they were close to the River of Light, and sure enough they soon caught sight of the Scourge's waters on the eastern horizon.

"Tomorrow we should make Carmel, if not tonight," Genewiu told them, and Nucial's head lifted. Chenesia could not tell if the news was welcomed or scorned by him, but her heart leapt at the thought of meeting good people and maybe receiving their hospitality.

When they reached a group of trees near the River of Light, a strange sight caught their attention. Clothes, weapons and other items were haphazardly lying around.

"Finally!" Chenesia said, holding an emerald dress over the height of her body.

"There was a fight here," Nucial said.

"Yes, I agree," Genewiu said, smelling the scuffled footprints on the sand. She saw a group of hooves, but one large set stood out from the others and she looked up at the mountains in deep consideration.

"Ursula?" she whispered inaudibly, and when the other two questioned, she simply said, "Nothing."

"I guess we should leave these for their owners," Chenesia said forlornly, "but maybe they won't miss this dress."

Chenesia strode with the dress to the embankment and, having no regard for company, she dropped her filthy dress on the grass. The nudity did not seem to bother Nucial, for the dirt on her skin was so abundant it was like another set of clothes.

She laid the emerald dress gently over the grass and with a bounding run dived into the River of Light.

***

They had passed many tunnels and the cut in his calf had become nothing but a mild throbbing. Darcwulf walked beside him with Nelnar in the lead.

It was obvious that the wolf had not been this far, for it took to smelling and searching for prints to ensure that they took the right tunnels. A thrumming sound had started, and Shadowolf had a feeling that they were on the right path. He was also sure someone had noted the wolf's absence and something was preparing for their arrival.

The thrumming was deep and almost guttural. Darcwulf tried not to surmise what kind of beast could make such a sound, but eventually his thoughts became words that danced along the depth of the unknown baritone.

"Besides the dragons," Shadowolf added his assumptions, "the largest creature I have seen in his army is the Ma-Wreth, and even that isn't big enough to make that sound."

"Maybe it's a group of them," Darcwulf offered.

"Let's hope not. One is bad enough."

They stumbled as the tunnel shook beneath them. The groan of the unknown broke through them as a hammer through ice. Shadowolf called the wind and floated between the floor and roof, but the soil was loosening above him and hit him on the head, so he decided against it.

"Run?" Darcwulf asked.

Shadowolf nodded and they picked up the pace. This was extremely strenuous on Nelnar, as the wolf had to pick up the Clan's trail within seconds at a time.

The groan ceased as they entered a gigantic cavern. There was no light in the area, but he could sense that the roof was far above them. It was cold and neglected and the ground was coarse with broken stone.

Nelnar whined softly. Shadowolf and Darcwulf could feel eyes watching them. They tried hard to tread carefully, but almost inevitably they stumbled over rubble. Shadowolf tripped and hit his forehead hard against a wooden structure.

"Damn this!" Darcwulf cursed and lit the tip of his staff. "They know we're here anyway."

The huts and buildings lay before them across the inside of the cavern. More towards the centre, there was actually grass and fields that ran to the other end. A lake of lava flowed on the left of the mountain valley, bubbling and spewing silently.

Yet the lava was dim and showed no light, so he assumed that it was the last embers of magma flowing to a standstill. A soft groan was emitted throughout the cavern.

Armour and weapons lay amongst dead dwarves. Their skins were scorched, but no recent burns could be smelled from the corpses.

"Look at this," Darcwulf bent down and pulled off a chain-mail vest that still clung to a dead arm; "dwarven mail-armour."

"See if any fits," Shadowolf said, doing the same. "Although these things do smell like the dead."

"Rather smell like it, than be it, I always say."

Soon they both were wearing chain-mail over their shirts, but Darcwulf found something else that intrigued him, holstered in its viperous sheath.

He removed the sword and held it above the light of the staff. It was one blade, but a hand's length from the hilt it split into two, and a groove smoothly separated the one side from the other. The tip of the sword resembled a serpent's sharp tongue.

"Nice," he said, replacing the sheath and tying it to his waist. "Anything you like?"

"Well, I am quite happy with Ruben-Will..." Shadowolf stopped as he saw something he did indeed fancy.

"The hilt hurts my hands a bit though," Darcwulf said as Shadowolf bent down over a corpse.

"Just tie a cloth over it until we can have a wooden hilt carved," he replied as he retrieved a small blade.

"What's that?" Darcwulf asked as he searched for a torn cloth, found one and then proceeded to wrap the steel hilt tightly.

"Looks like a short-sword, or maybe a dagger."

He found the sheath for the dagger at his feet. The blade was curved and only single-edged, but the tip hooked forwards like a barb and the back was serrated. It was as long as his forearm, about half Ruben-Willow's length.

He tied the large dagger to his right hip, as Ruben already occupied his left. A low growl caught his attention, and he recognized the warning instantly.

"Darcwulf, get down!"

Nelnar's timing was impeccable. The arrows missed them as they dived within shambled huts, sharing the darkness with the dead. Then a different type of growl reached his ears. Nelnar was sitting by his knees staring out into the darkness in silence.

"Shado," Darcwulf called softly from the opposite hut where he had a better view of the stagnant lava pit, "there are strange silhouettes creeping out there."

"Can you make it out?"

"Barely. It is crouching towards us. It seems as though it is a beast or…wait a second. Is that a wolf?"

Shadowolf moved to the opening to look out. It was very dark, but he too could see the shape of several wolves moving to them.

"Friends?" he asked Nelnar. It groaned in disagreement.

"Their legs are knock-kneed," Darcwulf said. "There is something wrong with them."

"And we have more Dra-hu'Mar to deal with," Shadowolf sighed.

"Let's wait for the wolves to come to us. We can kill between the huts, and it will hopefully confuse the Hu'Mar."

Shadowolf nodded in agreement and drew Ruben-Willow. He hadn't had a chance to wrap the dagger, so he left it in its sheath. He heard Darcwulf pull the serpent sword.

Out of the darkness came a noise they did not expect to hear. A woman's voice called incantations and the steps of the wolves faltered. The voice became deeper and echoed. The lava pit began to bubble and a little light broke through its cracked surface.

From the light, Shadowolf saw a line of twelve Dra-hu'Mar on a ridge above the molten river. One by one they fell to their knees as the intensity of the spell increased. They clutched their hearts and blood trickled from their lips.

One by one they fell off the cliff and into the opening lava. The wolves turned to their new prey, frustrated by this new disturbance.

"Heula!" Shadowolf screamed in warning.

Heula turned to see nine wolves racing towards her. She knew these were not ordinary wolves. She had played a part in rousing them once. And she also knew that she could not stop them all.

Nelnar broke from the huts, along with a newly-transformed wolf and white tiger. The three yapped and whined, trying to draw the attention of the enemy.

The rear five made a turn and faced the three. The front four continued to Heula who began muttering under her breath. The lava grew warmer and a warmer, orange light starting to glow from the one corner of the cavern. As Shadowolf rushed to save the witch, he realised something else was coming across the river from behind a hidden passage.

It was an intense battle of claws and teeth. Shadowolf did everything he could to quickly kill by lunging at their throats or kicking their jaws just to make it through to Heula. He knew the tiger and Nelnar could survive, but the witch was alone. The warm light grew brighter and warmer, and the lava erupted with new life, spewing flames onto the land.

He leapt off two wolves' heads and bit into the spine of one of the wolves at the fore. He struck a paw into its deformed, almost humanoid face and defended against an attack to his gullet. He rolled on his back and sent the wolf flying over to the tiger.

He transformed and, drawing his sword with his human hand, he lunged three times in quick succession. The wolves closest to Heula dropped to the floor, their lives gone. Only two wolves remained, and they fled from the group into the darkness of the tunnels.

When Darcwulf had returned to his natural state, he leaned upon the staff until he joined the others.

"Are you hurt?" Heula asked. The fire reflecting against the back wall of the cavern was growing tremendously larger.

"I need to tend to that, before you turn into one of them," Heula warned Darcwulf and knelt to nurse his leg with cloth and spell. Shadowolf and Darcwulf gaped as the dead wolves turned into naked human corpses.

"What...are they?" Darcwulf asked, wincing at the painful healing in his calf.

"Crethans," Heula replied, standing from her healing. "I will tell you about them later, but right now we have to defeat the Firestrom if we are to make it to the Clan."

"Firestrom? What is happening in this mountain!?" Shadowolf exclaimed.

"Le'Mar is taking dominion of the dwarves' holdings in the same way he anticipates defeating the elves," Heula said. "A large part of the mountains already belongs to him."

"Great," Darcwulf said.

All conversation was killed by the arrival of the Firestrom. The first sight was daunting enough that they all retreated a few steps. A fire beast twenty times Shadowolf's height turned the corner upon the boiling lava river.

There was no place that its light did not reach, or its heat did not penetrate. Sweat broke from Shadowolf's pores, over his eyes and down his cheeks.

It had no legs, but drifted on its own heat. Its face was in the shape of one of the creatures that Shadowolf had fought in Orion years before, but he could not remember its name.

"Lion," Heula muttered softly as if reading his mind.

Its face towered over them, but it was slowly rotating to the right. As the rest of its ethereal body appeared, they realised in shock that the Firestrom had four heads.

"Horse, silverback gorilla and shark," Heula said.

"Where did they get these creatures?!" Darcwulf cursed. "I have never even heard of a silver-gorilla back...what did you call it?"

"Darc, not now," Shadowolf cautioned. The beast was now over them, ready for the attack...and then hordes of hurorcs and purorcs broke from the crevices and tunnels.

"We're going to die," Heula said, but Shadowolf unsheathed his sword and dagger, ignoring the searing pain in his left palm from the steel. Darcwulf held his staff in both hands, fire breaking out from its timber. Nelnar simply bore its teeth...

***

The Blue Periwinkle was a hive of activity. It seemed as if the people of Carmel wished to get particularly drunk this evening. Lucian attended the bar and belittled a man who was having a little too much.

But as was his nature, he turned the scolding to a joke about a Froth Hun that went fishing with a Saneth.

Telgar was busy with the tables, as only two of her staff were available to work the night. She swayed from one customer to the other, making sure that their orders were taken down with precision.

"How do you think Kailan will feel knowing you abandoned your quest for me?" Telgar asked when she rested at the bar for a moment.

"I have already sent her an eagle," Lucian said. "She will understand. Besides, my quest does not have that much haste at the moment. However..."

"I know," she interjected. "When the time comes, you will have to leave. Not the first time, remember?"

"Yes," he smiled sadly.

"I have him!" a drunken man tittered on the small stage, pulling an equally sloshed man beside him. "This 'ere man told me the riddle! The 'ragonrida one I been speaks about!"

The crowd cheered and the few that knew the man personally called his name.

"Was a long time ago that I had to rehearse the tale," the riddle-man proclaimed. "Had to know it by heart, I did."

Lucian studied him for a moment and saw that the man was well aged. His beard and long hair hid his age well, but Lucian stopped his examination in anticipation for what he assumed the man would speak about: The DragonRider Prophecy.

The Periwinkle went silent as the man cleared his throat and for the length of the riddle, the inn seemed sober:

"He serves none; he walks alone in the passages of time,
For he has bound his soul with another; their powers are one.
He rides upon the wind as if it were his own,
He rides the dragon as if he were its king,
To finally destroy all those before his throne.

He journeys the world; fear is the tool of his power.
His name spreads over the earth, and they tremble.
With bow, horn, staff, dagger and sword he will kill the Sadgi,
With fire, wind, earth, water and soul he will rectify.
He rules the phoenix by becoming one with his ensemble.

Earth, ocean, sky and mountain will be his command.
Yet, with these powers, the land will be his battlefield.
In the end, blood will run from his hands.
In the end, with victory he will leave the land,
With his powers as his conquest and shield.

The Masaran Phenomenon will awaken his power.
He is the Windfarer, the DragonRider, the Sadgi."

The crowd cheered, but Lucian frowned and after a moment of contemplation shouted, "That's the *Enodhim* prophecy, you idiot!"

The old man stared dumb-founded back at him and then smiled ruthlessly, more from his stupor than anything else.

"You are correct, laddy," he replied, and Telgar laughed. "My mistake. The prophecy of the *Wisoum* should go something like this…

"Darkness comes; he wades across the fields of time,
For he has bound his soul with a dragon, and fears none.
Having commanded the wind under his soul,
He rules the dragon with only a word.
But a time of foreboded testing still comes.

He journeys the elements; for in the end he will be contested.
False claims to his name produce showers of confusion.
Yet, in the end his power will be not be denied,
All armies under his hand will be unified,
To destroy that which has always only been an illusion.

He will lose those he loves, only to set them free.
For the dragons he rules will demand a part of him.
Fear will drive his veins
Until it is fear that he tames.
Then the elements will reign in his kingdom.

The Masaran Phenomenon will awaken his power.
He is the Windfarer, the DragonRider, the Sadgi."

The crowd looked at Lucian, who nodded snidely, and then they cheered once more.

***

Le'Mar let them sleep and removed himself from their presence. The castle was before him and he stepped through the air into his throne room. He walked to the wall and released Sonersaat.

He fell to the ground gargling for fresh air and strength for his weakened muscles.

"I once taught you how to tame your fear, but it seems it has made you arrogant," Le'Mar said to the kneeling man. "Do not make that mistake again."

"What do you want me to do, my lord?" he said meekly.

"Go to Morkom Falls," Le'Mar instructed him. "Prepare the march on Horlorn's Gate. My army within the mountains will attack from the rear. We take Dwarf Mountains in two days."

Le'Mar walked to the throne seat and vanished. Sonersaat rose unsteadily and touched the crude amulet hanging from his neck. He ran for the opening in the wall of the room and jumped out of the castle.

Maneto swerved under him and caught him on his back. They flew east under the cover of darkness.

***

"Do you realise that the last time I had a good night's rest was Shenama?" Darcwulf asked.

"My body and mind are reminding me constantly, don't worry," Shadowolf said.

"How do you reckon we can deal with them?" he asked, watching the orcs approaching.

"You deal with the orcs," Shadowolf replied. "I'll fight the Firestrom."

"You expect me to fight all these things? Look at them!?"

Shadowolf ran forward with sword and dagger. He met the first rushing orcs and sliced open a neck, severed a shoulder and lodged the dagger into a forehead before rising upon the wind to face the Firestrom.

"THANKS!" Darcwulf shouted sarcastically, and then attacked the orcs. Nelnar took to biting into them while Heula used her spells to thrust them aside or into the fiery furnace beneath the Firestrom.

Shadowolf crossed his arms over to sheath the blades, knowing they would be useless. Even at eye-level with the beast, one of the heads outsized him five to one.

Shadowolf enveloped the wind about him as the Firestrom moved in for the bite. The lion attacked him first, and he moved over its head in time, but the searing heat blistered against his skin. The wind just kept the shirt from catching alight.

The gorilla swirled to hit at him with a fist of fire. He could barely discern its face within the flames, but it seemed to distort in anger. Shadowolf thought it humorous that the battle resembled a human trying to swat a pesky insect.

Putting aside his mirth, he flew into the hand of fire, concentrating as much wind as he could into its core. He also seeped water from his open palm, but the fire eradicated it before it appeared. The wind caught alight and twisted around his body and mind.

Without warning, a hoof lunged into his abdomen and he flew out of the malignant fire towards the lava. He righted his body and called the wind to lift him up. He turned around to see the four beasts charging for him.

Growling deeply, he flew towards them, arms at his side. Before he struck them, he stretched his palms out and turned his body into wind. Having undergone the trial made it easier, but during battle it required more determination. Soon his flesh became air and he dived into the horse's eye.

The gorilla's hands gripped the horse's head in agony as the equine's jaws roared open in protest. The flames of the beast flickered brighter as it increased its power and, as if flung by an in invisible hand, Shadowolf reappeared on the other side and hit the cavern's wall.

The light in the cave disappeared as the Firestrom vanished, and just as suddenly turned back on when it reappeared pinning Shadowolf against the wall.

The flames burnt into his face. He could feel his skin singeing and his hair burning. At the same time, he was losing air in his lungs. He felt his shirt fall off his body and his pants were up to his knees. The only thing keeping him relatively cool was the chain-mail now wrapped around his naked torso.

He glared his eyes ferociously at the Firestrom and became wind again. He traveled through the fire to the hottest point in its centre. The elementël buffeted him, striking at his forehead and shoulders as he pushed down further to the creature's abdomen.

When he reached the core of the four beasts, he stretched out his legs and arms, releasing as much wind as he could without expending all his energy. All four creatures roared and bent over, trying to release the man.

The orcs and Shadowolf's friends watched as the beasts separated at the abdomen. Fire fell everywhere on the cavern floor, and the ceiling started to crumble from the amount of power released.

The light went out. From the remaining flames on the lava river, Darcwulf could see an exhausted Shadowolf drifting in the air with nothing but the remains of his pants covering his tender parts. No sign of the beast was visible, but there was a slight power still lingering in the air.

Fire returned as the Firestrom burst into the air, this time as four separate creatures. The horse, gorilla, lion and shark stood in a circle around the floating man.

"Great," Heula said, dropping a dead orc from the grip of her palm. "That's a first, and probably the last."

The shark left the foursome and swam around the cave, going for the others. Heula, Darcwulf and Nelnar dived within shattered huts, but the orcs burnt in the flames.

"How am I supposed to fight fire with fire?" Darcwulf shouted in frustration. The roofs of their huts were ripped off by the gorilla and horse while the lion remained to challenge Shadowolf.

"Fire with fire…I wonder," Shadowolf thought out loud. His mind went back to the trial of the elements. He remembered having removed wind from a creature before. Could he also remove fire?

He raised his palm towards the lion before him and focused on removing the elementël's fire. He watched as the lion's mane stirred slightly and dimmed, but almost in result it redoubled in power.

"Fine," Shadowolf lowered his gaze. "If it's the *Enodhim* you want, it's he that you'll get."

Shadowolf arced his back and stretched his arms to the sides, opening his palms. The lion became apprehensive as he summoned the wind into his hands. The air from the cave gathered around him as he focused, and the wind swirled around his face. He could smell the singed hair, and something in his back felt like it was going to break, but he held on.

Soon his eyes flared sky blue from the intensity of his power. The lion sensed the danger and ran to bite at Shadowolf. Shadowolf became transparent as the wind took him, but the lion was quicker and rammed its jaws into him, hurtling him to the cavern floor beside the river.

Shadowolf's body cracked as he hit the floor. He pried open his eyelids to see the lion descend upon him. Darcwulf tried to get to him, but the shark swam between them and he was blocked by battle.

Shadowolf saw a shimmer in the air. It looked similar to a heat wave usually seen on the horizon with the rising of the sun, except that it hung in mid-air. It twisted and pulled left and then right, up and then down again.

He realised it moved in conjunction with the creatures, and

further study revealed that it stayed precisely in the centre of all four creatures, no matter where they moved.

Even though he felt like every rib was broken, he forced himself to stand up. A ring sounded through the cavern as he drew Ruben-Willow still at his side, but kept the dagger sheathed.

The wooden hilt was as singed as his face felt, but he gripped it hard as the lion and gorilla moved towards him. They roared out loud and landed their final blow down upon him. Their paw and fist struck the ground hard, causing the cavern to shake. Satisfied that their quarry was dead, they lifted their legs.

A pain shot their elements. All four beasts fell to the ground and screamed in a horrific downpour of agony. Shadowolf stood poised above the central line between the four beasts with Ruben-Willow lodged in its centre. He drew the power of wind and fire from the elements, his arms straining and his head under a rain of sweat.

Lines of flames and wind traversed between the beasts and the sword, drawing their power from them to the steel blade. With a desperate attempt, the lion wheeled around and charged him. But before his paw could strike, all warmth and light left the cavern, and Shadowolf fell to a cold ground surrounded by dead orcs.

He breathed with difficulty as Heula, Darcwulf and Nelnar reached him.

"That has never been done before," Heula informed him.

He couldn't speak. Darcwulf and Nelnar both collapsed and laid their heads on either side of his chest to rest and, as Heula laid her palms over his cheeks, he fell asleep.

PLIGHT OF THE MERLANI
CHAPTER THREE

A warm breeze drifted over his face and he felt the pressure rising and falling on his chest. Fire swept through his mind like a mellifluous river, soothing his spine and aching back. His calf stung and throbbed slightly, his shoulders crying in silent agony.

He awoke to noiseless screams. He would have jerked up in anguish and shock had the three heads not been resting on his lying body. Shadowolf reached up to his face and found that the burns he had experienced from the elementël beast were gone.

His cheeks were smooth to the touch, but as he ran his hands through his hair he found that it was shorter and broken in certain areas. He would have to get it cut the first chance he got.

The chain-mail lay lazily upon him, surprisingly not stinging his naked torso. The dragon amulet lay on the side of his neck against the cavern floor, amazingly still attached to the chain. Ruben-Willow was beneath Darcwulf on his left and his dagger attached to his right hip beneath Nelnar.

They must have been asleep for a day or so, for the lava river had somehow dimmed. It still flowed with warmth, but had diminished since their last battle. Shadowolf's internal clock also told him that he had had plenty of hours of sleep, and the stench of the dead orcs concluded that it must be so.

"Darcwulf, Heula," he whispered loud enough to stir them. Nelnar simply turned its head to look at him. The wolf had been awake for some time now.

After a few minutes they were all standing staring at the chaos surrounding them. Dead orcs covered the already littered floor and the only way further through the mountain was on a small ledge hanging over the river of dying fire.

"Alright," Shadowolf said determinately to Heula, "I don't want to be the interrogator, but I need answers."

"I know," she replied. "I don't expect less."

"First of all, where are the Clan?" he asked.

"Over the ledge and through the mountain further on," she said hastily.

"What happened?" he asked more kindly, realising she felt intimidated.

"We were waiting for you to surface, when an army of twenty orcs and five Ma-Wreths captured us and led us into the mountain."

"Five Wreths?!!" Darcwulf exclaimed. "What is going on?"

"I overheard one of the generals speaking about an army that is waiting on Le'Mar's command within the mountain. He is planning on attacking the northern villages above the Dark River."

"Any idea what this army consists of?" Shadowolf asked.

"None," she replied. "I only made it this far before I managed to escape and hide in one of the huts."

Darcwulf looked at her suspiciously.

"I knew a spell to unlock my shackles and was hoping you'd be following," she countered his glare. "But I couldn't do it for all of us; otherwise it would be too obvious."

"Relax," Shadowolf said to Darcwulf. "I trust her."

"She'll have my staff to deal with if…"

"I am on your side!!" she shouted. "If it were not for me, you would be a Crethan right now!"

"That was my second question," Shadowolf said with an air of expectancy.

"Those wolves you saw were once men, but by the power of a demon were transformed into flesh-predators. In the presence of a Creth-Demon, or Creths as we oft-times refer to them, the humans transform against their will into Crethans and will obey any command given them by their Creth-master."

"Did you get all that?" Shadowolf asked.

"She lost me at flesh-predator," Darcwulf joked, but Heula's stare meant that she did not find the two humorous.

"So, the bite from one of the Crethans will lead to the victim becoming a Crethan," Shadowolf said with as much sophistication as he could, but his mind reeled at the sentence.

"Within a day, yes," Heula said.

"Well done," Darcwulf applauded him, and Shadowolf smiled broadly.

"Oh, you guys are ridiculous!" Heula turned and stormed to the river's ledge.

"Wait, I'm sorry!" Shadowolf called. "Darcwulf and I tend to get into a teasing mood now and again just to cheer up."

Heula stopped for a moment and then turned with a small smile.

"No, I'm sorry," she said. "I tend to get crabby when I am anxious."

"So, if I have it right," Darcwulf said more seriously, "if these Crethans were in wolf form, then that means there is a Creth near-by?"

"Yes, with the Clan."

"We're in for another battle, then?" Shadowolf asked.

"A greater one than this," Heula replied, "for I have yet to find out what lies between us and the Clan."

Without saying another word, Shadowolf looked for clothes to place over his chain-mail and legs, and replaced his sword in its sheath. Darcwulf made preparations to leave, taking some time to pull his shirt over his chain-mail too, and finally they made their way to the ledge.

By the nose of Nelnar they followed passages and winding tunnels after the ledge returned to the main land of the mountain. The trio almost gave up their search for a period of rest when they suddenly heard voices coming down the tunnel.

Shadowolf crept slowly forward with the group behind him until he found the entrance to the next open expanse. He fell to his knees at the immense army gathered within it.

"I cannot fight so many," Shadowolf shook his head.

"The Clan," Darcwulf pointed.

Past the three Firestroms, past the five Ma-Wreths, past the approximately two hundred purorcs and eight hundred hurorcs, past the five hundred Crethans and eventually past the three hundred Dra-hu'Mar, sat the lonely group of humans. Their hands were tied behind their backs and they were seated in a circle facing outward.

"What is that light?" Darcwulf asked. Far to the left, a large light-blue circle rippled like water across the wall's surface. But instead of seeing the wall's rocky substance, they could see out onto the land.

"That is an illusion," Heula said, and Shadowolf found that her knowledge of the dark lord's arts was becoming somewhat useful. "They have created an opening through the wall of the mountain to the northern lands. The illusion is there so that anyone from the land cannot see the army in waiting. All they see is the mountain's 'side'."

"And when Le'Mar commands them to attack, they can march right through?" Darcwulf asked, his earlier antagonism towards her gone.

"He will drop the illusion first, but yes. They will march through the hole and then to their target."

"Why have they not killed the Clan?" Shadowolf asked.

"That I cannot answer," Heula replied sadly. "But perhaps it has something to do with our confrontation with Sonersaat. Ever since your reappearance, Shadowolf, it seems the dark lord is stirred to find you."

"What is your plan?" Darcwulf asked Shadowolf.

"I don't know quite yet," he replied, but something caught his attention to the right wall, and he saw that Nelnar had already begun its silent approach.

"Darcwulf..." he started to say.

"I'm on it," he replied and transformed into a black tiger with dark green stripes and soft red eyes.

"Heula..." he turned, but saw that she was muttering a spell and soon was invisible. He could sense that she walked to the others.

He didn't want to join the tiger and wolf, afraid that too many in one group would call attention. Neither did he want to teleport in case he needed his strength. Instead he relied on an old trick he remembered from college. He walked back into the tunnel a distance and then turned and sprinted towards the entrance. When he reached it he jumped and transformed into an eagle, soaring to the roof of the massive cave and towards the Clan.

He marveled at how organized the army was. The Wreths were the front line. Behind them, the purorcs stood in a square of ten wide by twenty long. Next were the hurorcs in four groups of ten wide by twenty long.

The Dra-hu'Mar simply stood in five long lines of sixty each, and the Firestroms brought up the rear. The Crethans were haphazardly scattered in the remaining open areas. He could not find the Creth that controlled them.

Between the front Wreths and the illusion wall was the lava river, blazing with fire and magma. It churned and bubbled, but somehow the steel bridge between the land and the illusion remained unharmed.

He turned his focus back on the Clan and saw that Darcwulf and Heula had returned to visibility and were pretending to be captured. Their arms were folded behind their backs unrestrained while there were quiet discussions between Darcwulf and Fransiska.

He banked his flight to land softly on Dren's shoulder. Dren stared at it, but Heula told him who it was, and Dren simply nodded. Shadowolf frantically turned and looked at each member of the circle, but his eagle-sight had not misled him; Shedaaij was absent.

Ursula, Millon and Kentaur were also not present, as were none of the horses. This was not going to be easy, he mused.

He transformed to human and sat quietly with his hands behind his back.

"How much do you know about Firestroms?" he asked Dren, Angelia listening on his right.

"Only that they are almost impossible to kill," he replied.

"If it comes to battle, I will separate them," Shadowolf said to an incredulous look from the gargoyle. "Get Rennick and Tinonte and any who can to use their elemental powers at the core of the stroms."

"I don't understand," he replied.

"You will when it happens."

A bang erupted on the wall ahead of him, and for the first time he saw a drawbridge hanging flush in the wall. Its colour was that of the wall and he would never have made the distinction had it not been for the loud, incessant banging.

"Everyone join hands," Darcwulf commanded.

Shadowolf had to shift the weight of his swords first before he could comfortably grab Angelia and Dren's hands. When they were ready, Darcwulf passed a ring of flame from one wrist to the other until all the ropes had burnt and fallen to the floor.

The Clan remained in their "restrained" position while some guards walked to the drawbridge in investigation.

"Someone tell me where Shedaaij is," Shadowolf muttered.

"For reasons unknown," Angelia said, "she was taken to the lava river and thrown in."

Shadowolf gasped involuntarily and one of the orc guards turned from the bridge and looked at the Clan. He walked to Shadowolf, clearly not recognizing him. The banging on the drawbridge grew louder and the army became restless.

"It was a command from an unknown source, and the orcs obeyed," Angelia continued sympathetically.

"Shado," Heula said before the guard was in audio range, "sirens and demon-queens can sense other mermaids."

"Can they live in lava?" he asked.

"Sirens and demon-queens, yes," she replied. "I am not sure about mermaids though."

"I have to hope," he said as the guard stooped over him. "Otherwise I will die here today."

"You stand," the purorc commanded him. The drawbridge exploded and, as the guard turned in horror, Ruben-Willow ate through its neck and the orc's headless body fell to the floor.

The Clan arose in a hurry as Ursula, Millon and Kentaur raced into the arena followed by a host of armed dwarves. Those in the Clan without weapons were hastily given axes and rough swords. Shadowolf's hope soared and he saw that there were nearly five hundred dwarves, followed closely by three hundred humans. His joy was further elated when he sensed that half of them were elementals.

"Remember what I told you," Shadowolf instructed Dren as he called the wind and rose to challenge the Firestroms.

"Wait!!!" Skywolf shouted.

"Don't worry," Darcwulf comforted her. "He knows what he is doing."

Dren quickly relayed Shadowolf's instructions to the Clan and the other elementals that hastened to their side. They looked up in confusion at the lone man that went to face the stroms.

Shadowolf didn't waste any time. The ground army was already moving towards the Clan, the Crethans moving the quickest. The stroms must have noticed his approach as all three turned towards him, each with their own horse, shark, gorilla and lion heads.

Yet another creature crawled out of the lava river that he had not seen before. It was taller than him, but when it stood up-right on two legs it reached a Ma-Wreth's height.

Its body was made of an earthly core, but its skin was fire. It had the head of a wolf and the body of a man with deep blazing pits for eyes. It held an emerald staff in its left hand. He could only assume that this was the Creth that controlled the Crethans, for it had no deformity at all and walked majestically amongst the dark lord's army.

He thrust himself into the first strom and became wind. He struggled through the flames and found its core, forcing his power into it. When the strom dissipated, he immediately teleported to the next strom.

The beast sensed him within it, and that was enough to reform his reality and complete the teleportation. He again forced the wind into its core, mixing a small measure of his spirit within it, and threw the Firestrom into darkness.

The last one suffered the same fate, but he could sense that it did so willingly. Obviously it knew that it would be better off separated as four instead of one and welcomed the first demise.

When the light in the cave declined and Shadowolf stood alone in the air, he waited for the next step. He looked down and saw that the battle was underway. What worried him was that most of the elementals were occupied fighting Wreths or orcs, but at least Rennick, Tinonte and Darcwulf were waiting below for the stroms' return.

And just as expected, the twelve fire creatures reawakened the light and flew over the battleground. Shadowolf was satisfied when he saw the three cores dancing between the main central lines, and left it up to his friends.

Power erupted from staff and axe as Rennick, Tinonte and Darcwulf simultaneously let loose their elements of fire and spirit at the cores upon Darcwulf's instructions. The creatures whelped in surprise and agony as they began to die their second and permanent death.

Shadowolf was about to dive into the lava pit when one of the sharks gripped him in its teeth in a final attempt at retribution. More from frustration than reflex, Shadowolf became wind and spun around in quick successions creating a tornado of fire.

Rennick, who was holding this particular shark's core, fell to one knee as the power to hold it became increasing difficult to maintain. Fransiska looked around for Darcwulf, and when she found him she ran to him and pulled the rose pendant from his pants pocket.

"Hey!" he exclaimed, but she had already disappeared into the fighting chaos and he had to contend with a line of orcs.

Shadowolf raged within the shark and pulled the tornado towards the river. With as much power and speed as he could muster within the battling shark, the tornado hit the Creth in the chest and lifted it up into the air above the river.

The Creth and the shark twisted around him. They reached the illusion wall and Shadowolf drove Ruben-Willow into the Creth's heart as Rennick finally managed to destroy the shark's core. The Creth was pinned to the wall, but Shadowolf removed the blade and sliced it through the demon's thick neck.

He spared no further moment to dive into the lava river. He missed the shimmering of the illusion wall as it dimmed and vanished. He wove fire around his body and entered the lava.

He heard a splash behind him, but the tension inside him was so great he no longer cared who was after him. The lava burnt around him, but the fire covering him like a cocoon was enough to keep him alive.

His gills flared open. Somehow the pendant reacted to the river of fire as it would have with water. He could feel the lava enter his neck and, although he was in a hurry to find Shedaaij, he attempted to breathe.

Coarse smoke and fire broke into his lungs, and he coughed. It seared his throat and he tried to scream. Yet, he was definitely breathing. Amazingly, he was breathing.

His revelation almost caused him to forget about the fire cocoon, and the heat caught at his eyes and hair. With renewed vigor, he called flames to surround his body and draw the lava away. He swam further down.

Cold water touched his arm. He turned in surprise. A body of water was drifting beside him, holding his arm. He saw a light shine from its sternum. The lava was eating at it, but it managed to sustain the element of water.

Fransiska? he realised.

Let's go, she said, grasping his arm firmly. *I can't hold out forever.* He nodded and he held her hand as he pulled her down.

It took three minutes of swimming before they found something. The bed of the river hit Shadowolf's head unexpectantly and then he swam horizontally. Eventually they found a crack in one of the walls. It was too thin to allow Shadowolf passage, but Fransiska leaked through in the state of water, and so Shadowolf decided to turn into wind and blow through.

On the other side they encountered a lake of water held within the mountain. His gills burnt as they changed to filter salt water instead of fire, but he saw that Fransiska had no such problem. Water was her natural element after all. The rose pendant hung useless on her chest.

When he refocused his attention to the lake, he saw sirens everywhere. There were at least a hundred of them, and in the centre was a demon-queen. It was not just any demon-queen he realised, but one that he knew.

Shadowolf, she said. *I see we finally meet again.*

She had not looked like this before. When he had first met her in *Marsandil* she had been a mermaid, with beautiful skin and proud breasts. Then she had been transformed into an aVampeyer, joining Mercius's side with a pale face and sharpened teeth.

Now she held a dark trident in her hands. Long snakes curled down from her hair. Scars were etched on her cheeks and her twin tails. On her abdomen protruded two extra two arms that held two coral swords, one glowing blue and the other purple. She had nothing to cover her breasts though, but he knew Blosom always liked being as seductive as possible.

I thought I was rid of you, he replied, and finally spotted Shedaaij tied by seaweed and strong rope to a reef against the wall, three sirens holding daggers to her neck. Her tail dangled helplessly below her.

You were never rid of me, she said. *I see you still fancy mermaids, though. Wasn't I good enough for you?*

Enough of this rubbish! Shadowolf said and moved forward with Fransiska at his side.

They stopped when they saw hammerhead and tiger-tail sharks moving around the waters.

Do you know what happens when sharks detect blood? Blosom continued. *You're about to see my 'Feed the sharks' exhibition.*

The sirens cut Shedaaij along the legs and abdomen, just small enough that the blood attracted the sharks. In a swarm they fought each other to reach her.

Shadowolf left Fransiska's side and swam for her. The sirens ignored him and headed for Fransiska who proceeded to remove a sword from a belt at her side. She became part of the water again.

The trident threw lights of power towards him, but he twisted and turned to dodge them. He closed his eyes and appeared next to Shedaaij's side. He raised his palms outward and released wind. Whirlpools and current thrust the sharks in all directions, some fatally hitting the bed while others met Blosom's trident.

He soothed and caressed the Argo Stir holding Shedaaij. The stimulant plants eased back from their tight, ferocious grasp, enjoying his comforting touch. He then used the dagger on his right side to cut the ropes.

Shedaaij kissed him and leaped into his arms. Her embrace was weak. They turned and started to swim to Fransiska.

Eight sirens were upon her. Three held her head back while another two had their palms placed upon her breasts. Two held her legs and the last one pushed behind her abdomen. They were humming.

The power emanating from them coursed through her. Shadowolf and Shedaaij raced to free her, receiving blows from Blosom's trident. The army of sirens descended upon them.

He grasped Shedaaij's hand and teleported. The eight sirens sprang back in shock as they appeared beside Fransiska. He removed Ruben-Willow and the dagger.

Get her out of here, he instructed the Merlani. Shedaaij grasped Fransiska's arm and swam away. They did not head to the crack, but rather the opposite direction. He could only assume this was the way Shedaaij was brought in.

Forget them, Blosom said to Shadowolf's intense relief. *Sacrifice him instead.*

He was now their main focus. He concentrated on his power as they made their way over. His eyes began to glow dully as his power grew. Ruben-Willow's blade gleamed with a soft light.

He arced his blade around and decapitated two sirens. Spinning horizontally, he kicked two sirens in the chest, and snapped the neck of another. He reversed his hold on the dagger and drove it backwards into an abdomen, severing a hand with his sword and then slicing a tail.

He twisted and struck up with his dagger, using the wind to shove three sirens away. The girls were almost out, but he could still sense their presence in the water. Ruben-Willow forced his arm to swerve in a full circle and then up, to the right and backwards with the dagger. The seven sirens sank to their deaths.

A tail hit him in the chest and another in his face. He turned and kicked it in the face and pushed the sword through its neck. Removing the sword, he crossed his arms to sheath the two weapons.

The girls had left the water and he hoped they were safely on land. He bunched his muscles up, clawing his hands as he pushed the power through his veins.

His veins glowed white beneath his skin and his eyes flared effervescently. It flowed rapidly from his mind and heart to the very existence of his being. Without his knowledge, an ethereal pair of fiery wings flickered momentarily from his back. His hands were burning with power, and he stretched out his limbs to release it.

Lightning broke into the water. Light flickered and crashed against every surface and siren. They shook and convulsed as the power ruptured their hearts and arteries. Blood filled the cavern as eyes exploded and tails ripped apart at the scales.

And still the lightning spread between Shadowolf's hands and feet to every crevice in the lake. Fire teased his eyes as they burned blue and then red, and streaks of fire broke into the water.

The corpses turned to dust and ash. The red of the blood was replaced by a muddy brown. As the power in his soul subsided, the noise of the lightning and fire died down and he lowered his arms.

Where did that power come from? he thought to himself. He could not see anything, due to the blood and flesh. He so dearly wanted to see if he had gotten Blosom, for he could not feel her presence any more.

He closed his eyes and used the last of his energy to teleport to the Clan. He appeared as they were slaying the last of the dark lord's army. Bodies and the remnants of the spiritual opponents cluttered the floor of the cavern.

As Darcwulf made his way over to his brother, Shadowolf's knees buckled and he fell with his cheek to the floor. He smiled softly as he saw Shedaaij and Fransiska enter through the far opening.

TRIAL OF THE *KARIEMSAPH*
CHAPTER FOUR

He felt warm. His body was soothed and caressed. He should have been in turmoil. Every bone should have ached and his energy should have been spent. Yet he felt rejuvenated and relaxed.

He opened his eyes slowly. The light burnt on his eyes and he recoiled. He looked all around and saw flames everywhere.

Shadowolf jumped up. Fire raged everywhere and all around him without burning him. Had he dreamt about teleporting to the Clan? Was he still trapped within the lava river?

He walked forward, determined to find the source of the fire. He looked down when he realised none of his swords were with him.

A lady appeared before him. Although the fire was everywhere, there was a distance between the two of them.

"You again?" Shadowolf asked. "I thought I had completed my exam?"

The lady's body was completely composed of water. She walked lithely closer and then stopped, watching him. Suddenly, a fist of wind struck the back of his head and he fell headlong forward.

The water element hit him from the front and he doubled over backwards. He twisted and landed on his feet. A lady composed only of air walked beside the water element.

Remembering his previous trial, he summoned wind. He pulled the air around him to force the two back. He walked sturdily forward, raising his palms to lift them off their feet. Nothing happened, except that he was knocked aside by an earthly rock.

They were more subdued than last time, almost as if they were disappointed in him. Water, earth and wind faced him, the male earth in the centre.

He ran to them, calling the wind. But the lady sneered at him and lifted him off his feet with a rush of air. As earth landed a fist in his stomach, Shadowolf grabbed his throat and forced fire into it.

Wind and water raced over to him and buffeted him. Wind lifted him up and twisted him around while water covered his face and started to drown him. He threw fire to the wind and a haling tornado ripped the water away as the tornado dissipated. Earth hit him in the face and stomach, but on the third approach Shadowolf caught his fists and pushed fire into the rocks. Earth turned muddy and fell to the floor of the flames.

Shadowolf stood coughing. He was getting tired now... so many battles. He just wanted to be rid of the dark lord, but so many other beings wanted to kill him at the same time.

Without warning, fire broke against him and thrashed at his eyes. It burnt his skin and face. He cried out as he wrestled with the element. They twisted and rolled through the flames.

Thinking that wind could subdue the flames, he again used wind. But the flames only enraged further and burned inside his blood. Not even perspiration could break his skin with the amount of heat that was generated.

He found the fire coursing through his veins and attacked it. He became one with the molecules of the element and calmed its progress. He removed the flames from around him and soon the fire attacking him was no more.

He was on his knees. He really didn't want to do this again. His energy resources were at an all-time low. If he came to, he really needed to take a vacation. Maybe he would return to Asgorna's land with Shedaaij.

The flames started to die. He knew it wasn't over; otherwise he would have woken up already. As the fire died and a barren, burned landscape was revealed, he started to shake. He hugged himself as it became increasingly cold.

He lost the feeling in his fingers and toes. The cold crept up through his veins and nerves, and he lost the feeling in his face. His lips turned blue.

The absence of the fire was more devastation than its omnipresence. He cuddled on the floor, trying to rub warmth back into him. He called fire to his palm, but it was not enough.

As he faded away, he closed his eyes and concentrated. He called the essence of fire within himself. He focused his mind on its existence until his body was a pyre of fire from his position on the floor. Soon he became fire, and no part of his body was visible. The tower surrounded him as the warmth and colour returned to him, and he stood.

The landscape lit up as a beast arose on the horizon. With incredible speed contradicting its size and bulk, it moved over the land towards him.

"I remember this," he said, but could not remember what the trial was. The beast descended upon him and he tried to rise up in the air, but the wind remained silent.

Becoming fire, he burnt into the air. The beast slashed and struck at him several times, and once landed a strike to his head. He used the heat of the flames to pull up and over, trying as hard as he could to hit the beast hard.

But no strike was powerful enough. It dawned on him what he had to do and below he could see the three elementëls waiting.

He raised his fiery arms and concentrated on the heat within the beast. He manipulated it and found the core of the heat that sustained it. Slowly, he removed the heat from its body, and it slowed its attacks on him. He swerved and turned, but continued to remove the heat.

The numbed beast collapsed to the ground. He landed beside it and touched its skin, making sure that every last bit of warmth was gone.

Now the two ladies and one man stared at him complacently. They were waiting for him to release them.

Shadowolf closed his eyes and focused on the fire. He absorbed as much of it as he could and let it suffuse into his soul. The power hummed from his body and his aura burned red from his burning skin. His body began to repair as the fire became one with him, and soon there was no body.

His skin was replaced with raging waves of fire that swirled in organized chaos. He opened his spiritual eyes, and received a nod of approval from each elementël as before. He was the fire, and the fire was one with him.

The Earth moved up into the air and soon stone and rock fell down over them. Trees and plants, animals and birds were born in seconds. The scorched land was repairing, but not fast enough.

Water moved up and rained down upon the earth, creating the rivers and oceans, fish and predators of the waters. The damaged earth repaired faster and soon was whole, as green as a paradise heaven.

Wind spread across earth and water and provided life to the fauna and flora. The earth was still, and no movement took place. There was coldness upon the land, as if joy had never touched it.

Shadowolf meditated into his spirit. He separated his element across the sky, letting it fall to the earth. He filled them with warmth, life and love. They reproduced, forming part of the cycle of life. Soon, animals were running across plains and grasslands, rivers were flowing to the oceans. Celenic Earth was alive...

He looked up and saw the Clan, dwarves and humans hiding behind shelters and bodies staring at him in fear. Darcwulf's staff lay next to him, the fire around the wood dying down. He could feel the weight of the swords at his waist. His red, pulsating aura was fading.

"The *KariemsaPh*," Malanite muttered. Shadowolf passed out within the circle of burnt debris that he had caused.

STORY OF THE VALE
CHAPTER FIVE

You have done what must be done. You have wandered the earth in mist and ignorance, but with your eyes now wide open you cannot escape the truth. You have been hardened and shaped for this purpose. Many will die, but many more will live because of you.

The time of the Sadgi is coming. He who will claim the four elements and the power of the soul to harness them to his will, it is he who will decide the fate of us all. I believe that you are that Sadgi.

My time is almost up, but before I leave this world let me train you in the ways of old. As an Enodhim, the wind will be your sails. As a Merlandsi, you will be emperor of the waters. As a Goudlem, the earth will be your ally. As a KariemsaPh, the fires will rise from the deepest depths. And as a Solem, the soul will be mastered.

You will be the Sadgi. You must be, in order to face him, for he is greater than you. So I leave you with one last warning, Wisoum. Do not face him until you are ready…

Shadowolf awoke to a smooth caress on his forehead. The lingering words drifted through his mind like a scattered fog on an island. The sweat poured over his head, but it was wiped away with a damp cloth.

He moaned as he opened his eyes and tried to see where he was. The sun beat down on the land, but some sort of canopy was hanging above him to prevent the sun from striking him.

"Get some rest," a sweet, loving voice said in his ear.

"Where…?"

"Just relax," Shedaaij said. "We will camp tonight and I will tell you everything. No more fighting, ok? Just get some rest, please…"

Her voice trailed off as he fell asleep again...

***

They had travelled long and hard, but had taken the journey to Carmel slowly. They were almost at their last energy when the city finally loomed on the horizon.

The sun was at its apex and the city's shade was welcoming to Chenesia, Genewiu and Nucial. Even more welcoming would be the first bath she could find.

They found a building with a blue insignia hanging above the door. Her eyes were dazed and she could not identify the insignia as readily as she might have, and she slumped into the tavern with her last ounce of dignity.

The few visitors to the tavern stopped all conversation as they stared at the girl whose dress was dirty from her travels. Then their eyes moved to the pegasus behind her and the straggly old man swaying at the hinges of the door.

"Oh dear," Telgar said as she rushed over to the trio. "Old man..."

"Nucial," he informed her.

"Nucial, please accompany your friend to the stables," she said politely, receiving a nod from Genewiu. "There is food and water there for you, mighty one."

"Thank you," Genewiu replied and made her way to the stables.

"Can I help?" Lucian appeared.

"Yes," she said, seeing that Nucial had remained and was tottering on his last strength. "Care for the man while I run a bath for this girl and tend to her wounds."

Chenesia almost felt like a princess again. Telgar took such care to bath her and provide her with food and a new dress. She joked that she could use the old one for a new rag at the bar.

Chenesia, however, asked for leggings and a shirt, as she was tired of dresses. Once she had scoffed the food down and had ensured her travelling companions' safety, she promptly fell on the bed and passed out.

***

A fire crackled close by, and the wind comforted his burning face. He opened his eyes again and stared at the encampment, remaining silent so as not to draw attention to himself.

There were three large fires, which were not yet necessary as the sun was still an hour from setting. Around the closest fire were the Shadow Clan members.

Darcwulf sat beside Fransiska. He was holding her close and whispering in her ear, placing a kiss on her cheek every few seconds. He seemed to be reassuring her about something. Her black hair fell down over her cheeks neatly to her shoulders. Her green eyes were wet.

Darcwulf's bald head was beginning to grow some hair, but he knew that his brother would shave it in the morning, having a personal aversion to hair-growth.

Angelia, Skywolf, Heula and Gwyn sat beside Darcwulf around the fire. He remembered when he had first met Angelia at the college. Her face had lit his face with joy, and the music from the violin had sparked something in his soul. Now those feelings were but a dim memory compared to his love for Shedaaij.

"I wonder how Dredwolf is doing," he could barely hear Skywolf say.

"Do you think he misses you?" Gwyn asked.

"Yes," she replied. "We are set to get married once I return, but that is the last thing I am worried about."

"So he doesn't mind that you are off rescuing the world?" Heula joked.

"He is a kind man, and I know he cares a lot for me. He said he will wait. I think I will send him a note first thing in the morning."

Lastgorn and Sny-Ten were sitting at the second fire with the Orion. Shadowolf studied the pale green dress and blue face of Sorceress, the blond spiked hair and bulged muscles of Trevor, the brown skin, scarred face and bald head of Rennick, the rugged look of Tinonte, the vicious Scarlette, and finally the serene complexion of Shadowwe.

At the third fire were Dren, Trimistus and the old man, Malanite. His silver-grey hair reflected the dimming sunlight, his wrinkled face barely visible beneath the beard. They were accompanied by the humans and dwarves that had survived the mountain attack.

Ursula, Millon and Kentaur stood in their usual place amid the horses, which Shadowolf was glad included Mandy, his black mare.

Nelnar snored somewhere behind Shadowolf. As he turned to look up at Shedaaij upon whose lap his head was resting, she leaned over to kiss him.

"I didn't know you were awake, sorry," she apologised. "I was thinking about *Avalendil*."

"I am also worried about Lellian," he replied hoarsely, restraining a cough. "I hope the sirens aren't giving him too much hassle."

"Fransiska didn't leave unscathed," she said.

"What happened? I saw Darcwulf comforting her."

"That humming we heard was some sort of siren enchantment. It seems as if Fransiska has the power of the sirens. She has accidentally been charming the men and Darcwulf has been hard put to call her back.

"She also becomes transparent at times, although I have noticed that she is gaining control over it as time passes. I think we just saved her."

"How long have I been out?" he asked quickly.

"You gave us a scare when you fell and then erupted in flames," she said first. "Even Darcwulf has never felt such power from any fire elemental, including himself. Malanite says you have become a *KariemsaPh*."

"How long have I been out?" he repeated, only because he didn't want to discuss the trial.

"Not yet a day," she said, "Although I would like you to rest longer if you can manage."

"I don't think my bladder or my stomach will allow me to. Where are we?"

"We are north of the Dwarf Mountains and heading for a place called Horlorn's Gate. Ursula thought it wise that we rest there before going anywhere else so that we consider our next move."

"I don't know Horlorn's Gate, but we can worry about that when we get there."

A thought occurred to him and he almost sprang up, but Shedaaij pushed him down.

"Where is the horn? And our equipment…?"

"Relax," she said. "The dwarves followed Darcwulf's directions and returned with our things moments before you awoke. All that was missing was one of Sorceress's dresses."

"And the horn?"

"Ursula said she will wait until the Gate before the Transfer of Horns. But it is safe with Malanite."

"I have so many questions, but I guess I will reserve them for later," he said. "I have a feeling only Ursula and Malanite can answer them."

"Get your bladder and stomach sorted out, so that you can get more rest."

He nodded and kissed her again, savouring the taste. The jersey she wore was warm and he snuggled into it for a few seconds longer before he rose to tend to his bodily needs.

***

The sun arose the next day as she stirred in the sheets. It broke through the pane in the wall and warmed her skin from the cold of the night. A shadow passed across her face as a cloud shifted in the sky.

Chenesia awoke and moved to the bathroom. She took a quick shower and cleansed thoroughly. When she emerged and found new clothes lying on the made bed, she dressed and went downstairs to the tavern.

A man called her to one of the tables where five meals were set. The tavern was open, but there were no customers yet. Nucial sat by the man, the lady that helped her the night before, another man that she did not know, and an open seat.

"Join us for breakfast?" the lady asked.

She nodded and sat down at the open seat beside Nucial.

"I am Telgar, the owner of the tavern," the lady introduced herself. "This is Lucian Par'Mal, my fair lady. And the other is Simnab."

"Fair?" she asked shyly.

"Nucial has told us about your journey and who you are," Telgar replied. "I know Maren-Ti personally and am glad to my soul to hear that his daughter is finally safe. I have sent word to your father that you are here."

"Thank you," she said.

"I will have to leave soon," Nucial addressed her. "I must travel to the southern borders to my family in Avalion. I have much to tell them."

"Of course," she replied. "I understand. Thank you for your companionship."

They ate breakfast in silence before a thought occurred to Chenesia.

"Does my father still have the Heart of Tigers?"

"Well, we do not speak much of it, but I hear that the gem no longer resides there," Lucian said.

"Where is it now?" she asked, surprised.

"We do not know, as Eldor has decided it to be a matter of great importance not to speak of it."

Nucial tried not to express his anger, but the scowl on his face could not be controlled. Fortunately for him, no one at the table saw it.

"So I believe it is safe for you to travel home," Telgar expressed her relief. "I don't think the dark lord will be much concerned with you now."

"Nevertheless," Lucian said. "I have thought about it long into the night, and I have decided to travel with you to the Vale."

Chenesia detected a hint of sadness on Telgar's face, but was overjoyed to have another companion. Although Le'Mar's attention would be diverted, she wanted as much protection as she was offered.

"Wouldn't it be better if you just waited for her father to arrive?" Telgar asked, hiding her emotions.

"I don't want to wait any further," Chenesia interrupted Lucian's reply. "One night was enough delay. I enjoyed the hospitality, but I will leave after this meal."

"May I join you?" Simnab asked. "It will be better for me and Telgar if I do, although I might be putting you in danger."

"Why?" Chenesia asked.

"I am a Crethan," he replied, and then continued when he realised she did not know what that meant. "Whenever a Creth-

Demon comes too close to me, I transform into a deformed wolf which lusts after human flesh. I am driven to do what that demon commands."

"And are any of these 'demons' in Carmel?" she asked, horrified. The scraggy, short-haired man shook his head.

"But I felt its presence to the north and, until two nights ago, was almost compelled to follow it. The further away I am from the demon, the better it will be for those around me."

"Very well," Chenesia said, still unsure. "You may join us. Hang on....where's Nucial?"

Everyone looked around and saw that the old man had disappeared.

Nucial walked into the cavern. He looked around at the devastation that surrounded him. The illusion wall was gone. The Crethan-Demon was gone. The orcs and Crethans were dead.

He screamed out loud and then pounded the floor with his fists. Almost as quickly, he remained on his knees and looked at the scorched ground. He moved his palm over it and felt the waning power.

"It can't be," he whispered. "A *KariemsaPh*?"

He stood up and closed his eyes. The wind stirred and then Sonersaat was standing with his back to him. Sonersaat turned around and frowned.

"What is going on here?" he said. "Who are you?"

Nucial had forgotten, and with another stir of power transformed. Sonersaat fell to his knee and bowed his head.

"I beg your forgiveness, Lord Le'Mar," he said. "I did not recognize you."

"Do you know what happened here?" he asked his servant.

"No, my lord. I was waiting to the east of Horlorn's Gate as you instructed. I assumed your army was waiting here in the west for your command."

"Are you aware of a Firephoenix among the people of the Gate?"

"No, my lord. I felt no *KariemsaPh*."

Sonersaat raised his eyes and saw the scorched circle. He could also feel the remnants of the power.

"Return to the army," Le'Mar instructed. "The gem is beyond me for the moment. Once the last recruits have arrived, raid the defence and destroy the Gate; be merciful to no one."

"What of Shadowolf?" Sonersaat asked.

"What about him?"

"Where is he? I have heard no news…"

"HAVE I NOT SAID TO LEAVE HIM BE FOR NOW! HE IS OF LITTLE CONCERN TO ME AS IS YOUR LIFE!"

"Very well, my lord," he replied, and Le'Mar sent him back to the eastern army with a wave of the hand.

He stood within the throne room of his castle. Le'Mar sat down with a heavy weight on his shoulder. Not only did he not know where the Heart of Tigers was, but someone had destroyed his entire army within the mountains. He also regretted not killing everyone in the Blue Periwinkle when he had had the chance.

But his duty was now split between the search for the gem and the destruction of the Gate. And where was Shadowolf…?

HORLORN'S GATE
CHAPTER SIX

The sun was near setting again when a large hill broke the horizon. It looked like a mountain, but it was only a long sloping hill with green grass that ran up the height of it. The apex of the hill broke at the same height as Dwarf Mountains.

It was a long ride up to the middle of the hill's height where they finally reached a towering gate wrought of dwarven iron.

Shadowolf was not eager to enter another cavern again, but he was informed that the only other option was to the top of the hill and then a long drop off the cliff into Horlorn's Gate. He decided to tolerate more caverns and tunnels.

Once they were inside the dimly lit tunnels, making their way through the hill to Horlorn proper, Shadowolf rode to Malanite's side and indicated that he hop on Mandy behind him and rode away from the others.

"Do you understand what is happening to me?"

"Yur refers to the powers yur b'en receiving?" Malanite asked innocently. Shadowolf nodded. "Laddy, mer believes that it is in consequence to the node yur received power from two yeurs ago."

"The power of the *Enodhim*?"

"Was it really?" Malanite raised an eyebrow to the back of Shadowolf's head. "What did yur see that day?"

Shadowolf knew he would have to talk about it someday, although the memory was stale already.

"The orb held the four elements within it," he said. "When I joined on to it, the fifth element caused it to fuse with me."

"The reason," Malanite interrupted, "that it is called the Prophecy of the Windfarer is because only the true Windfarer could release the power. But the power yur received be the power of the

Sadgi."

"But I don't feel like a *Sadgi.*"

"Yur wouldn't. It resides within yur. What would takes decades or centuries for others to become, now takes yur faster thanks to this power."

"And the sudden explosion of trials?"

"The elemental masters need to be searched for by elemental practioners in order for them to pass their trials. Because the power was imposed upon yur, I assume the power is searching for the masters when yur are at your weakest."

"You speak of the power as if it were a person?" Shadowolf asked more than stated.

"I don't know much about these trials, me boy," Malanite finally acknowledged. "I only know what I had read and learnt these long hard years. Yur situation is unique."

Shadowolf rode in silence. It must have taken an hour in the tunnels before they reached a large foyer. An opening broke the rhythm of the tunnels and they faced a space in a wall with two columns reaching up into the mountainous roof.

The corridor ran to the left and right. Six men could walk abreast in the corridor and it was well lit. Although the roof formed part of the mountain, the walls and floor were smooth concrete.

Shadowolf looked left at the junction and saw that the corridor turned right at the end. A banner was hoisted on a stand in the corner with an insignia of a sword, a bow and a staff upon the material.

They all dismounted. Instead of heading for the banner, they turned right at the junction. A few minutes later the corridor turned left. Shadowolf stared at the left wall. The corridors seemed to surround a large room, but no doors were visible.

The right wall broke away and a large room was hidden behind curtains. Two massive pillars served as the support for the curtains.

"Those are the sleeping quarters for the army of the Sky Tier." One of the men had fallen back to announce this to the Clan.

"What is the Sky Tier?" Sorceress asked.

"I can only explain that later," he replied, "for it will make no sense to you now."

They continued passed the quarters back into a corridor ahead of them. The corridor turned to the left at the next corner, and Shadowolf still noticed that there was no door to the barred space to his left.

On the right of the new corridor was a large opening. Shadowolf peeked in to see a vast area filled with candle chandeliers, ropes, tables and dressings.

"The Hall, where we dine," the man said.

"So why not call it the Dining Hall?" Darcwulf asked.

"Because it is used for various other things too, like meetings," he replied.

"What do you call it then?" Dren asked.

"The Hall," the man replied sardonically.

They continued further down the corridor past the opening. Again they met a junction. The men led them right at the junction, but Shadowolf looked left and saw the corner with the banner. It obviously led back to the foyer, and still he saw no entrance to the mysterious room in the centre of the corridors. On the right wall, though, half-way to the banner, was a door.

Turning around, he followed the Clan. Another corridor broke off to the left, but they went past it and continued forward.

The corridor's roof disappeared as they walked out into the open air. An overhanging cliff provided shade for the opening. Hundreds of men, women and children surrounded them. A low wall was ahead of them, and when Shadowolf finally reached the wall and looked over, he almost fainted from vertigo.

There were two more tiers below them. The men on the lowest tier appeared as ants, due to how high the Sky Tier was. The lowest tier ran out much further from the mountain than the top tier, almost five times more in length. The middle tier was half the length of the bottom tier, although Shadowolf could only see the last half of it.

The tiers arced out in semi-circles from the hill, their apexes pointing east. Shadowolf moved away from the wall, barely keeping consciousness.

"The sleeping quarters cannot possibly hold all these people here," Shadowwe said.

"That is why we house them on the Mountain Tier below us," a different man approached them. "Good day, I am Treville, and I am the Lord of Horlorn's Gate."

"What is the lowest tier called?" Shadowolf asked, his mind reeling again.

"The Ground Tier," Treville replied.

"Not big on names, are you?" Scarlette said.

"We concern ourselves more with battle and defence than with fancy names."

"Fair enough," she responded.

"How long will you be staying?" Treville asked.

"A week or two at the most," Shedaaij said, looking with grave concern at Shadowolf.

"We need to discuss tactics and the way forward," Shadowolf said. "We ask only for rooms and provisions if you can spare."

"We have rooms and provisions, but you will have to abide by the limits set. The unicorn and fellow equestrians will have to stay on the tier. We also have separate rooms for elementals, but I will have a guide escort you there.

"If you don't mind, I have to attend to some business. I have reports of an army gathering to the east."

Shadowolf nodded and Treville left. He did not like the idea of another army, and Shedaaij's look of concern turned to panic.

"Maybe two weeks is too long," she smiled.

"Perhaps, but we can discuss that later," Shadowolf said.

The Clan broke away and started to mingle with the people of the tier.

It was obvious which people the elementals were and which were not. The difference was in the wooden weapons and fur armour compared to the cold steel swords and iron armour of the other men. Shadowolf and Shedaaij walked hand-in-hand through the crowds, enjoying the peace.

A trio caught his attention. Shadowolf nearly dropped his jaw in astonishment, but laughed out loud instead. He had to let go of Shedaaij's hand as the three former college friends stared in disbelief and ran into his arms, staves and bows falling to the floor.

"Shado! I can't believe it! It's been years!"

"I've missed you! I never thought I'd see you again!"

"Where've you been? Wish you'd come sooner."

He pulled himself away to introduce Shedaaij.

"Shedaaij, I think you should remember my best friends in the world," Shadowolf smiled. "Lanel, Mourna and Harmony…"

With Nelnar lying on his feet, Shadowolf spent a few hours recounting to them the tale of the power node and everything that had happened since his return from the land of the dragons. He then listened in silence to their story.

He heard how they had lived in Carmel for a year before accepting an invitation to serve Lord Treville at the Gate, and how they had been there since. Their tales were far shorter and less eventful, for which they were grateful.

The Hall began filling up with those ready for the evening meal. As the food was delivered to their tables, the Clan strode in bits at a time and filled the chairs around them.

"Lucian is in Avalion," Shadowolf said, unaware of his previous Wind-tutor's recent travels. "It seems as if he was once part of Le'Mar's army, but is on our side now."

"What happened to Kelsey?" Lanel sneered, remembering his hatred for the former Water-professor.

"Oh, I forgot," Shadowolf smiled. "Asgorna ripped her and Malferus to shreds."

Lanel couldn't contain his joy. He wooped and shouted, and Mourna kicked his heels rigorously. But, instead of berating him for his behaviour, she nodded to a space above Shadowolf's head.

"And I forgot," Lanel said ashamedly. "Nashela came with us."

Shadowolf's stomach churned as he turned. He remembered that she had asked him on a date the first day of his last year at college. He had failed to meet that commitment, less to various circumstances than to his inability to face his emotions for anyone of the opposite sex.

He had rescued her from Shenama when it had first fallen, and Lanel had taken her to Carmel. And now she was standing in his arms, embracing him firmly.

"I've missed you," she said as she looked into his eyes.

"Nashela, this is Shedaaij," he said quickly. Nashela looked down at the seat beside him and realised what he meant.

"Hi there, so pleased to meet you," she bent down to hug Shedaaij. The two went into a good-natured discussion which surprisingly went a long way into quelling Shedaaij's concern.

Having completed their discussions for the evening and their bodies nourished, they left the hall. Outside in the corridor, one of the men called to them.

"Elementals down this corridor," he told them, indicating to the right. "Non-elementals to the sleeping quarters."

Dren, Malanite, Heula, Lastgorn, Sny-Ten, Gwyn, Sorceress, Scarlette, Trevor, Shadowwe and Trimistus all followed a guard to the quarters. Ursula, Millon and Kentaur were already with Mandy and the other horses on the tier under the cliff canopy.

"I'll show them the elemental wards," Lanel told the other escort, and led them down the corridor to the right.

Shadowolf looked for Nelnar, wanting to know where it could lodge, but the wolf was nowhere to be seen. Frowning, he and Shedaaij led Mourna, Harmony, Nashela, Darcwulf, Fransiska, Angelia, Skywolf, Rennick and Tinonte under Lanel's direction.

When they reached the junction that would take them to the tier on the right, they turned left to the banner. Half-way down the passage, Lanel opened the door set into the right wall.

The passage within twisted like a snake, but for what purpose Shadowolf could not determine. When the passage ended, they entered a small room. There were no other exits, except the passage they had just passed through. The walls, floor and roof were made of earth.

"Through that wall," Lanel pointed to the right of the passage, "is the Elemental Armoury, where I will take you tomorrow. Through that wall," he now pointed to the wall opposite the passage, "is the Library."

Lanel walked to the wall left of the passage and raised his palms against the wall. Calling a bit of wind, his hair stirred as the air shifted the soil of the wall apart to reveal a hidden passage.

"This way please."

They entered a larger room filled with thirty elementals, beds and various luxury couches and items. A water bowl, illuminated from within, ran the length of one wall and fish swam within it surrounded by kelp.

"Akwaserpenta chambers," Lanel smiled at Shadowolf.

"You actually used the names from the college," Shadowolf said in awe.

"Lord Treville seems to like it," Mourna said.

"The water elementals can stay here," Lanel said, moving to a wall on the right. Shadowolf turned to see the sandy passage behind them close.

"Why the separation?" Shedaaij asked anxiously.

"They found that there was less tension in a chamber when the elements were confined to their own groups," Harmony told her. Shadowolf shrugged his shoulders when Shedaaij's pleading eyes reached him.

They left Fransiska, Skywolf and Angelia behind as Lanel created a new passage in the right wall. They walked through to another chamber filled with a sharp light and a resonating power, but stocked with similar luxuries as the chamber before.

Several crystal balls were present on hip-high pillars, and within them streaks of lightning broke from the core to the surface of the ball.

"Mageia," Lanel said. "Power of the soul."

He moved to the opposite wall as the rear one closed. They left Rennick and Tinonte in the chamber of twenty-five elementals.

The next chamber had a beautifully bejeweled furnace along the wall, and pillars of fire in the centre.

"Feniseraat," Shadowolf guessed, and Lanel nodded. Darcwulf bid them farewell, joining the forty elementals as Lanel opened the left wall. One of the fire elementals shouted something to Shadowolf, but he didn't hear what was said and chose to ignore it.

They walked into the next chamber where he knew he would have to say goodnight to Shedaaij. There were thirty earth elementals in the Centaurin chamber. There were also many plants and a few animals and birds present.

After a long session of bidding Shedaaij farewell, he made his way to the opening in the left wall. He followed Nashela, Mourna, Harmony and Lanel to the AegleDaele chambers.

The walls were made of a transparent substance similar to glass and clouds drifted across them. A draft of wind blew from the walls, keeping any humidity away.

The wall closed behind them and a few of the fifty wind

elementals surrounded him.

"He doesn't belong here," one of them said to Lanel.

"What do you mean?" Shadowolf asked.

"Wait, I can feel the essence of the *Enodhim* within him," another said in awe.

"But there is also fire," a woman said. "How can that be?"

"We all have some form of each element is us," Shadowolf countered, but knew it was useless.

"I sense the power of the *KariemsaPh*," a woman said. Her eyes widened. "Are you a *Sadgi*?"

"Oh, no!" Shadowolf laughed. "That I am not."

"You are too powerful in the way of the fire to be here," a man said politely and with some embarrassment. "He will have to stay in the courtyard."

"Very well," Lanel said with sadness in his voice. He turned to the corner of the left wall and the wall they had just entered, creating a domed passage.

Shadowolf, with much dislike for the elementals, turned and walked after him.

"I can feel his energy pass right through me," one of the women said softly.

They entered the courtyard. It was at least thirty times greater in volume than any of the chambers he had been in. He could feel that it held all the elements within in it in equal stature. And he was its only occupant.

"I am sorry about that," Lanel said, "but these elementals are a bit fussy when it comes to company. Did you notice Theroy in Feniseraat?"

"No, I didn't," Shadowolf replied, shocked again. Theroy had been his opponent in most of the sports he had played at the college.

"He has really changed, having a few scars on his face now," Lanel informed him. "You can meet him tomorrow. I'm off to bed."

They greeted each other and Lanel left him in the vast jungle of the courtyard. There was a light from above somewhere. It lit his way as he walked beneath the large oaks and upon the orange leaves on the ground. Eventually he found a comfortable little knoll that could serve as a bed.

A whine announced Nelnar's presence as the wolf bounded over a small hillock and cuddled with its master.

"I don't know how you got here," Shadowolf said, "but I am glad for your company."

They closed their eyes and the worries of the world faded away. The light in the courtyard went out as they fell asleep, but it didn't take long before Shedaaij found them and held Shadowolf in her arms…

"Would you like to wash?" Lanel asked Shedaaij and Shadowolf. They were back in the entry chamber where Lanel had first parted the earth walls. Nelnar sat at Shadowolf's heels, waiting for food.

It was still early in the morning, about four hours before noon. Lanel had woken them for breakfast, announcing that they were the last to rise.

"Yes, please," Shedaaij replied.

Lanel turned to face the wall opposite the chamber's entrance, to the right of the corner that Lanel had opened for the elemental chambers. In the centre of the wall, he created a new path.

They walked down the dark corridor that curved slightly every now and again. Soon a bright light broke the darkness and to the left was a large circular washroom.

The roof was too high to be seen, but the room was as large as the dining hall. The massive basin that spanned the diameter of the floor was porcelain white. The basin sank into the floor and in trays along the perimeter were bars of soap. The pool was filled with steaming water.

"I'll leave the path open for you," Lanel said as he turned back. Nelnar whined and tilted its head to its master.

"Is he permitted in?" Shadowolf asked.

"Of course," the reply trailed through the passage as Lanel dropped out of sight. "The bath filters the dirt every hour."

Shedaaij and Shadowolf removed their filthy garments. He helped her take off the coral armour that had been beneath her clothes and they slipped into the basin.

Nelnar was already paddling in the warm water when they reached the centre. The water took Shadowolf to his neck and

Shedaaij bobbed up and down, kicking to keep herself up.

He held her in his embrace and gave her a loving kiss.

"Do you know how much I love you?" she asked him.

"Possibly not as much as I do," he replied, grinning.

"Probably not, cause I love you more," she said.

"Oh, really?" he reached for her stomach and tickled her, chasing her around the water as she tried to escape. He could feel that her stomach had tightened, in all probability from the previous night's meal. But he chose not to tell her that she had picked up weight, knowing it would deserve a hardy smack from her.

Nelnar promptly climbed out the pool, shook itself and ran in the direction of the hall.

"He must be starving," Shadowolf remarked when they stopped running around.

"I am quite famished myself," she said.

"Oh," he said fretfully. "Then maybe we should..."

"I think I will start with dessert," she said and then dived on top of him, delivering him a kiss as they drifted to the bottom. She waited a few seconds for the rose pendant to activate his gill-lungs, and then proceeded to love him. They closed their eyes to enjoy the moment more.

Fiery, ethereal wings broke the surface of his back, spreading out around the pool and then embracing Shedaaij. His shoulder blades shifted slightly, and became warm, but it was lost to the heat pulsing through their veins.

By the time they opened their eyes to engage each other more passionately, the wings had already dissipated.

They arrived at a nearly empty hall an hour and a half later. Dren, Darcwulf, Fransiska, Sorceress and Nelnar were still there, finishing some pudding and cakes.

"I see you washed your clothes," Darcwulf commented.

"Well, the bath can be quite useful," he replied. "If I knew we were going to bathe, I would have brought some clothes from my bag."

They sat down as Harmony approached them.

"The chef says there is still some food left, and will conjure a platter for you soon," she said.

True to her words, the food arrived ten minutes later. He wanted to tell Shedaaij to take it easy on the food, but wasn't sure how to approach the topic.

Half way through the meal, Theroy approached the table. As Lanel had indicated, he had changed drastically. He had been a thin boy, tall and with a handsome complexion. Now, his muscle overshadowed his height. It was not a bulky muscle, but rather suited his body and was only gained through hard and experienced fighting.

His face held several scars, but one was darker than the rest and crossed from his left brow over his nose to his right cheek. He carried a red staff with white tips in his right hand, but it was obvious he did not need it for support.

His hair that had once been long was cut short and neat. Some scars were visible upon his skull.

"That reminds me," Shadowolf said softly to Shedaaij as he approached. "I need to cut my hair. It's still damaged from that strom attack."

"Good day, old friend," Theroy said in a husky voice Shadowolf did not recognise, and he rose to greet him.

"Theroy, I did not think I would meet you again," he said honestly.

"That's alright, Degron," he replied, and Shadowolf smiled for he was glad at least one thing hadn't changed. Theroy had never called him by his first name in college.

"Have you been here since Asbec closed?" he asked.

"Yes. My home was to the east, the area now known as Morkom Falls. When Morkom received the news at the time of Mercius that the northern tribes should unite as the southern tribes did in New Avalion, it was too late and we went into battle.

"Needless to say, we lost the city, and the three outlying defences of Dewville, Crane and Sunville. The fugitives fled to the hills and created Horlorn's Gate. We have been recruiting people since then."

A soft song ran through Shadowolf's mind, and he and Theroy turned to look at Fransiska. Her skin glowed beautifully and, although she was talking to Darcwulf, it seemed as if she were staring at him.

She was so gorgeous, and he could not believe he had ignored his love for her before. But now, with her eyes glistening and her skin so soft and smooth, he could not hide his feelings. He wanted her, wanted to kiss her, hold her in his embrace...

"Fransiska!" Shedaaij shouted, and the girl turned to look at the men in her close proximity entranced by her.

"Oh, sorry," she blushed. "I can't fully control it yet."

She concentrated, and the sirenic power subsided. The men shook their heads and as she apologised to Darcwulf, Shadowolf turned to apologise to Shedaaij.

"It's okay," she stopped him. "I know you couldn't help it."

"What was that?" Theroy asked.

"While we were in the mountains," Shedaaij explained, "Fransiska was attacked by a group of sirens that were trying to change her into one of them. Although we stopped the process, it did not prevent her from gaining some of their abilities."

"Incredible," he replied. "Anyhow, I have to go. Catch up with you later, Degron."

He was again interrupted, but this time by a commotion at the hall's opening. Six dwarves dragged a slim man onto one of the tables, followed shortly by Trimistus. Once he was slammed down on the wooden surface, Trimistus stood before him.

"The last time I met you, you were trying to kill me at Le'Mar's castle," he said to the pale man. "I have no doubt your quest continues."

"I will fulfil my mission," the assassin said.

"You are surrounded by enemies; you cannot escape," Trimistus said.

"Nothing stands in the way of the Semhum Kateth."

"Take him away," Trimistus ordered, and the dwarves carried the man out of the hall.

"Where did he come from?" Shadowolf asked.

"I realised someone was following me this morning, and apparently so did my dwarf companions. When he struck, we turned and captured him."

"How do you know him?" Darcwulf asked.

"He was the one who tried to kill me when I escaped Le'Mar and fell off the cliff," Trimistus answered. "We fell together, but I never knew what his fate was."

"So Le'Mar still wants you dead?" Fransiska asked.

"Either that or this assassin only seeks to fulfil his mission," he said. "I can't see Le'Mar wasting any more time on me, but I'll question the man later."

"Do you think he'll tell you anything?" Shadowolf asked dubiously.

"I have my ways," Trimistus grinned, and the red lights of his eyes burned brighter.

"This is really starting to be a weird day," Darcwulf muttered as Trimistus left the hall.

"It's about to get weirder," Lord Treville said as he entered the hall. "The army I was warned of; it is appearing on the eastern horizon."

***

Chenesia rode on Genewiu, while Lucian had Lancenat and Simnab the Crethan his stallion on her right. The sun was near noon and was causing her to perspire heavily in her new clothes.

She still felt shy riding with Lucian. He was an attractive man, and she could feel the power of the wind within him. It was difficult to keep her thoughts off the married elemental, but she managed by training her mind on reaching the Vale.

They weren't talking though. The heat was getting to her and making her feel sticky. It would possibly be another day, if not by the evening, before they reached her father's land.

The desert-like terrain started to look familiar. The folds and run of the land rolled through her mind of recognition. And as she was about to place it, Genewiu trod on something harder than the land around them, and it reverberated through her.

"What's wrong?" Lucian asked her as she stood still.

"No...nothing," she replied, not wanting to reveal the secret.

They continued further, and it made her heart glad that the entrance to the Fairiwell was still there.

NEWS OF THE HEART
CHAPTER SEVEN

Shadowolf let the breeze caress his face. Out in the distance he could see the army lining up in their formations, ready for the assault.

He realised that he still had not met Le'Mar personally. He had been fighting against his men, setting himself against them the best he could, fulfilling the prophecy, and yet he still had not met the dark lord.

The Clan stood on either side of him looking out from the Sky Tier. On the Mountain and Ground Tiers the warriors of Horlorn's Gate waited in anticipation. The elementals were given the higher tier.

The Shadow Clan had wasted no time in getting their weapons. Somehow it was reassuring to have Ruben-Willow and the dagger dangling on his hips again. Ruben-Willow especially had been there since the beginning of the war and was a veteran in taking life by now.

He looked down at Nelnar, his faithful wolf. It never gave up on him. It was always there to ensure that it could serve its master. Nothing else matter to it but that single devotion.

"You ready, my old friend?" he asked it, and patted its head. Nelnar looked up with a brow raised. I am not old, the expression said.

Lord Treville approached Shadowolf from behind and he turned at the sound of the footsteps.

"I am indebted to you, Shado, and your Clan," he said, sighing.

"How so?" Shadowolf asked.

"I was thinking about it while I was getting ready," he replied. "If it had not been for Ursula's warning when your Clan was in the mountain, or the assistance you offered against those demons, we would have been caught on by sides."

"Trust me when I say the gesture was accidental," Shadowolf smiled softly.

"Well, the odds have increased for the Gate, that's for sure," Lord Treville smiled back. "Now, don't let me be more in debt by actually fighting in this battle."

Shadowolf felt his pride strike against his temple. "What do you mean?"

"There is no need for you or any of the Clan to actually fight in this battle," he told them. "We have sufficient numbers. And even if we don't, at least you can make it out."

"Nevertheless," Shadowolf said deeply, "We will remain, even if only to watch the proceedings. I can't promise that I will restrain my will to assist where I can."

"Of course," Lord Treville obliged, with gratitude on his face, and turned back to his army.

"He was just being polite," Sorceress said.

"I know," Shadowolf said, and left it at that. "Feel free to relax. We will only get involved if things take a turn for the worse."

The day dragged on and eventually Creotos began to set to the west behind Horlorn's hill. Food was brought out on trays to the waiting soldiers while the army on the horizon remained stationary.

"Do they want an invitation?" Darcwulf asked between bites. They were sitting on chairs now, with their legs stretched up on the wall at the edge of the tier.

"I feel like I'm watching a show," Skywolf commented.

"I've never felt more relaxed in a battle before, I'll admit," Scarlette added.

Shadowolf was also uncomfortable with the delay. He felt like he should be doing something, but there was nothing to be done but wait. It was now dark and Sothos was rising, and still there was nothing but the flicker of torches on the horizon.

"We've got movement," Tinonte said.

"Finally," Shedaaij moved her legs off Shadowolf's, and they sat up straight, peering into the distance.

The torches shifted and the army moved towards them. He could hear wings and a cloud moved in the air.

"Fletchlings," Darcwulf muttered, remembering the small blue creatures that Le'Mar usually used to distract the archers.

The fletchlings broke into visibility, and fire elementals lodged flaming balls at them with their staffs.

"It's like a hundred Darcwulfs," Dren joked, causing Shadowolf to laugh.

Most of the front fletchlings fell to the ground, but the mid-group made it through. Rocks and arrows coursed through the air to meet the next group. The remaining mid-group and rear fletchlings were summoned back to the army and they retreated.

"So far, so good," Shadowolf said.

"You'd have thought he'd given up on the fletchlings already," Malanite commented from somewhere to the far left. Shadowolf frowned, being the only one that picked up that the old man had lost his accent for the moment.

He leaned over to look at Malanite, but the old man ignored him and looked straight ahead. Where had he heard that voice before?

"Look," Shedaaij whispered.

He turned his attention back to the battle. A single line of thirty Ma-Wreths was marching. Behind them, ten Froth Huns rode on black stallions and mares. Shadowolf heard Mandy stirring on the tier, and he could feel the tension emanating from her.

"That is a lot of Wreths," Darcwulf said, almost sounding impressed.

"I'd be more worried about the Froths," Shadowolf added. "If this is only the front of the army, I really don't want to know what is next."

"Do you think we should get ready?" Trimistus asked.

"We'll wait a moment longer," Shadowolf answered.

"Trimistus," a dwarf called from the corridors. "The prisoner wants to speak to you."

With confusion distorting his reptilian complexion, he arose and left the Clan.

"I am starting to feel like I'm dreaming," Shadowolf said, rubbing his eyes. "What a day."

"Don't worry, this is as real as it gets," Fransiska said, and then planted a quick kiss on Darcwulf's cheek.

"Thanks sweets," he smiled and returned the kiss.

Arrows soared into the air towards the Wreths, but as was the nature with these rocky giants, their massive arms moved with lightning speed to slap them aside. Even the arrows that struck bounced harmlessly off their tough skin.

The earth elementals raised their bows and loosed their ethereal arrows. At the apex of their fall they became hardened rock and when they struck the Wreths, they fell to their knees in hoarse wails.

"Interesting," Shadowwe said.

The Wreths simply rose and ran for the Gate. Dwarves broke out from the Ground Tier to face them, their axes gleaming in the firelight.

"What's taking Tri so long?" Darcwulf asked. "He's missing all the fun." Rennick grinned, but Fransiska slapped his arm.

Soon every elemental sent ethereal arrows soaring onto the approaching Wreths, but the Froths' skeletal heads gleamed from blue to red, and the arrows disintegrated in mid-flight.

"Oh, that's not good," Sorceress said.

As the first line of dwarves engaged the Wreths, striking where they could and flying when hit by the arms, a second line of dwarves and men broke into the plains from the Gate.

Two Wreths fell. The Froths joined the battle and even though the Wreths and Froths were outnumbered, they were rapidly succeeding in decreasing the Gate's army.

A tenth of each of the groups of elementals soared into the air and landed on the plains to fight the Froths. Water, wind, fire, earth and spirit fought against the beasts, assisting greatly in defeating them.

"That's better," Darcwulf said, sitting on the edge of his seat as Trimistus joined the group again.

Five Wreths were now dead. Surprisingly, the death toll of the Froths was the same. Shadowolf remembered how hard it had been to kill his first Froth and was really impressed by the elementals' skills.

Ruben-Willow stirred on his hip and Nelnar whined. Shadowolf looked out further back into the dark lord's army, but could not discern what had disturbed them. Yet, he felt something…

"Oh, great!" he exclaimed, as the familiar feeling arose within him. His chair fell from underneath him as he stood. He touched the amulet hanging beneath his top.

"What?" the Clan were up, instantly aware that something was wrong.

"They've got dragons," Shadowolf announced. "Sonersaat is with them."

"Oh, fantastic!" Darcwulf said and his staff flared with fire.

No sooner than his power emerged did the horde of purorcs and hurorcs charge onto the battlefield. There were three groups of a hundred each. Shadowolf could tell by the dim silhouettes on the horizon that there were more.

"They're hiding behind the hill," Shadowolf said. "Come on, Asgorna, get here faster!"

"Shado, he needs to get here from his world first," Ursula reminded him.

The remaining men, dwarves and elementals ran from the Gate. There were thousands of them, and they outnumbered the army on the field vastly. But Shadowolf knew that once Le'Mar's reserves were brought into play the ratio would change.

"He's coming," Shadowolf said.

"Who?" Shedaaij asked. "Sonersaat?"

"No; Asgorna," he replied. "I can feel him within me."

Shadowolf jumped off the tier without warning the others and landed on Asgorna's back. As he did so, Sonersaat and his nine dragons rose above the horizon.

"So this is what he has been saving the Dragon War for?" Shadowolf realised. "Not for the elves?"

"So it seems," Asgorna replied. "Call to Trimistus. Tell him the dragon Mynisna resides in the Gate. Instruct him to summon him."

Five dragons rose above the hill of the Gate and soared down upon them. Shadowolf recognised them from his travels in Asgorna's temple, and felt relieved.

With the power of Asgorna within him, he called to Trimistus. At first Trimistus was stunned at the voice in his head, but as the Clan raced to get down to the plains, and Millon and Kentaur leapt over the tier's edge and dropped the distance, Trimistus's eyes flared orange as he summoned the dragon.

"Hey, why couldn't I get that ability?" Shadowolf asked.

"Do you have eyes sunken into your soul?" Asgorna asked, turning his head to peer at him.

"Guess not," Shadowolf replied.

Shadowolf could feel the dragon awake within the secret room he had seen without any doors. He felt the shadow move through the roof of the room into the earth of the hill. It rose through the surface without disturbing the soil, and its spiritual form became solid in the fresh air.

Following Shadowolf's example, Trimistus leapt onto the dragon's back and joined Asgorna's side.

"I never thought I'd see you again," Trimistus told Mynisna.

"Never say never," the dragon replied.

"Let's rather say I had hoped I'd never require the circumstance again," Trimistus added.

"Glad to know you missed me," Mynisna replied.

The seven dragons watched as the nine others approached. A light appeared in the east and eight Creth-Demons rose with fifty Creth-wolves beneath each of them. Following them were ten Firestroms.

"We need to end this now," Shadowolf said, losing his voice in fear, "before they reach the Gate."

He looked back, but his other fear was confirmed. Shedaaij was on the battlefield already, having removed her outer clothes to fight freely in her coral armour. She deftly wielded her two deadly daggers, and most of her skin was already covered in orc blood.

"Let's go!"

Le'Mar sat up as he saw the dragons approach. He tried not to curse, but it inevitably escaped his lips.

"How can this be?" he muttered. He watched as Sonersaat engaged Shadowolf and the sixteen dragons were caught in a ferocious battle.

"SHADOWOLF, WHAT THE HELL ARE YOU DOING THERE?!?!"

As Sonersaat rose again to fly at Asgorna, a strong wind shoved him down. Le'Mar walked on the ground, his face hidden beneath the hood of his dark cloak.

With a simple shake of his hand, a wave of wind blew Shadowolf's dragons backwards. The Gate's army fell to the ground, but the dragons rose up into the air again.

Sonersaat flew down to his lord.

"I did not know he was here," Sonersaat said in fear.

Le'Mar's mind was in turmoil. He really needed this victory, but he could not risk the War of the Dragons. He needed it at another appointed time.

His other option was to take the dragons away and let his army continue the battle, but he knew they stood no chance against Asgorna.

In retrospect, he decided he had no choice. He summoned a hyperportal on the hill and mentally called the retreat to all his remaining units. They rushed from the centre of the Gate's forces back up the hill.

"Get them!" Shadowolf commanded. As they descended with fire, claw and fury, he saw Le'Mar raise his hand again. An ocean of wind blasted into the dragons, but Shadowolf turned Asgorna into the wind element and they passed harmlessly through them.

The other dragons fell to the ground again, but luckily there were no fatal injuries. Le'Mar stared at Shadowolf as he and his dragon materialised again.

"Sonersaat, I finally know who the *Enodhim* and the *KariemsaPh* is that destroyed my army in Dwarf Mountains."

"Shadowolf?" Sonersaat asked. "How can that be? You told me it takes decades to master just one element?"

"I underestimated the power he received from the node," Le'Mar answered. "And I sense the *Wisoum* growing within him. And not just him, but another."

"Three DragonRiders?"

"The prophecy said it would be contested," Le'Mar answered, looking up with hatred at Asgorna, "but it does not mention how many contestants there would be."

When the last units of his army entered the portal, Soneraat and Le'Mar teleported with the dragons. The portal closed, and the people of the Gate cheered.

Shadowolf closed his eyes and dropped his head.

"I guess he is saving it for the elves then."

**

Chenesia waited patiently before the gates. She heard the cogwheels turn and the wood bend, and eventually the double doors swung outward.

The three travelers rode in together. She was shaking, not from the night cold, but rather from the anxiety of seeing her father again.

When they reached the stables, they dismounted and allowed the stablers to take their mounts. The exception was Genewiu, whom Chenesia insisted should join them.

They went up to her father's chambers and the guard hurried in waking the baron. A sleepy-eyed Maren-Ti opened his eyes to the guard, his wife Larnesia stirring in the sheets beside him.

"What's the matter?" he croaked, the rims of his eyes still wet.

"It's your daughter, lord," the guard said quickly. "She's at the door."

Maren-ti jumped from the sheets in his shorts. Topless, he banged his doors open and almost ran right into Chenesia. He realised with embarrassment that the guard had meant his immediate door, but the agony had been too much and he grabbed Chenesia in his arms and lifted her off the ground in joy.

"I thought I would never see you again," he said, and their tears rolled onto each other's shoulders.

"Chenesia?" Larnesia asked from the corner of the door hugging her robe, and then ran to join them in the embrace.

"Come, let's go," Lucian motioned for Simnab to leave.

"No, wait!" Chenesia exclaimed and pulled away from her parents. "Dad, can we give them lodging?"

"Of course," Maren-ti turned to the guard. "Get the ladies to prepare fine rooms in the maroon suites and what else they need for comfort."

"I am so glad you are safe," Larnesia said as the men left for their rooms. "How did you get away?"

"It's a long story; one I don't have the energy for now."

"Yes, yes," Maren-Ti agreed. "You must be exhausted. But who are the men with you?"

"Lucian is a wind elemental. I met him in Carmel, but I believe he resides with his family in New Avalion. Simnab is a Crethan, but I'll explain that tomorrow."

"Very well," Marent-Ti replied. "Let me get someone..."

"I'll have the pleasure of escorting her," a dwarven voice called.

"Hargon!" Chenesia ran and picked the dwarf warden up, planting a kiss onto his scruffy cheek.

"I still have your room in the monastery as you left it," he said, tears brimming onto his beard.

"Goodnight mum; dad," she said and walked with the dwarf to the room.

He had been right. Everything was as she had left it the fatal night that she and the dwarf had left the Vale against her father's will to travel to Eldor's Forest.

The room was musty though and clearly was not cleaned every week. She wondered if they had given up on her at some point.

Finding a nice lavender nightdress in her cupboard and changing into them, she made her way under the blankets of her bed.

"I've missed you," she whispered to the pillow and fell asleep.

She sat and told them about everything since she had left for the forest two years before. In between questions, she helped herself to the hearty breakfast before her.

The shower had been delightful that morning, and she could still feel her skin tingling as she finished the tale. She promised herself that after breakfast she would have another one.

"I need to know something," she said and looked at Lucian as she addressed her father. "I was told that the Heart of Tigers has been taken from our custody.

"That is true," Maren-Ti replied. "Le'Mar made another attempt to take the Heart. He decimated the sanctuary and nearly succeeded. But Eldor was here and he stopped him."

"And Eldor took it away?" she asked.

"Yes," Larnesia replied. "Only your father, Eldor and the new bearer know the location of the Heart now."

"Will it help?" she continued.

"We can only hope," the baron said. "Eldor says there are other ways to enter the forest without the Heart, but that would require the might of a *Sadgi*."

"So, for the moment, it is safe," Hargon sighed.

"Won't he try and obtain the Heart at its new location?" Chenesia asked, wondering where that was.

"If he does succeed to find it, he will have a harder time acquiring it than he did in the sanctuary; that I can promise you."

"But the sanctuary is perfect," Chenesia argued.

"I have spoken to the new bearer," Maren-Ti said in a humbled voice, "and have seen his land. I assure you, he is a greater man than I to look after it."

"I don't believe that for one second," Chenesia said grumpily, and filled her mouth with food again.

"Your faith in me is comforting," the baron responded. "I have desired it for so long."

"Which brings me to the next topic," Chenesia said carefully. Her mother and father lowered their utensils and looked at each other. "I won't be staying long."

They started to retort and complain, but Chenesia stalled them by raising her palm.

"I need to continue forward," she told them, and the sadness returned to her father's eyes. "I feel that I have a part to play in this war yet, and my destiny is in the forest."

"There is no need for you…"

"Father," she interrupted. "Mother. Please don't make me run away again. I know that this is what I must do. If the dark lord does manage to enter the forest, then I will be there."

"I don't want to lose you again," Maren-Ti cried. "The first time, my heart almost failed me."

"Do you still get the muscle cramps?" she asked him with grave concern.

"It has increased since you disappeared," Larnesia replied on his behalf.

"I will stay as long as I can manage," Chenesia said, her resolve and her love fighting a battle within her heart.

***

Shadowolf landed on Sky Tier and bid the dragons farewell. Mynisna returned to his secret chamber while he others headed west to Bentley Strip.

He turned and saw Trimistus approaching him with the assassin at his side. Instead of being held down by dwarves, the man walked freely, a few blood stains on his skin.

"Oh, this is an interesting twist," he said as the Clan began to form on the tier. He heard Nelnar bark and saw the wolf by the corner near the hall. Shadowolf nodded, and the wolf went to find food.

"Somehow, this assassin found his way out of his confinement," Trimistus replied, sincerely bemused. "And instead of hunting me down again, he joined us in battle last night."

"A very interesting twist," Darcwulf added, clearly suspicious.

"What's your name, assassin?" Shadowolf asked.

"Nolraldun," he replied.

"And why have you decided to join us?" he continued to interrogate.

"I no longer care if the Semhum Kateth find me," Nolraldun answered. "I will die sooner if I continue to attempt to take his life."

"Look," Shadowolf placed his hand on Trimistus's shoulder. "His mission was to kill you, so if you think you can trust him, so be it. He's not my problem, and I have better things to worry about."

Trimistus nodded, and Shadowolf started to walk away.

"Did you find anything?" Darcwulf called.

Shadowolf turned to look at the Clan. The morning sunlight struck their backs and created a beautiful silhouette around their bodies. He humoured himself by imagining that he could see their auras.

"It seems as if Le'Mar returned his army to the east of the forest, although I could only find half of it."

"The rest must be to the north," Trimistus offered, "where his castle is."

"That is what Asgorna figured," he continued. "We had to head around Eldor's Forest though, because Mynisna said that the elves were getting apprehensive below us and were preparing to fire."

"I guess they don't trust anyone with a dragon," Sorceress said.

"Or they thought you were Sonersaat," Scarlette added.

"In any event," Shadowolf said, "I still plan to find a way to the elves."

"I know a way," Ursula said behind him. "It is through a mechanised tunnel, known as the Fairiwell. If the elves are being as cautious as you say, then I suggest we take that route."

"How can we get there?" Fransiska asked.

"We travel from the Scourge to Carmel and then to the secret entrance en-route to the Vale of Tigers."

Malanite dropped his head slightly, seemingly to consider something, and then looked up again.

"Then it's settled," Shadowolf said, turning to the corridors again. "Tomorrow we return to the Scourge."

The Clan mumbled in agreement and went their separate ways.

Nashela and Shedaaij were still in deep conversation when he finished his evening meal. He hadn't spoken much to anyone, except the occasional word to Dren. Nelnar slept passively by his feet.

The two girls were becoming good friends, much to Shadowolf's relief. But he held his breath, and it felt almost as if someone had dropped a bucket of ice on him.

"Will you be coming with us to the forest?" she asked Nashela. Shadowolf listened carefully.

"No," she said, and the air that he released exploded from his lungs, and he coughed.

"I'm fine, don't worry," he said to the staring girls, tears brimming on his eyes from the coughing.

"I must stay with these people," she replied with a smile. "Besides, I am interested in one of the elementals."

"Oh, really!? Which one?! Is it Norren?" And this was where Shadowolf stopped eavesdropping. He did not feel like listening to gossip.

He rose from his chair and wished the Clan a good night's rest.

"If you don't mind, I'm going to stay up for a while," Shedaaij told him. He nodded and left. Nelnar arose sleepily and followed.

When he reached the elemental courtyard, the roof was already lit with artificial sunlight. The autumn leaves drifted passed his feet as he strode to his comfortable knoll. The trees stirred in the breeze that Shadowolf summoned, and a bird sang along the top.

A mist arose in the courtyard and floated over his legs. Nelnar sniffed at it, but remained calm. It filled the courtyard with its wonderful presence until there was no leaf untouched.

"This feels familiar," he said softly as the mist calmed his nerves and he relaxed. The power and energy that had been surging deep within him subsided and the pain in his shoulders disappeared.

"We met in mists like this before," a voice said as equally soft as his, but he was not disturbed or alarmed.

"And when we did, Ursula, you tried to convince me not to go after Mercius and leave the node to him," he smiled.

"Not exactly in those words," she retorted kindly.

"How did you manage to recreate the Mists of Celene?" he asked her.

"I carry a part of it within me," she replied. "It is a secret lore that Eldor also carries, although he does so with water eggs. I, however, have enough power within me to carry it wherever I go."

"She says modestly," he laughed. "Speaking of power..."

"Yes, that brings me to my purpose here," she said.

"Where is it?" he asked.

"Behind you."

He turned and on the ground was the lengthy horn he had retrieved from the Scourge.

He gently picked it up and turned to ask Ursula how she wanted to do it. A sharp light broke the mist's veil, and the horn shifted on her forehead.

A red light shone beneath the edges where it was attached to her skin, and the horn fell to the floor. A pulsing sack of red veins glowed in a hollow on her head where the horn once was.

"Bring the new horn, and use your power to assist me," Ursula instructed.

"I don't know how," he replied honestly.

"You will."

He walked closer and placed the rim of the horn over the hollow. He saw that the diameter of the base was larger than the first and would allow more room for the sack to grow.

Energy flowed from Ursula as she fused the horn to her head. Her white coat glowed brilliant blue and the mist complemented it.

Shadowolf reached for the elements. He called the wind around him, raising his power. It passed from his mind into his palms and the horn sparkled.

Next he summoned fire, and watched as his hands turned orange and transfused into the horn. His power increased further. Without skipping a beat he added water and earth simultaneously, and finally his spirit.

The horn sprang into place and completed its fusion. Shadowolf fell back as the horn exploded with effervescent light, and Ursula reared up on her hind legs.

The light became an incandescence of power that flowed through the mist. Not even the Mists of Celene felt this strong. It filled Shadowolf with a joy he had long forgotten and all his ailments were healed. He was ready to take on the world again.

He even felt strong enough to defeat Le'Mar.

She returned to her hooves and the mist started to disappear from the courtyard.

"Before our shroud of secrecy disappears, Shado," she said, her head drooping from tiredness, "one thing I must reveal to you, so that your choice to travel to Eldor's Forest is well-informed.

"The Heart of Tigers for which Le'Mar strives so hard," she continued, "is now in the hands of your father."

He stared at her as the last of the mist vanished.

"How..."

"Don't," she warned. "I don't have the strength to call the mists again, even though my power has tripled. Be content with that knowledge and make your decision wisely."

"What about the old horn?" he asked, looking for it, but he couldn't see it.

"Masara healed me when I lost this one, and in doing so created that horn," she replied. "It rightfully belongs to him. He can decide what he wants to do."

"Where is it?"

"Do you see the butterfly pendant?"

He looked again and under a few leaves he found a fine chain and on it a beautiful butterfly made of various small gems.

"There are so many marvels in this world," he said and took the butterfly.

"I have already asked Sorceress to be the bearer, so the burden won't be added to you," she smiled. "And now I can walk among you again."

"What do you mean?" Shadowolf laughed. "You have always walked with us."

"But it has been a long time since I could be like you."

He watched as her body glowed and her coat pulled into the skin. The white turned blue, and skin formed on her back.

Her front hooves turned into gentle, smooth hands as she rose on her hind, long legs. A blue dress fell over her slender beautiful body and long, amber hair fell to her soft neck and shoulders. It highlighted the ocean blue of her eyes and the red, sumptuous lips beneath her lovely nose. The dress complimented her firm, small breasts and her curved hips.

"That's about as much energy as I can spare tonight," she smiled and Shadowolf's knees went weak. "Good night."

She placed a soft, friendly kiss on his lips and walked towards the exit of the courtyard. Her hips swayed gently and he could not say a word. His heart pounded and the blood pumped painfully through his veins.

"Oh, no," Ursula turned in alarm. "It's happening again. Shado, lie down!"

Nelnar whined as Shadowolf's arms turned to rock. The blood in his veins turned to sand and grass grew on his face.

"What the..." he said, and fell onto the knoll, the butterfly pendant still in his palm.

TRIAL OF THE *GOUDLEM*
CHAPTER EIGHT

He opened his eyes to a starless landscape. There was no light nor any objects in the sky. Only land and mountains surrounded him with a luscious green landscape.

It was similar to the elemental courtyard in many ways, except that there was no light on the land. He could still see the forest and trees, so the lack of light evidently did not hamper his sight.

When he rose, he marked an obvious difference to his previous two trials. Ursula stood in her human form before him and Nelnar was still by his feet.

"How did you get here?" he asked her.

"I have no clue," she replied, staring around her. "So this is where you do your trials?"

"If this is actually a place," he said. "The first time was in the sky, and the second in complete fire."

"Seems quiet," she looked around.

"Here comes one," he nodded behind her. Ursula moved aside as a lady made completely of wind walked in his direction.

Shadowolf tried to remember how the trial worked, but he had been through so much already it escaped him. He knew the element would be taken away from him at some stage, and that thought made him shiver.

And then he realised he was not that strong in earth. He had used wind all his life, and fire had also been a strong part of his journeys, but earth was mostly left unused. With that realisation came the knowledge that he also hardly dealt with water.

He turned around to kick the Fire Elementël, but his foot soared through him. The water lady hit him in the stomach and sent him flying into Wind's foot.

He summoned the earth around him, but the rocks formed too slowly. Fire etched around his arms and turned the rock into soft stone that slid down his body. The fire element slammed his fist into Shadowolf's jaw, and he stretched into the air and fell on his back.

"Your earth is too weak," Ursula commented.

"I know," Shadowolf said, rising.

He concentrated and increased the power within him. The stones from the ground started to lift, and the trees swayed. Wind charged at him and twisted into a tornado. He ran into her, sending rocks and sand into her core which flew wildly around. But she hit him and threw him out into a whirlwind of fire.

He knew he had to transform into earth. It was the only way he would pass this trial. He focused within the fire that was scarring his skin and strained every muscle, persuading the earth to become one with him.

His head turned to rock and his body became soil. He swirled with the fire and soon he flooded it with earth. The fire died down and he used the earth to fling the elementël aside. Water drove into him and he became weak, falling to the floor.

"Shado!" Ursula called. He turned to look as he became human again and saw that the elements were now approaching her and Nelnar. He could feel their power coursing through him.

He gritted his teeth and powered up. His muscles bulged and his eyes glowed as the earth responded. Roots broke from the grass and the trees reached down. The earth shook to break the elements as he used the trees to tear at them.

The water fell to the grass, the wind dissipated into the air and the fire broke into the branches. Shadowolf touched the ground and sand flew up into the air to kill the burning flames on the branches.

"That was quick," Ursula smiled.

"It's far from over," Shadowolf replied.

He could feel the earth elementël approach from behind. He turned and saw the earth goulem tense its fists. It called vines from the ground to grasp his wrists and as Shadowolf tried to break the restraints, the elementël planted his fist into Shadowolf's abdomen that sent him into the air.

The vines pulled him back to the forest. Once in range, the

earth elementël released the vine and hit him in the face. Shadowolf stopped sliding at Ursula's feet.

"Are you okay?" she gasped.

"This is a lot harder than the first two," he replied, trying to stand.

A centaur was charging at him, horns ready to strike into his chest. He jumped into the air and somersaulted over him, landing on the other side. Ursula and Nelnar ran away from its shoulders.

Before Shadowolf could turn around, the elementël kicked him in the back with a powerful blow that sent him flying towards a mountain. The velocity at which he flew tore at his face, but he suspected that the mountain was going to hurt more.

He held his palms out and threw massive rocks at the spot he was about to hit. He managed to gouge a few holes in it, but it wasn't enough. He slammed into the side of the wall and almost passed out.

Shadowolf rolled down the valley of the mountain, hitting brushes and twigs as he did. His hands were bleeding as he called branches from a nearby tree to catch him. The tree uprooted itself and ran towards him, grabbing him with a branch.

The element was flying towards him, soil and leaves bristling on the surface, his fist coiled to strike. Shadowolf called forth wolves from the earth and as the elementël landed he commanded them to attack.

The matter was resolved with efficiency. Earth raised his palm and the whining wolves were taken back to the ground.

"Shado!" Ursula shouted, but her following words were drowned when the element raised his palm to her and a vine yanked her to the ground. The grass grappled her to the floor and Nelnar was pulled down with her. They were sinking into the soil.

Shadowolf raised the earth and it struck the elementël in the chin. He ran to him and they exchanged rocky blows. The elementël hit Shadowolf in the chest, but he turned his body to sand and the fist passed through him.

He hit the elementël in the face, but the sand blew off and his face reformed. Shadowolf called a vine from the ground to restrain the elementël's arms, and with force he yanked the right arm off. The element laughed and regrew it, broke the vines and hit

Shadowolf into the air again.

Only the faces of his friends were visible in the grass. As Shadowolf soared into the air, he looked down and pointed his palms at them. He concentrated on the earth, and his abdomen tensed as the power increased beyond anything felt before. His arm glowed intensely and his skin hardened with emerald flowing in his veins as the grass withdrew and they were freed.

The element was upon him, but he was fed up now. With an enormous power increase, he raised the earth and a hillock raced to greet the elementël. Yet again, it simply brushed the earth aside with a wave of his hand. The hill crumbled down and landed on Ursula's ankle, trapping her.

The element plunged straight into him and they went hurtling towards the ground, which by now was a great distance. The earth element raised a rocky mountain, and it had a spire aimed for Shadowolf's back.

Shadowolf realised he would either fail and die, or pass and become the *Goudlem*. He twisted the element around in circles as the spire rose up, and Shadowolf forced his fist into the element's abdomen area.

With a great amount of energy, he forced stone and more soil into it. He changed its interior to rock, and when he had a grip on the handle, he yanked it out. The element broke in two in mid-air as Shadowolf dodged the spire, calling a tree from its side to catch him. He summoned vines and eagles from the mountain that gripped each limb of the element and pulled him apart.

The soil started to reform, but Shadowolf raised his palm and commanded the earth to subside. The soil sprinkled onto the mountain that had ceased its climbing.

"Well done," Ursula said as Shadowolf returned to the ground and freed her by commanding the crumbled soil to disintegrate into the earth.

She looked at his battered body. His shirt had been ripped off and his chest had several scrapes across it. A river of blood ran from the corner of his lips across his right cheek to his ear. Nelnar sniffed his bleeding calf.

Shadowolf groaned as he fell to his knees. As the grass under his hand receded and the trees wilted, he realised that the moment he had feared had finally arrived.

He watched as the skin on the back of his hand fell away into ash, and the red flesh was revealed. This too started to eat away as his blood coagulated within.

The sand and leaves turned black. Even the mountain was dying as the trees that he had summoned fell over. He coughed out sand which spewed from his bleeding lips. Two of his teeth fell out, and his hair withered.

He concentrated on his power. From within he willed the earth to regenerate his body. It took him a moment longer, to the point where the marrow ate through his bones, until he finally managed to command the earth.

The soil from the dying earth shifted onto him. From within him, his bones formed again and the blood wrestled free and became fluid. His heart pumped with renewed life.

His skin formed again over his flesh. Not ceasing with himself, he forced the element back into the landscape around him, and a new eco-system was formed. Bees and birds, mammals and reptiles moved in the jungle he had created.

He stood and kissed Ursula on the lips gently.

"How is that?" he asked, eyebrow raised.

"Real enough," she smiled, but he could tell from her eyes that it was not because she longed for him, but for another. "I could almost kiss the power from your lips. It reverberates against my skin. I might have to teach you how to lower your power level."

"You can do that?" he asked.

"Yes," she replied. "Masara was adept in it, although he isn't as powerful as you have become anymore."

"You and Masara were really close, weren't you?" Shadowolf asked. He could hear the beast approaching within the forest. Trees were breaking and animals were fleeing.

"We were lovers, you could say," she revealed. "As much as a unicorn and a man could be, I suppose. We set boundaries for our love, but ever since the Battle of T'Mar's Scourge, we've been apart really."

"We can discuss this later," he said, stroking her cheek. "It's not difficult to love a unicorn, Ursula, if that unicorn is you."

"Shedaaij is a lucky woman," she said.

"No," he laughed as he turned to face the beast. "I am a blessed man."

He rushed to meet the beast before it reached the others. When the long necked beast appeared, he used the trees and leaves to rise up into the air. When he was eye-level, a thought occurred to him and he rose higher.

When he was high enough and the beast reared on its hind legs, he faced both palms to the earth. Concentrating his mind on the area occupied by the beast and mumbling some runes he remembered from college, but modifying it for the occasion, he increased the gravitational pull of the landscape.

The beast's knees buckled as it was pulled to the earth. Shadowolf strained also, and so he minimized the area of the pull so that it only affected the beast. It fell crippled to the ground.

With one palm holding the increased gravity, he used the other palm to work on the beast. He focused on the skin and internal organs, his mind getting a headache. He closed his eyes and felt for the element and slowly extracted it.

The skin withdrew from the beast and the blood turned to sand as it coagulated. It choked on its own hardened phlegm, and its eyes bulged. He focused on its heart and main arteries, and slowly the pulsed ceased. The beast reared its head for one last cry, and then slumped down.

"Remind me," Shadowolf said as he returned to his friends, "never to use that ability again, no matter what the circumstances."

"It is quite disgusting, isn't it?" she replied, looking away. "How many more trials?"

"No more," he said. "The beast is last. Hold my hand."

Nelnar was high enough that he could rest his other hand on its head. Water, wind and fire walked through the forest towards them.

"So beautiful," Ursula said. "Where is earth?"

"You'll see," he told her.

Water fell to liquid onto the grass and became a river that swam past them. It created oceans and lakes to provide a source of life for the world.

Wind evaporated into the air and the breeze gave the grass and trees new life. The water was filled with air, and the sky formed clouds so that water could descend again to the earth.

Fire traveled through the breeze to the sky and further until it was no longer visible. Then, a vast sun appeared, providing warmth to the land. The fire journeyed through the rays and joined the other two elements in the wonder of life.

Finally, Shadowolf closed his eyes and Ursula, Nelnar and he crumbled into the earth. The grass expanded to every available landscape. Creatures of every kind were born onto the land, within the water and into the skies. Celenic Earth teemed with life...

He opened his eyes and saw the courtyard. Unlike the other times when he had had no strength to move after the trial, he found that he could stand.

Ursula was lying where she had stood before she had gone with to the trial, as did Nelnar. Shedaaij, Malanite, Lanel and Harmony stared at him from the entrance to the courtyard. All scars and wounds were gone.

"The *Goudlem*," Malanite whispered.

Shadowolf looked into his hand and saw that he still held the butterfly pendant within it. By doing so, he missed everyone's gaping faces that stared in fear at the ethereal wings that flared out into the courtyard behind him.

RETURN TO THE SCOURGE
CHAPTER NINE

The morning light filtered through the clouds. The clouds were not heavy with impending rain, but rather served as a beautiful adornment for the day ahead. The land of New Avalion still slept in the web of its slumber, unaware that a stranger was among them.

Even if they had wanted to see him, they could not. His spirit moved to the main Degron Castle, and in the wink of a thought he found the source of power.

How Eldor thought he could hide such a powerful object was beyond his understanding. The only other thing that had triggered his senses in the search for the Heart was Shadowolf. Somehow the man he had once ignored had once again become more powerful. He needed the Heart; he needed it now.

For he had finally obtained the ability to open the Heart and therefore gain access to the elvin forest. His army was ready, his *Wisoum* was growing restless with his dragons, and his patience was running out. Soon, Shadowolf would become impossible to stop; even for him.

More importantly, the *Wisoum* within Shadowolf was becoming stronger every time Shadowolf did. Sonersaat would be no match for him if it continued. There was a chance that Sonersaat would not fulfill the prophecy of the DragonRider, and that he would lose the forest. But that was a risk he was willing to take.

He found the room etched deep into the foundations of the castle. He moved through the magically-enforced door as if it were not there.

Eldor, you will have to do better, he thought to himself. The room he entered was vast and cubical in shape. There were no torches. Only a glass cabinet set into the far wall with a golden axe embedded in it.

He moved to the cabinet and smashed the glass. He moved his hand over the blade of the glowing axe.

A decoy. The axe exuded the power of the Heart, but was not the Heart itself. There was a minor distinct difference in its essence. In a fowl temper, he removed the axe from the wall and threw it across the room...

"Le'Mar has attempted the Heart," Eldor said to the gathering in the Jin Tai sanctuary.

"And?" Chenesia asked. Her father, Genewiu, Lucian, Simnab and Hargon waited in anticipation for the answer.

"He found the decoy, luckily," Eldor smiled. "It won't be long before he finds the Heart, though, and I think I should prepare.

"Do you still wish to travel to the forest?" he addressed Chenesia.

"I want to be there with you when he arrives," she replied stubbornly.

"What if he takes you again?" Maren-Ti asked.

"I will die before he gets the chance," she said to the discomfort of her father. "Besides, Hargon will be with me."

"I didn't do too well last time," the dwarf said grumpily.

"Which means you will try harder to make sure it doesn't happen again," Chenesia added.

She walked to Genewiu and mounted her back. Lucian assisted Hargon and placed him before her.

"Thank you again for repairing my wings, Eldor," Genewiu said. Simnab mounted his horse.

"It's my pleasure, Genewiu," he smiled, and raised his hand. A green portal opened up for them.

"Good luck finding uPendus," Chenesia said to Lucian before they rode through the portal to Eldor's Forest.

***

"What are they doing here?" Shadowolf asked. The Clan's members and Lord Treville were standing on Sky Tier facing the rising sun.

"We were left behind when the dark lord entered his portal," one of the four men said.

"I don't see how that is my problem," Shadowolf said. "I would kill you now if I were not tired of shedding blood."

"Please, elemental master," another man said, falling to his knees. "Our homes are on Celenic Earth, like yours."

"So why did you join *him*?" Shadowolf looked to Ursula briefly, and she nodded. She had to teach him how to lower his power level. Shedaaij looked between the two, wondering at the unspoken exchange.

"We are Crethans," the first man replied.

"And Crethines," one of the three women said. "We have no control of our actions."

"I cannot permit you to join us," Shadowolf concluded. "When we face a Creth-Demon, you will turn on us."

"But I can sense the earth and fire in you," another Crethine said.

"What has that to do with anything?" he asked.

"The Creth's primary source of power is earth and fire," Heula informed him. "A *Goudlem* and *KariemsaPh* can counter a Creth."

"If I knew how," Shadowolf replied.

"You can always practice," a Crethan said. "We feel our master Creth still roaming the mountain. If you kill him, we will serve you."

Shadowolf turned to Darcwulf, who shrugged in reply.

"Could always use the help," he said. "We're heading that way anyway."

"Ok," Shadowolf said to the Crethans. "But if I can't avoid it, I will kill anyone who becomes a problem."

"Agreed," they said in unison.

"So what are your names?" he said in a friendlier tone.

"The Crethines are Madisona, Trish and Dayna-wolf," the main Crethan answered.

"Dayna-wolf?" Shadowolf asked. "Of which southern tribe?"

"Former Iceland," she said.

"I am sorry to hear that," he dropped his head. "I was there when it fell."

"The Crethans are Teristé, Markors and Mino'Nelar," the

Crethan continued.

"Just call me Mino," Mino'Nelar informed them.

"And you?" Shadowolf asked the head Crethan.

"They call me Midnite," he answered. "But you might remember me as Morkom Larnesa."

"That can't be," Skywolf said suddenly. "My father Malkius received a report that your head was severed by one of the dragons."

"You mean this," he pulled down the collar of his shirt and revealed a crude scar. "Le'Mar's power is darker than you can imagine."

"You'd be surprised," Dren said, remembering the undead they had faced in Meëntis.

"After Le'Mar conquered the place they now call Morkom Falls," Midnite continued, "he resurrected me using the power of the dragon's heart. He then placed me under the enslavement of a Creth."

"That would explain where he gets the humans to make the hurorcs," Shadowolf said.

"You're saying that we could be killing our own friends in these battles?" Darcwulf said incredulously.

"How much of the dark lord's secrets do you hold?" he asked Midnite.

"Only what we heard. But that might be enough to assist you."

"We'll deal with that later, then," Shadowolf said, and marched off to breakfast.

"Welcome to the Shadow Clan," Sorceress said, the butterfly pendant gleaming on her blue chest.

"I've counted about thirty in the Clan," Shedaaij told Shadowolf over the bread, jam and cheese they were sharing.

"We've really grown," he smiled.

"It's nothing compared to Le'Mar's army though," Dren said next to him.

"We haven't lost anyone yet," he replied. He sighed with relief.

"I hear that the *Wisoum* has grown inside you?" Dren asked.

"Ursula says she can sense someone else with us that also has it growing inside, but it is minute. Every time she catches a glimpse of it, it disappears."

"She really is pretty in her human form," Shedaaij said, looking at Ursula.

"She is, isn't she?" Shadowolf replied, and then realised he'd fallen for her trap and countered quickly. "But you are the love of my life, and none can compare."

"What are our plans for today?" the gargoyle asked.

Shadowolf pondered the reply. He had the choice of heading for New Avalion where the Heart of Tigers was being kept or for Eldor's Forest where he suspected the final battle with Le'Mar would be.

Yet, he could not tell them of the choice, due to the confidence Ursula had placed in him in the mists of the elemental courtyard.

"I want to leave today," Shadowolf said. "I have had enough 'rest' as I can handle. We can head back through the mountain to find that hidden Creth, and then to the Scourge."

"We aren't such a small band and we'll be easier to spot," Dren warned.

"I know, but that will have to be our fate for now," he replied. "And then, we can head for Carmel en-route to this Fairiwell that Ursula told us about."

"It feels like you've hardly been here," Lanel said to Shadowolf among the gathered Clan as the sun reached its noon apex. "But somehow you managed to still leave a mark."

"And just yesterday we were merely kids in school," Shadowolf joked, embracing him in farewell.

"Good luck with the prophecy," Harmony said, placing a kiss on his cheek.

"Save the world like you always do," Mourna added as he hugged her.

"And save some for us," Theroy said, shaking his hand.

"Take care of yourselves," he replied.

The thirty-one members of the Shadow Clan entered the tunnel leading back into Dwarf Mountains, and left Horlorn's Gate behind.

Toward night's end they found the Creth-Demon. His wolf-head atop a man-body riddled with fire was the give-away. He held his emerald staff as he stood from his quiet contemplation.

Behind him the Crethans growled.

"I think it best to deal with them first," Ursula warned.

The men and women were curled on the floor. The Creth-master's staff gleamed as they transformed into their deformed wolf-state.

"Stand back," Shadowolf warned. As they cleared the area, Shadowolf stared at the ground beneath them. Steel cages rose from the earth and surrounded the rising beasts. They yapped and bit at the bars, blood curling around the edges of their lips in a rabid fever.

"If they escape," he instructed Sorceress and Darcwulf, "kill them."

He walked towards the Creth. The master raised his staff and fire flew in a ball from the top. Shadowolf allowed the fire to enter his body.

Trying again, the Creth threw rocks from the staff and Shadowolf raised his palm and simply cast them aside. Without warning, the Creth planted his staff in the ground and a sharp light broke forth.

It formed a wide arc of fire and earth that exploded towards him. He dug his feet into the ground and braced his arms, catching the power in his hands. His muscles burst through the shirt as he pushed against the wall of fire and rock.

Helixes of light issued between his pushing palms and the emerald staff. Both he and the master strained against each other, moving to and fro. The earth beneath his feet became a small trench as he pushed harder.

He manipulated the force of elements and grappled the Creth around his neck. He tossed the creature aside and then absorbed the power that was about to explode. The light slowly suffused into his soul and died down.

Before the beast could rise, he dropped the cage holding the Crethans. He shook his head to Sorceress and Darcwulf, and then controlled the minds of the seven Crethans. They stopped and watched as Shadowolf's forehead perspired with intensity.

The bond between them and the master snapped, and the wolves shook their heads to clear the confusion. When they realised they had been freed and their will had returned, they charged to the prostrate Creth-Demon.

He raised his elemental staff, but Shadowolf raised his palm and the staff turned to fire and ash with green emerald shards lying in between.

Once the master had been killed, Shadowolf called his wolves and listened to their spirits. He held touched their heads and transformed them to their human forms.

"We are yours," Midnite said.

"Good," Shadowolf said sternly. "I accept your service if only to prevent another master from using you against us."

"That is why we serve you willingly," Dayna-wolf said.

"When I find a cure or Le'Mar is killed," Shadowolf assured them, "I promise that your life will be yours again."

The sunshine of the third day's travel caught them as they exited the mountains. Dark River stood between them and the main land to the south, but the current was gentle.

"How will we get across?" Tinonte asked.

"I am more concerned with the travel to Carmel than that," Shadowolf replied. He knew the land was dry and barren. He was not looking forward to it. As a matter of fact, the water looked more pleasant.

He looked at the valley around him and found a central point on the beach. He called trees to grow from the sand that rose high into the air. The trees emerged from the ground, using their roots as legs and approached the river.

"Are you doing that?" Shedaaij asked, terrified.

He couldn't respond, as he was wrapped in his own power. The *Wisoum* wings emerged from his back and Shedaaij walked away from him.

The trees split into different sections and formed on the quiet waters. Rock broke into sediments and he found quartz and other minerals deep within the crust that he brought forth and added to the rock to form hard nails.

The nails were driven into the wood. The extra wood lying on the beach thinned out to form a flexible material, which he manipulated with his power to form sails. Within ten minutes, he calmed his spirit and the ship drifted on the waters.

He approached it and raised his palm to the bow. With fire, he etched the name 'The Windfarer'.

"Why 'The Windfarer'?" Shedaaij asked as the boarding plank dropped to the beach.

"Because that was the name of the ship that carried my family the night I was born," he replied. Shedaaij acknowledged the answer and boarded the new ship.

Darcwulf placed his hand on Shadowolf's shoulder and stared with hardness into his eyes.

"I mean this in a kind way," he said to his brother. "I feel like I don't know you anymore."

Shadowolf thought on this and his heart saddened. He placed his arm on Darcwulf's opposite shoulder.

"I will try and remedy that on the way to Carmel," he said with a soft smile.

"I think there are some things that are beyond remedy," Darcwulf said, "but we can try."

He left Shadowolf's side and boarded the Windfarer...

PART THREE

ELDOR'S FOREST

RUMOURS OF THE DRAGONRIDER
CHAPTER ONE

The wind blew softly into the sails of the Windfarer, managed by Shadowolf as he stood on its bow. He enjoyed the soft ripples of the water splashing against the hull. It calmed his taut nerves, and soothed his pulsing headache.

The River of Light carried them from the Scourge towards the shores of Carmel. The stars glittered down upon him, but Sothos was new and could not be seen.

The power he had gained thronged within him. He had yet to learn to soften its effect, but he did not wish to bother Ursula with that at the moment. He was enjoying the calming effect that the wide river had on his soul.

A dark border of trees rose on the west embankment of the river, and it only increased Shadowolf's joy. He could hear the birds twittering softly, his ears attuned to nature more than ever before. The trees murmured softly in their sleep-state, simply shifting in the breeze that carried the Windfarer south.

Shadowolf looked down at his open hands. So much had changed since he first encountered the Mer-Kingdom and the aVampyere. It felt like it should all have been a dream, or a story woven by a mad man. He felt sure that, if he ever had the will to sit down and write books for his grandchildren to read, that he could never have imagined to write about a life as complicated as his.

Yet, he could imagine sitting down by the fireplace and telling them about his adventures. He would thrill them about tales of the centaurs, and his two years in the land of the dragons. Imagine their faces when he told them about Ursula and the forest of the elves; about the four-armed Saneth that he and Darcwulf barely escaped.

Where would he be when he ever told those tales? Would he be comfortably sitting before the fireplace? Or would he be sitting in a prison of Le'Mar? Or would he never get the opportunity to tell anyone about the Shadow Clan's journeys?

He laughed when he thought of the Clan. He also vaguely wondered if it could still be referred to as a Clan, since it had grown so large. Maybe "The Shadow Entourage" would be more suitable; or "The Shadow Fanatics."

Nelnar walked up to him and lay at his feet, its stomach filled with food. It could sense that its master was preoccupied with thought and so left him alone. But something changed in the air and it raised its head to sniff at it.

Shadowolf also picked it up and recognized it. He didn't move as the feet landed softly behind him and the cape stirred with the breeze. He simply smiled and greeted the aVampeyer.

"You've changed," Nellice responded to his welcome.

"A lot of things have happened since Meëntis," Shadowolf replied.

The aVampeyer moved beside him and joined him in staring down the unlit river. His face was pale as usual and the nails on his fingers stretched over the wood of the railing. His long hair had no life to it and was stuck on either side of his head. When he spoke, his sharp, retracted canines peeked out from behind his lips.

"What have you been up to lately?" Shadowolf asked him.

"Hunting for food, mostly," Nellice replied. "Don't worry; I'm on a 'no-human' diet."

"That's good to know," he laughed.

"Orc doesn't taste too good though," Nellice added. "Really leaves a bad taste to the mouth."

"So what made you betray Le'Mar, by the way?" he turned to face Nellice.

"It wasn't really betrayal," he replied. "I just didn't want to work for him anymore. I don't like having a master or lord. I am my own servant."

"Well, I am glad we are friends."

"Oh? I thought it more a sense of us not being enemies."

Shadowolf laughed again. Here was at least one aVampeyer that he could enjoy the company of.

"I must tell you, though, that I am the last aVampeyer on Celenic Earth," Nellice said softly.

"Oh," Shadowolf replied, not sure if this was good or bad. "A few days ago I faced a demon-queen that was an old aVampeyeric acquaintance of mine."

"I think you're referring to Blosom," he said, and Shadowolf nodded. "She's not really aVampeyeric. We don't naturally swim and hold tridents."

"I understand what you are saying though."

"Your group has grown quite large," Nellice said after a moment of silence.

"We managed to get some Crethans, too," Shadowolf said.

"Crethans?"

"These guys that change..."

"No, I know what they are," Nellice interrupted. "How did you manage to get those to join you?"

"Long story, but I basically killed their master and inherited them."

"A hero that takes from the dark lord and uses it against him." Nellice perked his lips. "I like it."

Shadowolf just smiled again. He calmed the wind, deciding that the ship could take a break until morning. He walked to the port side and dropped a heavy rock attached to a chain. It anchored the boat and, once Shadowolf was satisfied that they had stopped, returned to Nellice.

"How is Mandy?" Nellice asked as they walked to the cabin. The black mare raised her head to find the person uttering her name. She was on the starboard stern with the other mounts and the two centaurs.

"Ever loyal, like the others," Shadowolf sighed. "Is that why you appeared? To join the Clan?"

"No, as much as that would honor me," Nellice said. "I heard in Lasglow that there have been sightings of dragons riding to the east. I was hoping for some more news."

Shadowolf broke into a litany of the battle at Horlorn's Gate and Sonersaat's withdrawal.

"Very interesting," Nellice frowned. "So I guess he plans to still take Eldor's Forest."

"So it seems," Shadowolf replied, glad he was not the only one that thought so. "I'll have to question the Crethans about that."

"Shado, I must warn you," Nellice said suddenly. "Sometimes another master, if stronger, can change the wolves' allegiance."

"I was not aware of that," he acknowledged, "but the thought crossed my mind. I just thought they could also assist with information on Le'Mar's army."

"Don't bother. I was on the eastern front before I reached Lasglow. Le'Mar has had many portals opening in his camps, and there are creatures even I have never seen before."

"Great," Shadowolf said.

"My advice; get rid of the Crethans before they turn on you."

"I once thought that of you, Nellice," Shadowolf said. "I will keep them until they become problematic."

"Very well," Nellice smiled. "Good luck, Shado. We will meet again. Maybe not in the forest, as I cannot enter there; but one day."

"One day," Shadowolf agreed as Nellice became part of the night.

Shadowolf left Shedaaij's side early the next morning to join Ursula on the deck. Dren, Millon and Kentaur raised the rocky anchor and the sails caught the wind that was already blowing.

"Are you ready to attempt the depowerment?" Ursula asked. Her amber hair blew forward over her cheeks. Her eyes were gentle and her lips a softer pink than when she had first transformed. Her deep blue dress fell to her ankles, and a neat gap at the top between the straps displayed the smooth skin below her neck.

"I think so," he replied.

Shadowolf shivered and his heart jumped when Ursula slipped out of her dress. She had a slender figure with beautiful long legs. He felt shy looking at her, and when he looked down he noticed how cute her toes looked.

"Let's go," she jumped overboard, covered only in a two-piece blue bikini. He removed his shirt and jumped over into the river with only his long joggens.

The Windfarer moved past them and they waited until the water calmed from the ship's movement. Ursula moved until she found a spot where the wind did not disturb the water's surface much.

Ursula stretched her hand under the water towards Shadowolf. From her fingertips little strobes of light swam into the water. The largest of them was the size of the nail on Shadowolf's little finger.

"What are they?" Shadowolf asked as two thirds of the lights surrounded Shadowolf's chest and hips.

"They are element-warders, also known in the elvin tongue as Sinokwe," Ursula said sweetly. Shadowolf was trying not to enjoy her smile so much. It wasn't that he felt more for her than Shedaaij. It was just that her smile had a way of penetrating the heart.

"What do they do?" he asked.

"They find any source of power relating to the elements," Ursula advised. "The stronger the power, the more that collect around the source. Also, their lights change in respect to the elements. Look."

He followed her hands, if only to have a longer look at the soft knuckles and tender fingers, but his sight changed to the warders. Many of them went white, another lot turned red, others turned green and only three turned a deep blue.

"I guess the blue is for Water," he said. Ursula nodded. "I must still undergo the *Merlandsi* trial."

He studied them further and wondered. "What colour would the spirit be?"

"Power of the soul is the total of all the Sinokwe that gather," Ursula replied. "For that is the power required to harness the elements."

"So what do you want me to do?" He was sure she was getting annoyed with his ignorance, but she replied calmly again, unperturbed.

"Summon the wind," she said.

He called on the wind like he always did and, as the wind picked up and the sails of the Windfarer stretched further, he noticed that a few of the loose warders swimming near Ursula turned and raced to his stomach. They became white and glowed brightly.

"I see," he finally said, entranced by the little blobs of light.

"You need to lower your power to the level where you have as little as possible visible to them."

"I must lose my power?" he asked, confused.

"No, you can't do that unless someone takes it from you," she said.

"Is that possible?" he asked, and she stared quizzically at him. Her eyes said: Is that a rhetorical question?

"All that happens," she continued, "is that, to the outsider, your level has decreased, when all you've done is store it where no one can see it."

She moved closer and touched his abdomen just beneath his chest with her fingers. He shivered.

"Getting cold?" she asked.

"Something like that," he replied. "So it goes into my diaphragm?"

"No, your soul," she said. "It is the core of your power, which spreads out to your spirit and aura. Once stored, the only way someone would be able to see your power is through your eyes."

She proceeded to explain how he should decrease his level by storing the power.

"Where's Shado?" Shedaaij asked Darcwulf.

Darcwulf looked up from his breakfast, Fransiska still eating beside him.

"I don't know," he replied. "I thought he was still asleep."

Shedaaij moved away from them and left the cabin. When she reached the deck, she looked around for him. She moved over to Rennick at the port railing.

"Have you seen Shado?" she asked again.

"No, not really," he replied, but she could tell he was hiding something.

"What's going on?" she asked earnestly.

"Nothing," he said and moved to the bow.

Shedaaij ignored him and moved to the stern of the ship to find Millon and Kentaur. The centaurs were staring aft of the ship.

She held her fingers to her lips as she gasped softly. They had drifted a distance from the two in the river, but she could clearly see who they were. And that Ursula was scantily dressed.

A hand touched her shoulder and she whirled around.

"She is teaching him how to lower his power level," Malanite answered, and then coughed. "You have nothing to fear from her, as she does not care for him like you do."

"I still don't trust her," she replied haughtily.

"Do you trust him?" Malanite asked, but she remained silent. "Surely he would not betray you? You were the first he committed to."

"But I've seen the way he looks at her," Shedaaij said, her tone changing a pitch. "How could he not fall for her?"

"Because he loves you," Malanite assured her, turning his face to cough again. "If his love could be measured, it would be greater than his elemental abilities."

"What if she tries to seduce him?" she asked.

"I assure you that she would not," Malanite replied. "Even if she were capable of such traits, her heart belongs to another that cannot be replaced."

Malanite coughed into his hand, and then he cleared his throat.

"Are you ok?" she asked him, but then her face of concern turned to doubt. "Don't think that I don't suspect you. I've noticed that your tone of voice has changed. You're not the old man we met in Meëntis. You seem more like..."

Malanite burst out in horrendous coughs. Blood spewed onto his beard from his lips and he doubled over.

"Oh, no!" she exclaimed. "Kentaur, help me!"

"Get Sorceress," Malanite whispered, his voice hoarse. "She can help."

"Come old man," Kentaur picked him up in his arms.

"Just remember," Malanite said to Shedaaij as he was carried off, "that you are not the only one that is permitted secrets."

Shadowolf could feel the core of his power. It was the centre of his energy, and from it the power of the elements streamed into his spirit and through his veins and arteries.

"Can you see it?" Ursula asked.

In the reflection of the water he made out a faint line surrounding his body.

"I think so," he replied.

"That is your aura, and at the same time that the warders swim away from you, your aura should diminish. The first thing Le'Mar will search for is your aura, as it is an indication of your power level. Also, there are different colours for different states of your power."

"So much information," he said. "I think I have it though."

"If you pull more power to your eyes, you can see my aura," she said. He raised his face slowly and with his spirit, the medium of his power, he transferred energy to his eyes. He could see the faint line of the aura, but not completely.

"Seeing the aura is essential when in battle with an elementalist," she continued as he stared at her. "You can detect where the enemy is transferring his power to, and be prepared to counter-attack."

The warders had not diminished though, because he was still learning how to decrease his level. By transferring his energy from body part to body part, they had simply shifted in colours.

"Shado!" a scream curled down the river to reach their ears. "Ma..nite is si...!"

"I didn't realise the ship had drifted that far already," he said, turning to look at Shedaaij's terrified face.

"I think we better head back," Ursula said. "Something is wrong."

She called the warders back to her fingers and then started swimming back to the ship.

"Wait, it will take too long," he said to her. "Let me teleport us."

"One more lesson," she said. "It will save you the energy and you won't be so tired doing it.

"The same way that you visualise where you are going to in your mind when you teleport, project that image through your hand above the water."

"I don't think we have time for this," Shadowolf said as he saw Kentaur and Darcwulf join Shedaaij on the stern.

"Ok, teleport us," she agreed.

He grabbed her hand beneath the water and closed his eyes. His spirit whispered into Shedaaij's ear, and as she turned they appeared on the deck.

"What's wrong?" he asked, and Shedaaij looked down at their locked hands. Shadowolf let go of Ursula.

"Malanite got sick," Kentaur informed them. Shedaaij was still staring into Shadowolf's eyes, her forehead frowning and a tear starting to form.

"Where is he?" Ursula said.

"With Sorceress in his room," Darcwulf said, looking at Shadowolf and Shedaaij. "He seems calm enough now, though."

Ursula rushed off, and Darcwulf and Kentaur left the two alone. Shedaaij was still silent and turned to lean over the stern rail.

"It's really not what you think, my love," Shadowolf said, feeling too uncomfortable to hold her.

"You were holding her hand," she snickered.

He remained quiet and stared at the spot in the river he and Ursula had been standing moments before. It had been an innocent act, yet suddenly everything he had done since he had awoken felt wrong.

"Do you remember when Sonersaat first attacked us?" he asked. "Do you remember I had to touch the dragon to teleport it?"

She wiped her eyes and nodded her head.

"Ursula was trying to teach me another way to do it, but that was the only way we could get back in time."

She rushed into his arms and held him tight, digging her head into his chest.

"I am sorry that I am so insecure," she said. "I really don't know what has become of me."

"I understand," he said, and kissed her head. "You need to realise that when I say I love you, I really mean just that."

She nodded and they remained there for a while longer staring out onto the river.

By the evening, Malanite was well enough to walk around. Shedaaij apologised for her behaviour, sure that she had caused the outbreak of coughs. However, he joked and assured her that it was due to an illness called age.

With Shedaaij's knowledge and apparent permission, Shadowolf and Ursula walked to the bow of the ship to continue the training.

"Are we going to jump in again?" Shadowolf asked.

"No, there's no need," Ursula replied, concern for Malanite evident in her expression. "I just wanted a refreshing swim this morning."

She raised her hand and the Sinokwe flew from the tips to his body. He found his core centre easier than before, and transferred the energy to his eyes. Ursula's green aura radiated around her skin, and when she released more warders the aura was denser around her fingers. Suddenly the aura deepened around her eyes.

"When you can truly see the complete aura," she told him, "I should appear to be webbed in it like a cocoon."

"How did you know I was looking for your aura?" he asked.

"I can also transfer my power." She smiled, but it was a sad gesture.

"So when your eyes are covered by the aura, it means you are searching my aura?"

"Not always, but if you see Le'Mar do that, then you should expect that he is doing so."

He looked down and saw the warders attached to his body.

"Your spirit is where most of your active elemental particles lie," she said. "If you can transfer them to your core, then to the outsider it will seem as if you have very little power.

"But be careful. It can become very dangerous if you don't manage it properly. A lot of heat will be produced from the storage, and I don't recommend doing it for long periods until you have mastered it and your spirit has become used to the change.

"Once we have got that part right, I will tell you how to release the energy only when required without killing everyone around you."

"What do you mean by 'killing'?" he asked in exasperation.

"If you release it too quickly or unwillingly, it can explode and hit everyone in your proximity."

Shadowolf widened his eyes as he realised how dangerous this training was. He calmed down and listened for his heartbeat. He mentally traveled down his blood into his spirit, until he found his centre with his mind.

Slowly he pulled the surrounding energy, starting with the retraction of his aura into his spirit. It was more difficult than the trials, as it required precision. Sweat flowed from his forehead while he concentrated. His headache returned.

He opened his eyes and looked down. His aura was faint, but still there. Two or three Sinokwe had left his side and floated towards Ursula, but the bulk remained with him.

"That's about as much as I can manage today," he told her.

"When you are successful, your aura will be gone and the warders will no longer stick to you. But your power will remain within you."

"What about the teleportation part?" he asked eagerly.

"I won't go into that now," she said. "Maybe when we reach Carmel."

He nodded and they went back to the others.

They reached Carmel in the mid-afternoon of the following day. The small port was filled with people and fishermen tackling their hard day's work.

Shadowolf used the wind to push them onto a beach north of the port. They collected their things and made their way down the boarding plank. When all thirty-one members were on the beach, he bid farewell to the Windfarer.

The ship's timber fell apart and after five minutes lay drifting on the water. He raised his palm and the timber burst into flames and turned to ash that floated to the bed of the river.

"Such a pity," Darcwulf said once Shadowolf joined him.

"Would be more a pity if I left her there to be abused by someone else," he said and mounted Mandy. A glint of metal shone into his eye. "Oh, I forgot you had that sword."

"Yeah, I kept it with my clothes," Darcwulf readjusted the serpent sword on his hip. "But seeing as we are the royal procession today…"

They rode to the city of Carmel. The haze of heat drifted over it like a veil over a bunch of flowers. The walls were grey with a hint that it had once been white. It was the same size as Avalion had been before New Avalion had been formed.

The Carmelite people stared at the strangers, some with awe etched on their faces, others with boredom. New-comers would not have labeled them as friendly, but Shadowolf remembered times that had been better.

If they survived the next two years, they would again celebrate the Masaran Phenomenon within this city. They would have food and wine, and the tables would be filled with gifts for families and friends.

Most of the stares were focused on Mandy. Her mane was still tattered and swayed like a ghost in the breeze. Her deep eyes sank into her black head and red pupils glared from within. Her coat was dark and looked as if she were constantly wet. Her tail was beautifully long, but only added to her eerie atmosphere.

In more ways than one, she looked like she had been spawned by the dark lord from the deepest pits of his castle. And then there was the reptilian form of Trimistus and the gargoyle that traveled under the sun.

It was not easy for him to ride through the wave of special attention paid to the Clan. He was just thankful that Shedaaij was wearing pants and top over her coral armour.

He was trying to find the tavern that Lucian had mentioned to him before. His directions through Carmel had been somewhat dulled since his disappearance from Celenic Earth. When he realised that he was totally lost, he turned to another expert in taverns.

"Darcwulf, where is the Blue Periwinkle?"

"This way," he replied and took the lead.

It was close to the centre of Carmel. Where roads and courtyards emerged, Darcwulf took a path north and then north-east until the tavern with the blue sign was before them.

The stablemen took their mounts by the reins and led them away. Shadowolf could see passed the fence that they had ample space in their backyard for over a hundred horses.

"Shado," Millon addressed him, "Kentaur and I are going to have a look around the city."

"Can you manage with all these glares?" Dren asked.

"Working for Kraakis," Kentaur replied, "we did not have much time to visit civilisations."

"And this expedition with the Clan has afforded us little opportunity for that too," Millon added.

"Enjoy it," Shadowolf smiled, and waved as they left. "As a matter of fact, don't any of you feel obliged to stay by my side. You're as free as them to travel through the city."

"We intend to," Skywolf said, "but I want to make sure you get us decent rooms."

They entered the tavern as a lady approached them.

"I am Telgar," the lady said, eyeing the group. "Will you be seeking quarters in the tavern?"

"Yes," Shadowolf replied. "We don't have much to trade with unfortunately, but…"

"Don't worry about payment, laddy," Malanite stepped forward, and shook a beige, leather bag. "I have some gems and gold here that will suffice."

"I only have five rooms available, though," Telgar said.

"We'll pay per head, instead of per room," Malanite offered. "And I am sure we can make a plan with the rooms."

"Whose name shall I book it in?" she asked the old man.

"Place it under Shadowolf," Malanite said.

"Oh," she replied, confused. "I expected you to be a bit…if I may say, younger."

"I am Shado," Shadowolf smiled.

"Lucian told me a lot about you," she said. "Come, let me show you the rooms and then I'll prepare some lunch while you unpack."

Lunch turned to supper as they took a while to get settled and arrive back at the dining rooms. The furnaces were lit and the entertainers and musicians arrived. It became a jolly affair and Shadowolf felt light-hearted again. When Millon and Kentaur returned, Telgar invited them inside and they thoroughly accepted.

Shadowolf was conversing softly with his friends when a nearby table caught his attention. He could not make it out, but the word "DragonRider" struck a nerve, and he turned to the table to listen better.

"He said he saw the dragons flying low over the valley," a woman said.

"Do you think the time has come, Elsmidya?" a man asked.

"Heaven knows, Toller," she replied. "We don't know if that old fool was making those things up."

Just then, Telgar walked passed him and Shadowolf grabbed her wrist.

"Did something happen here concerning the DragonRider?"

"While Lucian was here, a drunken guy spoke the *Enodhim* and *Wisoum* prophecies and now Carmel is in a buzz concerning the DragonRider."

"Thanks Telgar," he said, and let her continue her duties.

"Let's just hope your wings don't flare out again," Shedaaij said. "Otherwise you will be the talk of the town."

"I don't need any publicity at the moment," Shadowolf agreed.

"I heard Gingos was captured by the DragonRider last week." New conversation reached his ears from an adjacent table.

"What did he want?" a woman asked in alarm.

"He was trying to determine the location of some kind of portal," the man replied.

"Why did he ask Gingos?" the woman asked.

"I have no idea," the man laughed. "The fool probably spoke too much to the wrong person, and it reached Sonersaat's ears."

"Wow," she said. "I wonder where this portal is."

"I do too," he agreed. "Hold on, here he comes."

A shaggy man of about thirty years of age entered the tavern and walked over to the two.

"Stella, Manory," Gingos greeted them.

"Sit down," Stella offered politely, but her eyes were filled with curiousity. "I heard about your contact with the DragonRider."

Shadowolf realised that the Clan had fallen silent and were eavesdropping with him. Malanite clung to his staff and his eyes didn't blink as he caught every word.

"It was scary," he said, intensifying every word in dramatic effect and adding a sigh at the end. "When he is flying in the air with the dragons, he seems pathetic. Up close though, your opinion changes quickly."

"What is this portal all about?" the woman continued to pursue.

"He wants to find a way to Eldor's Forest," Gingos replied. "I happen to know one that is situated in Lasglow, in the ruins of Barnot Villa."

Malanite and Ursula stared at one another in confusion.

"Lasglow?" Manory asked, scratching his head. "That close to Carmel?"

"Yip," he replied. "But I told him to beware. That way is guarded by Eldor's power. Strange creatures live down there."

"What do you…"

"There is something wrong with that story," Malanite said, interrupting their eavesdropping. "That is not where the portal is located."

The Clan fell silent as their food arrived and they began dining. But the matter they had overheard bugged Shadowolf.

"Do you think we should investigate the portal he mentioned?" he asked. "We must pass through Lasglow anyway."

"Yes, indeed," Malanite agreed. "Eldor did not create an entrance in Lasglow, and no other path but the one we know leads to the Fairiwell."

"So could Le'Mar have created it?" Sorceress asked.

"No," Malanite replied firmly. "Then Sonersaat would not have asked for its location."

"Masara?" Shadowolf tried.

"Definitely not," Ursula said. "I have no knowledge of him ever creating another portal."

"Then we have no choice but to investigate and warn Eldor if what he says is true," Shadowolf concluded.

They continued their meals. Gingos was satisfied with the result and smiled maliciously as he left the tavern. He marched across town to his humble hut, making his way to his quiet room.

He touched a painting of a mansion on a hill, and the portrait changed in colour as Sonersaat's face appeared.

"Did you succeed?" the DragonRider asked.

"Yes, my lord," Gingos replied. "The rumours of the Clan were true. He is indeed in Carmel."

"Did you do as I asked?" he asked again.

"I have given them the location of the false portal," he replied happily. "From what I have heard, they will indeed be heading for Lasglow."

"Very good," Sonersaat said.

"Did you manage to find the true portal?" Gringos asked, rubbing his hands together in excitement.

"Yes, your directions were precise," Sonersaat replied. "We will be invading very soon. What will you do if the Baron discovers your treachery and send the Vale's army after you?"

"I will deny all knowledge," he said stubbornly. "No one will know, anyway."

"Except the Clan," Sonersaat raised an eyebrow. "I cannot allow anyone to learn of our plans."

"But you will take care of them," he said, and then shifted his stance. "Have I earned my reward?"

Sonersaat nodded. Three orcs stepped out of the shadows and silently drove their blades through his back.

"Every bit of it," Sonersaat smiled, and the image of the lonely mansion returned.

THE FAKE PORTAL
CHAPTER TWO

The Clan rose before daybreak to start their journey to Lasglow. Shadowolf was getting anxious and frustrated with the traveling, but he knew that as incircumstantial as the little problems seemed, it might be necessary in preventing Le'Mar from entering the elvin forest.

Mandy was also jittery beneath him, fed-up with the long days and short nights. Yet, she preferred the glaring sun to the pouring rain; the favonian breeze to the barren humidity.

He used the time between cities to spend moments with the members of the Clan. There was comfort in the fact that they found things to laugh at and that there were no long-lasting tension between any of them.

Fransiska had her sirenic powers under control, and found that she could call up her powers to seduce at will. Darcwulf constantly joked that he wondered if he really loved her or if he was under her seduction, much to her chagrin.

Shadowolf thought on his father. It was a privilege that Nighthale had been given in keeping the Heart of Tigers, but it was also an unwanted danger. He did not know to what lengths Le'Mar would go to find the gem, but he knew the dark lord would not wage war against New Avalion if he could avoid it. He needed his armies for Eldor's Forest; at least, Shadowolf hoped he did.

They saw Lasglow appear south of them, just above Little River. It would take another hour's ride before they reached the gates, but the sight was a relief to their hot bodies and travel-weary minds.

When they entered the city Malanite once again paid for their board, this time at the Cherry Tom inn. The third-floor room had several three-bunks beds in it, and was sufficient for the entire Clan to stay in. The red curtains shone brightly against the blue walls, and the chimes sang beautiful against the wonderful breeze.

"Hard to believe anything evil occurs in this city," Sorceress muttered, her butterfly pendant shining on her light blue chest.

Shadowolf had to agree with her. There was serenity in Lasglow that he had somehow expected he would find in Carmel. But, just like everything he had discovered since his return, things had changed.

"Will we be searching for the ruins soon?" Shedaaij asked, also affected by the calm.

"I think Shadowolf and I should practice his leveling first," Ursula suggested, and Shedaaij simply nodded her head.

They found a quiet spot in a field central to Lasglow. Sitting down on a patch of grass, Shadowolf closed his eyes and calmed his spirit. He found the centre of his power while Ursula emitted the Sinokwe. As usual, they changed their colour once they found the elements within him and clung to his body.

After half an hour only three had left him to drift over to Ursula. His forehead was wet from the effort, but he felt that he couldn't manage any further.

"Controlling your power is harder than using it," he acknowledged.

"Don't worry," she replied. "Once you have the ability, it will be as easy as walking."

She started to walk away but Shadowolf forestalled her.

"I know who Malanite really is," he said carefully. "And I understand why you care for him so much, Ursula. Do you think it wise for him to be here?"

"That is for him to decide," Ursula replied. "He is concerned about a few things."

"Like the Fairiwell?" he asked.

"Yes, amongst other things."

"And that is why he, or you for that fact, haven't taken us directly to the forest," he said.

"I am afraid so," she replied. "We have the time to have a look, and I believe it to be in the interest of the forest."

"Why doesn't Eldor just send his own elves?" Shadowolf asked.

"If Eldor really knew what he was up to, do you think he would permit him to be here with us?" she asked.

"No, I guess not," he answered. Leaving the other questions and doubts in the silence of his mind, he followed her back to the inn.

They left the inn later in the afternoon, leaving the horses behind in the stables and their spare provisions in the room. Shedaaij had opted to wear her coral outfit with her two daggers hanging at her sides, but the people they passed in the busy streets were so preoccupied that not even the Merlani drew any unwanted attention.

They stopped at an armoury shop to buy an extra staff. Malanite paid for it and handed it to Shadowolf.

"It's for the training," Ursula advised him. "I need you to practice transferring your power to the staff like Darcwulf does. It will assist you in lowering your internal power levels."

"I have Ruben-Willow," he replied.

"That sword is unique," she said, "and has bonded well with you. I need you to use a weapon that is separate from you, that will not assist you in your training."

"Ruben-Willow has already fused with the dagger you wear on your other hip," Malanite added. "Its essence possesses each blade."

"How is that possible?" Shadowolf asked. "Does the sword have a soul too?"

"No," Malanite smiled. "It is your growing power that gives it that ability. Unwillingly, you have created the essence of Ruben-Willow by your fondness for it, and now you have split it across the blades.

"At some time, Ursula, you will have to teach Shadowolf the principles of what he has accomplished and what he can still accomplish. You will also have to teach him the things he needs to avoid."

"So that I do not become a danger to myself and the Clan," Shadowolf said, and received a nod from the old man.

The Clan reached the ruins of Barnot Villa in the south of Lasglow. The stones stood as a monument to time. The cracks and rubble lay around the pillars and foundations to the formers homes and library. Where once was a fabulous garden, there now stood an arid landscape no longer irrigated or inhabited. The nets and supports were forlornly lying over the once raked and farmed ground.

No one wanted to change the memory of the Villa. The wind still whispered the happiness of the town before the battle that had changed Lasglow's culture and life. But the battle had passed, and although the tale was as stale as forgotten bread, everyone still remembered the Villa and stayed outside its border. It was in loving memory to those that had defended Lasglow with their lives.

The wind now stirred the dust as Shadowolf walked onto the sands of the village. His green pants collected the dust and his blue top was damp with his sweat. Ruben-Willow and the dagger dangled on his sides, and in his right hand he held on to the staff.

"Looks like this used to be a vineyard," Darcwulf said, stepping under support-trestles. The dried-out remains of the vines had fallen to the ground. The building was more intact than the rest of the Villa. Only the roof was missing, and a few cracks showed on the brick walls.

Millon cantered over to a patch where rose bushes use to grow and found baby cacti between the dead roots of the roses.

"At least there is some sort of life here," he said gruffly.

"You don't happen to remember if Gingos mentioned where in the ruins the portal is?" Darcwulf asked.

"No, unfortunately not," Shadowolf replied.

Dan..k... He turned quickly towards the vineyard building.

"Did you hear that?" he asked.

"Hear what?" Shedaaij asked.

"That voice…" D..aka

It carried lightly in the air from the building to his mind. He lifted his fingers to his temple as a pain shot through it.

"Are you ok?" Sorceress asked. The Clan gathered around him.

"There is someone in the building," he pointed with his staff hand, still massaging his brow with the other. "I can hear it calling to me."

"Then it is obviously a trap," Ursula warned. "It's no coincidence that Gingos speaks of an elvin portal never created and now someone is calling for you."

"Maybe not," Shadowolf said, unsure of her theory. "But even if it is, I would like to be released of this headache."

...anak.., the voice called again and he walked to the only entrance. The interior was lit through the roofless top, and some of the floorboards were gone. In the centre of the floor was a gaping hole that was too obvious to be missed. The woody, splintered rim of the hole was covered in dried blood.

"Shall we?" Darcwulf dared him.

"Of course," he smiled.

"This isn't time for games," Shedaaij said.

"I concur," Fransiska added, crossing her arms.

"I am in the mood for an investigation," Kentaur said. He walked over to the hole, but realised that it was too small for a centaur.

"Move," Shadowolf laughed. He raised his palm to the floorboards and used the wind to tug it apart. He added some earth and used fresh vines to pull them further out. Soon the hole was big enough to allow two centaurs abreast.

Kentaur descended into the hole, followed shortly by Millon.

"You can stay if you want," Shadowolf offered Shedaaij and Fransiska.

"Forget it," Shedaaij said, unsheathing her daggers. "You need someone to watch your back."

"I sense a long journey coming on again," Darcwulf said and jumped into the hole and landing shortly thereafter. "Ok, maybe I was wrong."

It was a small chamber, not big enough to hold the whole Clan. Shadowolf, Nelnar, Fransiska and Shedaaij landed in the room, but the rest remained above.

"Very quaint," Fransiska said.

"Here's something here," Shadowolf said and shifted the sand with his feet. "Can't seem to get the grime off though."

"I think it's time I show off a bit," Fransiska smiled, and then closed her eyes. "Uhmm, not much water around here. Give me a moment."

As if her legs had begun to leak, water dripped down her skin onto the ground. In sweeping motions it flowed over the area Shadowolf had indicated and washed the grime away.

"I have a bad feeling about this," Sorceress said, and she and Trimistus joined them in the chamber. There was barely room for them all.

"It looks just like the true entrance," Ursula said from above.

There was a circular line etched in the ground. It was large enough in diameter that even Millon could have stood on it. There were two holes in the centre; the one was a thin line, as long as from the tip of person's finger to the centre knuckle, the other was as long as Shadowolf's hand.

"Except," Malanite corrected, "that the original's second key was made for a dwarven axe. That one has been modified for a sword."

"You've lost me," Shadowolf admitted.

"There are two keyholes on the platform to the tunnel," Malanite informed them. "The thin linear key hole is for an elvin bow. The second was supposed to be for an axe, but it is only long enough for a sword."

"So what do I do to activate the platform?"

"Insert your sword in the key hole," Ursula said. "The platform will take us to the tunnel, I assume."

"Alright," he said. "We'll go first, and then one of you can use your sword to activate it again."

Shadowolf unsheathed Ruben and held it over the key hole. He breathed deeply and drove it in. Red rays of light rose up from the floor, and then the group in the chamber vanished.

"What happened?!" Rennick exclaimed.

"I don't know," Malanite stood dumb-founded. "Lastgorn, your sword."

Ursula, Malanite, Sny-Ten, Skywolf and Trevor joined him in the chamber as he poised the falchion-blade over the hole. As he lowered the sword, the key holes closed and the sword clanged against the metal surface. Lastgorn cursed out loud as the sword stung his hands.

"What are we going to do?" Shadowwe asked.

"Wait for their return," Malanite replied, and sat down in meditation.

Shadowolf was staring at the brown sand. He was on his hands and knees with Ruben beneath him. Nelnar sat beside him. He looked up and saw the centaurs rise from their front knees.

Shedaaij, Fransiska and Darcwulf were kneeling beside him, with Sorceress behind him. Trimistus had already begun walking towards the buildings.

"Where are we?" Sorceress asked, but her voice was strange. The wind blew roughly against them. It felt like they were close to a tornado.

"I don't know," he replied, and his voice squeaked.

"You sound like Shedaaij," Darcwulf said in a rough voice.

"And you sound like Kentaur," Millon said in a voice resembling Fransiska's.

"What on earth is going on here?" Shedaaij said with Darcwulf's voice.

There were ruins everywhere, and they weren't simple buildings. These were towering skyscrapers where only their steel frames stood against the wind. Broken mountains and sunken craters were on each horizon, and there was no sign of life.

"What kind of creature could live here?" Shedaaij asked, sheathing her blades.

"My kind," Trimistus said when he returned. "This used to be my home."

Shadowolf gulped as any word of comfort escaped his mind. Even without eyeballs, the expression on Trimistus's face conveyed extreme sadness and rage.

"This was meant for me," he said, and dropped to the floor. "It was meant to destroy me."

"Trimistus," Shadowolf said, recovering from his stupor. "From the time I have spent with you, I know that Le'Mar underestimates your strength and your ability."

"Look at this world," Trimistus said. His red eyes turned blue. Shadowolf couldn't be sure, but it seemed as if he were crying. "This is what will become of your world, and we will become his slaves."

"What happened?" Shadowolf asked, sitting beside him. The others resumed surveying the planet.

"A man arrived here, someone called the Gemetrashef," he said. "In our tongue that means 'Tyrranic Governor'. In much the same way that Le'Mar has battled Celenic Earth, the Gemetrashef took out our most valuable defences.

"When we finally succumbed to his will, a black fog filled the land. After a decade, we forgot that the fog was there. Prophets said that they had travelled to the mountains and could look down upon the fog. They said we could still be freed from the sickness of the fog, and so we built the skyscrapers."

Trimistus indicated the desolate buildings.

"But the Gemetrashef learnt of our plans," Trimistus continued. "The fog fought against us, and in the end we were called to a council with him. He informed us that he would offer us the opportunity to be freed of the fog.

"He told us of the wars he planned for other planets and systems and that he was building an army of Saneths, or Kings of the Knight as we referred to it. If we agreed, he would lift the fog.

"I was assigned to Celenic Earth with Lister, Ma'Kanak and Rumaak."

"But they seem so different to you," Shadowolf said, and then spat out the sand that the wind had kicked up into his face. He focused on the wind and tried to calm it. It only softened slightly before raging against him again.

"They were from other conquered planets," he said. "We were then given to the service of Le'Mar."

"Where does he fit into Gemetrashef's plans?"

"Some power called the Governor to your planet," Trimistus said, his eyes turning red again as he composed himself. "It was only after you told us about the vision in the unicorn chamber that I realised it was the Battle of T'Mar's Scourge that had alerted him."

"How so?" Shadowolf asked.

"The story that the horn doesn't tell you is that Le'Mar took the dead T'Mar to his home to be confronted by the Gemetrashef. The Governor now had someone from your world that hated his home and would assist him in conquering it. He gave Le'Mar the charge to conquer Celenic Earth and rule over it.

"Le'Mar spent a long time in the Gemetrashef's charge learning his ways and becoming stronger. Even though the Governor did not understand the concept of the 'Sagdi', he agreed to help him achieve this power."

"Why did you not mention this before?" Shadowolf asked politely, but he was feeling frustrated at this lack of sharing.

"Shado, I tried to forget my past life," he replied honestly. "While I was with the dragons, it gave me time to accept the fact that I had lost my world. But I cannot let it happen to my new home."

"At first I thought Mercius was the mastermind," Shadowolf said. "Then I learnt it was Le'Mar. And now you say there is someone else giving him orders."

Trimistus couldn't answer. Shadowolf looked at the planet, but his mind was at home.

"I am going to have to teleport us all home," he finally said.

"Can you do that?" Trimistus asked, staring up into the star-glittered sky with two beautiful moons overhead.

"I have no idea," he replied, realising how ridiculous his suggestion sounded.

"There is a room," Trimistus said, "that was used to teleport me to the Governor's ship. Maybe, if we can make our way there, we can use it to take us home."

"Do you think it still exists?" he asked.

"The problem is if we can reach another destination besides the ship."

"Where is this ship located?" he frowned, looking around for a river or alternative source of water.

"Up there," Trimistus pointed to the night shy, "in space. He travels on it between planets and stars. We call it 'Banusqi', but you might refer to it as a starship."

Shadowolf absorbed this news. He had never heard of a ship travelling through space. It confused him, and so he chose to ignore it for the time-being.

"Were you always referred to as 'Trimistus'?"

"No," he replied. "My name was Lord Danaka. I took on Trimistus when I was hired as a mercenary for Le'Mar."

"Well, Lord Danaka," Shadowolf forced a smile. "Somehow, someway we must find a way home.

Shadowolf rose from the dust and swirling sand. Besides Trimistus, only Nelnar was close at hand. He did not know where the others had disappeared to, but at least it gave him a moment of peace.

He raised his palm and concentrated it in the air before him.

"Ok, Ursula," Shadowolf whispered. "Let's see what it is you wanted to show me."

He closed his eyes and envisioned Celenic Earth. He remembered the barren vineyard and saw the broken building with the gaping hole in the centre. He remembered the others standing around it.

Yet it was not the same as spiritual projection. He was not travelling in mind, but only recalling a memory from the dusty files in his brain.

He increased his mind's power, trying to transfer some of it to his palm from the memory, but it was to no effect. When he opened his eyes, the dust and sand still swirled around his ankles.

"Shado!" he heard Shedaaij's voice reach him through the hailing wind. When she came closer, he saw that the stones had battered her exposed arms, legs and sternum. She held her hands by her face, and he realised that he himself was blinking faster to keep the sand out of his eyes.

"There are elementëls here," she informed him as she leapt into his arms, hiding from the storm.

"Great," he replied. "Where are the others?"

He needed no answer, for he heard a loud crash in the direction of the battle. Grasping firmly on the staff, he took Shedaaij's hand and raced towards them. He heard Trimistus's footsteps behind them.

There were indeed elementëls; two winds, one water, three fires and six earths. A shadow flickered in the tossing wind and sand, and just before it slammed into one of the ruined buildings he saw that it was Darcwulf.

Fransiska was locked in an elementël battle with one of the water elementëls. Their arms were braced as water rushed between Fransiska's palms and the masculine elementël's arms. Shadowolf called up the earth from behind the elementël, and the beast was shoved forward. Fransiska responded rapidly by placing her palms together and then splitting them. The elementël shred in two and the water rose into the tornado.

Rain and mud fell upon them. Darcwulf broke from the ruins and was faced by an earth and a fire elementël. Shedaaij ran forward to Fransiska's side as wind and fire challenged her. Millon, Nelnar and Kentaur were occupied with three earths and one fire.

Sorceress fought against wind.

During his observation, the remaining two earth elementëls had walked up to him and Trimistus. He looked into their sand encrusted crevasses that should have been eyes. Their bodily earth swirled in time with the twisting atmosphere.

"Does everything turn around here?" Shadowolf asked.

"I think elementëls find our atmosphere difficult to work with," Trimistus smiled.

Shadowolf held up his palm and brought forth fire. The fire leapt up and twisted in the air, joining the cyclonic chaos of the tornado.

"That just makes things a bit more complicated for me too," Shadowolf said.

"Do you guys mind helping us out a little!?" Shedaaij shouted. Having hardly uttered the last word, fire sent her up into the air and she slid on her back, dropping one of the daggers. Millon kicked at the earth elementël, and as it sunk to the ground and reappeared before his chest, he slammed his fist into its face. The sand snapped off its neck, and reformed into a head.

Shedaaij raised her hand at Millon's earth elementël. As it tried to walk, its feet fell into the ground. Millon grabbed its shoulders and separated its arms from its chest. As it tried to reform, Shedaaij severed the element with her mind, and the earth joined the tornado.

The fire that had sent her sprawling to the ground rose up in the air and descended upon her. Just before it could kill her, Darcwulf landed above her and thrust his staff between him and the fire. He pushed it back up, cast his staff aside and his skin became fire. The two grappled and wrestled each other to the ground, and every piece of ground they touched became black from the power emitted.

The two elementëls before Shadowolf and Trimistus looked at each other. In the silence of their stares they communicated and it seemed as if their minds were far away.

"Should we do something?" Trimistus asked. Shadowolf shrugged his shoulders. The flames of the elementël battling Darcwulf subsided and embraced the ground, but did not join the tornado.

Soon the other elementëls backed away from the fight, leaving the Clan to halt their violence. Millon unfortunately did not realise the sudden change and his fist sent an earth elementël flying into the core of the tornado. Fransiska grabbed his arm, and only then did he notice that something was amiss.

"Will you speak to the elements?" one of the two elementëls asked Shadowolf.

"I have need to return to my world," he answered carefully.

"We can provide that means, if you will seek the council of the elements."

"Is it far?" Trimistus asked.

"Are the elements hindered by distance?" the elementël responded.

"We will go," Shadowolf agreed, and the elementëls turned away.

They moved away from the approaching tornado, but the earth elementëls sank into the ground and the Clan were left alone. Shadowolf frowned in frustration, trying to site any guide that would show them the way.

Suddenly, the earth shifted beneath him. The sands twirled in tune with the cyclone and the wind beat at their legs. Small hillocks rose beneath each of them, rising to their thighs and lifting them into the air.

The earth stretched out and supported them. The heads formed and the legs grew out from underneath them. The brown stallions kicked and neighed. On their backs they supported the Clan with beautifully gemmed saddles.

Shadowolf looked down at Nelnar, and the panting face told him that the wolf found this humorous. He offered Nelnar a comforting smile before urging the horse forward with a kick.

The earth rose and dropped, barren hillock after barren hillock. It felt as if he were riding through a land of dreams, where the silhouette of his friends tore at the fragments of his vision onto the dreary surface of his existence. The warmth of Shedaaij's love drifted from her heart onto the musical waves of the listing air, distorted and damaged by the chaos they were leaving behind.

He could almost hear her call his name. He could almost hear her words of love, but because it was carried in the undertone of Darcwulf's voice it did not quite have the right effect.

To the left they passed a large crater, but as his senses were highly attuned to the elements he could tell there was once water in the gaping nook. Nelnar's paws echoed in the air to the right, but Shadowolf looked and could not find it. When he looked down to the left of the horse, Nelnar was still running beside him.

There was no need to steer the stallion. Whenever the horse had to change its direction by a few degrees, the wind would push the horse slightly. Shadowolf could feel that this was not part of the cyclone, but a deliberate change in the air.

If you ever left me, my soul would be empty...

He could not recognise the voice, but his heart was moved by the affection. Through the hailing sand storm and wailing wind he saw Fransiska ride closer to Darcwulf. Something in the wind urged the horses to ride faster, and the sound of the hooves' clatter increased on the rock hard earth.

An outcropping rose ahead of them and the whirling sand subsided a little. The air became clearer and Shadowolf no longer had to narrow his eyes or manage the wind to avoid blasts of sand striking his face. Signs of grass and shrubs became common along the ground and the ruins and buildings disappeared.

The horses slowed their approach. The outcropping was a cave with a wide foyer for an entrance. There was nothing grand about it, for it was only earth and grass. The inner walls of the cave were dilapidated, very unlike the fine craft of the dwarves.

The horses decayed back into the ground, saving them the effort of dismounting. The two earth elementëls of earlier greeted them from within the entrance and beckoned them to follow. Shadowolf looked at his friends, but they simply shrugged and walked into the gloom of the musty cave. Shedaaij grabbed his arm and placed her head against his shoulder.

"Nanoo nanoo," Darcwulf said and plugged Fransiska's ears with his index fingers.

"Hey!" she jumped, laughing.

"Where did you get that saying from?" Shadowolf smiled.

"I just made it up," Darcwulf replied and lunged to tickle her. "Nanoo nanoo!"

"Stop it!" Her jovial voice rang down the cave's tunnel. Shedaaij held Shadowolf closer and looked into his eyes. It was becoming increasingly clear that each of the couples were neglecting their love for each other. The war was not only affecting their freedom and peace, but also their love.

But love was now finding a way to intervene. It conquered his heart and the dilemma of the situation floated away as he fell into her eyes and swam around the vast vista of her soul. While the others continued walking and laughing to a destination unknown, the two stopped and faced each other.

"If it is in my power, I will protect and love you for all eternity," he smiled.

"I want you to be mine for all time, Shado," she said, kissing his lips. "Only my love for Bontu is greater."

"As it should be," he replied. "I love you, sweetheart."

"I love you too," she laid her head on his chest and he embraced her.

"Oi!" Darcwulf's voice trailed towards them. "The elementëls are waiting; hurry up!"

"Coming!" he shouted, and they clasped hands as they followed the Clan.

They entered a small open area with concave walls and a domed roof. It was not constructed that way but was rather the rudimentary design of nature. A rough stage wide enough for one person to stand on and long enough for four was set against the one wall. In the walls on either side of the small platform were niches that disappeared into darkness.

The platform was now their focus of attention, for it had its four occupants on it already. The elementëls stood facing them with calm demeanours. Their forms were composed wholly of their respective elements, fine waves rising from the platform into the tense air.

"Welcome Darcwulf," the fire being's voice spoke. His tone resembled the cracking of a warm fireplace. "My name is *KariemsaPh*, and I recognise myself within you."

"Welcome Fransiska," the water element said, her words trailed by the flowing sound of water. "My name is *Merlandsi*, and I recognise myself within you."

"Welcome Shedaaij," the earth element said, his words rumbling and deep. "I am *Goudlem* and I recognise myself in you."

The wind element drifted down from the stage to Shadowolf and placed her ethereal hands on his shoulders. Nelnar whined softly at his side, but she looked down at it and the wolf calmed and lay down.

"Welcome Shadowolf," she said, joined simultaneously by *Goudlem* and *KariemsaPh*. She then proceeded to address him alone. "I am *Enodhim*, and we recognise ourselves in you. But I the most, knowing that I have the strongest presence within you."

Shadowolf remained silent and waited for the rest if the Clan to be greeted. However, the elements said nothing further and *Enodhim* returned to the stage.

"What of the others?" he asked, still stunned by their welcome.

"We do not sense any form of the elements present within them," *Enodhim* informed them. "Our Lord Bontu guides their paths, but they have no knowledge of us."

"Are you gods?" he asked carefully.

"No," she replied. "We are all servants of Bontu, angels sent to lord over the elements and fulfil His divine will."

Merlandsi smiled and raised her liquid arm. She waved her hand in a circle and soft waves of atmospheric vapour poured over them. The cave changed, taking a more beautiful form. There were no solid structures, only ethereal flames of different colours.

Shadowolf looked at his hands. His skin had turned to earth, but within it he felt the pumping wind pulse through his veins. Where the air escaped the soil and rock of his arm, fire broke out like minute volcanoes and burst into blue-red flames.

He turned to see the others. He recognised Darcwulf by his staff. His body consisted solely of fire, resembling *KariemsaPh*. Shedaaij and Fransiska likewise resembled their elements.

Trimistus was a green silhouette. An aura of green surrounded the form, but he did not resemble any of the elements. Millon and Kentaur were large four-legged beasts with two arms that were brown in silhouette and aura. To the side, Sorceress was a blue shadow and Nelnar was a cloud of grey by his feet.

"This is how we see the world," *Enodhim* told them.

"What happened to this world, *Enodhim*?" Shadowolf asked.

"Le'Mar, sent by Gemetrashef, came and destroyed everything sacred to this world," she replied sadly. "As you can see he turned the elements into turmoil, and we have been sent by Bontu to restore it to its previous beauty."

"In all fairness," *KariemsaPh* added, looking at Trimistus, "he did try and change the Governor's mind. He had made a promise to the one once known as Lord Danaka, but Gemetrashef would not abide by promises, and had no empathy towards Le'Mar."

"But Le'Mar is no longer one of us," *Merlandsi* said, "having turned his soul to darkness ages ago. That is why he will never be Sagdi."

Shadowolf was about to speak again, but *Enodhim* forestalled him.

"We need to know your purpose here, Shadowolf," she said. "We have not summoned you, nor is it time for your last elementël trial."

He gaped. The realisation hit him like an arrow through his head, and the sharp pain pounded against his skull.

"You are the elements from my trials?"

"Yes, we are," she smiled. "You are not ready for the final trial, but somehow I sense that is not the reason you are here."

"It is an accident that we are here," he replied. "We entered a portal that should have taken us to Eldor's Forest, but lead us here instead."

"We do not know of that portal," *KariemsaPh* said, "but we can take you back should you wish."

"Is that possible?" Trimistus asked.

"Wherever the elements are found, we can go," *Enodhim* said.

"He's here," *Goudlem* said sternly. The other elements raised their heads, calm dislike and disgust reflected in their ethereal eyes. Shadowolf was about to question them, but *Enodhim* flicked her hand and the Clan were instantaneously moved to the dark niches on either side of the stage.

Their eyes were still attuned to the world of the elementëls. From the soft light emanating by the cave's entrance he entered. The sand stirred by his feet, almost fleeting from his presence. The wind curled away from his body and pushed up against the walls.

His aura was completely red. A deep black pulsed at the centre of his abdomen that coursed like spider webs through his veins and up his spine. He stopped before the platform, hands folded behind his back. His red aura drifted like a large cloak around his body, his purple eyes barley hidden by the hood that he wore.

"Le'Mar," *Enodhim* addressed him. "What an unwelcome surprise."

"I have come to complete what I started centuries before," he said to them. There was no greeting in his voice; it was utterly demanding as if the very elements were meant to obey him.

"You know we cannot complete your trials," *KariemsaPh* replied. "You have turned your soul from Bontu and offered it to a darker being. The elements do not recognise you anymore."

"I am *KariemsaPh*, *Merlandsi*, *Enodhim* and *Goudlem*," the dark lord growled. A chill ran over Shadowolf's spine. "I have control of the elements and mastery over their natures. I demand that my training as *Sadgi* be finalised."

"Do you see what your mastery has done?" *Enodhim* spread her arms. "Look at the destruction of this world."

"I will repair it," he said, shaking his head. "In the end, all things will be returned to their beauty."

"By sacrificing how many souls?" *Goudlem* shouted, the earth from his being rising up, enraged. "How many dead do you require before you return to Bontu?"

"As much as it takes!" Le'Mar shouted. Wind broke into the cave, a chaotic element that had nothing to do with the goodness of *Enodhim*. A foul stench followed in the wind, but *Enodhim* raised her hand and her essence pervaded the area. The chaos returned to the planet outside.

Goudlem raised his palm, and as the gravity increased Le'Mar fell to his knees.

"I can feel what you are doing," *Merlandsi* said. "I can feel you sensing around our home, searching for someone."

"I do not know of what you speak," Le'Mar denied.

"You have not come here for your trial," *Enodhim* said. "You have indeed come here in search for another."

Le'Mar remained silent. He raised his eyes to glare at the elements.

"In the end, I will defeat your champion," he said in conclusion. "Even if he is the *Wisoum*, I will defeat him. Centuries of training and power cannot be outdone by his damned ignorant youth."

"But he has someone greater on his side and within his spirit," *Goudlem* said.

"And who is that?"

"Bontu," *Enodhim* said.

"Let Bontu and his angels come," Le'Mar sneered. "I am ready for them too. Now, release me."

Goudlem stared at the dark lord, but the elements communicated silently to one another and the earth released its grip on him.

"Do not deign to approach us again," *Enodhim* said dismissively.

"The next time we meet," he said as he left the cave, "I will have my own masters on your thrones."

It is not safe for me to reveal you now, Enodhim spoke in Shadowolf's mind, and he nodded. Cold sweat ran down his arms and he shivered from the cold dread within him.

Familiar mists surrounded them in the niches. He saw that it was coming from *Merlandsi*. The Mists of Celene clouded their vision and after a few seconds they were staring at the building of the abandoned vineyard.

"Shado!" Ursula shouted and the Clan rose from their seats.

"Ursula," he said, his voice shaking. "You must teach me about the elements. Time is running out."

THE FALLEN FAIRIWELL
CHAPTER THREE

Shadowolf looked over the dark plains of the east. The Clan was asleep in one of the inns of Lourdes, just north of Lasglow and its abandoned vineyard.

He could barely make out the dusty moon-lit horizon, knitted with minute silhouettes of the Vale of Tigers. His mind drifted for a second from his constant worries to this quaint little desert city. He remembered the Heart of Tigers that somehow was part of the war, but not part of his immediate concern.

But when he remembered that it had been Ursula that had told him about the gem, her words once again returned to his mind. After they had left the vineyard and approached the inn, she pulled him aside and looked sadly into his eyes.

Teaching you about the matter of the elements is not something I can do within days, Shado. You must learn to grow in the skill of the power you have obtained. Only you can learn what the elements will teach you. I cannot pursue this road with you, but I will add guidance where I can. If only I had been with you the two years you were gone. I could have taught you so much.

There were so many problems to the matter in his mind. One main aspect was the fact that he would have liked to push his power to the limits and see what he was capable of, but he was afraid it would draw Le'Mar's unwanted attention.

"The night holds many secrets, my boy," the old voice croaked behind him, followed by a cough.

"Too many to be unraveled, old man," he replied as Malanite sat beside him on the low wall.

"Anything I can help with?" the old man asked.

"No, I think it's mostly up to me," Shadowolf replied

sarcastically. "Why did you return to the earth?"

"Wouldn't you, Shado?"

He thought long in silence on this answer and realised he was right.

"I will be returning to the forest tonight," the old man said.

"I thought it was only Mercius that would dare to split his soul," Shadowolf said with a polite laugh.

"Sometimes you have to do what's best for what you care about so much."

"What about the Fairiwell?"

"Ursula and you can provide me with feedback when you reach the Elvin Throne," he answered. "I believe you are more than capable, Shado, to protect her."

"You love her, don't you?"

"More than you know," he replied, with a soft smile. "Do you think my son Elgoth was raised by the dust?"

Shadowolf gaped at this revelation, realising he had never thought on the maternal origin of the strange man sent to assist the Degron Tribe. Before he could comment, the old man turned away. He stretched his aged hands and gripped his staff for support. His eyes gleamed and the wind stirred with the power.

"Oh, and thank you for paying for our accommodation and travel," he remembered.

Masara smiled as his body transformed back to its proper state. Shadowolf watched as the ancient saint became one with the wind and journeyed to bond with his body waiting in Eldor's Forest.

"Shado?" Shedaaij's voice called from the empty darkness behind him. She joined him on the wall where Masara had been sitting.

"I saw Malanite leaving, but can't find him," she said, looking at his complacent face.

"Remember how you said he seems strange to you?"

"Yeah," she said.

"Well, I couldn't say it before, but it's safe now," Shadowolf smiled. "He was Masara."

She didn't betray any surprise. She nodded simply as if deep within her she had always known.

"What's bothering you, my love?" she asked, tucking her arm

under his.

"I want to exercise my power, but am at a loss as to what to do," he replied honestly.

"Make love to me," she said, smiling mischievously.

"What?! Here?" he blurted out, blushing.

"Up there," she looked up at the star-filled sky.

Shadowolf looked east again and thought about it before jumping onto the ground and walking to the open land. He turned and waited for her to reach him. She placed her hands in his palms.

The wind moved by their feet and they rose up to into the air. Shadowolf turned them in circles, careful not to create a cyclone. The wind was chill but comforting. The world shrank beneath them, and they were covered by the blanket of the night, Sothos in the east.

"I need something to lie on," she whispered, her eyes glistening.

He smiled and stretched his palm to the earth. Only a slight rumble shook the ground as a twisting tree broke free and rose into the air to meet them. It then spread out at the top to form soft earth covered with grass. On the borders of the earthly bed, roses sprouted. Shadowolf let them settle down on the bed, and Shedaaij lay down.

"And now," she said, and smiled lovingly, "the fire…"

The sun broke the horizon and the birds' songs awoke him from his sleep. Shedaaij was sleeping with her head on his chest, their clothes still lying on the side. He moved his head, and the many birds lodged in the tree and rose bushes made a noise as they fluttered away.

Shedaaij stirred her head and looked through misty eyes at him. A faint smile creased her cheeks and then she put her head down again.

A faint voice travelled upon the wind to his ears. He focused on the sound which became howling. The realisation that the Clan were waiting for him struck with a deep headache.

"Dearest," he whispered, moving his chest slightly to get her attention. "We must get moving."

"I feel so tired," she said, sitting up. Shadowolf warmed up inside as he looked at her naked body. She moved so lithely, even in her morning state. Her skin shone in the sunlight, accentuating the curves of her breasts and thighs.

As if he had been pulled by a rope around his neck, the scene obscenely changed as she got sick in front of him. She turned and vomited on the bed, clutching her stomach. He moved to her side and rubbed her back stupidly.

"Are you ok?" he asked, concern altering the pitch in his voice.

"I don't know," she said, not sure how to say what she wanted to say. "But ever since Shenama I have been feeling a bit strange. My skin grows warm for no reason now and again. I've been eating more than usual."

Shadowolf looked in her sleepy eyes and realised what she was saying.

"You sure it was Shenama?" he asked.

"Didn't you ask me if I was eating for two at Horlorn's Gate?" she said, holding her stomach.

"And here I thought you were just getting fa....". He stopped in mid-sentence as she stared daggers at him. "Sorry."

"We better get dressed," Shedaaij said bravely.

Once they were dressed, Shadowolf looked down over the edge of the bed and saw how high up they were.

"Well, I guess I can't leave this here," he said, stretching his arm to the tree.

"Wait!" Shedaaij shouted. "I can feel the animals, birds and insects in this tree. Please leave it for them?"

Shadowolf smiled softly, but frowned at the huge tower. Deciding to leave it, he used the wind to return them to the ground.

"About time," Darcwulf grumbled. "Come one, we're heading for the Fairiwell."

The dust of the drying land was soon covered by the shadow of grey clouds. By early afternoon a mist rolled over the land, broken by a small shower of rain.

The horses neighed as they rode through the watery mud holes. Shadowolf and the few Clan members that could pulled their hoods over their heads while the others made the use of tops or blankets. Yet, even with that scant protection, Shadowolf felt the water break through to his hair and down his cheeks to his chin.

He was glad though for the rain. The desert plains of the Vale hardly saw rain through the year. The *Goudlem* in him sensed the joy running through the creatures below the surface crust of the earth.

It was another two hours of rain and travel before they reached the site of the Fairiwell portal. It was hidden beneath the mud and sand, but with his mind he shifted it to clear the disc.

True to Masara and Ursula's observation in the abandoned vineyard, the portal was exactly like the fake one. Shadowolf bent down to inspect the key lines, and the sword line was indeed replaced by a line thick and long enough for a dwarven axe. The arrow line was the same.

"Sny," Shadowolf muttered and Sny-Ten deftly swung his axe forward and unstrapped it from his shoulders. He grasped the handle firmly, lifting the one edge high in the air and bringing it down into the hole.

Shadowolf and Sny-Ten walked off the platform as it descended into the earth. Mechanisms ground harshly and wheels whined, struggling to bring the disc to the floor of the waiting tunnel.

"A tight fit for thirty people," Shadowolf said to Ursula, his hands on his hips.

"We will have to walk single file," she said, and then looked at Millon and Kentaur. "I'm not sure about the centaurs through."

"We'll manage," Millon said gruffly. "We're not leaving the quest."

"You don't have to," Ursula said. "I can request a portal for you to the forest. At least then our packages and horses won't have to be left behind."

"I thought no one can enter the forest with a portal?" Kentaur asked the question on everybody's mind.

"When we enter the forest, I will ask Eldor to open the portal," she replied.

"I don't like this idea," Shadowolf said, frowning deeply against the rain drops. "What if they are discovered here? And we can't leave them in the rain."

"I have an idea," Darcwulf said. "Why not send them to Horlorn's Gate?"

"Good idea," Shadowolf beamed.

"Very well," Kentaur said, obviously displeased.

"The fight will be in the forest, good friend," Shadowolf tapped his muscular arm. "The Fairiwell is merely a detour."

"Ok Shado, let's not waste any more time," Ursula said.

"Excuse me?" he turned to her.

"It's time for you to learn how to open a portal," she said.

Shadowolf looked her in the eyes a moment later, shocked that she expected this of him now, but he relinquished and walked to her.

"Close your eyes," she tutored. He relaxed his body and followed her instructions.

The wind stirred against his body as he called the power to his mind. The power moved to his eyes and after a moment, he was able to look with his spirit through his eyelids at the assembled Clan. Ursula continued with her instructions.

He was standing on the Sky Tier of Horlorn's Gate, staring at the moving people. He raised his arm and transferred some power down his arm to his open palm. His mind was caught in the rift between Horlorn's Gate and the Vale of Tigers.

He tried to release the power to open the connection between the two areas. The wind buffeted him, the rain falling hard against the crown of his head. In the area where the portal should have opened, a shimmer appeared and vanished.

He tried again. The two lands were before him, and he knew that he was doing this part correctly. The power thrummed in his head and the fire coursed through his veins to his palm. The rain stirred and formed a soft circle before him, but dissipated again.

"Ok, Shado," Ursula said. "That's enough for now."

He slowly calmed his spirit. Without warning, Ursula released the Sinokwe. The element-warders floated up to his eyes and his hand. As he relaxed his power and they drifted away, Ursula raised her hand and opened a portal to the Gate. The Sinokwe left him immediately and surrounded her white aura.

Shadowolf opened his eyes. The rain still poured over them, and the centaurs and horses passed through the portal. When the last were through, Shadowolf addressed the Clan.

"Anyone who wants to wait with them is welcome."

The Clan looked back and forth between him and portal, but

decided to remain with him. Nelnar panted silently beside him, drenched all over. Ursula dropped her palm, and the portal closed.

"Let's go," Darcwulf said, and dropped down to the tunnel, followed by Fransiska. The seven Crethans, Madison, Trish, Dayna-wolf, Teristé, Markors, Mino'Nelar, and Midnite jumped down, with the six Orion on their tail.

Ursula decided not to wait for last and entered with Dren, Trimistus and Nolraldun the assassin. Lastgorn, Sny-ten, Gwyn, Angelia, Skywolf and Heula jumped down, leaving Shadowolf, Shedaaij and Nelnar for last.

"Quite the group," Shedaaij smiled.

"Yes it is," Shadowolf agreed, and the three of them entered the Fairiwell tunnel.

The entrance rose up on its own and closed behind him. As Ursula had warned, due to the lack of width in the semi-circular tunnel, they were forced to walk single file. Shadowolf felt like he was walking blind at the back, not being able to see anything except the walls around him and Shedaaij's back before him.

The tunnel was humid, and although their damp clothes dried in the soft heat, it still clung to their bodies uncomfortably. The sand was smooth beneath their feet.

A few minutes later they passed green bunks on either side of the tunnel. Although Shadowolf would have enjoyed a rest, the urgency of reaching the forest outweighed any other concern. His ignorance of Le'Mar's plans and strategy was working on the edge of his nerves and every second wasted plucked at the tired streams his mind.

"Something is wrong," Ursula mumbled in the centre of the moving line. Someone said something at the front, but Shadowolf could only hear Ursula's response. Suddenly his head reeled and he leaned on the wall as they spoke.

"We should have seen the fairdievells by now," she said.

"Are you ok?" Shedaaij whispered and touched his back, not wanting to disturb the others.

"Yeah," he replied as someone spoke at the front again. "Just feeling dizzy."

"Maybe you should rest?" she offered, pointing at a bunk.

"They are a species of fairies found in the Fairiwell," Ursula continued to explain to the others. The words echoed distantly in his head, till he found the words to speak.

"We must reach Eldor," he said. "I have a feeling that our time is running out."

Something knocked at his mind. Warmth flowed from Shedaaij, and he looked at her to find the source. He transferred power to his eyes and found the heat by her belly. A small form was lying in her uterus. The joy filled his heart at the sight of their forming baby, but then he sank to the bunk as his head reeled again.

Shedaaij was about to exclaim, but he forestalled her by grabbing her arm.

"The dark lord is coming," Shadowolf warned, images of Le'Mar filling his head. "We need to hurry."

The line was moving again and Shedaaij helped him stand and put his arm across her shoulders.

The tunnel felt like it would never end. He grew warmer and began seeing everyone's auras. The light from the torches in the tunnel accentuated their silhouettes. His head was burning from within.

"Please not now," Shadowolf groaned.

"What?"

"I hope it's not another trial of the elements," he replied.

"Shado," she gasped softly.

"What's the matter?"

"You've got those strange, ghostly wings on your back," she replied. The ethereal wings were tucked neatly behind his back, not having much room to expand. His eyes were burning, and everyone's auras brightened. Suddenly he could see passed everyone to Darcwulf in the front, and then back again to Shedaaij.

"If I don't use my energy soon, I am going to explode," he warned.

"Try to contain it, Shado," Ursula said as she broke through the line to him. "Darcwulf! Let me know when we reach a dead end!"

Darcwulf acknowledged the command and the Clan continued. Ursula helped carry Shadowolf as they trudged along.

"It's the *Wisoum*," Ursula informed him. "The War of the Dragons is approaching. It means that Sonersaat is getting ready for battle, and the dragon power within you is awakening."

"That also means that Le'Mar must have found a way to enter the forest," Shedaaij assumed.

"Maybe," was all Ursula could muster to say on the topic. "Where's the staff Masara bought you?"

"It's with Mandy," he said forlornly.

"Great."

They continued for a while until the Clan stopped and Darcwulf uttered that they had reached a dead end. Ursula left his side and scrambled to the front. Shadowolf lifted his eyes and looked past all the auras and flesh until he found the wall she was facing.

With her finger she etched a strange design on the wall. He couldn't follow it, but the design remained etched in his memory. When she had completed her design, a door opened and the Clan hastily passed through the opening. Shadowolf returned to his sight.

"I....can't... hold it....any....more!!!" he shouted and pushed Shedaaij to the side. He butted everyone with his shoulder until he finally reached the door.

"No Shado wait!" Ursula shouted and Darcwulf tried to stop him. But Shadowolf's heightened senses had betrayed him and he missed the step of the ledge that led along the large cavern down into the Fairiwell. He slipped of the rocky surface and descended into the depths.

Not swayed by fear or vertigo, power exploded from him. Wind rose up from the ground and cycloned around him. His hair swayed wildly around his bright blue eyes, and he held his fists at his side as the power surged through his veins.

Something broke from his chest. Although the flesh was unharmed, fire rose all around him into the air. His hair rose up with the fire and he exclaimed, the energy forcing his muscles to spasm.

Just as quickly as it had started, he calmed down. The fire was an aura around his body, and he looked down at the vast cavern of the Fairiwell.

"What happened?" Darcwulf asked.

"The power was too much, I had to expend it," he replied gruffly.

"Well, you're going to get that chance," his brother replied.

Before them the Fairiwell was in battle. Every inch of the cavern was written in colour as the multi-coloured fairies fought against the blue creatures of the dark lord. The fletchlings were bigger in bulk than the fairdievells and had bat-like wings, but the fairies were faster and more experienced in lore.

"This might be a little difficult," Shadowolf said.

"How do we help them without hurting them?" Darcwulf agreed.

"Moths to a flame..." Shadowolf thought out loud.

"Mmm...good idea."

The two went to either side of the cavern. Shadowolf closed his eyes and focused on the essence of fire and spirit. Deep in the kernel of his soul the power grew stronger. The wings of the *Wisoum* slowly retracted out of sight as the energy reached a peak within him.

And then he released it. Fire ate at him and coursed around him like a ferocious bonfire billowed by wind. The heat increased and the flames shone a dull combination of white and blue. On the other side Darcwulf was having the same success in releasing his power. The two torches lit the roof of the cavern, and the battle in the Fairiwell ceased.

The fletchlings looked up at them, unsure of their next move. The fairdievells flew back to their homes in equal uncertainty. Shadowolf looked through white, shining eyes at the destruction caused to the living quarters of the fairies. Although he had never personally visited their abode before, he had heard tales and knew that it had once been fairer.

Pock marks on the floor revealed moisture that had once been bodies of water; probably lakes or pools. Scattered timber lay across the earth as testament to hubs of previous habitation. And the colour that had been the life of the Fairiwell was now grey and brown.

The fletchlings flew up to the brothers in trepidation. Shadowolf and Darcwulf lifted their arms and aimed with their palms at the ascending beasts. In one fluid flow, their power streamed down.

Rivers of fire and spirit roared into the cavern. The flames burnt every beast it encountered, their muffled cries outdone by the noise of the energy.

"No!" Heula shouted, but no one could hear her on the ledge. Unaware to the brothers, their flames were reaching the homes of the fairdievells. She hastily mumbled words and closed her eyes.

The sound of hooves passed behind her.

Soon the unicorn was below the fiery blaze, her horn shining and raised, keeping the fire from harming the fairdievells. The level remained above Ursula's horn, never once passing closer to the floor of the Fairiwell.

The flames dimmed and died. Shadowolf drew the power within himself, his eyes becoming blue again. The last vestiges of the ethereal wings vanished as Ursula changed from her unicorn state back to her human figure.

"Have you gone mad?!" she asked them, but keeping her piercing gaze on Shadowolf. He simply looked back at her, not answering. "I expected this from Le'Mar, not you."

"We simply protected the fairdievells," Darcwulf countered.

"A *KariemsaPh* would know better than to set everyone's life in jeopardy for the sake of killing the enemy," she addressed him, and looked back at Shadowolf. "Maybe Masara was right. Perhaps you are not as ready as I thought."

Ursula turned to scout the fairies and to assess the situation. The Clan members reached the floor from the ledge and waited for the two to float down. It was difficult to think of anything to say in the aftermath of Ursula's belittling rebuke. He turned to Shedaaij for comfort, but found it only in her smile.

"You were irresponsible," she told him, but held him when she saw the effect of her words through his eyes. He could tell from the look on Darcwulf's face that Fransiska was giving him the same treatment.

The fire blazed before him. The restored lakes glittered in the cavern and the fairies brought food and fruit juices from their havens to the occupied tables. Although the Fairiwell looked splendid and alive with colour and underground forest growth, Ursula had informed the Clan that it was a mere shadow of what it once was.

But the unicorn lady was nowhere to be seen now. She was the only member of the Clan not seated at the festive table. Shadowolf wanted to speak to her; he longed to make things right, but it was as if there was a wall between the two of them. Was he really becoming like the dark lord? Was he taking the same path Le'Mar had taken many centuries before, forgetting everything he cared about in pursuit of power?

"I have to find Ursula," he said to Shedaaij beside him. She nodded in understanding and he rose. His faithful wolf stood and walked beside him.

He walked between the trees and under the lit candle-lanterns. The leaves crunched under his dirty bare feet, but Nelnar's soft paws barely made a noise. The sound of trickling water reached his ears to the left and right, but the scent of Ursula's body mingled with steam and sweet perfume led him forward.

His mind drifted as it usually did when he was alone. Her words echoed in his mind like the sting of a scorpion poisoning his veins. He calmed his thoughts and nerves, deciding rather to practice lowering his power level. But Le'Mar was there in his mind, the impending war an alert to his senses and he could feel the energy coursing from his soul into his body.

He stumbled and stood dead still as he realised he had found Ursula. She was bathing in a small pool lit from a source under the water. It lit her wet skin delicately and her hair dazzled from the fairies above her.

She turned and gasped as she saw him and sank below water level. He quickly dived behind a tree, Nelnar jumping behind an adjacent one politely.

"I am really sorry," he said, sitting with his back against the trunk of the tree. Nelnar lay down on the dry leaves.

"Were you looking for me?" she asked.

"Yes, I was, but we can discuss it later."

Ursula was silent. Shadowolf counted his breaths, his heartbeat slowing as he awaited any word from her. When he was absolutely sure she was going to say nothing further, he started to rise.

"What was the purpose of your search?" she asked. He could hear the water moving as she continued bathing, and he sat down again.

"Did you mean what you said?" he asked. "About Le'Mar?"

"Shado, you abused your power," she said kindly. "What you did served nothing but destruction."

"Don't I always?" he said half light-heartedly.

"Usually you use precision and call on the elements for

assistance, not slaughter. You must overcome the *Wisoum*, not the other way around."

He knew she was right. The power had arisen from something deep inside him, and not something he had mentally summoned.

"Is the *Wisoum* inherently evil?"

"Why would you ask that?"

"I have never felt something so strong within me before. But its purpose seems bent on exhausting my power. Like you said, I was almost as bad as Le'Mar."

Ursula was silent again. He was tempted to look around the bark to see what was keeping her. He heard a rustle of material and footsteps on dry stone and assumed she was getting dressed. A few footsteps later her smooth ankle covered by the cyan straps of her sandals appeared around the tree, followed by a flowing blue dress. Her shoulders were bare of any straps, and the light accentuated her neck.

She smiled and her red lips held his gaze, until he looked up past her soft nose into her ocean blue eyes. He breathed deeply, managing not to kiss her and they walked back to the festival.

"The *Wisoum* is not a person, but an attributable power," she informed him. "You have gained it from your experience with Asgorna, as did Sonersaat with Maneto. As did one other…"

"One other?" he frowned.

"I will leave that up to you to discover," she said.

"Of course," he realised. "Will he take part in the prophecy?"

"Only time will tell."

"But why can't I control it?"

"Because its power is still greater than you can maintain," she said. "There is a long, technical theory about it that I have no desire to go into now, but as you grow and learn the *Wisoum*, the more it will adhere to your will and the less it will control you.

"Just remember my warning," she said as they reached the festive tables. "If you release your stored power too quickly without training, you could kill everyone around you."

They managed to sleep a few hours until the fairies woke them and indicated that the sun was rising. Shadowolf moved with tired eyes, eating the finely laid breakfast prepared for him. His blood pumped fast again as his metabolism awoke, and his senses stirred with the gentle breeze in the cavern.

When they were done, they followed a ledge on the wall up to the opposite side of the entrance. Once again they had to walk single file to avoid falling off the ledge. They reached the wall at the top where Ursula drew her insignia on the wall, and a door opened for them.

A tunnel similar to the one they had entered through led them out of the Fairiwell. Green bunks lined the side walls on occasion and the trip was more onerous than the first.

When Shadowolf was about to open his mouth to complain, the sweat sticking to his top, they entered a dark room. The torches of the tunnel could not penetrate the room because of the opening's angle. Darcwulf held his palm open and small flames blazed from his raised fingertips.

Along the far wall Shadowolf spied what was once a lever. Its handle was gone, but the base mechanism was still attached to a concrete slab on the wall.

"Now what?" Sorceress asked.

Almost in reply, the roof of the wall opened to noon sunlight and twelve archers aimed their arrows at them.

"Is this the Clan?" an archer asked.

An old man moved with his staff to the edge of the roof and peered down, smiling affectionately at Ursula.

"Yes," Masara confirmed. "It is."

SHEPHERD'S FESTIVAL
CHAPTER FOUR

"Shepherd's Gate," Masara said, indicating the village ahead of them. They rode on fresh mounts provided by the elves towards the looming trees of the village.

"Horlorn's Gate, Shepherd's Gate," Darcwulf said, "I feel like a gate already."

"Sometimes I wish I could find the latch," Fransiska teased, but he didn't find it amusing.

The village had two layers of trees. One layer consisted of tall, towering trunks reaching into the clouds. The others were short, stout stems reaching only half the height of the first group. Yet the two layers complimented each other, and held the abodes of the elves within their branches.

At first glance, it appeared as if there were three settlements in Shepherd's Gate. This was due to the ghostly lights that shifted around groups of homes. The closest group shone a pale sky blue, mingling with the chorus of voices that danced on the breeze of the noon sun. Masara led them past these homes to another group of trees with homes that glistened with deep purple lights.

When they dismounted, Shadowolf leaned back in curiosity to look at the last batch of trees. Almost in answer to his prying, the trees shone dull, ochre-brown lights around the homes built into the high branches.

"You should see them in the evening," Masara smiled, and handed the reins of his horse to the nearest elf. The horses were led to green lawns beside a still river to the north of Shepherd's Gate.

"Is Eldor here?" Shadowolf asked as they approached the trees with the purple lights.

"No, his throne is in the centre of the forest." Shadowolf followed Masara's pointing finger, and even in the density of the forest could see the tall spires of Eldor's Throne peeking into the sky.

"Then why are we stopping?" Darcwulf asked, equally anxious about the delay.

"The elves," Ursula broke into the conversation, "are holding a feast tonight, to welcome the Clan."

Shadowolf and Shedaaij frowned at each other, clearly not believing her. The Orion stirred and looked around at the forest.

"Eldor will meet us here tonight and after the festival we will travel to his throne," Ursula added to ease their doubts. "He has a message for us."

Shadowolf held his tongue, deciding to leave them to their secrecy. He was no longer in the mood for talking and simply nodded at her.

He shifted the weight of Ruben-Willow on either side of his hips, the dagger bouncing off his thigh and the sword slapping his knee. He wished he had kept the staff with him, if only to support him as he walked slightly up-hill towards the purple village.

"The village with the cyan lights," Masara pointed at the first group of trees they had passed, "is called *Karei-Mehr* by the elves; Fire's Ice."

Shadowolf saw that most of the activity was in the lower layer of trees in *Karei-Mehr*. The higher branches were empty, if one excused the abundant presence of marble homes, fairy nests and birds lodged between the branches and leaves.

"The violet village before us," Masara continued, breaking Shadowolf's observations, "is *Tholoi-Temh*; Light's Shade."

Tholoi-Temh had the most activity compared to the other two. As the name suggested, the purple lights did indeed seem to shade the inhabitants from the light of the sun. Trays devoid of any food or substance were carted up ladders to the topmost layer of trees, while trays filled to the brim with finger dishes and meats descended down spiraling staircases bound to the trunks of the trees. Tables were set in the vast opening between the trees, and this was where the feast was being prepared.

"And the last, brown village," Masara concluded, "is *Creoto-*

Goume; Sun's Nature."

This was the village where life was teeming, not in the sense of activity, but rather where nature was concerned. Creepers rose from the grass and wrapped around the trees, reaching the top branches of both layers and hanging down like tear drops. Squirrels ran up and down the trees, and beautiful birds that Shadowolf had never seen before bathed in its shade.

Shadowolf turned his attention to the festive tables. The elves were spreading their purple-hued hands over the trays of food. He gaped at their purple tinged faces, and frowned at Masara enquiringly.

"I thought elves were slightly green?" Shadowolf asked.

"Not all elves," Masara replied, smiling as if it were a mistake everybody made. "And the elves of these three villages correspond to the lights surrounding their villages."

Shadowolf looked back to the lower layer of *Karei-Mehr*, and after intense study through the distance he thought he could see the soft blue skin of the elves.

They walked past the table-setting elves to the trees. Masara reached one of the ladders and pulled himself onto it. Behind him, Shadowolf heard the wings of Dren push against the air as he rose.

"Nelnar," he started to say, but the wolf had already made up its mind and went running through the forest.

"We are going to have a look around," Teristé said, and the other six Crethans nodded their heads in agreement. Once they moved off, Shadowolf saw that the other Clan members had already started ascending the six ladders before him. He moved beneath Shedaaij, and climbed.

When they reached the low layer's platform, they stepped off. Masara let the Clan pass waiting for Shadowolf to join them and then proceeded to lead them through marble corridors.

The mist of purple light pervaded the air, but thankfully the walls were beige and not purple too. In contrast, the skins of the elves were deeper in colour when walking passed them and stood out against the walls.

Shadowolf started imagining just how large the village must be, as just the one forest of *Tholoi-Temh* was vast from the outside. His imagination was not far off it seemed as they passed room after splendid room, until Masara led them to a courtyard of bedrooms with a fountain in the centre.

Even though the roof of the courtyard was covered with overlaying leaves and branches, light still shone into the grass as if the sun were directly above them. No shadow or silhouette of the trees darkened the light, and even the silver fountain of a unicorn shimmered in the artificial rays.

Where they entered the courtyard, pebbles served as a circular path around the perimeter. The wall was lavender marble, and set in the wall were twelve doors. Shadowolf assumed they were the bedrooms.

"You will need rest for the festival," Masara said, and smiled at the Clan's gestures of relief. "If you need anything…"

He moved over to the unicorn-statue set in the midst of the fountain's water, and pulled down on the horn of the unicorn. The horn sank into the skull of the statue and a soft, violinic tune sounded through the trees. The purple mist deepened in the passage leading to the courtyard, as if it had become a beacon to the sound of the horn.

A movement caught Shadowolf's eye, and he turned his head to see Sorceress touching the gemmed butterfly pendant below her neck. She smiled softly, her eyes distant in thought.

Masara moved to the passage they had entered through and touched a decorated knob on the wall. The purple mist subsided to its usual hue. Masara and Ursula greeted them and left the courtyard.

Shadowolf doubted he would have the nerve to summon any of the elves. He felt queasy at the thought of calling any of them to his bidding when he could walk and assist himself. But then the idea of walking through the corridors of *Tholoi-Temh* without guidance struck him, and he realised that it might inevitably be necessary.

"Shall we share a room?" Shedaaij said teasingly, tucking her arm into his.

"Yeah, next to the lavatories," he smiled. "Just in case you…" Her eyes warned him, and he left the sentence incomplete. Yet, she took his advice and walked to the opposite side of the courtyard. There were two lavatory rooms, one for each gender. She turned the knob of the door to the left of the ladies' toilets and opened the room.

"Wait a second," Shadowolf turned and walked back to the courtyard, glancing around. The other members were settling into the rooms too, trying to pick ones that would best suit them.

Darcwulf and Fransiska took the room beside the men's lavatory. Angelia, Skywolf and Heula decided to stick together and took the room next to Darcwulf. He smiled shyly at the girls in greeting as they entered.

It was only now that he realised how much the three girls complimented each other. Although Angelia was slightly tanned in complexion compared to the other two, Heula the palest, their faces were almost identical. But their differences were marked by the shades in their hair, the varied beauty in their smiles and the experience in their eyes. Angelia giggled at his staring, and they disappeared into the room.

"Where are you going?" Lastgorn called as he and Sny-Ten chose a room.

"I am not staying with you two buffoons again," Gwyn replied tartly and entered a room that Sorceress and Scarlette had picked.

"I told you not to..." Sny-Ten was saying to Lastgorn, but Shadowolf could not hear what the Costen boys had done to cause her to react like that for they had disappeared behind the closed door.

Shadowwe and Tinonte decided to bunk the afternoon together, while Rennick and Trevor chose another. Dren and Trimistus decided to stay alone in individual rooms, leaving four rooms unoccupied.

Although they had already slept in the Fairiwell the previous night, Shadowolf knew all of them would enjoy another few hours rest.

"What wrong?" Shedaaij said behind him, tugging at his arm.

"How will Nelnar and the Crethans find us?" he asked turning to her.

"I am sure they can find their own way," she replied. "In the meantime..."

She walked back into the room, and he closed the door and followed.

***

"You summoned," Sonersaat said as he entered Le'Mar's chamber. He moved to the table and leaned on the surface awaiting his lord's response.

"Are the armies ready?" Le'Mar asked. He sat quietly staring out his opening in the wall over the Alcove of Light to the lands of the south.

"Yes. We are as ready as we can ever be," he replied. Le'Mar swiveled in his seat and faced the DragonRider sternly.

"Are you ready?" he asked.

From Sonersaat's back, bright ethereal wings emerged. They spread out passed his shoulders and Sonersaat grinned wildly as the power raced through him. Le'Mar could almost see the golden scales of the dragon wings become real.

"Good," the lord said, locking his fingers together and lifting them to his lips. "I see the *Wisoum* no longer controls you."

"What are your orders?"

"Alert my castle and eastern armies for war," Le'Mar looked up into his eyes.

"Very well," Sonersaat grinned even broader and tucked his wings in. He left without greeting.

Le'Mar stood up. As he walked to the centre of the room, the stone walls closed over the doors and the opening. He calmly sat down on a rug on the floor and crossed his legs, laying his wrists gently on his knees. He slowed his breathing and felt his heartbeat pulse softly against his forehead.

He closed his eyes. Nothing existed to him at that moment. It felt like the world was removed from him, although he was very much still part of it. His spirit stirred within him, and his body remained motionless in the meditative position as his spirit left it.

He could have passed to his objective with a single thought, but chose not to. Instead, he moved through the stone walls and moved spiritually over his land. He could see through his ethereal eyes the *Wisoum* moving through his army and giving the command. Ahead was a portal in preparation for his trip to the east.

Le'Mar moved over Sonersaat's portal and dropped down the steep cliff to the ends of the waterfall and the deep, beautiful forest at the bottom of the Alcove of Light. He moved south until he reached the start of the mountains of Bentley Strip and soared above the highest peaks covered with light, melting snow and hidden in stratospheric clouds.

What would have taken a traveler a few months to traverse the mountains took him mere seconds. He moved east to the River of Light, looking down at his Dark Boundary as he did so. He saw the area once called the Nether Region by the first elves to walk the earth and crossed the River of Light.

He was careful to avoid the Mists of Celene. He knew that the forest would reject him, as powerful as he was. Indeed, the forest would repel him the most because of his power and the nature of it. The tower of the War Council rose into the sunny sky with the Degron Castle attached to it.

He could feel the elemental wards placed in New Avalion's walls. The crude skill of the elementals and elves stung his nerves like a dire needle, but did not prevent him from entering the city. Their lore was not as strong as the ancient magic of the elvin forest. He smirked within his effervescent veil; while they grew weaker, he grew stronger.

He passed through the tower walls and entered the occupied circular room. The members of the War Council were deliberating, but their words did not pass into his hearing. He was not concerned with their plans. He was only interested in the man that sat at the head of the table.

Nighthale's aura glowed around his body. The element of wind was strong in him. It was odd to Le'Mar that Nighthale was stronger than most Windfarers he had met, but chose not to follow the path of the *Enodhim*.

He floated on the polished wooden table. He moved closer until he could sense his spirit. He entered though his pores into his arms, up his veins until he met the shoulder. He drifted through his chest until he found the aorta pumping blood into the heart. He floated in the blood awaiting entry.

When he entered, it was not the blood-filled heart that he found. Instead, it was the heart that he was hoping for. The ruby-coloured gem glistened within the fleshy heart. The Heart of Tigers pulsed with the power to open Eldor's Forest. Le'Mar passed through the wall of the gem.

He fell onto a rocky, grey surface, his left knee leaning onto the ground. It seemed as if his body had reunited with his spirit, because the pain of striking the surface shot up his leg. He was clothed in a green robe with a hood dangling down his back. He looked carefully around not quite knowing what to expect.

The grey surface was but an illusion to hide the red, burning obelisks that rose beneath him. He did not know what lay down the chasms between the rocks, but he did not want to know either. He was certain that Eldor would ensure the entrapment or death of any who tried to break the secret of the Heart.

His hair waved around his neck as he stood, the pain still shaking his leg. The wind whistled softly, blowing the fog surrounding him. He concentrated for any sound of attack, lowering his power level within by storing it in his soul but keeping it ready for defence.

There was nothing. No movement marred the crusty clouds that prevailed in the air. Feeling secure in his solitude he transferred power to his eyes, searching for an aura. The only existent being in the Heart seemed to be him.

"How is this supposed to be the Key to the Forest?" he whispered. Echoes shouted and whispered back to him from every direction, repeating his words. He spun around, desperately trying to find anyone in the desolate landscape and still there was nothing.

This will drive me mad, he thought.

"Oh will it?" three voices said.

"Drive me mad," another two said.

"What is a mad?" another four asked.

"Mad as a cow," one said.

In the distance a warm glow was approaching. It hopped from obelisk to obelisk. Its aura was strong until Le'Mar no longer needed power to see the four-legged beast before him. It had a white coat speckled with large black shapes. It looked at him strangely, and emitted a low 'moo' sound.

"What is this?" Le'Mar cursed at the foul Heart.

"What is what?"

"That is what."

"A cow is what?"

"That is a cow."

The cow reacted by bellowing again. Le'Mar hadn't cursed about the cow, but rather the predicament he was in. Yet the answer he had elicited from the voices made him realise there might be a solution after all.

"What is the Key of the Heart?" he tried.

At first there was no reply. The red obelisks glowed warmly for a moment and the cow grew bored and hopped away. Le'Mar was about to rephrase the question, when the various voices spoke.

"A key opens a door."

"A door is a covered hole."

"A covered hole is a door to what?"

"A watt is the unit of measure for power."

Out of the fog a door appeared. It was a plain door with a black knob on the side. Le'Mar hesitated before jumping over each grey surface until he reached it. He leaned against the door and turned the knob. The door opened slowly to a void. Le'Mar stepped into the opening.

As his foot landed, something passed through his body. He stood rigidly shaking, as if lightning coursed from the door knob through his body to the floor. With a violent jerk, he flew back and barely managed to catch the tip of a sharp obelisk. His legs dangled towards the chasm below.

He pulled his body up and jumped to a grey platform. The door was still there and he stared at it as he lay on the obelisk.

How do I stop this? Le'Mar thought, realising too late he should have stilled his mind. He sighed as the voices started again.

"Power cannot be stopped, for it is always in motion."

"Momentum is the product of mass multiplied by velocity."

"Speed and mass of a cow?"

"A quantity of cows."

The air moved around him and he looked up and saw a multitude of cows storming over the obelisks. Their speed belied their weight, for they moved as fast as fairies. Before he could teleport or jump, a cow rammed into him and he was carried on its head from obelisk to obelisk.

Le'Mar raised his hand and drew fire to attack the cow.

"Fire draws air."

"Fire dries water."

"Water erodes earth."

"Earth displaces water."

From the chasms elementëls of every sort arose into the air. While Le'Mar climbed the back of the cow and held on, several elementëls flew before them. Rocks and fire and water and cyclones of wind rained down on the stampeding cows.

"How do I get out of this hell hole!" he shouted, dodging several balls of flame by steering the cow, while avoiding the gaping chasm beneath the obelisks.

"Hell is the home of the wicked."

"Hell burns with brimstone and evil."

"The undead and demons burn in hell."

"Hell smells like acrid smoke."

Suddenly fire broke from within the chasm and deep, black smoke rose up. Le'Mar choked, his eyes burning with tears. Hoarse cries filled the Heart, and he looked through watery eyes as demons and skeletons crept up onto the obelisks and began killing the cows in an attempt to reach Le'Mar.

Without a further word or thought, he jumped off his charging cow and rammed his fiery fist through the skull of a skeleton…

***

Shedaaij woke up in the late afternoon to an empty bed. The cover was neatly closed on the pillow, but the head that should have been there was gone. She got out of the bed and reached for the top and skirt hanging in the wardrobe.

She contemplated her coral armour for a moment, but decided to leave without it. The weight in her stomach was effort enough without the armour pressing on her breasts.

Shedaaij walked out of the room into the circular courtyard. She easily found her way down the tunnels, the earth essence in the trees guiding her to the spiral staircase leading to the elvin homes. She walked down the stairs, running her fingers along the trunk and watching the approaching fields for any sign of her lover.

Creotos glinted in the northwest as it approached the horizon. It opened her eyes to the feast preparation; the hordes of tables and food, the jolly elves and company of dwarves. But she could not spy Shadowolf within *Tholoi-Temh*.

She reached the grass of the fields and spotted the Crethine Dayna-wolf chatting to Trimistus. The former Saneth smiled at her until she reached them, and pointed to a hedged training ground in response to her question. Shedaaij walked to the indicated hedge, hearing a whistling sound end in a thud.

Shadowolf notched another arrow and aimed for the sack of corn. He heard Shedaaij's footsteps behind him, but kept his focus on the swaying sack hanging from a branch. When the momentum of the previous shot died and the sack was still, he loosed the arrow.

"Nice aim," she said as she stood beside him. He notched another arrow and waited for the sack to stop swinging. Nelnar emerged from undergrowth and lay down chewing a dead hare. "I see you are both in a hunting mood."

"It helps me clear my mind," he replied, loosing his arrow.

"What's disturbing you?"

He calmly pulled out an arrow and notched it. The sack swayed left-back and then right-forward. As it reared back again, he aimed and loosed. The arrow struck the sack dead-centre and sent it swinging further back and up.

"Many things," he said and leaned on the bow as he looked at her. "Our child; Le'Mar's war; the War of the Dragons; Eldor's message tonight; Darcwulf's distant mood lately…"

"Ok, ok, I get it," she sympathised and embraced him. She could see the weary look around his eyes and felt the tension inside him.

"Sometimes I let it all out by expending my power," he said, and she heard his voice crack. She knew it was difficult for him to be open like this with her, but when he did she felt appreciated. "At other times…"

He whirled around, drew an arrow and shot the sack in the instant of a second. Shedaaij did not turn away in shock or apprehension, but walked to face him and placed her fingers on his cheeks. His eyes were wet and as much as he tried to hold them back, a tear trickled down each cheek onto her fingers.

"It's not a shame to cry over heavy matters like yours," she said, trying her best to console him. Shadowolf heard footsteps enter the training yard and used the wind to dry his cheeks.

Shedaaij watched as the cold image set over his visage; it was his mask that he wore, not for Shedaaij, but the others. It was a mask designed to give hope and confidence to the Clan, a mask that Shedaaij had long since learnt to look past. It was a mask that he inherited from his father.

The two turned to greet Masara. His advance was subtle for he did not wish to disturb them. But there seemed to be a purpose to his visit, and Shedaaij smiled at Shadowolf before leaving the two men alone.

"I seem to be popular today," Shadowolf smiled heartily, although his heart was still damp.

"I wanted to speak to you before Eldor's arrival," Masara said. "Not about his purpose, but other matters relating to you…and your sword."

"Ruben-Willow?" he asked, looking down at the blade and dagger hanging from his hips. The dagger's handle was now covered with a green, woven cloth. While Shedaaij had still been sleeping he had approached one of the elves to assist him and in a matter of an hour the task had been completed.

"Indeed," Masara replied. "I too have a sword that is as much part of me as Ruben-Willow is to you."

Shadowolf looked incredulously at Masara's robe, but he only saw the staff that the old saint leaned on.

"It cannot be seen, for our union is complete," he continued. "Draw your sword to attack me, and I shall show you."

Shadowolf did not doubt him and knew he had a trick up his sleeve. He reached down for the blade on his left hip. Before he could draw it Masara had lengthened his arm and a sword as white as pearl touched his neck, the sound of its unsheathing ringing in his ears.

"Ok," Shadowolf said calmly. Masara frowned at his behaviour. "How did you manage that?"

"It is a bond with my sword that enables me to make it one with me," he explained. The sword sheathed back into his arm, the ringing sound scaring the nearby birds. "It is useful in surprising the enemy, and you don't have to disarm yourself when sleeping, bathing, or any other such duties."

"How do I do it?" Shadowolf replied sincerely, lowering his defences and smiling. He knew closing himself to the world was no answer to his troubles, although it did give him a moment's reprieve.

"I will do it for you," Masara said. "You have enough on your mind."

He moved towards Shadowolf. He placed his hands on Shadowolf's shoulders and look into his eyes. Shadowolf breathed deeply, waiting for anything to happen when he felt power surging around them. The light suddenly became brighter until it felt like they were floating in the air.

He was alone. Everything was white around him. Although he could feel the power of Masara, the saint was not visible before him. He drifted in the light until a sharp pain penetrated his soul.

His hips seared with a sharp sting. Soon, the sting travelled through him like a quick poison. Ruben-Willow glimmered on his hips momentarily, and then faded from sight.

Although he could not see the weapons, he could feel Ruben-Willow as part of him. It was as if a long lost piece of him had been returned after years of separation. Ruben-Willow shared with him the knowledge of its power and filled his mind with their combined capabilities.

The forest loomed over him as the light faded. The shade of the leaves overhead glimmered over his eyes as he stared at the sky.

"It is done," Masara sighed and coughed. He moved from Shadowolf's body on the grass to the hedges, his feet creating echoes of shuffling on Shadowolf's power-enhanced senses.

He continued to stare up at the sky. He could feel Bontu all around him. The trees whispered his power, and the air brimmed with his omnipotence. His heart held joy in his heart that he had not felt in some time. It was different from the happiness he shared with Shedaaij…it was peace.

Once his communion with Bontu was over, he rose up slowly. Masara was almost out of the clearing on his way to the preparation.

"Thank you Masara," Shadowolf said.

"The grace of the Lord be with you, Shado," he replied with a soft smile. "Without it, we are all like Le'Mar."

The night crept on them like a velvet shield, the stars shining down like studs of quartz and Sothos like a diamond sword. The jolly fires leapt in *Tholoi-Temh* and the tables were filled with various meats, breads, cheeses, jams, elvin kuitar, juices, wines, salads cold and warm, tomatoes, potatoes and every other food and drink that leaves the lips watering with desire.

Shadowolf ate to his heart's content, but anxious for the arrival of Eldor. Darcwulf eventually arrived with Fransiska attached to his hip, and it was the happiest that he had seen his brother in a long time. Darcwulf promptly landed into the vacant seat beside Shadowolf.

"Has the elderly elf showed himself yet?" he jibed, dishing his plate. "Ooh, wild boar! My favourite."

"Not as yet," Shadowolf laughed, but silence reigned further as they ate.

Sothos was a quarter-way up the sky when Masara walked up a temporary wooden stage with Ursula. Fairy and elvin lights lit their faces and the crowds kept their mouths in anticipation.

Seeing the two of them together on the stage made Shadowolf realise something: was Masara's prolonged longevity really due to the magic of the forest, or was it partly aided by Ursula? Did legend not tell that unicorn blood prolonged a man's life?

He shuddered at the thought of drinking Ursula's blood. Yet, in a sense it did explain how Masara's health survived as Malanite. He was thinking about her reaction on the Windfarer when she heard he was sick, but was cut off by the sound of Masara's voice.

"Ladies, gentlemen, elves, dwarves, Crethans, Crethines, etc, etc," he smiled at the laughter. "It is good to see you all so happy. I announce with pleasure that the time has come for Eldor to present his message."

Masara and Ursula separated and walked to either side of the stage. The old saint tapped his staff thrice on the floorboards. In the centre of the stage the air shimmered with air and power until the silhouette of a wide circle was visible.

The circle grew steadily clearer until the portal streaked with green lightning and someone stepped through. It was not the deep, aged elvin face that everyone was expecting, but Elgoth who stepped to join his father.

Next a staff passed through and the expected elvin lord Eldor walked onto the stage, who was greeted by thousands of cheers. He raised his palms in supplication for silence, and they waited.

He walked away from the portal, but it did not close. Next a woman in a gorgeous, glittering green dress exited. She had light freckles on her face and dark hair, but Shadowolf could see by the strain in her face that she had overcome a great ordeal. The smile was polite and sweet, but held no real affection to it.

She was followed by another man that he did not recognise, but the Crethans seated near him suddenly looked at each other and he assumed the stranger must have been one of them. He was clothed in hard, brown leather and auburn shoulder pads encrusted with rubies.

Another elf walked through. He held a regal appearance, and Shadowolf heard some voices whisper "Prince Lesan." The elf prince stood beside the woman, his splendid elvin robe and bow shadowed by her beautiful dress.

The portal closed. Eldor walked to the centre of the stage and faced the crowd with a faint, yet comforting, smile.

"Thank you all for leaving your villages and burrows to attend the feast," Eldor said. "I have many others to visit in the forest tonight, but there is purpose in presenting it to Shepherd's Gate first."

Shadowolf stirred and Shedaaij snuggled closer into his arms. He watched with intense concentration, feeling that this was the most exciting event that had happened since his return to Celenic Earth.

"Our guests are the reason," Eldor indicated the Shadow Clan seated across six tables. "I needed them to see the decision I have made before anyone else."

This seemed to concern the elves and dwarves the most. Fear chorused in the voices that carried across the wind to Shadowolf's senses.

"We have long sheltered our forest from evil," he continued, determined to present his case. "At first the only access was through *Pernonil*, the forest gate to the west."

The woman in green shivered at the mention of the gate.

"We waged a battle for the magical forest with Le'Mar two years ago, during the Windfarer Prophecy." Eldor looked up at Shadowolf and smiled. "*Enodhim*, would you be so kind as to join us?"

Darcwulf and Shedaaij were the first amongst the Clan to look at him enquiringly, but deferred from asking as his face was covered in confusion. He rose from his seat and took to the stage. He walked up the stairs, his heart beating harder than ever before. He looked up at the beautiful woman's eyes across the stage.

"When the power of the *Enodhim* was released, the gate of *Pernonil* fell," Eldor continued, addressing the crowds. "At first I thought Mercius had succeeded, as we all had thought he was the Windfarer. But Ursula feared we had misunderstood the prophecy, and based on Masara's assumptions she approached Shadowolf."

His face grew warm from all the attention.

"Shadowolf had conquered Mercius," against the will of Ursula and Asgorna, Shadowolf thought to himself, "and released the power of the *Enodhim*. Maybe if we had explained the peril of the forest to him, he would have desisted from doing so."

Shadowolf looked up at Eldor and frowned.

"Mercius was but a pawn for Le'Mar's greater plan," the elf lord said. "He knew how great the power of the node was. He calculated that there might be a chance that the release of the power would destroy the magic of *Pernonil*. He was right."

"Why did he not attempt the power node?" Shadowolf asked, and Eldor seemed pleased at the question.

"For two reasons," Eldor replied. "Firstly, because he wanted to be present when the gate fell, before I had the opportunity of rebuilding our defences. Secondly, because he had a servant that had been nicknamed "the Windfarer" for decades.

"But they did not understand the true nature of the Windfarer, and therefore Mercius could not release the power. So when Le'Mar felt the demise of Mercius and the rise of the true *Enodhim* he panicked. He must have thought that we had secretly sent Shadowolf to claim the power and that Shadowolf was on his way to defend us."

Shadowolf laughed, but stopped when Eldor looked at him.

"But I thought he needed the Heart of Tigers?" Shadowolf asked, trying as hard as he could not to realise that if he had left the power node as Ursula had advised, *Pernonil* would not have fallen. Perhaps Le'Mar would have been defeated too. He pushed the guilt away.

"He did, but he also counted on the release of the power to assist him," Eldor said. "To redeem his moment of dread he took the only other treasure that Baron Maren-Ti held dear; his daughter."

Eldor stepped aside so that Shadowolf could see the woman.

"Her name is Chenesia," Masara introduced. "And she has played a large role in pursuing the safety of the Heart until her capture."

"How did you escape?" Shadowolf asked, intrigued.

"It took me two years," she replied in a crystal clear voice. "And it is a long tale."

"She also confirmed Trimistus's news of Le'Mar's castle above the Alcove of Light," Masara said.

"Lucian and Simnab the Crethan," Eldor indicated the man in the hard leather, "met her and the pegasus Genewiu at Carmel on the way home."

"That can't be right," Shadowolf interrupted. "I saw Lucian in New Avalion with my father."

"He is on a journey to find uPendus," Chenesia informed him.

Shadowolf held his silence. He recalled Telgar mentioning Lucian's presence in Carmel. He had many thoughts and questions, but they only converged into a renewed headache.

"So where is the pegasus?" he asked stupidly.

"On her way as we speak," Eldor pointed to the sky.

The crowds looked up. In the dim light of Sothos they saw white wings gliding through the air. On her back was a human that they could not clearly see, as he was clothed by the night. It took a minute for her to land, and when she trotted into the light Shadowolf almost choked.

"Father?" he ran down and greeted Nighthale. Their embrace was broken by the deep rumbling of thunder. The two Degrons looked up at the sky and saw green flashes of light pass over, and then the sky cleared.

Nighthale and Shadowolf walked onto the stage. Eldor greeted and faced the crowds again.

"The Heart of Tigers was passed from Baron Maren-Ti to Nighthale Degron as keeper," he informed them. "I believe that Le'Mar will stop at nothing to enter the forest, and to put the lives of others at risk for our sake is no longer acceptable.

"It is time we fight our own battles."

Eldor looked at Nighthale and Shadowolf's father simply nodded. Eldor placed his palm gently on Nighthale's chest. An aura of red surrounded the chest and palm, and slowly Eldor retracted his arm. A large red gem emerged through the chest's skin, but the skin was unharmed.

Eldor turned and held the Heart of Tigers before all of them.

"The magical defence of the forest is broken," Eldor announced. "We prepare for war!"

POOL OF RADIANCE
CHAPTER FIVE

"Prepare for war," Darcwulf snorted. "What a joke. Haven't we been at war for the last few years?"

Those were the words that now echoed in Shadowolf's head early in the morning as Shedaaij still slept beside him. He had only closed his eyes for two hours before he had awoken to the thoughts in his mind.

Eldor was going to allow Le'Mar to start the War of the Dragons in his forest. Shadowolf turned his head to see the dragon amulet dangling from the knob of the wardrobe. He had communicated through the amulet with Asgorna to prepare the army. Asgorna simply reminded him of their bargain and left to command the dragons.

He had also spoken a few words to his father after the speech of Eldor, but his father had decided to return to Avalion as he suspected Le'Mar might try an assault there too. Shadowolf wished he could return to his home, but facing Le'Mar in the forest was his greater priority.

When the Clan had arisen and gathered their goods outside in the fields of *Tholoi-Temh*, they were addressed by Masara. Shadowolf could not see Ursula, but he assumed she was with Eldor.

"We will not be heading immediately for the throne," he informed them. Several of the members groaned. "We will be going to the Pool of Radiance first to open a portal to Horlorn's Gate."

"Oh ok," Darcwulf jibed and merrily saddled his stallion. "In that case..."

***

"Death will free you."

"You are death"

"Taste blood tingling."

"World of blood."

Clouds gathered in the Heart and blood rained down on Le'Mar. He rose into the air and avoided the slash of the FireStrom. He dived down and decapitated one of the undead. Phoenixes cried at him. Dragons clawed the air at him. Blood, ice and fire stormed around him.

Death was the only answer. The Chasm. The chasm was where the creatures were crawling out of. He dodged several aVampyere, barely moving faster than them, used wind to parry something the Heart referred to as a "kettle", and fell down the chasm.

The darkness surrounded him; darker still was the fear that clung in his throat. And he hit ground, his legs aching from the pain. He lay on his back, sunlight reaching his weary, blood-crusted eyes. He could smell nature and hear birds and animals rustling nearby.

He had failed. The secret of the Heart was still unknown to him, but he knew he had failed. Hate and anger built up in him, his longing to destroy Eldor's home sinking into despair. If he couldn't even destroy the elves, how was he going to ever find Masara?

A bird hopped on a windowsill and looked down at him. He opened his eyes very carefully, shielding the sun with his hand. He glanced around the tiled lavender room and saw the Heart glistening in a bracket set in a wall. On either side of the bracket were shelves of books, scrolls and artefacts.

He dared not speak, for fear that it was another world bent on answering his everything thought, word or action. His curiosity only permitted him to stand and look out the window. The bird flew away from his stench.

"It cannot be!" he exclaimed softly, and then ducked in fear of the voices from the Heart. Only the wake of his words still echoed in the room and the sounds of nature outside.

Down below he saw the fields, trees and villages. The mountains rose to the west, south and north. The tower he was in was substantially high, but he could see a large group traveling in a caravan to the south.

"Am I in the forest?" he mumbled, not daring to believe it. He moved to the only door of the room and opened it minutely. He heard footsteps and chatter, but elves and dwarves walking in the corridors confirmed his suspicion. When he caught sight of Chenesia he almost slammed the door hard, but stopped at the last moment and closed it softly.

"How did this happen?" he said, cradling his forehead in his hands. "I know I failed."

Many suggestions crept into his head, but none of them mattered. He was in the forest. He needed to contact Sonersaat and inform him of success. And then he would have a look for Eldor's army and see what he was up against.

Yes. That was what he would do.

Le'Mar ran for the window opposite the traveling caravan and jumped into the wind, becoming part of it.

Shadowolf rode with Masara and Darcwulf at the head of the caravan. Shedaaij and Fransiska spent time with Heula and Skywolf near the centre. They had already heard Shadowolf's concerns earlier and decided to search for alternative discussions.

"You know," Shadowolf said, "when we met in the ruins so long ago, I never dreamed we would be traveling in the forest together."

"It is strange," Masara agreed.

"There is so much that I still don't understand about this war," Darcwulf said. "Le'Mar's motives being one. I understand the whole "Battle of T'Mar" thing…"

"Not as much as you ought to," Masara said. "But Eldor will be explaining it when we reach the throne. It's time you are told the complete reason behind the war."

Shadowolf and Darcwulf looked at each other in surprise.

"You have always had special interest in me, haven't you?" Shadowolf asked.

"In the Clan, you mean?" Darcwulf countered.

"No, in me," Shadowolf said, looking at Masara. The saint smiled. "You met in me in the ruins when this war started."

"Elgoth merely warmed my interest when he mentioned this boy that was running around trying to save the world," Masara teased.

"There was not much that I could do from the Far Isles, but Elgoth kept an eye on you."

"But it's more than that now," Shadowolf pushed for an answer. "You bought me that staff so that Ursula could teach me to store my power. You joined my soul to Ruben-Willow. Everything Ursula has done for me was upon your advice."

"What makes you think that?" Masara laughed.

"I realised it when Eldor said it was based on your assumptions that Ursula first approached me in the Mists of Celene."

Masara stared at the grass as the horses rode on. He was deep in thought and sighed at least twice before he answered Shadowolf.

"You have done what must be done," Masara said. "You have wondered the earth in mist and ignorance, but with your eyes now wide open you cannot escape the truth. You have been hardened and shaped for this purpose. Many will die, but many more will live because of you.

"The time of the *Sadgi* is coming," Masara held Shadowolf's concentration intensely. "He who will claim the four elements and the power of the soul to harness them to his will, it is he who will decide the fate of us all. I believe that you, Shadowolf, are that *Sadgi*.

"My time is almost up, but before I leave this world I have asked that you be trained in the ways of old. As an *Enodhim*, the wind will be your sails. As a *Merlandsi*, you will be emperor of the waters. As a *Goudlem*, the earth will be your ally. As a *KariemsaPh*, the fires will rise from the deepest depths. And as a Solem, the soul will be mastered.

"You will be the *Sadgi*. You must be, in order to face him, for Le'Mar is greater than you. So I leave you with one last warning, Shadowolf. Do not face the dark lord until you are ready."

Shadowolf's head reeled as the words of his dream passed through Masara's lips. He focused back on his surroundings and rage burnt within him.

"It was you!" he exclaimed. "You put me through the trials!"

"No," he sighed again, "but it was I that initiated it."

Shadowolf was angry but he kept quiet, hoping Masara would explain and too scared he would not control his temper.

"I approached the elementëls to teach you the way of the Sagdi," Masara explained.

"Why?" Shadowolf asked.

"You fulfilled the Prophecy of the Windfarer," Masara continued. "And by doing so, you initiated the cycle of the prophecies set out by Philgarn Asmuth so many years ago.

"It was inevitable that the Prophecy of the DragonRider would follow, and we already know Le'Mar has prepared Sonersaat to take that title. Sonersaat is an accomplished *Enodhim* by now, and therefore by right may challenge you for the *Wisoum*."

"I don't understand," Darcwulf asked of both of them. "He has a right to challenge Shado?"

"Philgarn mentions in his 'Latos-Formos' theory," Masara explained, "that the position of the latter may only be challenged by the fulfilment of the former."

"Say again?" Darcwulf said.

"It means that the position of *Wisoum* will be competed for by *Enodhim*'s," Masara helped. "Position of *Sadgi* will be competed for by *Wisoum*'s."

"Oh," Shadowolf said. "So Trimistus won't play a role as he is not an *Enodhim*."

"We assume," Masara said.

"Wait, wait, WAIT!" Darcwulf shouted in frustration. "Too much information! Trimistus?"

"I have seen the *Wisoum* in him too," Shadowolf said. "It's faint, but it's there."

"But I thought you got it by spending years with Asgorna?" Darcwulf asked. "And Sonersaat was with Maneto."

"Trimistus never told us what he and the dragon Mynisna did with his two years away from the earth," Shadowolf explained. "When I saw the *Wisoum* in him and when he summoned Mynisna at Horlorn, I realised."

"So he might become a *Wisoum*, but not necessarily contest the prophecy," Darcwulf realised.

"There is a chance," Masara said with caution in his voice, "that Le'Mar has seen the *Wisoum* in him too. If Le'Mar is ignorant of the "Latos-Formos" theory, he might send Sonersaat to kill him too."

"That's been on his agenda anyway," Darcwulf said, turning in his saddle to look at Nolraldun.

"Wait a minute," Shadowolf said suddenly. "Le'Mar met with the elementëls and said he had undergone the trials. So, he is *Enodhim* too."

Masara nodded.

"Does he contain the *Wisoum*?" Darcwulf asked.

"I don't know," Masara asked.

Shadowolf relaxed in his saddle and let his thoughts roam freely in his head, trying to reach a conclusion.

"I don't think Le'Mar will allow Sonersaat to become a Sagdi," Darcwulf concluded for him.

"We will have to see."

Masara's warning not to challenge Le'Mar stayed with Shadowolf on their journey south to the Pool of Radiance. When they passed Eldor's Throne to their left, the Pool shone brightly in the mid-afternoon sun.

"Why the Pool of Radiance?" Shadowolf asked.

"*Pernonil* was the only magical entrance into the forest, the Fairiwell being the non-magical," Masara said when they were on the southern banks of the Pool. "After the fall of the gate, Eldor decided to create a magical entrance within the forest, the Pool of Radiance."

The Clan dismounted. Masara whistled two low notes, and the elvin horses loaned to them ran back towards Shepherd's Gate. The old saint beckoned that Shadowolf and Darcwulf follow him to the beach.

The lake of the Pool of Radiance shone before them as Masara drew his staff before him. He closed his eyes in heavy concentration.

As was expected, a portal shimmered in the air before Masara. It intensified until it was a solid, swirling opening between Eldor's Forest and Horlorn's Gate. Masara lowered his stance and prepared to walk through to the other side, but was stopped by a sandal that made it through first.

The man proceeded to step through; he was apparently not concerned by the thought that anyone else might be attempting the portal. His regal figure stepped on the beach until his complete body was through.

"Lord Treville?" Shadowolf frowned. Horlorn's Gate's leader smiled and bowed to Masara.

"So you have returned?" he asked the saint.

"Indeed," Masara replied. "You have heard that we intend transferring our horses and equipment from Horlorn to the Forest?"

"Yes I have," Treville responded, a more serious connotation in his voice. "After Millon and Kentaur returned to our camps, we wondered if it would not be wise in joining the forest too."

Masara widened his eyes and looked at Shadowolf for a moment. He had obviously not been expecting this. Shadowolf stepped forward to assist him.

"What made you reach this decision?" he asked the lord of Horlorn.

"We missed our opportunity in facing the dark lord," Treville replied with a malicious grin. "And we thought that the forest would stand a better chance of survival if we assisted."

"Your numbers would greatly increase our odds," Masara agreed. "I might have to speak to Eldor about this..."

"I don't think we have time," Darcwulf said. "Le'Mar could be preparing for the war as we speak."

"It will only take a moment," Masara replied and, true to his word, he vanished from the beach. The portal closed behind Treville, leaving the trio alone.

"Well, I guess we better make ourselves comfortable," Shadowolf said, leading them to the waiting Clan.

He was deep in thought about Lord Treville's decision when the sight of Trimistus brought him to another matter. He walked over to the former Saneth. Without being called, Nelnar left Shedaaij's side and joined them.

"Is Mynisna ready for the war?" Shadowolf asked. Trimistus sat down on a box containing supplies from the elves and squinted up at Shadowolf with his dark, red pupils.

"Mynisna is ready to aid Asgorna, whatever the cost," he replied sternly. Shadowolf could see he was uncomfortable, and had no doubt what was troubling him.

"Do you know what is happening to you?" Shadowolf asked casually, sitting beside him on the box.

"I can feel it growing in me," the reptilian-man replied.

"Sometimes I can see wings on you, and the thing that squirms to be released. Is it the *Wisoum*?"

"Yes, I believe so," Shadowolf said.

"Does that mean what I think it does? Will I have to partake in the prophecy?"

"I don't think the answer is as readily available as that," he replied humorously. "No one knows what will happen. We don't even know if Le'Mar realises that the forest's seal of defence has been removed."

"Why me?" Trimistus asked.

"Because, like Sonersaat and I, you have been trained by a dragon," Shadowolf replied. "It is interesting that two of us have been taken by dragons and returned to this world at the same time, and I wonder what the dragons had in mind doing so."

"I spent many years with Mynisna," Trimistus informed him. "Not once did he mention that this would happen."

"Well, as Mynisna's rider," Shadowolf stood, "we hope that you will assist in the battle."

"I will fight until my dying breath."

"Do you think your old buddies Lister and Ru-maak will be present?" Shadowolf asked tentatively.

"I do believe so, Shado," he replied. "We will need all the help we can get to survive this battle. The dark lord hungers for this forest. He will stop at nothing to ensure its demise."

"Eldor has accepted," Masara said behind Shadowolf. "He has expressed concern about your Crethans though."

Shadowolf looked towards the spread Clan and found the Crethans. They were relaxed, talking to the others and walking around the woods.

"If Le'Mar has a Creth-Demon with greater command over them than I," Shadowolf said sadly, "then I will personally take care of it."

"Very well," Masara said. "I will need you and Darcwulf to assist me with the next portal."

Shadowolf's questioning gaze was ignored as the saint turned and walked to the Pool. Darcwulf joined him on route to the lake, carrying his fire staff in his hand. When Shadowolf reached the beach, Masara tossed him his staff.

"I want you two to split up to either end of the lake, but in line with me," he uttered. "As you leave me, use the end of the staves to draw a line to each end. I will call your names when to stop. At that point, plant the staff into the soil and hold tight."

They did as they were told. They used the staves to draw the lines, trying not to curse at stones that got in the way. After seven minutes of dragging, Darcwulf heard his named called and planted the end of the staff in the soil. It took another minute for Shadowolf to do the same.

Masara turned to face the elvin throne and spread his arms to each staff. His toes pointed along the line to the staves and he lifted his eyes to the heavens, speaking softly.

The silence in the fields became deafening. The animals and birds didn't mutter a cry, but as an eagle descended and screeched he realised it wasn't for lack of trying. Shadowolf spoke to test it, and although his vocal chords vibrated in his throat no sound emitted.

It was not that he could not speak, but the thrum of the portal's power over-rode every other sound. Masara looked at him with a hard face and he realised he was not gripping the staff properly.

The staff rocked to and fro in the sand. The water was receding from them and the power was overwhelming. He was sweating and even across the vast distance, he could see Darcwulf was having a difficult time with his staff too.

Masara strained where he was standing, and in an explosive appearance that almost threw Shadowolf back into the air, the portal spread between the staves with Masara in the centre.

The portal was as high as it was long. It was by far the largest portal he had ever seen and he wondered if there had been any larger in the history of Celenic Earth. The power through his staff remained constant albeit extremely potent. Masara relaxed his arms and body and beckoned for the brothers to join him.

It was a relieving three-minute jog to Masara. The old man watched the portal carefully waiting for any sign of the army.

"We forgot to ask if they were ready to come through," Masara smiled.

"I prepared them," Treville said behind them. "I could see no reason why we would be denied, but thought we could easily repack the mountain if we were."

"How long did it take you?" Darcwulf marveled.

"Ever since the centaurs appeared," Treville replied proudly.

"Well done, Lord Treville," Masara said. "We need a few more like you in this world."

Masara, Darcwulf and Shadowolf stared agape as the first walked through. With Treville, they slowly retreated backwards as the army moved forward towards them through the portal.

There was not one area of the length of the portal that was not filled with the crossing army. Some barely made it passed the staves as they walked onto the lush grass of the forest. A variety of people murmured in awe at the sight of Eldor's kingdom, while Masara, Shadowolf and Darcwulf marveled at the army of Horlorn.

It was not that they had not seen the army before; it was the fact that they had been split between three tiers when the Clan had last seen them. Now, all formed in crowds walking through the portal, the immensity of the army was truly revealed, and Shadowolf wondered if there was any place in Eldor's Forest to house them.

"Where do you want us?" Treville shouted to Masara, who croaked to find his throat.

"Down to the south at Lard's Den!" Masara shouted over the great crowd, for their murmurs had grown loud and still people were entering the forest from Horlorn. He pointed at ten elf riders. "Follow the elf scouts."

Treville nodded his head and instructed several generals concerning the Den. The army moved over the plains, forming into groups and waiting for the word to proceed. Shadowolf was watching the generals group their troops, the others still walking through the portal and passed them, when Masara pulled his arm.

"We have to ride to the Throne!" he shouted, although Shadowolf could hear him well enough. The wind carried it to his ears. "Eldor will have to give his presentation in the Den!"

"Isn't the Throne large enough?" Shadowolf said upon the wind, and Masara sheepishly smiled realising he didn't have to shout.

"It is, but can you imagine getting these troops in and out of the trees," Masara replied.

Shadowolf laughed, seeing the logic in Masara's statement. He nodded and followed Masara and Darcwulf to the Clan. Millon and

Kentaur had joined them with their supplies, and he stroked Mandy's dark fur and looked into her deep eyes. His staff still dangled from her saddle.

"Thank you for letting Mandy in," he said to Masara, knowing the world's tendency to disdain her due to her dark nature.

"I convinced Eldor that she is with you," the saint replied, "but the Crethans still bother him. Do you mind getting my staff while I confer with Treville?"

Shadowolf frowned at Masara for a moment, and then left Mandy to get Masara's staff. Darcwulf similarly left to the opposite end to get his.

Shadowolf ran down to the beach, wondering when the crowd would finally diminish and the last of the army would be through. His toes touched the soft sand as he held the staff.

During his patient wait, he spotted Theroy marching between elementals, and he wondered if he would see Lanel, Harmony and Mourna again. He hadn't spotted them earlier, but he was sure they must be with the army. Then he remembered that Nashela would be with them too, and his insides knotted.

The final group passed through the portal and, at a nod from Treville, Shadowolf and Darcwulf proceeded to remove the staves, with Masara lifting his palms in the distance. The portal closed.

Shadowolf started walking back, when his head grew faint. He cupped his fingers on his forehead and dropped the staff in the water. The world started to reel around him as he staggered.

"Not now!" he shouted, and as he fell he saw he saw a satisfied smile on Masara's face. His head hit the water and the last thing his eyes beheld was Darcwulf running towards him …

TRIAL OF THE *MERLANDSI*
CHAPTER SIX

Shadowolf stirred from the ground, and inwardly groaned. He was about to ask if the trial was necessary, when bubbles escaped his lips. Everywhere he looked was water.

His rose pendant lit up the area on his sternum. His gills reopened along his neck and he breathed. He looked up, but he could not see the surface of the water.

I don't even know if I can use water, he thought forlornly, realising that he had never really tried. A soft change in current made him turn around.

A figure in wind moved towards him, but she hardly seemed ready to attack. Her waist whirled elegantly in the soft cyclone until he could almost see the shape of her eyes.

Do I need to do this now? he asked mentally.

It is pertinent, yes, she replied. She moved what looked like a hand to his cheeks, caressing them as it passed down his neck to his chest. He wondered if the last trial was one of seduction.

When she reached his chest, she stopped on the glowing pendant.

I think you have had this privilege long enough, she whispered and her fingers passed through the skin of his chest and ripped the pendant out.

He immediately flailed around as the air left him. His gills hung like dead skin on his neck and air bubbles raced around his face as he tried hopelessly to keep his breath. A fist of fire moved through the ocean and hit him straight across the face, soon followed by a kick of earth from the back.

Shadowolf tumbled down and down. There was no bed now to catch him. The depths of the ocean were endless, and he could barely see through all the water. He coughed as more air left him and he could feel the pressure build in his lungs as the stale air yearned for release.

They were going to kill him this time. He opened his mouth as last of his air left him, his eyes closing. He saw the mental image of Darcwulf running down the beach, staff in hand. Nelnar was licking him, trying to wake him up. Masara's staff drifted slowly passed his face. Somewhere in the distance he could hear Shedaaij shouting in vain. And he felt Le'Mar's presence in the forest…

Shadowolf yanked his eyes open and saw the ocean again. His deepest fear contorted his face into anger. He would not allow Le'Mar to win.

He focused on his lungs, feeling the dirty air in them, and called the wind into them. He demanded that his biological system replace the carbon dioxide with fresh oxygen and somehow it worked. The air stirred in his body and the blood did the transfer with his lungs. He let the water pass in and out of him, slowly becoming attuned to the current passing through him.

Excellent, he said, but was knocked off-course by an earthly fist. He lost concentration on creating air for his lungs and started drowning again. It took him a moment to recreate it, but the moment was disturbed by an assault of wind. He could not block and attack while creating air and releasing the water.

The rage inside him grew and he knew what to do. He transformed his body completely into water. His skin and organs vanished as it became liquid. He grinned at the elements as they attacked. Now there was no need to breathe.

They were as relentless as usual. Earth, wind and fire struck him from all directions. Even in the density of the water, fire glared as bright as ever. It burnt at his liquid form. He blocked and counter-attacked trying to find their weakness.

When he next blocked fire, he used the water to grab him around the neck and poured it into his chest. Fire struggled and screamed writhing in its grasp. In the depths of the ocean, Shadowolf created bodies of sharks consisting solely of water packed together. The water shark buffeted wind, and bit into fire's body.

Earth summoned vines, but Shadowolf dodged them and

stretched out his hands, producing shards of ice. The ice struck cleanly in earth's chest and another shark's tail hit it. Mud flew everywhere and rock slapped Shadowolf's face.

Wind attacked from behind, and when he turned she struck his side. He simply summoned two liquid eels and they floated into the cyclone, shocks of lightning coursing through the air molecules and separating them until she was no more.

He waited. He knew that she was somewhere close. Although water surrounded him, he knew *Merlandsi* would attack him through some sort of ethereal form. Although the trials were tiring, he actually enjoyed this one. He felt cold, but relieved that his only concern at the moment was surviving the trial, and not the war.

She smacked his face. He recoiled slightly and looked in front of him. She hit the back of his liquid head, and he spun around to see that she was gone. A punch in the stomach and a flick on the nose, but still she was not visible.

Something came to mind, something that had happened between him and Mercius. He had moved as a spirit into Mercius's camp, and the dark Windfarer had chased him around and they had fought as spirits. Is this what she expected of him? Did he have to sense her to know where she was?

She smacked his considerations aside with a hit to the cheek, followed by a kick to his back. This was more frustrating than intimidating, and he stretched his senses out to try and feel her. He moved along the water, being liquid himself, trying to find her.

When she next attacked, he felt the power of water move towards his face and he blocked. His arm didn't rise, but his liquid entwined with hers and she released. Now she increased the tempo of her attacks and he managed to block three out of every five.

She seemed to have decided to use his tactic against him as liquid bodies of sharks arose in the water to meet him. They swam for his head and he dodged reflexively. Unfortunately, he had not controlled the dodge and he ended up on top of another shark. Being liquid was much more difficult than human, and distance was harder to estimate than he was used to with wind.

He swam over and around the shark until he found her again. Their powers locked as they embraced each other, exchanging jabs and blows until he actually thought he felt physical pain in his abdominal region.

You don't really seem to be into this, he said to her.

The power already resides in you, she said. *You just need to learn how to use it.*

I am about to face the dark lord, he said prophetically. *I would appreciate it if you gave me your all.*

She seemed to smile and disappeared. He looked around with watery eyes as the sharks vanished too.

The current pulled him. The water streamed from a source unknown and as he tried to drift away, a large black hole formed. It swirled and swallowed the water around it until it was as tall as Shadowolf. He moved against the water, not swimming but as one with the ocean, but still the hole tried to swallow him.

His toes touched the hole. Pain screamed into his mind. He increased his power, straining to lodge his liquid body from its pull, but he only managed to get his toes out.

He twisted into a ball until he faced the hole. He added his own current to the fury of the black whirlpool, thrusting his power at it. His face was upon the hole when it changed into a ball, an eclipse and then nothing.

Behind him he heard explosions, but he was too late to stop the balls of ice that hit him. His liquid body separated with each strike. He dodged, curved his abdomen and swirled over another. One hit him in the face. He lifted his arms in anger and caught one. He threw it back at her.

She continued this only ten more times, until he was returning each one. Suddenly he was right in front of her. He had moved through the expanse of water in the matter of a second and was pinning her against a hardened wall of water.

Didn't see that coming, did you? he smiled.

No, she replied. *I guess I didn't. Before we continue, I must just say that you need to constantly practise the elements. The more you practise, the greater you will become. Do not forget that.*

She was gone. Shadowolf exclaimed as the desert rock hit his knee. The ocean had vanished, and he was kneeling in his human form on rough sand with a strong sun in the sky.

He coughed. His throat was scratchy. He ran his hands over his throat trying to figure out why it was so dry.

Dry…no water…dehydration. He had forgotten the next step of the trial was withdrawal of the element. He coughed and spat, but only air emerged. He fell to the floor with his face on the hard clay, trying to swallow to get water down his throat.

It was no use. His throat constricted and tightened. He concentrated on his power, trying to call it from his core. Deep within he managed to create water, which seemed to seep through his body, up his spine and into the organs that required it the most. Feeling better and relieved, he sat up and spat again. This time phlegm did emerge with strands of sand. He cleaned his mouth with the back of his palm. The water continued to race from his core into his body producing a steady stream.

The water began to form sweat on his skin and he urgently needed to urinate. He slowed the amount of water coursing through his body until it was acceptable. He was about to urinate, when a sound of heavy feet thundered behind him.

He turned to see the huge beast that he had conquered so many times before. It loomed above him and roared furiously. Shadowolf was too tired and anxious to waste time fighting it, so he simply raised his hand and sensed where the water lay in its body.

The beast raced to confront him, but stopped as soon as it started dehydrating. It cried out mournfully as Shadowolf pulled the water out of its scaly skin and mouth, falling like a waterfall. The beast roared and then fell with its face on the ground. Its skin was extremely dry and soon became dust.

The four elementals walked over the arid land to him. They all smiled sadly in unison, and he knew what was expected of him. This time, however, he interrupted them.

"Can Le'Mar do all that I have done?" he asked.

"That, and more," *Enodhim* replied.

"And that is why you prepared me," he said, looking up in thought. "To defend myself against his elements, to attack with my elements, to create the elements if he removes them and to remove them from him if need be."

"Yes," *KariemsaPh* said, glad that he understood. "It is only the basic initiation of a *Sadgi*."

"But you won't continue his training?" Shadowolf asked.

"There are other types of *Sadgi*'s, ones who use evil to abuse the elements" *Goudlem* said. "You saw what he did to the world of Lord Danaka. When he is done with your world, he will do the same."

"I see," was all Shadowolf managed to say.

The elements moved away. *Enodhim* moved into the air and formed the winds. The sand stirred as it was cooled from the heat of the sun. *Goudlem* sank into the earth and filled the barren wasteland with life. *KariemsaPh* joined the rays of the sun in managing the heat of the land.

Shadowolf returned to his water form and fused with *Merlandsi*. They dropped into cracks and assisted *Goudlem* in creating grass and trees, animals and fish.

Celenic Earth teemed with life...

ELDOR'S RECEPTION
CHAPTER SEVEN

Sonersaat marched up and down the tent for the hundredth time. He had heard no news from Le'Mar. It was too quiet. His army waited outside, ready to take Eldor's Forest.

Yet, their master was still. He sat down on the chair, a servant handing him a warm drink. The sky that had been clear outside was starting to gather its clouds. He was anxious; Maneto and his dragons were just as anxious.

He jumped up as a red portal appeared on the wall of the tent. It was not a travelling portal, but rather a window of communication.

The dark, dirty face of Le'Mar appeared. Sonersaat was shocked to see the dark lord so, but held his comment. He moved closer to speak to him, but Le'Mar's head was turning constantly to make sure no one was seeing him.

"My lord?" Sonersaat greeted.

"Move the first wave of troops down the gorge into the forest," Le'Mar instructed with a broad smile on his face.

"What of the elvin protection?" the DragonRider asked.

"It has been removed," Le'Mar stated. "They are awaiting us."

"Can I expect any problems?" Sonersaat asked cautiously.

"Eldor is giving them a lecture," Le'Mar replied. "It would seem Horlorn has joined them, and they will be meeting to the south. It is close to the gorge, so it is perfect for an attack. Keep the men on guard until I give the signal."

"What of the drago…"

He was cut off as Le'Mar looked desperately back and the portal vanished.

Sonersaat rushed outside and commanded the vast troops to enter the gorge.

***

Eldor sat quietly in the Throne Room alone. The vast hall was empty as he had commanded his son to take the elves south. They had planned to go south after the visitors had been to the throne, but after seeing the vast army enter the forest, he decided not to delay it any longer.

He had procrastinated too many times. He considered that maybe his centuries on this earth had caused him to be slothful. Maybe he should have returned the Heart of Tigers before the fall of *Pernonil* forest? Maybe he should have dealt with Le'Mar then? And maybe he should have sent the elves south when his scouts had first seen Le'Mar's army gather at the southern gorge?

Too many 'should-haves'; too many decisions that might have been mistakes. He tapped his long, green fingers on the table, his thoughts curdling in his mind, when he was gratefully disturbed by three men.

"The three elementeers," Eldor teased them once they gained the stage. At least he could afford them some humour, he thought.

"Shall we go to Lard's Den?" Masara asked, foregoing the pleasantries.

"Yes," the elf lord replied. "Let's not waste any more time. Did you teleport here?"

"We used a portal," Shadowolf said. "Our horses are waiting at the Pool of Radiance."

"Ok, then we shall go there," Eldor said and whistled loudly. Eldor stood from his seat and took his white staff. He walked down the stairs with them to the bottom of the hall and opened a portal to the Pool.

They waited for a moment and Eldor's white pegasus entered the hall. Beside him walked Ursula, but she was no longer in her human form. Her long, reclaimed horn jabbed the air before her in pristine power, and together they went through the portal to the Pool.

By the time Eldor, Shadowolf, Darcwulf and Masara had ridden upon their mounts to the back line of the elvin army, the clouds above had darkened the sky and the sun was near setting in the west.

Chenesia was riding elegantly upon Genewiu towards them, and Hargon the dwarf rode another horse beside her. Eldor pointed out that it was under very special circumstances that any pegasus would allow someone to ride them.

"What about unicorns?" Darcwulf asked. Masara looked down at Ursula and smiled fondly. Although they knew the love the two felt for each other, Darcwulf shuddered at the thought of loving a horse.

Another thought occurred to Darcwulf and he reached down to the base of his saddle where a loin bag was dangling and pulled his serpent sword from it. He strapped it around his waist and looked up at Shadowolf's amused expression.

"You never know," he smiled back.

Prince Lesan left his post between the elvin and Horlorn armies and joined the group, followed shortly by Shedaaij. They all trotted beside each other, watching the storm clouds gather, knowing it was ominous for the battle that was approaching.

"You know the 'Battle of T'Mar's Scourge'?" Darcwulf said.

"Yeah?" Shadowolf replied light-heartedly, knowing by his tone that his brother was about to add a snide comment.

"Do you think they will call this 'The Battle of Eldor's Forest'?" he jibed.

"If Le'Mar wins, they won't be able to call it anything," Shedaaij answered, the tone in her voice indicating she was not impressed with his attitude. Shadowolf sighed.

"Are you going to fight?" Shadowolf asked silently, looking at her stomach to indicate his reference.

"Hasn't stopped me yet," she replied just as softly, but Darcwulf's frown showed that he had picked up on the conversation.

"Are you with child?" Chenesia asked, apparently also noting the discussion. Shedaaij nodded, knowing she could not avoid the topic.

"Is it safe?" Hargon said beneath his rough beard.

"Leave it," Shadowolf warned, and saw from the corner of his eye that Shedaaij looked at him sharply. She evidently decided not to respond.

He saw the rear of Fransiska's mount pop out of the back line of the elves. She had slowed down so that they could catch up to her and within a few minutes trotted beside Darcwulf.

"How is the Clan?" Darcwulf asked.

"Restless as usual," she said. "They want to get to the Den and stop journeying."

"I can't blame them," Eldor said. "They have almost been all over Celenic Earth."

Shadowolf wanted to ask Eldor to give them the speech while they were riding, but he knew the elf would not oblige. The small talk was a tiny respite to his tense veins, but he knew that once Eldor explained everything, it would clear a lot of questions.

After an hour's slow journey he could see the front line of Horlorn's army disappear over a dip. Another half hour later and the elvin army joined them. It was a matter of moments before the nine riders stood on the lip of the hill and looked down into the valley of Lard's Den.

There were many trees and bushes occupied by the original inhabitants of the Den. Shadowolf also spotted many unoccupied trees and heights which he assumed would be taken by the Throne's elves. Between the trees on the ground were newly constructed tents and temporary buildings which he knew had to be for the visitors.

"You didn't waste time," Treville said as he rode up to Eldor.

"We have none to waste," Eldor replied. "As we speak, Sonersaat is moving the dark lord's army towards us."

"Should we prepare?" Treville asked, his eyes betraying surprise at the revelation.

"Yes," Eldor said quietly. "When you hear a dwarven horn sounded, I want your men to sit and listen."

Eldor looked at Hargon and the dwarf nodded. Treville noticed the exchange, but decided not to comment. He turned and rode back to his army.

"How on earth are you going to convey a message to all of us spread through the Den?" Darcwulf asked.

Eldor rode down the valley into Lard's Den.

"Leave that to me," Ursula said and followed Eldor.

"I hate it when they are cryptic," Darcwulf muttered.

***

"Night," Franklin said as he entered the War Council. The tower was empty except for the one man stubborn enough not to leave his seat.

Karla had left Nighthale alone after ten minutes of trying to convince him to attend dinner. Malkius, Sjedwolf, Jasnon and Kailan had been adjourned to their villages. Nowles and Elgoth were in the Degron dining hall.

After Lucian had left for uPendus, his wife Kailan had decided to take the role of the Orion representative for Harhonsa Village. Nighthale had laughed at the image of Lucian's shocked face when he eventually returned from the Pegasi.

But the mirth was far from his heart now. Only the impending doom of the earth haunted his mind.

"Yes, Frank?" Nighthale said, keeping his eyes fastened to the east through the one-way, elvin windows.

"It seems that you were correct," Franklin said, sitting down beside him and facing the western window. Nighthale swiveled in his chair to join him.

"He is preparing the Dark Boundary?" he guessed.

"Yes," Franklin agreed. "Le'Mar's forces have started moving towards the southern gates of the Boundary. They will cross the River of Light by midnight and be by our walls by morning."

"Who leads them?" he asked.

"The Saneths Lister and Ru-Maak seem to have taken the charge, along with a witch by the name of Maerlesa."

"Then prepare the troops and elementals," Nighthale sighed. "Prepare for war."

"And the Mer-Kingdom?"

"Send a message to *Avalendil* to prepare too," he responded, nodding in appreciation to Franklin's thoughtfulness. "If I know Le'Mar, he will send his sirens."

***

Shadowolf was seated outside one of the tents, preferring not to be hidden from view. The Clan sat with him at a long table with five elvin fires that floated on the surface. The fires were bright green and did not damage the wood of the table. The elves had provided them with some food and water, knowing that the warriors would need the energy.

For an unknown reason, Darcwulf was in an extremely good mood. Shadowolf tried to share in the joy, but when Darcwulf tickled his ear with a long spring onion and said "nanoo nanoo" it took most of his self-control not to whirl around and hit him.

"Relax," Darcwulf smiled and diced the onion for the salad he was concocting. Thankfully, Darcwulf discarded the piece he had used on his brother's ear.

Shadowolf returned the smile if only to keep the atmosphere as joyful as he could. He had to however burst out in laughter when Darcwulf tried to nanoo Fransiska's cheek with a celery stick and she turned in heated frustration and whacked him with a chicken wing across his nose.

A soft sound echoed through the forest trees. Shadowolf realised it as a dwarven horn, only because Eldor had told them to listen for it. The horn resounded softly over the grass and on their tables. Even though it seemed that Hargon had stopped blowing, the sound of the horn continued to permeate the forest.

Another sound entered their minds, but the horn still rang sweetly in the background. He knew it was Eldor, for the aged elf's voice could not be mistaken so easily. It was crisp like summer leaves, and soft like winter snow. Shadowolf managed to relax more than ever listening to his voice, despite the marching troops to the south.

"We have some time to meditate on the past," Eldor started. "Le'Mar's army approaches and although it is possible that he could use a portal to bring them through, I honestly believe that he will not do so."

Shadowolf considered the logic in this, but perhaps Eldor was right. If Le'Mar had wanted to portal his army, he would have done so the moment that the protection of the forest had fallen away. Was the dark lord that confident of victory, or was his ego bigger than Shadowolf had realised?

"If our estimates are correct, we have four hours until his army reaches a critical point above us," the elf continued. "Sufficient time to show you all what must be retold.

"I was wondering where to start. Usually the beginning suffices, but in a case where the end raises more questions than the beginning, it is best that I start with a volume written by Nighthale Degron."

Shadowolf stirred on his seat. Although he was intensely focused solely on Eldor's words, he felt the others in the Clan look his way.

"He aptly entitled the small work 'The Fulfillment of the Windfarer Prophecy'", Eldor explained. Suddenly, his voice changed into that of Nighthale's. It was only because of Shadowolf's years and bond with his father that he could detect the slight difference in the pitch of the voice and realise that it was still Eldor narrating.

"'It has been a year since the fulfilment of the Windfarer Prophecy. I pen this down in the hopes that there will be a generation to read it. It may be that my knowledge of what had transpired last year will be essential in the event of my death...'"

Shadowolf sat quietly and listened. Although he knew exactly what had happened to him two years before, listening to the words of his father did in fact open his mind to a few revelations he hadn't thought of before.

"'Although my son Shadowolf played the essential role in the prophecy...'"

He smiled. He remembered how glad his father had been upon his return to Avalion, and how the prophecy seemed insignificant compared to the safety of his son.

The tale went on to explain the happenings before Shadowolf's birth. He listened intently, every word examined by his mind. Then it changed to Shadowolf's involvement with the power node, until his father started to explain the prophecy in detail.

"'The writings of Philgarn became widely accepted...'"

It was interesting to hear his father's thoughts on the prophecy, and Masara's meetings with him. Masara seemed to have a hand in everything, for which he was half grateful.

Nighthale then summarised everything that had led up to the

release of the power node. Shadowolf marveled that his father knew so much about his adventures, but guessed it was mostly thanks to Masara.

"'Masara found the bodies of two of the Sandrihelin, with no knowledge of where the third and fourth were.' "

Shadowolf realised that he too had forgotten about one of the Sandrihelin. He knew that Lucian had changed, but what had ever happened to Sona Nelma? He waited for the letter to end.

"'It seems that Le'Mar has already chosen his champion for the DragonRider Prophecy. And still, I do not know when my son will return to us…' "

Shadowolf turned quickly and leaned over the table to Trimistus.

"Did you ever see a Sandrihelin by the name of Sona Nelma in Mercius's army?"

"Not that I recall," Trimistus said. "When the Saneths came to Celenic Earth, I only met Malferus and Kelsey."

This disturbed Shadowolf greatly but he had no idea why. Sona had been an Earth professor at Asbec College, and he remembered that Lanel had told him that all of the Elemental[1] professors had met with the Headmaster, except the Natural[1] professor that had taught of the pure power of the soul.

Lucian, Malferus and Kelsey were all accounted for in Shadowolf's mind, but the last time he had seen Sona was at the College.

Shadowolf looked towards Heula at the end of the table, but she had not heard him speak and was still waiting for Eldor to continue.

"Now many questions still arise," Eldor returned to his own voice. "Mostly concerning Le'Mar's true motives and concerning the prophecies.

"It would be nice to say that he is purely evil and bent on destruction, but I am afraid it is not that simple. Many have seen and heard some truths, but there is one essential truth that has escaped the ages.

"It is now time that the essential truth is revealed."

Shadowolf noticed that there was a difference in the air, and it took him a moment to realise that the dwarven horn had gone silent. It was replaced with a soft violin, and in the centre of the forest a white light spread out.

They were all enveloped by the light until it was all they could see. Shadowolf did not feel like he was watching the scene progress before him; instead he felt like he was time itself, passing over the ages. He was the walls and trees that had been witness to the eons since the creation of the world.

The white faded, the violin went silent and once again they were surrounded by forest in the village of Malay. The sun shone pleasantly through the leaves from overhead onto the earth and grass.

A boy of six sat playing on the grass. His father Namara was in the village working with the town smiths and his mother Levon was busy in the house.

"Brighton!" his mother called. "Please assist me with these clothes!"

A small, yellow bird sat perched on Brighton's finger tittering to him. He replied and conversed with it, enjoying the frivolity, when he looked over the bird's head and gawked at the elf approaching him.

"I see I have found you at last," the elf said, but Brighton did not reply, too afraid he would say the wrong thing. Levon stepped out, wondering why he had not responded to her calling and held her hand to her mouth when she saw the elf.

"My name is Elmerion," the elf greeted and bowed.

"Oh my," she whispered. "Are you not the son of Saldheron, the elf lord?"

"Yes," Elmerion replied. "But my father is stepping down to another. He has reigned for a dozen centuries, and now it is Eldorion's turn."

"Your elder brother?" she asked uncertainly, and he nodded in reply.

"May I speak to your son?" he asked.

"If he so wishes," she replied.

"Oh, I do, I do mama!" Brighton shouted.

"Now, now, young one," Elmerion said politely, but sternly. "That is no way to behave towards your mother."

Brighton remained still, the fear written across his small face.

"Masara, the silver heart, is what you shall be called from now on," the elf stated. "Your spirit has called me forth in dreams and I joy at this meeting."

"My name isn't Masara," Brighton said as his face screwed up. His mother hushed him, but he persisted. "What's a spirit?"

Elmerion laughed at this before answering.

"I am here to take you to a place where I may prepare your mind for the power you hold within," the elf said.

Brighton widened his eyes in shock and stared at his mother momentarily. Humans had stopped practicing the elements and powers, as greed and evil desire had always swayed men's hearts to dark deeds. His mother simply smiled, offering no words.

"Be assured," Elmerion continued, "you are to be great, but be not bold in your abilities for you must not fall to the same inhibitions as your forefather. You will school the future generations and will build the path for the pure one to tread."

Levon readied Brighton for the departure and before Namara had returned from his duties, the newly-christened Masara had been taken away...

The white light faded the scene and the violin played in the intermission. Soon the light disappeared to be replaced by a new scene.

A little boy of nine with bright blond hair and a handsome face sat on a tree stump. He was bent over a scroll, scratching on it with a feather pen, the ink bottle drifting in the air beside him.

He paid no notice to the birds chirping overhead, neither to the wind that rattled the dead leaves on the ground nor to the elf that walked into the glade. The only sign that the little boy knew he was there was the appearance of a slight smile on his face.

Elmerion simply watched the little boy. To the side was a wooden building leaning against and between trees. On the door was a large note with the words 'Masara; Widgen Glade; Carmel.'

"Masara," the elf spoke, and the boy looked up. The smile remained on his face. "Your parents are here to see you."

This seemed to please the boy even more. He dropped his notes and pen, the ink drifting to the grass. He nodded to the elf.

"You remember the hospitality I taught you?" the elf asked.

"Yes," Masara said, and aimed his right palm at the hut. The door opened instantly and four sofas flew out and settled in the glade. A table joined them in the centre and soon four mugs rested on the surface of the table.

"What of the contents of the mugs?" the elf asked in a way that revealed he expected a certain reply.

"I will personally serve them with my labour," Masara smiled broadly.

"You are so young, but Bontu is strong with you," the elf said proudly. He turned to face an opening between two trees. "Namara! Levon! You may enter."

Masara's parents entered the glade. They looked around them and marveled at his home. They sat down at the table and stared at their son.

"Namara, he doesn't look so small anymore," his mother commented.

"I agree, Levon," his father said. "You've grown these last three years."

"I still see the six year old though," Levon said. While they had been greeting and commenting on his age, he had already boiled the water over a small fire and begun to pour their warm drinks. The elvin tea was not something they would be used to, but it was mild enough…

The scene faded back to the white light and the violin sounded briefly until the next scene appeared.

The young face of Masara had grown into a mature twenty-five year old. Namara watched with fond pride as his son left him and returned to the forest of Carmel. Many wondered what he did during the afternoons in the forest, but the presence of Bontu was so strong that they dared not enter.

On this particular day after Masara had been in the heat of training with Elmerion, a twelve year old boy entered the woods. Lucas Benight had a love for elvin lore, and he would not let the admonitions of his parents stop him. The power within the forest attracted him strongly, and he desired it.

When he entered the glade, he looked up at Masara floating in the air with a table stacked with books beside him. Masara turned his gaze to the boy and Lucas fled.

Lucas ran far. He was ashamed of his actions and knew his

mother would berate him if she found out. As he fell from exhaustion, he heard a pup wailing somewhere in the bushes.

He investigated and found a litter of wolf pups suckling on their mother. The wolf growled, but she was obviously tired. Lucas drew an elvin slupe fruit from his pocket, knowing its abilities for invigoration. The wolf ate and obtained strength and health. She permitted Lucas to pet her pups.

From that day, Lucas would return to feed and care for the small wolf family...

The light appeared to clear the scene.

"I see many things rising within Lanesara," Elmerion said to a thirty-year old Masara.

"Why must elves always have other names for humans?" Masara jibed. "Just call him Lucas."

"Very well, Lucas then," Elmerion laughed. "Yet his boldness is the thing I fear the most."

"You said he would be a good student to recruit for my new school," Masara smiled. "Anyway, here are my exam papers."

"I already know the result," Elmerion said broodily. "I want to show you something."

They traveled to the outskirts of the desert until they were above Eldor's Forest.

"I remember when it was called 'Saldher's Forest'," Masara said fondly.

"My brother will make a great king," Elmerion stated, turning to Masara. "One day, when your battles are fought and all think you dead, you will live in harmony with us here until you rise to Bontu."

"I look forward to staying in the forest," Masara said. "Besides being with Bontu, this is my greatest goal."

Before they left to return to Carmel, Eldor raised his palm from his throne towards them, and called upon Bontu to lengthen Masara's life and strengthen his righteousness.

Masara and Elmerion landed in Carmel. Levon was waiting for them, and Masara ran to her when he saw the state she was in.

"It's your father," she cried on his shoulder. "The building collapsed. They did everything they could."

Masara teleported to his father's workshop and held his father's body in his arms. He didn't scream; he didn't wail. A single tear fell from his eye onto his father's cheeks.

"Go with Bontu…"

The light; the violin; fade back to scene.

At thirty-five, Masara was used to teaching. He stood in the open classroom with no walls. The pillars held up the corners and mid-sections, and between the marble the air rushed from the gardens.

Twenty-two year old Lucas was his top student. The boy excelled in elvin lore, and quickly learned the nature of the elements. There were two dozen students, all eager to learn of the arts that had been forgotten by humans. Masara only hoped that his humility and lack of greed was a prime example to them.

He adjourned the class.

"How are your wolves, Lucas?" he asked.

"Very well, thank you," Lucas replied. "The mother wolf just had a new litter the other day."

When Masara thought the class was empty, he walked towards the back garden sipping a glass of water. His mother sat on a bench under a tree reading a book.

"Did it go well?" Levon asked.

"Yes," Masara replied. "I just hope that one day the people of Carmel will release their fears of the lore and let their kids train too. The life of Bontu is so fulfilling."

"Teacher," an elderly voice called behind him. Masara turned and smiled at the man that was a little older than his mother. "Sorry for bothering."

"Not a problem," he replied, but caught the man looking passed him at Levon. "Did you have a question?"

"I was wondering if I can have private lessons concerning the teachings of animals, spirit imbuement and transformation."

"Sure, T'Mar," he replied. "We can start as soon as you have free time…"

The scene changed again and the light cleared to another time.

"I guess you were right about his boldness," thirty-nine year old Masara said.

"I did not think he would go this far though," Elmerion commented.

They looked down from the clouds at the new city of Mai-Wolf, which meant 'Mother Wolf', and saw Lucas teaching thirty of Masara's former students.

"How did he obtain the staff?" Masara murmured, his gaze focused on the land below them.

"I do not know," was all Elmerion was able to say.

"My name is no longer Lucas or Lanesara," the former pupil of Masara said to the students. "From now on I will be referred to as Firewolf. I will be continuing your past training with Masara, as well as the training that he claims are forbidden by the elves."

"We can't let this continue Masara," Elmerion said. "But you go to your mother; we can discuss this later."

Masara nodded and teleported to the nursery. The building was well maintained and allowed the cool breeze to clear the humid air contained in the rooms.

He saw his step-father waiting outside his mother's room.

"Shouldn't you be with your new teacher?" he sneered at T'Mar.

"My first duty is to my wife, Masara," T'Mar replied. "Even Firewolf understands family responsibility."

"His name is Lucas," Masara grumbled and entered his mother's ward.

The baby lay swathed in white linen, cradled in Levon's arms. He was breathing deeply in his sleep, and from above his forehead Levon stared at her older son.

"Hello Brighton," she greeted.

Masara smiled in return and leaned over to rub the baby's forehead.

"Will he follow his father's footsteps?" Masara asked.

"Don't start that again," Levon said. "If you teach him the ways..."

"If T'Mar follows Lucas's teachings, the baby will surely walk in his footsteps," he interrupted.

"It was your decision to stop teaching," Levon said.

"Only because Elmerion told me this birth would shorten your life and you will only have a year left to live."

"At least you have students loyal to you that would never follow Lucas," she said, changing the topic. The same tear he had shed for his father now rolled down his other cheek.

"What have you named him?" Masara asked.

"We wanted something that had both our names in," Levon replied, looking at the sleeping baby. "So we took 'Le' from my name, and 'shaimar' from his father's."

"Well, Le'Mar," Masara said, stroking his head again. "Welcome to Falgaran Earth…"

The light washed the scene and presented another.

"What will you do?" Elmerion asked.

Masara looked down at the grave of his mother. She had lasted two years longer. When she passed away in Masara's arms, T'Mar had left the house to return to Mai-Wolf. He didn't wish Masara farewell, nor waited for the funeral rites. He had simply taken Le'Mar and returned to Lucas.

"I need to continue my training," Masara said sadly. "I need to place myself in Bontu's presence again, because my spirit is in disarray. Will you help me?"

"No, Masara, I am afraid I cannot," Elmerion said. "Eldor has asked me to visit the Far Isles. This matter of Lanesara is a growing concern to us. We need to make a decision, for he is growing stronger in the dark ways and forsaking the path of Bontu. He is greedy for power."

"Then what must I do?" Masara looked at him in supplication.

A lady walked from behind the elf towards Masara. She was splendid and beautiful. She wore a long red dress with butterfly beads around her left wrist.

"You're a unicorn," Masara observed, looking at her aura.

"He is as powerful and observant as you warned," the lady said to Elmerion, and then addressed Masara. "My name is Ursula, and I will be guiding your training from now on."

The sound of hooves exploded into the field. The three turned their attention to the approaching black pegasus. A two year old was seated on its back and Masara ran to help him dismount.

"What are you doing here, child?" Masara asked, but the boy ignored him and ran for the grave.

"Mama!" Le'Mar shouted.

"He insisted I bring him to you," the pegasus said. "Will you care for him?"

"What of T'Mar?" he asked.

"T'Mar will search for him," the pegasus warned. "I do not know when he will realise the child is with you."

Masara nodded and the pegasus flew away.

The flash of light and violin changed the scene.

"Have you heard the news?" Ursula asked the meditating Masara. "Lucas and T'Mar had a fight concerning the lessons and curriculum."

"Who won?" Masara asked non-chalantly.

"T'Mar killed Lucas," Ursula pronounced. "He is proclaiming himself the new Firewolf."

"So he has resorted to murder," Masara muttered.

"There are ways which seem right to men," Ursula said with a sorrowful tone, "but the ends thereof are always the ways of death; you know that."

"What of the staff Lucas found?" he asked tentatively.

"He wrested it from Lucas's charred hand," Ursula replied.

Twenty-year old Le'Mar turned from his eavesdropping and left the forest contemplating the discussion.

There was another scene change.

"He's coming for Le'Mar!" Ursula shouted. Masara was now seventy-nine and had a short, white beard to compliment his long white hair. Yet his energy and complexion resembled a Masara that was once thirty.

"Le'Mar is old enough to care for himself," Masara stated.

They heard voices outside the forest of Carmel. Masara left the seat and went to listen.

"…this idiocy," T'Mar was saying. "You are my son, and I forbid you to continue this training. I can teach you so much more…"

"I don't want to hear it!" Le'Mar shouted. "My brother has been called the saint of the ages…"

"And yet he teaches no one anymore!" T'Mar pointed out. "Ever since that mother of his died…"

"She was my mother too!" Le'Mar erupted with rage. "Stop blaming her for an illness she could not avoid! It's not her fault she died!"

"SHUT UP!!" T'Mar recoiled. "You are coming with me and that's final!"

Masara ran into the glade. From beneath the ground, demons rose to pin Le'Mar's arms. Before Masara could shout, Le'Mar had already disappeared to Mai-Wolf.

"There is nothing you can do, Masara," T'Mar grinned. "He is mine, and mine alone!"

T'Mar rose into the air upon the black pegasus that had once brought Le'Mar to Masara as a toddler. Masara ran after them, but they disappeared into the sky.

"Get on!" Ursula shouted, running beside him in her unicorn form. He jumped and they rose in the air towards Mai-Wolf.

When they reached the barren land to the north where the River of Light passed Mai-Wolf, T'Mar turned to face them.

"I don't suppose you will just let us be?" he asked.

"I will not allow Le'Mar to be corrupted by you," Masara said, sensing that Le'Mar was still trapped within the walls of Mai-Wolf.

Suddenly something pulled at his spirit, and he groaned as evil spirits tore at his soul. Ursula remained strong beneath him, and soon enough Masara over-powered them.

"Just because it is not the way of Bontu," T'Mar said, removing a staff strapped to his back, "does not mean it is evil."

"All power comes from Bontu," Masara said, a white staff appearing in his hands from the air. "There is no other."

"Let me show you another," T'Mar muttered.

The pegasus leered forward, following the will of its master. The staves clanged together and the mounts butted each other as they fought. The power ran through the hills and the still river below.

After several minutes of combat, they were both exhausted, the sweat falling upon their brows.

"T'Mar," Masara muttered, "this madness must stop."

"I cannot lay it to rest, Masara," T'Mar replied. "These are my ways."

"Have you not learnt anything from me?" Masara asked.

"Your ways are old," T'Mar said, panting. "I cannot let it be so unadapted. We must have recourse to better powers."

"These powers that you seek are dark. Let it be, for the sake of our world and under the grace of Bontu."

"I cannot lay it to rest," T'Mar repeated. "I have found my way, and I will teach it to all, including my son."

"Firewolf, please…" Masara said, more calmly.

"Do not utter that name!" T'Mar screamed. "I am no longer

Firewolf. My name is T'Mar!"

T'Mar erupted with even more power and foul wind was summoned. Demons rose from nowhere and Masara was forced to not only fend off the dark devils, but T'Mar too. Ursula used her powerful horn to vanquish any demon that came in contact with her.

The power was too great for the earth. The plates shifted beneath them as they wrestled, arms tensed and locked, power flowing from their souls into their bodies and through their staves.

Soon a rift formed in the earth, so much so that T'Mar and Masara lost balance as a vast canyon split the earth. The land dropped and rose simultaneously, but T'Mar continued to fight. He threw balls of fire and lightning at Masara but the saint simply caught them and hurled them aside. It crashed into the earth creating craters and peaks.

The River of Light split at the formation of the new mountains. The canyon emptied its waters from the sea through the top of the mountains into a new waterfall.

Their staves made contact again and fell to the waters. Masara and T'Mar hit each other, but the mounts got too close. The pegasus and unicorn banged hard together and the two riders were dislodged as the mounts fell to the junction of the river.

T'Mar and Masara continued to fight, power rising from them as was never seen on the earth before. When they hit the waterfall, the water rose high into the air. With one last violent move, Masara summoned his staff and thrust it right through T'Mar's heart. Ursula stabbed the pegasus, but as she released the horn the pegasus gave one last kick that broke the horn off her head.

T'Mar's face went vacant as he died and fell to the depths of the waterfall. Masara used the last of his energy in an attempt to make the surface, but it gave out. He took his last breath and felt the gravity pull him down.

Le'Mar broke free of the demons and teleported to a gap in the peaks of the new mountain range. He watched carefully at the spot where the waterfall was swirling furiously, waiting for his father to rise.

After what seemed like a lifetime, a man emerged from the water. Ursula was bleeding on her forehead. Her horn was gone, but she managed to drag Masara to dry ground. Soon, Eldor and Elmerion were there to portal the two to Eldor's Forest.

Le'Mar dived into the water in search of his father. When he reached the bed, he saw the pegasus lying in the sand with the horn lying hidden beneath the sand. Beside it lay T'Mar with a gaping hole through his chest.

Le'Mar reached for his father. When he touched his face, screams of pain and death sang through his nerves and he clutched his head in agony.

When he was relieved of the noise, he reached down again but this time it was silent. He grabbed his father and teleported his body to Mai-Wolf.

He spent the remainder of the afternoon mourning his father. By evening, a strange man approached the house.

"I bring condolences for your father," the man said. Le'Mar ignored him, sitting with his face in his hands. "Would you like to avenge your father? I can teach you the greatest powers of the universe."

Le'Mar looked up now, very interested.

"I am called many names," the man said. "But you can call me Gemetrashef."

Le'Mar looked to the far wall and saw his father's staff. It was black with a blood-red, flame-like design on its wooden, elemental surface.

A flash of light, the last violin chord and the forest returned to their eyes.

"Wow," Darcwulf said, truly amazed. "Wow…"

"It is time," Eldor said. "Le'Mar will be here within the hour. "Get ready…"

DARKEST HOUR
CHAPTER EIGHT

On any other day it would have been a wonderful sight to behold. Any human would have loved to see its depths, the colour that washes their eyes and the beautiful civilisation that thrives upon its life.

Avalendil had many tunnels and domes that were attached on the walls, those that rose from the floor and those that were simply suspended by webbed bridges between caverns. The mermen and maids usually swam in the brilliance of the kaleidoscopic corals and the warm ocean current. The white bridges and domes drifted in the water without care.

But the time of peace was passed. No longer could they resign to the quiet life they once knew. War had already begun and they were fighting for survival.

The water swirled furiously. Flashes of light broke the dark depths and sand rose from the burning bed. Howls of death echoed in the ocean and the warrens of *Avalendil* were surrounded with chaos.

Lellian slashed his trident through a siren's chest and turned to block a ray of red light from a demon-queen's trident.

There's too many, James yelled mentally.

Keep fighting! Lellian shouted back.

James whirled his daggers to kill a siren and swung his tail to deflect a crude knife.

Walls crumbled around the warrens as sirens and mermaids were thrown to their deaths. Lights of power missed their targets and broke into the coral.

The Mer-Kingdom, in the midst of power and light, fought to overcome the hordes…

***

Nighthale felt the ground tremor slightly beneath the parapet he stood on. The night had finally reached them, but the sight on the northwestern border was not a welcome one. The air stank of the evil approaching and, although Avalion was protected by elemental powers, he feared for the worst. The mass of the army was far larger than he had ever expected.

The archers stood along the topmost walls that touched the Mists of Celene. Their bows were ready to be fired. The horses were being saddled for war. Those with swords sharpened their blades. The elementals called their powers.

Nighthale's memory was recalled to the day his son was born as the elementals had fought to save their lives. Tonight the Degrons fought, not only with the Saphin Tribe, but with the Lowle, Watre and Orion tribes too.

Tonight they fought for survival…

***

Shadowolf saw them rushing through the trees of the forest. The purorcs and hurorcs wore cold steel armour and carried swords and spikes. He let the fire within warm him as the night chill sank in. He really wished that he did not have to fight. He had had enough of war and blood and death.

He heard the sound of their armour clinking. It reflected off the thoughts in his mind. It was not that he feared them. He had killed enough of Le'Mar's army as target practice. They had all known this night was coming.

It was not that he was afraid for the others. He knew their skill was so far unmatched. He dropped his head, wondering why he suddenly felt a cold indifference to the orcs rushing to kill him.

"Brooding again, are we?" Shedaaij said next to him, her daggers in hand. She was dressed only in her coral armour. He looked down at her muscled stomach that was starting to show a small lump where the baby was.

"You could say that," he replied. Mandy stirred on his left,

Nelnar calmly standing behind him. "Don't worry, girl. When I need you I will call."

"Don't you think you should draw your sword?" Shedaaij asked nervously, getting her stance ready for the attack.

"I'll see if I need it," he said, taking the staff from Mandy's saddle. He looked into the forest and saw Darcwulf and Fransiska waiting for the orcs.

Shadowolf closed his eyes and breathed. This was it. This was what he had returned to Celenic Earth for.

The dragons aren't here yet, Masara's voice carried to his mind. *Maybe you should wait before you summon Asgorna.*

Shadowolf simply nodded, because he had not intended summoning them before Sonersaat did. He focused on his inner core, slowly drawing his power into his soul. He could feel the level of his aura descend, and he hoped that Le'Mar would not be able to detect it.

The wind blew softly against his head, warning him of the foul orcs around the tree. As the breeze caressed his cheeks, he could feel a little power rise up again. The elements were so attuned to his being he wondered if he would ever fully master lowering his power.

The orcs crossed the tree line he stood behind. He whirled his staff immediately and caught an orc in the lower jaw. He lifted the fallen orc sword with his staff and kicked it into the abdomen of another hurorc.

Mandy kicked and butted orcs that passed her. She trotted off to join Nelnar in battling purorcs and hurorcs, although the animals were struggling to find weak points between their armour.

As Shadowolf used his staff to knock a tenth orc back, and wind to lift three orcs into the waiting weapons of Lastgorn, Gwyn and Sorceress, he heard fluttering. In anxiety he looked up and saw the blue fletchlings break through the tree tops. He built up arrows of fire from his arm, but it was not necessary for fairdievells had suddenly appeared out of the tree trunks and fought them.

Shadowolf continued to fight on as the Horlorn swordsmen ran passed him. The forest was crowded with fighters and screams of death. There were so many orcs he had to use the fastest way to kill them his mind could come up with.

He tripped three orcs and stood over them with lightning arcing from his palm. He blocked several blows when Darcwulf was suddenly there covered in an aura of flames. His staff drove through them like wild fire through the forest. His eyes shone bright red as he burned into their acrid flesh and through the cold armour on their chests.

Sorceress and Shadowwe ran past him and started decapitating orcs. Sorceress removed her bow from her back and split three arrows across orcs' open necks. Rennick shoved his palm out and several hurorcs fell to the ground. He moved quickly to drive his glowing white sword through their armour into their chests.

Shedaaij leapt in the air and placed her legs around a purorc's neck. She twisted and snapped it, rising in mid-air again to drive her daggers into orc necks and knees. She raised her palms up, and stones and rocks rose up and assaulted a line of orcs. Before the five could regain their sight, their deaths were delivered to them by her fatal prowess.

Shadowolf looked back as he removed his staff from an orc's face and saw that the forest was full of orcs. The elves and elementals were winning the battle though. There were more orc corpses on the ground than any other.

He also saw Masara riding upon Ursula, his white staff blinding orcs and then his sword being released from his soul into the heart of an orc. Eldor was upon his pegasus, dealing death the same way.

Shadowolf raised his staff to block a sword. As he was about to kill the orc, a thunderous quake shook the ground and trees started flying through the forest. He barely ducked beneath a soaring trunk and saw two giant Ma-Wreths breaking into the forest. Further away he could hear more pounding and assumed there were more Wreths.

The giants whirled their massive arms in unbelievable speed as they crushed trees. Orcs scattered out of their path, still trying to kill any of the dark lord's foes. Shadowolf's eyes turned black for a second and then returned to blue.

He knocked an orc's head and jumped on its shoulder, rising in the air to land on Mandy's saddle as she ran passed. He placed the staff back in the saddle rope and raced to meet the Wreths. More hooves sounded in the forest, but to his consternation he realised it was in the direction he was heading and not from behind. Black horses as dark as Mandy rose upon the far hilltop and upon their backs were the Froth Huns.

The Froths leered at the forest, racing down the hill in glee. Their skulls burnt with the blue flames they were known for, with their bony fingers in steel gloves clutching the reins. The dark horses seethed bloody fumes of cold air and their pitted eyes held the red pupils that gleamed like retsinic rubies.

Mandy raced beneath him to meet her former allies. Her mane was blown by the wind to form a ghostly weave that touched Shadowolf's neck. Her tail flared up in abysmal black that tickled the night with her bloodlust.

Several orcs grouped together to stop the approach of the elemental rider, but Shadowolf merely glanced their way and the earth sprang up with thorny vines that wrenched them to the ground and throttled them. He rode through them, the hooves of his mare echoing across the landscape to the Wreths that he would have to face first.

This sound was soon joined by a silent patter. Shadowolf could feel Nelnar stride beside him, keeping the pace of the horse with a simple trot. Its face gleamed as it growled deep, ready to kill the first that would harm its master.

Shadowolf jumped off Mandy's back as they approached the first Wreth. He rose in the air with the wind powering his arm and he unsheathed Ruben-Willow from his soul and aimed for the back of its neck. With incredible speed, the Wreth turned and hit him to the ground.

Sny-Ten ran up to assist him. The man deftly carried his large axe and swung it at the Ma-Wreth. The Wreth countered, but the axe lodged in its thick arm and it bellowed a deep cry in pain.

Sny-Ten pulled the axe out again, and aimed for its waist. Unfortunately, he could not move the heavy double-edged axe as fast as the beast could move its arm. When the Wreth hit him in the face, he whirled around and struck at the beast's knees. The beast fell on its injured knee.

Another Wreth had made its way over to them. Shadowolf stood up from the sand he had slid on and ran to confront the second Wreth while Sny-Ten continued to combat the first. Nelnar was already there, dodging its fast, lumpy feet as it tried to find a spot to bite into.

The second Wreth raised its oak-like hand to pummel Nelnar. As the hand fell, the arm blurred and went towards its own neck. It coughed and choked, flailing around at the unknown aggressor. The air moved from its lungs into the air, and its face went darker and it gave one last gulp and collapsed.

Shadowolf dropped his palm. He had no time to spare for the Wreth he had just suffocated, for a scream resounded behind him. He turned and ran back, but it was too late.

The Wreth hit Sny-Ten in his abdomen and then his chest, sending him into the air, barely conscious. Before Sny-Ten was even pulled back to earth by gravity, the Wreth had snatched Sny's axe and hurled it at him. The axe bit with a sick noise into his chest, and the body hit the ground with a dull thud. The life of Sny disappeared from his eyes.

If anyone felt fear from that attack, it was not Shadowolf. His face was set with anger and fury and the power raged within him. The wind picked up and stormed towards the Wreth. The Wreth faced the elemental, seeing its dead ally on the ground.

In the two seconds it took to swing at Shadowolf five times, Shadowolf became part of the wind, drifted behind the Wreth up to its neck, unsheathed the dagger Ruben-Willow from his soul and cut the beast's neck. When he realised it wasn't enough, he also drew the sword and the blade past neatly through its back.

The Wreth shouted and cursed into the air, falling on the knee that Sny had injured again. Shadowolf flared with fire and it passed into the Ma-Wreth's body. Smoke curled from its eyes and mouth and finally it collapsed to the ground.

Shadowolf stood and a Froth Hun and its horse toppled onto the dead Wreth before him. Before he or the Froth could work out what had happened, Nelnar jumped up and bit into the skull, the blue flames dying with the Froth. The fragments of the skull fell over the Wreth's corpse as Shadowolf turned to defend against the others.

Several Froths rode passed into the forest, but four remained to challenge him. Mandy appeared and he rose into the saddle, sword and dagger still in his hands. Shedaaij walked to his left. Her face and body had blood streaked over it. Some of it was from wounds on her arms.

Shadowwe, Tinonté, Angelia and Skywolf stood on his right, equally painted with blood. Skywolf had a green bow and a quiver on her back, and a staff in hand. Shadowwe and Tinonté had their swords and Angelia held her staff.

"Glad you could join me," he mumbled.

"We got tired of you having all the fun," Angelia said.

The Froths seemed indecisive, but after a moment they dismounted. Their flames turned amber around their skulls when they touched the ground. They unsheathed their large, two-handed swords and approached the group.

Shadowolf heard arrows being loosed into the air, but he knew it wasn't Skywolf. He peered into the night sky and narrowed his eyes. Thousands of arrows were creeping across the blanket of stars towards the elvin forest, soaring over the combatants before the Froths.

When the arrows reached their apex, elvin arrows launched from the trees towards the hill that the Froths had descended. Shadowolf saw lines of Dra-hu'Mar lower their bows and take cover from the falling elvin arrows. Cries and screams spread from the forest and the dark lord's outpost on the hill, filling the land with dread.

Mandy suddenly jerked forward to attack the Froths' mounts. Shadowolf reflexively jumped off and landed next to Nelnar who was growling deeply at the orange-skulled creatures.

The Froths' swords were easily twice as long and thick as Ruben-Willow. Their orange flames roared above the sounds of the battles behind them, while the swords glinted in the little moonlight available between the clouds.

Shadowolf moved wind into the sword and dagger, holding them tighter. All at once, the four Froths attacked the group.

Shadowolf parried the large sword aside, careful not to let the full impact break his sword. He lunged at the Froth with his leg, and ducked an arm. Nelnar attacked its legs, and jumped away from a kick.

Shadowwe blocked and turned full circle at the skull of his Froth Hun. The swords clang together, and the beast kicked him in the stomach, sending him sliding. He rose up and sheathed his sword, standing in his *ru-maak* stance, the martial arts style of the Orion.

Tinonté slashed at his Froth's legs, trying to change the beast's focus of attention. The Froth staggered backwards, trying to match the speed of Tinonté's fighting style. But the Orion was quicker and managed to slide his sword into its chest and arms.

Angelia and Skywolf shared a Froth. The sand was getting slippery now, as a small mist from the moisture in the air was making the soil damp. It was only a matter of time before the gathering clouds exploded their contents onto the land, adding to the tension of the fighters.

The girls jumped and hit at the Froth. The more he tried to attack one, the more the other one hit him hard and off-balance. Angelia's staff caught a few blows to his skull, and the cranium showed slight cracks on the spots where she got him the worst. Skywolf took turns between striking her staff and lodging arrows at him.

Tinonté feinted a blow to the beast's shoulder, and as it moved to block it, he twisted the blade and drove it through its chest. The beast fumbled with his sword, and then the Orion removed his blade and swiped it horizontally through its skull.

In victory, Tinonté watched as the remains of the Froth slipped to the ground. He glared happily down at it, but then gasped in horror as three Dra-hu'Mar arrows entered his chest. The blood dripped off the shafts onto the ground and Tinonté fell to his knees.

Angelia was hit aside and Skywolf pushed to the ground. Their Froth's flames flared with evil and he turned and looked at Tinonté kneeling and sputtering blood. Tinonté shouted as his body was consumed by dark, red flames. His ashes drifted to the soil as the Froth faced the girls again.

Whatever anguish and sadness should have been felt for Tinonté's death was quickly replaced by fury as Skywolf ran to attack the Froth. She shot two arrows into its head, one actually going through its eye socket and protruding out the back. Angelia lifted her palm and, from the moisture in the air, water formed into a solid orb that grabbed the pointed tips behind the skull, yanking down hard.

The Froth Hun fell backwards, its skull splitting in three as the flames died and the body hit the ground.

Shadowolf punched his Froth in the gut, moved swiftly over the Froth's blade, sheathed Ruben-Willow while whirling his arms in circular motions to gather power, and hit the Froth with both fists against its chest. Lightning and wind went into the beast's body and its head burst into pieces of bone.

Shadowwe exclaimed as the Froth's blade entered his chest. The Froth moved the sword down into Shadowwe's ribs and out his side. Shadowwe limped down and fell, looking up mournfully as his life left him.

Shadowolf jumped over the fallen Orion's body as Angelia and Skywolf attacked the Froth that had killed Shadowwe. While Angelia tripped the Froth with her staff, Skywolf loosed three arrows into its chest and Shadowolf split its skull with his dagger.

"Where's Shedaaij?" he turned, realising she wasn't with them. He saw her a few steps towards the forest, triumphantly removing one of her daggers from a Froth that she had taken care off.

She moved up the hill towards them smiling, regardless of the fact that there was a battle around them. But the face turned to confusion and then horror as she raised her hand to her mouth and pointed with the other to the hill.

Shadowolf, Angelia, Skywolf and Nelnar looked around. Past Mandy who had scared the other Froth horses away, on the top peak of the hill where the Dra-hu'Mar still stood loosing arrows, were four Creth-Demons.

Their brilliant golden sceptres shone dully in the night, their wolf heads grinning deeply in anticipation for the fight. Their human torsos and abdomens were naked, revealing the hard muscles and deep scars. Their human legs were open too, with cloths dangling down from sashes on their waists.

"How are we going to contend with them too?" Skywolf asked.

Wolves howled from within Lard's Den and Shadowolf realised that the Crethans from the Clan must have transformed. At the same time, wolves howled from behind Le'Mar's hill, and he guessed that there were Crethans waiting to meet them in battle.

"More Crethans?" Angelia gasped.

"You told Eldor that you would personally kill..." Shedaaij said, but fell silent.

Shadowolf was emitting power before them. His body language suggested a calm spirit, one lost in meditation. Yet his aura stretched out and touched them as he called on the elements.

Water climbed up his legs from the soil. The clouds overhead burst and rain poured over Eldor's Forest. The water sprayed everywhere, but was especially concentrated around Shadowolf. The liquid seeped into the pores of his skin and then the core of his soul.

Earth creaked softly as sand moved into his feet. His body went from a sandy base to a stony exterior. He held his eyes closed, consuming the energy the earth provided.

Wind whistled passed his ears and around his body, whipping his hair into a frenzy.

"Get back to the Den!" Angelia shouted as the hill Crethans descended towards them, the Creth-Demons walking placidly at the rear.

The wind carried the sounds of the hundreds of Crethan wolves to him. It lashed out in all directions before being absorbed into his body to his lungs.

"Shado..." Shedaaij whispered.

"Go," Shadowolf instructed above the sound of the gathering power, trying to maintain his focus. He has spoken softly, but somehow she had heard him. He listened as her steps took her away from him.

Fire shot up from his aura and lit the ground around him. He opened his eyes to the sky and released the energy. The fire rose like a torch towards the heavens, and then was replaced by ethereal wings that drifted on his back.

He ran down to the forest with a yellow aura of power surrounding him. Even to the non-elemental eye, Shadowolf's skin glowed softly. He jumped up Mandy's saddle as she passed him, with Nelnar sprinting ahead.

Ruben-Willow's blade and dagger sprang from his arms as he killed orcs on his way. Several Ma-Wreths had managed to break down nearly every tree into the Den. Splinters and timbers were strewn amongst the dead orcs and humans. Froth Huns maimed elementals while swordsmen succeeded slowly in killing Froths.

Shadowolf saw six of the Clan Crethans running amongst the elves, biting and killing where they got the chance. Their hairy wolf bodies were covered in the blood of their victims and the power of the Creth filled their eyes with sinister light.

He tried to command them with his spirit when one of the Crethans jumped up to push Mandy, but Shadowolf raised his blade through its gullet. He watched dismally as it transformed into Teristé before shuddering to death.

He was hoping that he could stop the Crethans from attacking, but seeing them only convinced him that they were cursed to obey the Creth-Demon.

A Crethan lunged for Nolraldun, who was killing orcs with stealth, but Nelnar rammed its body into it and they rolled down the hill together. Mandy breathed blood-stenched mist from its nostrils, eager to join the fight.

Shadowolf jumped off her back as she went in another direction, keen to attack Froth mounts again. Two orcs approached and he sliced through them without thought. He watched Shedaaij and Dren each kill a Crethan. The bodies of Mino'Nelar and Madison lay twitching on the floor.

Soon the Clan Crethans were not alone in the forest. The other Crethans had entered and it was difficult to tell the two apart. The Creth-Demons were running down the hill to join their servants in battle, their golden scepters glinting through the rain.

Shadowolf ignored the hordes of Crethans and decided to confront the Creth-Demons. He ran back to the hill, seeing Trimistus in the distance. He shouted to the reptilian-man, who looked up at him and nodded.

Trimistus started to join him in the run, when a Crethan leapt on top of him. The deformed wolf growled and yapped at his face, its drool falling over him.

Trimistus's dragon sword lay trapped beneath his body. He was holding it tightly on its throat, fur falling on his shoulders and teeth gleaming near his cheeks.

Trimistus face contorted with the effort of keeping the Crethan back. It was twisting and turning its body to get into a better position for the kill. Shadowolf altered his course to assist him. Orcs got in his way again, but he simply shoved them aside with bursts of wind.

When Shadowolf finally made it, he was thrown back by a powerful force. His back hit a broken tree trunk and he groaned as the pain swept through his body. He forced his eyes open to a brilliant light before him.

Trimistus was still lying on the ground, the Crethan still above him, when the sparkling ethereal wings had reached out from his scapulae. The wings twisted around his shoulders, passed his elbows and into the chest of the Crethan dying above him. It slowly transformed into Trish, blood dripping from her lips onto his shoulder.

Trimistus used his gleaming wings to toss her aside. He strode over to Shadowolf and offered him a hand. Shadowolf stood up and searched for Nelnar. His wolf was in the distance, standing beside the body of the Crethan Midnite and fighting several of Le'Mar's Crethans simultaneously.

"We need to take care of the Creths," he said hoarsely, trying to regain his breath.

"Then let's g..." Trimistus had turned to run up the hill, but stopped when he saw the two Crethans before them.

Their backs were towards them and they were glaring at the Creths. They stood on their hind legs, their bodies twisting in agony and soft moans escaping their lips. The faces of Dayna-wolf and Markors appeared briefly before returning to that of rabid wolves.

The two Crethans took off and ran for their masters. Their claws dug into any orc or Froth that got in the way, clambering over fallen stumps and shattered timber. Markors flew back as an arrow from a Dra-hu'Mar entered swiftly into its chest. When it fell on its back, a Froth ran its two-handed blade into its heart.

Dayna-wolf reached a Creth-Demon and slashed at it. The Demon used its staff to deflect her claws, striking her in the chest and face. She continued to assault until the Demon held his staff before her and it glowed sharply. She fell to her knees, howling in agony. Before she could react, two Crethans jumped at her and killed her.

Shadowolf removed his sword from an orc while Trimistus retrieved his dragon blade.

"Ready?" Trimistus asked, his wings still gleaming.

"You know what I just realised?" Shadowolf said meditatively, blocking an orc sword and thrusting Ruben-Willow through its abdomen.

"No," he replied, doing the same with a Crethan.

"If you hadn't betrayed Le'Mar," Shadowolf said, "you would have been in Sonersaat's place right now."

The two continued to fight, making a path to the closest Creth-Demons. Shadowolf looked passed the fighting hordes and saw the Dra-hu'Mar change their bows into swords and descending the hill.

"Not necessarily," Trimistus said heavily, dispatching an orc. "If I hadn't fallen off that cliff, Mynisna would not have found me and I would still be a Saneth."

Shadowolf contemplated this, deciding this was not the time to enter into a philosophical discussion about dragon motives. The Creth-Demons were up ahead and he had yet to conjure a brilliant plan to kill them. Should he simply get rid of them, or show off a bit? He grinned mischievously at himself.

Trimistus ran with his glorious wings to face one, while Shadowolf idled up to another with the elements burning for release within. He grinned at the wolf-head of the Demon. The Creth leered back, apparently anxious for this fight.

It swung the ends of the staff at him. Shadowolf deftly blocked and parried blows, trying to tear the human skin of the Creth. There were times when the tips of the blades nearly drew blood, but somehow the Creth had narrowly twisted the staff to move it away.

The Creth hit at his ankles, turning in a circle to bring the end up into Shadowolf's chin. Shadowolf jumped back, somersaulting in the air and slashing his blade to the side and the dagger in a forward lunge. The staff swept sideward and up, catching both blades and pulling it from his grasp.

The metal clanged against rocks. The Creth moved forward and the staff glowed. The amulet-tip changed into a blade. He hit at Shadowolf, using the stem of the staff to manoeuvre the blade at his target.

Shadowolf moved the sweat out his eyes with a sleeve as he ducked. He was breathing deeply, trying to preserve his strength. He focused on the earth element, drawing the energy from beneath his feet into his soul and body.

He straightened his back waiting from for the blow. The blade of the scepter passed through Shadowolf's solar plexus and out his back. The Creth bore its fangs in a deep smile, a growl escaping its mouth.

But the Creth quickly lost its grin when he realised Shadowolf wasn't dying. The man smiled back, his eyes turning an opulent green. Where the staff-blade was stuck, his skin became a swirling vortex of sand and wind. The Creth tried to remove his weapon, but Shadowolf's ribs moved up and grasped it firmly.

Out of his back, where the vortex continued to swirl and the golden blade emerged, the sand twisted and curled into vines. The sand rose up over his shoulders into thick cords of rope. The Creth released his grasp on the scepter and stammered backwards.

The ropes flew at the Creth's head and arms. It promptly pulled his arms from its shoulders and snapped its neck. The Creth's body fell to the ground as Shadowolf's ribs snapped the staff within him and spat it out.

Shadowolf fell to one knee. Trimistus ran over, his *Wisoum* wings glaring from the Creth it had just killed.

"Are you alright?" Trimistus asked. He looked down at Shadowolf's torn shirt. The skin was a bruised blue, but the sand had become flesh again and his ribs and diaphragm settled back into place.

"We need to help kill the Creth-Demons," Shadowolf said. "The Crethans are humans and we can't keep killing our own people. We must…"

But he stopped as the warm warning filled his mind. He knew what was approaching before it even topped the hill. He sighed deeply, anguish and despair inches away. How much more? When would Le'Mar stop?

The Firestroms lit the hill with their burning fires. Gorilla, shark, horse and lion heads sat atop six fiery, gigantic bodies that drifted over what was left of the grassy plains. Shadowolf shuddered in pain and tiredness as he stood as watched their descent.

"We have to let the Horlorn elementals know how to kill them," Shadowolf said.

"The Clan elementals can inform them," Trimistus replied. "You taught them how last time."

Shadowolf nodded and looked back at the forest.

"You need to rest, Shado," he implored. "It is not only your world to save."

"I need to regroup with Shedaaij," he said, and Trimistus nodded. Shadowolf didn't have much strength to run down, so he summoned Mandy. Both Mandy and Nelnar heeded his call.

"Good luck, Lord Danaka," Shadowolf smirked and rode into the crumbling Den.

Mandy had a hard time leaping over fallen trunks as Shadowolf searched for Shedaaij. Crethans, orcs, Froth Huns, Dra-hu'Mar and the few remaining Ma-Wreths pillaged the forest, fighting against elves, elementals, the Clan, and swordsmen. Shadowolf only drew his gaze from his search when he caught sight of a few dwarves hurtling orcs off their axes. He wondered when they had arrived.

He spotted Darcwulf flaring, his body made wholly of fire and his staff whipping into enemy faces. He was a dancing coloumn of fire. A small glint showed that the unused serpent sword was still on his hip within the flames. Shadowolf rode over to him and looked down.

"Where is Shedaaij?" he said, his voice raised high now to overcome the din of battle.

"She left with Fransiska to assist Eldor and Masara," Darcwulf said, softening the body of flames slightly.

"We have Firestroms coming," he warned.

"We know," Darcwulf said, looking around for something. "Rennick and Sorceress went to inform the elementals what to do."

"Good," Shadowolf said, too tired to dismount again. Nelnar panted heavily by Mandy's feet, but its eyes showed that it had plenty of fight left.

Shadowolf was thrown off Mandy as she lurched to the side and fell to the ground. She quickly recovered and got off his leg as Darcwulf assisted with the attacking Crethans. Shadowolf jumped to his feet, and limped as the numbing pain travelled through his leg.

A Crethan jumped up from a broken stump and hit Darcwulf in his chest. He fell on his back, his staff bouncing away. The Crethan raised its paw, claw ready to strike his cheek. Darcwulf became flames again, but the Crethan lowered its paw.

The Crethan had a sad expression on its furry face. It drooped over him and sniffed the fiery shadow that was his head. Darcwulf killed the flames and stared back.

Shadowolf pulled his blade from a Crethan and was about to pierce the beast on Darcwulf, but his brother raised his hand to stop him.

The Crethan got on its hind legs. It looked at its hands and then held its head in agony. A low growl turned into a torrentuous scream as the body began to transform. Slowly the human behind the Crethan mask completed the change.

Unlike the Clan Crethans, Le'Mar's were not clothed. When they died and their bodies returned to human, their naked bodies lay where they had fallen. For Angelicus, it was no different.

Her short body was shivering slightly. The anguish and sadness in her eyes were only slightly marred by the awkwardness of her nudity. Where once she had worn glasses, dark rings circled her eyes and caused a ridge on her cheeks. She looked at Darcwulf with fond recognition.

Shadowolf looked passed the frowning face of Darcwulf and saw Fransiska beside Shedaaij. Fransiska was standing still, watching with insecure attention at the scene unravelling. Before Angelicus could say anything, before Darcwulf could reach out and comfort her, before anything more could go wrong, Shadowolf decided on a plan of action.

"Angelicus," he said, wrenching her attention from her former fiancé, "we need to stop the Creth-Demons. We are killing humans."

Angelicus looked at him, a vacant expression in her wet eyes.

"Is there a way we can stop them?" he asked, but she looked at Darcwulf again, who was watching Fransiska waiting anxiously in the distance. Angelicus joined his gaze and closed her gaping mouth. She looked back at Darcwulf's eyes that were apologising to her silently. A hard resolution filled her demeanour as she turned to look at Le'Mar's hill.

Light pulsed from within her body. Her arms stretched out as the light spread over her skin until she was no longer visible beneath it. The light rose up into the air, pulsing softly to its own serene beat.

The noise in the forest seemed to settle as the Crethans quietly looked up at the pulsing light. They turned from their quarries and slowly circled around, gazing intently at the light. All fights and skirmishes stopped as the light turned a deep yellow, and the Crethans let off an almighty howl. The song filled the air, and it coursed through the veins of everyone present.

The light moved west out of the forest. The Crethans followed in a maddened frenzy. Shadowolf turned around when he felt more power and saw the scepters of all the Creth-Demons glowing. They were chanting coarse sounds indiscernible to him.

Yet the Crethans continued to charge. They left the battle scene and moved towards the western Elvin Mountains, apparently prepared to cross it should the light of Angelicus command it.

Shadowolf looked at all the naked Crethan corpses littering the forest. It was a dismal picture and the only seven that were clothed were the Clan Crethans. The Creths' scepters had stopped glowing and Le'Mar's men looked around in confusion.

A thunderous wind broke over the land and roared through the forest. It sounded like a command, and Shadowolf had no doubt who had conjured it. In fear, Le'Mar's armies continued the assault, and the Firestroms moved down to Lard's Den again.

"What do you want to do?" Darcwulf said, his face stained with anger. Nelnar sneezed softly in the rain. Fransiska and Shedaaij joined them, followed shortly by Sorceress, Scarlette and Gwyn.

"I think we have over enough elementals to deal with the Firestroms, but I want to help where I can," Shadowolf said, looking at the blood covering Shedaaij. He transferred power to his eyes and looked at her stomach.

"How is the baby?" she asked. Fransiska and Darcwulf exchanged worried glances.

"The baby is well," Shadowolf said. "Do you need rest?"

"No, I can fight," she replied, twirling her daggers.

"You guys take care of as many Froths and Hu'Mar as you can," he instructed, looking around and seeing that only three Ma-Wreths remained in Le'Mar's army. "Darcwulf and I will assist with the Firestroms."

The friends nodded in agreement while Shadowolf and

Darcwulf turned into wind and fire bodies. They flew up into the air where two of the Stroms were already separated and their inner cores dancing in the drizzle. A gap in the clouds allowed a little moonlight to penetrate into the forest, and glinted off the silvery orbs connecting the Stroms.

Other small figures glinted also in the light and Shadowolf spared only a minimal moment to look down. Dead fairdievells lay among the burnt grass blades, their wings and bodies still reflecting a pure light. Dead fletchlings lay among them too, no light refracting off their dull, midnight-blue forms.

Shadowolf wondered if any still remained and saw a small group of lights fighting dark, winged objects just outside the perimeter of the Den. Further study revealed that there were several of these small groups fighting over the middle of the forest.

He heard fire roar and barely missed a ball of flame that had been hurtled at him from a Firestrom. He dodged several more of these missiles and made to attack its open core.

Shedaaij twisted her dagger into the bony neck of the Froth Hun and snapped it off. She had to admit, almost self-appraisingly, that experience in killing Froths did count for something. She raised rocks from the ground with her power to trip one of the two Froths running at her.

She blocked the heavy blow of the other Froth's blade and swung at its knees. The Froth lifted to kick into her stomach, and in panic she changed her stomach lining to stone. The foot landed on it and she flew back, sliding in the sand and mud until she hit a tree.

Shedaaij looked at her stomach. The Froth's boot print was embedded in the stone, but the baby was alright. She used the element of nature to warm the womb and nurture the baby.

Scarlette hit the Froth on its shoulder with her single-edged blade. Its metal was covered with crusts of blood, only enhancing its maroon sheen. She kicked and hit with the sword, managing to draw some blood from its chest and a crack in its skull.

A giant Wreth's arm shoved the Froth aside and hit Scarlette in her face. He took her sword and thrust it aside, the blade travelling sharply through the air. From a barrage of attacks from its oak arms, blood trickled out the corner of her mouth over her clothes.

Scarlette looked up at the beast's eyes, her mouth locked in pain. The Wreth slammed his fist into her abdomen and her body limply rose into the air. Her head slumped back and she saw with her waning sight that her blade was protruding from Gwyn's back; the girl fell down on her knees and keeled over.

Scarlette groaned out loud as her body hit the ground, her neck snapping on a rock. The sound of the battle died from her as Lastgorn jumped over her body and reached Gwyn. He held her tightly and removed Scarlette's blade. Tears flowed down his eyes as he stared at the sky and screamed in anger and pain.

The Wreth looked over at Shedaaij, who had just risen and was staring at Gwyn. She shifted her glance to the Wreth as it marched over, its arms bracing for the attack. She held her daggers tightly, but with despair creeping into her mind.

The Wreth raised its hand, but twisted around as Nelnar bit into its calf. The beast smashed down at the wolf, but Nelnar jumped and the arm hit the calf and a snap resounded.

Shedaaij watched as the wolf pounced on the beast's other calf, running through its legs to evade the fast, brutal punches. The black fur on its back was turning a slight grey. It looked almost like showers of snow scattered along the ridge, but she assumed it was the drizzle that was making it glitter.

Nelnar bit deeply into its spine, and the Ma-Wreth expanded its chest to roar in pain. Shedaaij drove her twin daggers deeply into its biceps, followed by a fatal grip by Nelnar on the back of its neck. The Wreth fell over to its death.

Shadowolf drove his blade into his second Firestrom's core. Like the first, it writhed and squirmed until it faded from view and the ashes fell to the muddy earth. Rennick and a Horlorn elemental were busy separating another Strom.

Nelnar left Shedaaij's side and ran towards the hill. The rain suddenly pelted down with a heavy shower, but it didn't slow the wolf. It jumped over logs and between Froth legs, racing to join its master.

Nolraldun tripped over a stump, but twisted in time to dodge a Dra-hu'Mar's sword. He bent back as an arrow narrowly skimmed his cheek and kicked the hu'Mar's blade to the side.

The hu'Mar thrust forward, but Nolraldun moved his hips,

grabbed its sword arm and shoved the blade into the Froth that had approached behind him. With the sword stuck in the Froth's chest, Nolraldun cut the hu'Mar's head cleanly off and drove the bloody sword into the Froth's skull.

Nelnar passed Millon and Kentaur. The two centaurs were faring the best against the enemies. Their equine bodies had minor scratches, although splattered with the blood of their victims. Killing orcs was a mere matter of grabbing their necks and snapping. Dra-hu'Mar were a tad more difficult with their bows, but the centaurs were managing.

Dren swooped over the running wolf. He was almost as invincible as the centaurs. His aerial advantage gave him the chance to swing down and grab any orc and kill it in mid-air. The arrows were a constant pestilence and every now and again he resorted to landing to face the archers.

Nelnar passed between Masara and Eldor on unicorn and pegasus. Power and staves were flying from their hands as they countered enemy after enemy, awaiting the arrival of the dark lord.

Chenesia, Hargon and Prince Lesan formed a trio in bow, axe and sword. They were the focus of three hu'Mar, two Froths and the final Ma-Wreth. The trio were assisted by the remaining Clan Orion of Rennick, Trevor and Sorceress.

Heula muttered curses as the wolf passed her. Orc skin turned putrid and they fell in the pus of their own boils. Skywolf loosed an arrow into a hu'Mar and used her staff as a purorc attacked her. Angelia snapped the orc on the back of its neck, and Skywolf thanked her under heavy breath.

Mandy's trotting hooves joined the muted pads of Nelnar's paws. The two ran in Shadowolf's direction as he left the final Strom to the other elementals. He was completely drenched in the stench of his own sweat and used the wind to clear his wet brow. He turned at the sound of the wolf and mare's approach and offered a weak smile.

"Glad you could join me," he muttered.

A rumble ran over the hills. Shadowolf held his ground and looked up the hill, his dragon amulet gleaming under his torn shirt. At the top he saw a cloaked figure with his staff staring down at him. Shadowolf grinned in anger at the dark lord, hoping they could finally meet in battle.

But he knew the dark lord was not going to meet him soon. He could smell and sense the vast amount of dragons waiting behind the hill. Sonersaat sat on Maneto's back, awaiting the order of his lord.

Shadowolf touched Asgorna's amulet, summoning the dragons. He rolled over immediately as a Froth Hun's blade swiped for his neck. Le'Mar was going to do everything in his power to kill Shadowolf now.

But Shadowolf was relentless as he drove Ruben-Willow through its skull. Arrows rose to fall upon him and he rolled and dodged, using the elements to assist him.

A yelp reached his ears, and in shock he turned to see Sonersaat stand above Nelnar's body. His sword was in Nelnar side, penetrating deep into the wolf's heart. Nelnar lay on the floor, panting heavily as its life left its body. It black back was covered with its own blood now, mottled with tiny specks of white.

But Shadowolf paid no heed to this snowy appearance on Nelnar's fur. His heart sank as he watched in dulled shock the life leave his beloved wolf. Sadness filled its eyes, staring at Shadowolf apologetically, and Nelnar sighed softly and left the world.

Shadowolf wanted to hold Nelnar in his arms. He wanted to weep for hours and mourn its death, cradling it in his embrace as his tears rolled down its mottled fur. Sonersaat, however, would allow no such luxury.

Sonersaat's body was glowing from the red wings spread out behind his back. Down the slope, he could see the white wings of Trimistus flying up to meet them. Sonersaat walked up to Mandy, preparing to kill her and speaking words that were meant to bite into his last resolve.

Shadowolf heard none of these words and screamed in anger. The *Wisoum* in him suddenly awoke and bright green wings broke from the skin of his back, no longer ethereal in appearance. He roared out loud, his anger burning deep within him and a great release of wind sent Sonersaat rolling down the hill towards Trimistus.

Shadowolf rose up in the air and touched his dragon amulet again. He could feel the dragons approaching, and knew that

Asgorna would be there soon.

Without warning, Maneto's tail hit him in the back and he went soaring into the air. He passed over Nelnar's dead body. He passed over Trimistus and Sonersaat now wrestling with each other, their wings striking for a hit.

He passed over the first line of trees that had been smashed by the Ma-Wreths. He passed the remaining Clan members and elves fighting for survival, and the elementals of Horlorn.

Finally he passed where Eldor and Masara were fighting, who looked up to see his battered body flying over them. Shadowolf used the wind to pull up his descent and turned around.

His wings were flapping in the air and he no longer had to use the wind to keep him levitated. His aura was a rage of fire that burnt yellow off his skin, his eyes glaring green towards the dark lord's DragonRider. His hair rose up in madness against the aura that pulsed against gravity.

Asgorna and his army of a hundred dragons flew behind Shadowolf's back. The dragon's warm breath touched his neck as Sonersaat's army of dragons cropped the hill and roared in defiance.

"You have impeccable timing, as usual," Shadowolf grunted, his loss still ringing in his nerves.

WAR OF THE DRAGONS
CHAPTER NINE

Nighthale swung his staff up. The edge of the wood became as sharp as a sword of wind and cut through the orc. Dra-hu'Mar archers were still loosing their arrows over the outer walls of Avalion, but merely dropped down onto the grass of the inner defences.

Avalion was as yet impenetrable. As much as Lister and Ru-Maak tried to force entry, the elementals used their arrows and elements to buffet their forces. The elemental walls also held any dark creatures back that tried to scale them. Nighthale had watched in relief as the ladders broke the moment it touched the walls, or the orcs tried climbing and simply slid down onto a waiting spear.

Lister and Ru-Maak solely concentrated on the army outside Avalion's walls. Nighthale had considered signaling the men to return within its safety, but they, like him, were too stubborn to wait inside.

Nighthale swung the end of his staff in a wide arc, and three arrows of wind flew across the field into orc chests. Two centaurs ran around him about to hit his head, when he struck the one's front legs and thrust a pointy end through the other's chest.

Looking passed the first centaur he had toppled he saw Malkius Saphin lying on his back blocking blows from three orcs. Nighthale jumped on the shoulders of the rising centaur and became wind. He travelled to the fallen comrade and twisted his sword-edged staff around into the orcs.

As Malkius rose in gratitude, ten orcs charged to them. Nighthale's eyes burnt white and the wind lifted the orcs up into the air. Malkius released shards of ice from his palms towards each of the suspended orcs and they fell to their deaths.

"How long do you think we can keep them out?" Malkius murmured.

"As long as the elements ward against them," Nighthale breathed back.

Six machines rolled up the hill. They were wooden in structure and the arm of the machine held a ball in its pit. The orcs put torches to the balls and they were engulfed in flames. Nighthale turned as he heard the machines release the balls into the air and they descended on the walls.

The six flaming balls hit the wall and crumbled to the grass. The wall showed no sign of damage or stain, but Nighthale could feel the power in the wall drop slightly before rising to its former level.

"We need to take care of those machines!" Nighthale shouted as the cries of the enemy grew louder.

Unexpectedly Malkius and Nighthale were thrown to the floor by two Dra-hu'Mar. Their swords twinkled in the firelight and their eyes shone in victory. They dropped the tips of their swords down on the two lords and then were jerked off them by two beasts.

Nighthale blinked and watched the Crethans storm over the plains. A bright light was hovering in the sky above, a faint power resonating between it and the deformed wolves.

And instead of attacking Avalion's army, the beasts were assisting them.

"Need some help?" Elgoth said, holding a hand down to Nighthale and smiling...

The hurorc stirred. She looked around the hut, hugging the human blanket to her chest. After they had taken her from the edge of the desert where she had fallen from dehydration, the humans had cared for her in Avalion as one of their own. But she could feel the familiar power of the dark lord's attack from the outside and instead of being drawn to it she hid in fear.

The humans had shown her love again, and Lowle Hills was a better abode than she could have ever wished for. But the orc blood that ran within her cried out for release, and the only rewards she received for denying it an outlet were constant headaches and spinal pains.

"Jelina, wait!" someone shouted outside the house. She heard scuffling of feet and then a short cry and an eruption of flames. The hurorc, even in her cold dread, managed to get up and look through the open gap in the doorway.

A young woman walked quickly passed the door. Her hair was wild and honey blond, kept above her shoulders. She seemed tense, but on a determined mission.

"On my way, lord Le'Mar," she whispered as she turned a corner of the house. The hurorc could feel the essence of the dark lord within her, and wondered how the elemental happened to get within Avalion.

The hurorc left the safety of the house and rushed after the elemental. She saw the remains of a body that had been pulled by vines to the ground and burnt by fire. Its ashes lay smouldering in the blades of brown grass.

She ran around the house, eager to see what the emissary of Le'Mar was up to. When she reached the walls that were guarded by the power of the elements, she saw the elemental with her palm against the wall. Her eyes were closed and she could feel power being drawn from the wall into her body.

The hurorc panicked and ran to attack the elemental with her hands. The woman turned quickly and thrust her hand out. Gravity yanked the hurorc and pinned her to the soggy grass.

Once again, the woman proceeded to draw power from the walls.

"I know you," the hurorc said in a bad, grunting sound. "You were one of those professors. One of Mercius's kind."

Sona Nelma completed her mission. She drew the last of the power from the wall. To her left she heard a loud crash against the outer wall, and smiled in satisfaction as it broke and crumbled.

"Why are you doing this?!" the hurorc shouted.

"Because I have been waiting all these years for this moment of victory for my lord," the dark *Goudlem* smirked in joy.

Sona raised her palm to the pinned hurorc. The woman began to cry as her skin and organs collapsed and turned to sand. Her scream became a gargle as she choked from the dust that collected in her failing throat. Her bones turned to earth and filtered through her pores to the earth until the hurorc was nothing but ash.

"It is accomplished," she said.

Good, Sona, Le'Mar said sweetly to her mind. *You may proceed to kill at will.*

Lellian released another blow from his trident. The demon-queen disintegrated in the water, her dark blood spreading into the blackened waters.

We have to escape into the oceans, my lord! James communicated in anger. *We will choke to death in Avalendil!*

The mer-King knew this to be true. There was nothing left of the warren to salvage, and he could not see or filter air through his gills from the dirty water properly. Even the trident was waning in its ability to produce sufficient light.

Lellian! James shouted again, swinging his blade to kill another siren.

The trident flared in rage and the Mer-Kindgom received the signal to abandon *Avalendil*. Lellian could feel the currents swaying against him as the mer-people hastened to leave, and saw that the sirens also made for the exit.

Among them were sharks and other predators that had been attracted by the blood, but Lellian had been too occupied by the demon-queens to command them to attack. They swam in the evil water trying to find siren, queen or mer-victims to sage their appetites.

Lellian was last in line to leave and stopped when the water cleared enough for him to see the exit to the oceans. The foundations of the earth above served as the canopy of the exit, and beneath the canopy stood a demon-queen covered in red light.

The demon-queen's eyes blazed with purple fire and the sirens swayed in ghostly silence behind her. There was no doubt in the mer-people's minds, still watching from within the warren, that this demon-queen led the sirens.

What was worse was the fact that every mermaid and merman once knew this queen.

Blosom, Lellian called. *You don't need to do this. Return to us.*

You place your trust in a fool! Blosom shouted.

You once fell for that fool, James grunted.

And Shadowolf never loved me back, Blosom leered. *Mercius was a much better man, and Shadowolf took him away from me too.*

Blosom raised her dark, purple trident to the lip of the warren's opening. They could feel the power surge through the instrument, ready to collapse the warren around them.

Lellian swam fast, breaking away from the mer-people. He was a wave of light that travelled through the water to Blosom, a moment away from striking her with his trident's force.

James barely saw the movement, but her shadow trailed her as she moved faster than Lellian and drove her trident into his back. The snakes on her head lengthened and lashed at his neck and hair, pulling his face up. A silent scream escaped his lips as Blosom drove the trident through his chest for the fatal blow.

Lellian closed his mouth and eyes softly as he died. His hand dropped the golden trident that began to drift to the bed of the warren far below. Blosom let Lellian's body fall and was about to grab the handle when the trident mysteriously disappeared.

She gulped out loud as the prongs entered her stomach. Before she could respond, the trident was removed and thrust through her neck, the snakes hissing and twisting for escape. The attacker pinned her neck against the warren wall and the power of the trident exploded into her.

As her body died, the warren started collapsing upon itself. Rocks and buildings fell upon the mer-people, smashing into their heads and carrying them to the depths of *Avalendil*.

James grasped the trident firmly, his body lit with glorious light. He was about to strike at the sirens outside with its power, about to throw some of the falling spikes at them, when a rock twice his size hit him against his neck.

James drifted unconsciously with the trident to the bed of *Avalendil*, trapped with his kingdom within its prison.

***

Shadowolf lowered his power as he dropped onto Asgorna's shoulders. He kept his *Wisoum* wings open, flapping in the cold air that was the remnant of the clearing clouds.

Trimistus rode on Mynisna and they pulled up beside them. His dragon sword was gleaming on his hip, the red eyes in his sockets the most intense that Shadowolf had seen it.

Although Sonersaat was still on the opposite hill they could both feel his power. His army of dragons was marginally smaller than Asgorna's, and this gave Shadowolf the hope that they stood a chance.

Asgorna and Maneto rumbled roars at the same time, signalling the start of the Dragon War. Shadowolf's body lurched back as the dragon surged forward. Wings, scales, talons and fangs the size of an adult human raced passed him. Maneto also seemed to drop back to allow the bulk of his army to charge forward.

"What about the earth below us?" Shadowolf said, remembering the casualties during the war in Asgorna's world.

"Let's hope the elves can move as fast as they are famed for," Asgorna said solemnly.

"Can't we take the war elsewhere?" he tried again.

"You can always ask him, or him," the dragon said, indicating Sonersaat and then Le'Mar. "But I doubt they will concede."

"That must be why they reserved the dragons for now," Shadowolf realised, and then held on tighter as Asgorna swayed.

The first dragons struck with powerful rage. It was hard for many in the forest to tell who was fighting who. The clearest difference was that Maneto's dragons had an essence of evil within that was palpable to those as sensitive as Shadowolf was to it.

Wings broke as claws dug in. Trimistus seemed to be making headway to Sonersaat much quicker than Shadowolf as Asgorna was faced by five dragons simultaneously.

Shadowolf jumped off the dragon's back and used his own wings. Ruben-Willow sprang out in both hands and he lost Asgorna among the tails and bodies than hurtled into him.

He ran along the spine of a dragon and jumped off to deliver his sword into the side of its body. It cried out as he slid down tearing its scales and kicked off to cut another's neck.

The second dragon looked down and roared fire at him and he changed his body into fire. When the roar stopped, Shadowolf became wind and passed through the dragon's scales and body, passing through its back with the sword of wind ripping its insides.

He stuck his sword in a swinging tail and used it as leverage to swing up to Asgorna, but a separate tail hit him in the chest and he accidentally let go of Ruben-Willow. He flew up again to retrieve it from the tail, when another roar erupted and a dead dragon's body tumbled from above towards him.

As the corpse reached him, he ran up its body with his wings as support. When it passed, he kicked off its stomach and flew for his sword. He ducked a claw and swerved passed fangs that bit at him.

The fangs came back and tried to kill him. He dodged and dived, hurtling balls of ice and rock at its face. In a fast, serpentine move, the dragon lashed out for the fatal blow that would have ended any man's life. But Shadowolf called Ruben-Willow with his soul and the sword vanished from the dragon's tail and leapt into his arms.

The blade passed neatly into the beast's upper palate. It roared out but was silenced when he cut through its neck. He turned to face other dragons and heard a dull thud as the dragon hit the earth. He hoped no allies were getting killed from the falling bodies.

From the quick glances he could steal he saw that Trimistus had begun battling Sonersaat. For some reason this didn't bother him. His concern for the land and people below was greater than for the prophecy, and he had no doubt that Trimistus was a match for Sonersaat.

Yet he questioned his own doubt... he could feel that Sonersaat's power was greater than the two allies together. Shadowolf had no idea how he had become so strong, but he was determined to keep fighting until the dark DragonRider was defeated.

Shadowolf continued to scale dragon backs and slide his blade into them. Asgorna was at his side again and he quickly mounted his shoulders. As the dragon breathed flames to assist his army, the man threw balls of elements at the dragons while swinging his sword up at bellies that passed.

He vaguely wondered if he should attack Le'Mar while the DragonRiders were busy. It would be unexpected and maybe he might get lucky. But Masara's words crept back into his mind and, even though Nelnar's loss still plagued his heart, he decided to listen to the old man this time.

Do not face him until you are ready...

Grey wings passed by them and Shadowolf raised his sword in

greeting. Dren had obtained a sword somewhere and was now jumping between dragons trying to kill them. His skin seemed to glow like the moon lighting a stone wall each time he approached one of Maneto's dragons.

"Can he sense them too?" Shadowolf asked Asgorna. "How can he tell the difference?"

"The curse of the gargoyle is also a gift," Asgorna replied during a reprieve of battle. "They were set as guardians against evil in their original world."

"Ahhh," he replied. "That would explain why Masara wanted them in Eldor's dungeons. Asgorna…"

Shadowolf had ducked and cut the claw diving down on him. Maybe this wasn't the time to discuss probabilities, but something worked on his mind even in the midst of battle.

"Yes, Shado?" Asgorna rumbled and a glow passed up the dragon's neck and was belched out in a wall of flame.

"What will happen if Trimistus kills Sonersaat?" he asked reflectively.

"Then he will have to take the roll of DragonWourd and Mynisna will become the new Dragon King; unless you challenge Trimistus for the position."

Shadowolf went silent, another thought on his mind, but Asgorna seemed to have picked it up.

"Our bargain still stands, Shadowolf, should Maneto be defeated."

Shadowolf nodded his head, but chose not to speak. Once again he looked down at Le'Mar at the top of the hill, but decided against it.

"Let's get Maneto," Asgorna said and Shadowolf lurched back again as the dragon picked up speed.

Suddenly the attacks on Shadowolf and Asgorna increased. It was like a wall of dragons had moved up to stop them from gaining the DragonRiders. Shadowolf could feel Trimistus's power ebbing, but Sonersaat was still as strong as before.

"Is there any way I can help?" Darcwulf asked as he rose to meet them. His body was still completely made of fire, but now he held the serpent sword. Shadowolf saw a soft, silver light at the place where the metal hilt touched the flames and he wondered if it hurt at all.

"Yes," Shadowolf said, turning his body and sword into wind. "Let's create a path to Sonersaat."

"See you on the other side," Asgorna said, falling away from them.

They took turns dashing between bodies and cutting into their hard scales. Shadowolf ran along ally dragon backs, which he quite took a liking to now, and jumped off to cut into an opponent's belly.

A dragon tail swerved and he unsheathed the dagger in time to cut into it. Unfortunately his angle had been wrong and he hit a tailbone. As the momentum of the tail pulled him down, forgetting to let go, it threw him at immense velocity to the earth.

He curved his body, using his wings and the wind to pull him from the gravitational force. He cleared the lowest layer of dragons and saw the earth below him again. They were still fighting among the littered tree trunks and dead dragons, killing the few remaining Froths and the many Dra-hu'Mar.

He realised that the elf and Horlorn numbers were also dwindling and flew up in new resolve to end the Dragon War. He saw a clear path to Sonersaat and wondered why he hadn't thought of flying below the dragons before.

Several dragons dropped from the sky and he saw that it was to no avail either. The dragons were going to stop him from reaching the *Wisoum*s.

Something told him to watch Trimistus. Maneto had turned from killing a dragon, a ferocious expression on its scaly head. He curled and flew for Trimistus, ready to snap his head off.

Shadowolf teleported instantly. He had surprised himself and barely raised his blade in time to cut into Maneto's chest. The dragon reared up, and Shadowolf could hear Trimistus and Sonersaat's swords meet behind him.

"Uh oh," Shadowolf breathed, his body still in the form of wind. Maneto leered down at him and roared in anger. Shadowolf flew passed his jaws and made to move away from Trimistus. Maneto followed, chasing Shadowolf through the throng of dragons.

On the earth, Shadowolf's former school friend Theroy ran and hit a Dra-hu'Mar with his red staff. The elementals of Horlorn were now together as a group fighting the dark lord's remaining army.

The swordsmen were nearly depleted, many having removed themselves from Lard's Den to the open fields.

"Leave the Froths to the elves and Clan!" Treville shouted. The lord of Horlorn looked at Theroy. "All elementals kill as many hu'Mar as you can!"

Theroy nodded and rushed over the dead body of a dragon. An arrow passed his head and he somersaulted over a slashing blade. As he blocked the returning sword, his staff turned into a red rope and coiled around the steel. He pulled the sword from the blond man's grasp and flicked it back into the Dra-hu'Mar's chest.

Millon and Kentaur took it upon themselves to dispose of the remaining Froths. The centaurs now had wide, open gashes on their hinds and sides. Their faces were pockmarked with blood and dirt. But their fists were doing immense damage and with a power unknown to the others seemed to be able to deal with the Froths quite comfortably.

Millon rammed his back legs into the chest of a Froth and tottered his front hooves in the air before crashing down on its skull. Kentaur caught the two-edged sword of another and threw it aside, broadening his shoulders and slapping his palms over the flaming, bony head.

"Kentaur, Millon!" they heard Theroy shouting. "Move!"

They didn't waste time looking up and then ran to the side. They could feel the weight of the dead dragon falling towards them and barely missed the crushing drop.

The earth rumbled in their vicinity in the aftermath and Kentaur lost his balance. He slipped over a trunk and fell with his equine chest into the blade of a Froth. He was about to hit the beast, but it removed the blade and drove it into his human chest.

Kentaur stared dumbly as blood trickled from his mouth and nose onto the Froth's gloved hand. His vision faded as Millon trotted over and killed the Froth.

"Kentaur, can you hear me?" Millon said, but the centaur stared at him. His eyes went white as he tried to speak and then he fell onto his front knees. Millon stared at his friend, suspended on his legs, head bowed down in death.

Millon clenched his fists in rage and stomped the ground furiously. He ran to find the first Froth he could and launched him into the air with a bounding leap of his fist. Theroy hit the body aside with his staff, more from defence than any other reason.

Heula chanted and sparks ignited before three Dra-hu'Mar. Sorceress held her palm out and each spark turned into coils that grabbed their long blond hairs and flung them to the ground. Shedaaij summoned shards of rock from the earth into their bodies.

"This could be a problem," Angelia said beside them.

They had ignored the Froth horses roaming around the Den blindly. Mandy had joined Ursula in battle and it was hard enough telling the difference between her and them.

But the Dra-hu'Mar had tentatively tried to mount the black beasts and the horses were not opposing them. One by one the remaining horses were mounted and the hu'Mar charged with bows and swords.

Theroy ran up and released balls of fire from his palms at the horses. One reared up and, as it landed again, Theroy jumped up and hit the end of his staff across the hu'Mar's face. It fell to the earth and was trodden to its death by the other horses.

To the north, on the outskirts of the Den and along the hill that Le'Mar stood on, Hargon fought the only group of orcs left with the Vale's dwarves. He swung his axe around, covering his beard and short body with even more orc blood.

He swung again, but the weight moved him back and he toppled over a body. While he tried to recover, a purorc moved over him and raised his crude blade. Hargon screamed in defiance and as he drove the edge of his axe into its stomach, Lesan's elvin sword passed through its back and Chenesia's arrow through its head.

"Effective," the dwarf grumbled. "Gruesome, but effective."

Chenesia rode on Genewiu to him. Concern was etched across her face but she smiled encouragingly to him.

"Chenesia!" a voice shouted, but it wasn't Hargon's. She turned her head to the Vale's army that was fighting orcs to the left and saw the man approach her. She dropped her jaw in surprise, but smiled fondly as he rode up.

"Father! I didn't know you were here," she said, pride shining in her eyes.

"Baron Maren-Ti," Prince Lesan said. "I need to regroup with my father. I leave Chenesia…"

"No, no," Maren-Ti said. "She will be in better care with you."

"Don't lie," his daughter laughed.

"I, too, wish to see your father, Lesan," he said, looking down the hill into the Den. "Eldor seems to be planning something."

They followed his gaze. Opposite Le'Mar's hill, on the other end of the Den, Eldor sat upon his pegasus talking to Masara upon Ursula. There was tension between the group as they looked up at the dragons that filled the sky.

Chenesia also looked up and saw Shadowolf and Darcwulf letting balls of flame pass through them. When three dragons spat at Darcwulf, he twisted his arms and gathered the fire. He then straightened his arms again and threw the balls back at them.

"Let's go," Lesan said. Hargon ran up to him, who automatically reached down and pulled him onto the back of his horse. Chenesia followed on Genewiu and Maren-Ti beside her.

They rode through the Den, only defending when it was necessary. Several thuds resounded over the land when dragons plummeted onto the earth. Blood curdled the sand beneath them in rivers of death.

After long moments of hard riding they finally reached them. The area was clear of any bodies and Ursula was speaking to Masara.

"Can you manage?" she said. Masara looked worse than ever. His head hung down, his skin taut with sickness. He coughed and put his palm to his chest.

"Shouldn't you return to the Far Isles?" Chenesia interrupted, unsure how to help.

"We need to finish this," Masara said, glaring through the distance at Le'Mar.

"But we still have the *Sadgi* prophecy to go through," Ursula pleaded. "We will need you the most there."

"Bontu will provide in my stead," he groaned. "My time is coming to an end."

"What is he planning on doing?" Lesan said to his father.

"Not he alone," Eldor said. "But we are going up there to assist the *Wisoum*s. Le'Mar is using the dragons to distract Shado, Darc and Dren while Sonersaat defeats Trimistus."

"That scoundrel!" Chenesia shouted.

"Chenesia, relax," Maren-ti said in a paternal manner. Instead of relaxing her, it incensed her more. "What..."

"We are going with," Chenesia said, and Genewiu rode forward to join Ursula and Eldor's pegasus.

"Chene..." Maren-ti started to plead again as he always did, but he caught the expression on Eldor's face and turned his horse around.

Behind Le'Mar a black pegasus rode onto the hill. It stretched its wings and tucked it neatly again as Le'Mar mounted it, staff in saddle-sheath. The group waited, but Le'Mar simply sat on the pegasus.

"Do you think he knows?" Chenesia asked.

"Anything is possible," Masara said. "The question is what he plans to do about it."

Without being commanded, Genewiu ran passed Maren-ti and rose into the air. The Baron and Hargon were busy protesting when Masara and Eldor joined her. Hargon looked up at Maren-ti, who sighed and dismounted to continue fighting.

"I am starting to feel nostalgic," Masara said as they approached the wall of dragons.

"What do you mean?" Chenesia called back.

"It feels like the Battle of T'Mar's Scourge," Ursula completed for him, "only on a larger scale."

"I still can't believe he is your brother," Chenesia said to Masara and prepared for the dragons.

"Chenesia, here!" Masara shouted, ignoring her comment. He threw his soul-bound sword to her. "Your arrows will be useless."

"What about you?" she asked, but he brandished his white staff and smiled.

Le'Mar's pegasus stirred and its front hooves scraped the sand. The dark lord watched them rise into the sky. It was time to do what he had come to do; to do what he had been yearning for all the centuries. The black pegasus rose in the air towards the dragons.

Shadowolf watched them fly up and saw the dragons block them too. Masara and Eldor were using their staves to release power, while Chenesia used the sword to carve her way through. He could see she didn't know how to use a sword, but if it was like

Ruben-Willow, he was sure the sword was doing most of the work.

What distracted him from Sonersaat was Le'Mar. The dark lord was finally joining the battle and Shadowolf suddenly realised that Le'Mar didn't care what happened to the *Wisoum*s. It seemed like he only wanted Masara.

Shadowolf left them to their own devices and made for Sonersaat again. He raised his blade as he approached, for Sonersaat had stabbed at him.

Power surged around the two. The wind circled around them as they tried to throw each other aside. Shadowolf turned his blade into fire as Sonersaat thrashed his spiked wings at him.

Shadowolf dropped down as Maneto's tail flew over his head. He circled around Maneto and grabbed onto Asgorna's shoulders and the dragons circled each other. Their claws scraped against each other's bellies and then Mynisna slammed into Maneto with Trimistus jumping off and flying to attack Sonersaat.

Masara raised his staff and hit a power orb aside. Le'Mar's hood had fallen to reveal his dark sneering face. Eldor and Chenesia tried to reach them, but Le'Mar avoided them and the dragons kept them aside, no longer interested in the *Wisoum*s.

Le'Mar swayed his staff again and held his palm out to send two balls of black fire at him. Ursula twisted and Masara back-handed the second ball, which fell towards the earth. Where it hit, the earth shuddered and a wide circle of grass turned black.

The dark lord held his black staff with red flames horizontal with both hands and a stream of red waves cascaded to them. Masara held his staff up and the wave hit them. He strained, holding back the immense strength of the younger lord.

While the two held the staves tight, the stream of power locked between the two of them, Shadowolf jumped on Maneto's back. Sonersaat turned around and walked down. The dragon twisted and fought with Asgorna and Mynisna, dodging their flames, but the two men walked on his back as if he were standing still.

Shadowolf sheathed Ruben-Willow in his soul, prepared to face Sonersaat without it. Sonersaat found this amusing and sheathed his sword on his hip.

The two moved forward and locked hands. Their faces glared at each other as their wings intensified in light and the power grew from both of them.

Their elbows moved as they pushed harder against each other, but none fell back. Unexpectedly, Sonersaat kicked Shadowolf's stomach and he fell down. Trimistus flew into Sonersaat and carried him off the dragon's back.

The two wings interlocked as they hit each other's faces. They fell to the earth with Shadowolf letting gravity pull him down behind them. When Trimistus broke free, Dren crashed into Sonersaat and landed stone fists into his chest.

Sonersaat's face screwed up in anger. He grabbed the Lapis Pin on the gargoyles chest and ripped it off. Dren opened his eyes in horror as Sonersaat slammed an open palm into his chest and sharp sunlight erupted.

Dren's face and chest went still as rock and he fell down. Shadowolf tried to fly passed Sonersaat and catch up with Dren before he smashed into the ground, but Sonersaat pulled Shadowolf's hair and threw him up in the direction of the dragons.

Shadowolf twisted and looked down. Fire hit his face and he was knocked over. When he tried again, he couldn't see any trace of the gargoyle on the earth.

The loss of the gargoyle stung his nerves again, reminding him of Nelnar's demise. The image of his pet wolf came in his mind, and he saw Sonersaat driving the blade into it. He bunched his fists together, raising his power as high as he could, and flew down to meet the *Wisoum*.

The power-lock between Masara and Le'Mar erupted and threw them back but they turned raced to meet each other again regardless. The pegasus and unicorn nearly collided as the staves met, turning into blades of wind and chaos. The mounts kicked at each other in an attempt to dislodge the riders.

Trimistus had his hands on Sonersaat's throat. Sonersaat kicked at the reptilian man and unsheathed his sword. Trimistus pulled out the dragon blade and they battled each other. Shadowolf was almost upon them when Sonersaat raised his palm and wind that Shadowolf couldn't control threw him aside like a weak puppet.

Trimistus thrust his blade at Sonersaat's neck, but he evaporated and appeared behind Trimistus. He pushed the blade through Trimistus's wing and flew up to tear a large hole in it.

Trimistus screamed in pain. Sonersaat fell down and kicked hard into his face, power blasting through his legs into Trimistus's cheeks. A sizzle escaped as Trimistus's reptile face burnt open and he fell.

He tried to correct his fall, but the torn wing wouldn't permit it. His body turned and turned as he fell, the dead wing fluttering sickly in the air.

The two Orion, Rennick and Trevor, watched as Trimistus fell towards them. They sheathed their blades and held their hands up. Rennick was getting his spirit power ready to slow his descent while Trevor was getting ready to catch him.

Le'Mar hit Masara in the face and shoved him aside with wind. He stared down at the earth and saw the two male Orion getting ready to save the *Wisoum*.

He teleported and thrust his staff through Rennick's body. When it felt like Rennick was going to turn around on the staff and face him, Le'Mar removed the staff and hit him across the back and then his neck. A crack resounded as the neck broke.

Trevor had nearly hit him, but the dark lord lifted his hand and the staff smacked him across the face. It was evident that some power had accompanied the hit, for Trevor soared across the land and his spine broke on a broken tree stump.

Le'Mar looked up at Trimistus burnt face. The wing still fluttered uselessly and the dark lord smile up in satisfaction; the traitor would be paid his dues.

Le'Mar gave a final wave and moved out of the way. Trimistus contracted his muscles, gathering the power of the *Wisoum*, and struck out with fist and legs into the earth. The ground shook and Le'Mar was cast aside at the power that was released.

The dark lord stood up and waited for the white dust to settle. A shadowy figure moved within the newly formed crater, but Le'Mar couldn't see any wings. When the man walked from the smoke, Le'Mar grinned.

"Come, Masara," he said. "Let's finish this."

Shadowolf waited anxiously for the smoke to clear, but when it did he only saw Trimistus's body lying in the crater. The wings covered his body like a blanket. He transferred power to his eyes and sighed in relief when he saw that Trimistus still lived.

To the side in the fields, Le'Mar and Masara fought alone, their staves twinkling with power and the earth reverberating beneath them. Shadowolf looked around and saw Sonersaat looking up at him glumly.

"I thought you'd be happier," Shadowolf said conversationally.

"You two are harder to kill than a pair of flies," Sonersaat said and rose to meet him. Above them, Asgorna and Maneto lunged at each other, Mynisna leaving them to attend to Trimistus.

Nolraldun walked through the broken land, looking at the crater. The dragon landed beside the hole as the assassin looked down. He remembered vaguely how he had been sent to kill this reptilian man, and wondered if death by another hand counted.

He twisted his head as a familiar scent reached his nose. He looked everywhere, suddenly aware of his surroundings. Could it be that the Semhum Kateth had sent someone to kill him for his failure? Had Le'Mar contracted someone to kill him too?

He kicked out as the other assassin pinned him to the floor. They rolled passed the crater, clutching each other's wrists.

"Master assassin Jutbacca?" Nolraldun smiled. "I am honoured. They sent the best."

But as was the assassin code, which Nolraldun had quite forgotten thanks to the Clan, the assassin would not speak when addressed. He had one mission: kill.

Jutbacca used his toes to draw a knife up to Nolraldun's stomach, but Nolraldun used his knees to wipe it aside. They rolled up and down the hill again until Nolraldun broke loose and made for the broken trees of the Den.

Shadowolf hit Sonersaat in the face. Maneto loomed down to bite him, but Asgorna bit into his tail and flung him aside. Maneto released balls of flame at him, but Asgorna flew around them and attacked again.

Sonersaat hit his palm into Shadowolf's chest and then drove his sword into Shadowolf's sternum. Like before, Shadowolf turned his skin into earth and the blade passed through sand.

Sonersaat laughed loud. Shadowolf was about to question his mirth when power pulsed from Sonersaat's core, up his shoulders and through his arms and into the blade. With a screaming pain, Shadowolf's body returned to flesh, hanging from the sword, and then he was thrown off the blade.

Shadowolf fell backwards. The blood oozed over his chest and down his neck. It trickled behind his ears and into his hair.

The world around him began to fade as death came closer. He saw Le'Mar and Masara still fighting, the body of Trimistus in the crater and the dead lying all over the forest.

The searing heat of his chest was numb to him. He gulped and coughed as his life left him. His wings drooped to the earth as he had no more left to give.

Maneto curled into Asgorna's arms and bit into his neck. They thrashed around in the air, but Maneto refused to let go. Blood gushed into Maneto's mouth as Asgorna went limp.

Shadowolf looked through misty eyes at the land one last time. His eyes swept over Nelnar. The wolf's fur had completely turned white. Beside the wolf knelt Shedaaij, watching him fall with pain on her face, shouting for him not to die.

His chest grew warm. A red glow pulsed around the sword wound on his sternum. Before he could explain how or why, he had reverted his fall and was floating in the air. Asgorna's dragon blood pulsed through his veins and he could feel the power that came with it.

Shadowolf flew up with massive velocity, his renewed wings searing the sky with heat. He rushed passed the gaping Sonersaat and struck Maneto in the belly with his fist. A bang echoed across the skies as the dragon cried out in pain and released Asgorna, falling down to Sonersaat's side.

Shadowolf placed his hand on Asgorna's neck wound and watched as the dragon's eyes lit up again.

"We share the same blood now," Shadowolf and Asgorna said at the same time. "Let's finish the prophecy."

He mounted Asgorna again and watched Sonersaat mount Maneto with trepidation. Shadowolf smiled down at them, knowing what he had to do.

Asgorna sailed down, rumbling with the fires that burnt within. Maneto flew up, casting balls of flame up at them. The fires passed them as Asgorna swerved from side to side, getting ready for the final attack.

When they met, Shadowolf and Sonersaat jumped off.

Shadowolf spread his arms and wings majestically and he changed. Asgorna pulled Maneto's arms and legs apart and rumbled deeper.

Sonersaat dropped his sword in horror.

Go for his heart, Asgorna said to Shadowolf's mind.

Shadowolf's wings turned to those of a dragon. His face contorted until he had a snout and fangs too. As one, Shadowolf and Asgorna bit into Sonersaat and Maneto's hearts. The light and life of the hearts flickered as they killed them, and the bodies fell with defeat to the earth.

The dragons stopped. One by one the dragons surrounded them. Shadowolf watched as a dazed Trimistus was flying on Mynisna up to them. In total there were seventy-three dragons left in the sky and they all waited on Shadowolf's command.

"It is time," Asgorna said, retaining his position as Dragon King. "Your time has come to fulfil your end of the bargain."

"What does he mean?" Darcwulf said, killing his flames and joining them.

"We had a bargain," Shadowolf replied, "that if they assisted in the war then I would return to their world and finish what we started."

Darcwulf remained silent. Shadowolf looked down at Masara and Le'Mar still fighting, the earth transforming from their power.

"I can't leave," Shadowolf said, feeling the anger rise in Asgorna.

"You dare turn your word on a dragon?" the Dragon King responded.

"The war isn't over," Shadowolf said, looking at Asgorna. The dragon leered at him.

"Do not use technicalities with me," he said. "Do not..."

"How do we serve you, Asgorna?" one of Maneto's dragons asked. "We've been fighting a war against you for decades. How do we serve you?"

Shadowolf and Asgorna looked down at them. The dark dragons still held hatred for Asgorna although Maneto wasn't there. To get them to obey him now might create a terrible situation for Asgorna.

"I have an idea," Shadowolf said. Asgorna groaned, knowing

fully well what he was going to say. "Trimistus is a *Wisoum*. Will the dragons swear allegiance to Mynisna and Lord Danaka as the DragonWourd until I am able to complete my end of the bargain?"

The dragons murmured among themselves until they had made a decision.

"So be it," they said.

"I humbly accept," Trimistus and Mynisna said with the same voice.

"Very well," Shadowolf said, changing his face back to human. "See you soon."

"Do you need us?" Trimistus asked.

"No," Shadowolf said. "You will more than likely just get in the way."

Trimistus and Mynisna flew back to Bentley Strip, leading the dragons.

"I won't forget this," the former Dragon King said, and flew after them to his temple.

THE DARK LORD
CHAPTER TEN

Shadowolf soared down with the wind and landed hard on the forest earth. He saw Masara and Le'Mar using their powers in combat on the hill, no one interfering, but he ignored them. At the moment he felt anger at the dragons, and mostly at himself for making the bargain in the first place.

Shedaaij ran up to him and looked in his eyes, apparently wanting to say something but then just embracing him. Chenesia and Eldor landed on the ground beside them.

"How is he doing?" Shadowolf said coldly, enjoying Shedaaij's head on his chest. Darcwulf, without flames around his body and the sword back in its scabbard, joined Fransiska as she walked up to them.

"He will manage," said Eldor said. Ursula trotted up to join them and Shadowolf scouted the forest and saw Le'Mar's pegasus watching them through the distance.

"Let's go," Shadowolf said and started walking towards the combatants.

"No, Shado," Ursula trotted in front of him. "We cannot get involved."

Shadowolf watched her with calculating eyes and then looked up at Masara. He transferred power to his eyes and saw a towering aura of red clashing against an equal aura of yellow. Within Masara's soul, a stronger power waited to be released.

"Why doesn't he just finish him?" he asked. "He has the ability to."

"It's not as easy as that," Eldor replied.

"Because he is Masara's brother?"

"And not as easy as that either," Ursula said. "It is because

Le'Mar's power is so evil and unstable that Masara prolongs killing him."

Shadowolf doubted as much, wondering if Masara just chose not to defeat his half-brother.

"Sorry, but I need a better explanation why I should not go up there and help kick Le'Mar's ass," Shadowolf said.

"I agree," Darcwulf said. "The three of us can take him."

"You underestimate Le'Mar," Eldor said sadly. "Masara made that mistake too. But you need to understand the essence of evil before you destroy everything you love."

"I thought we wanted Le'Mar dead?" Chenesia asked, perplexed.

"Le'Mar's evil power is so great," Ursula said, "that if we killed him now, all his power would explode and kill everyone around him."

"It's one of the principles of power," Eldor said. "If evil is not restrained, it can destroy itself and everything around it."

"So we need to drain him of his power before we kill him," Darcwulf said to the nodding agreement of Eldor and Ursula.

"And the only thing restraining evil is Le'Mar," Shadowolf concluded, "and if he dies, he takes us all with him."

"So, is Masara weakening him?" Chenesia asked.

"Something to that effect," Ursula said.

Shadowolf turned when he heard a rumble behind him. From the western mountains of Eldor's Forest, he saw a beast with four arms running into the forest. Not much remained of Le'Mar's army, and even if Le'Mar managed to defeat Masara he didn't have much of an army to go on any more.

"Hey, I remember him," Darcwulf said, watching the four-armed Saneth approach. "Isn't that our old buddy, Lister?"

"Yeah," Shadowolf said. "I wasn't expecting to see him."

"Pity Trimistus left," Darcwulf said. "They could have had a tea party together."

"I wonder where he came from and where Ru-Maak is?" Shadowolf thought darkly.

"Do you think they are attacking Avalion?" Darcwulf asked, but the look on his brother's face confirmed it.

"Let's go take care of him," Shadowolf smirked, "for old time's sake."

Shadowolf unsheathed his sword and Darcwulf his serpent blade. The blades turned from metal to wind and fire.

"I see you are getting the hang of it," Shadowolf said, but they remained silent as they ran for Lister.

Nolraldun crouched awkwardly behind the fallen tree splinters. He sniffed the air, listened to every move. He carefully discerned between the remaining battles and the sly footsteps of the master assassin that searched him out.

A twitch betrayed Jutbacca and Nolraldun scampered like a rat beneath the splinters and pounced upon the assassin. He pulled the orc blade with his teeth from Jutbacca's grasp and kicked him in the throat.

Jutbacca fell back but recovered fast enough to tackle Nolraldun before he landed on the earth. Sharp nails like daggers raked at Nolraldun's chest, but only a sigh escaped as evidence of pain. Nolraldun used his toes to scrape at Jutbacca's belly and the two rolled around the earth again trying to outdo the other.

They rolled over a low, angled stump and flew into the air, twisting and biting. Nolraldun moved on top of Jutbacca and hit him through his cheeks. Then he kicked with all his might on his chest and ricocheted in the air.

Jutbacca turned, but too late. A spear's snapped handle broke through the alien flesh of his chest and he slid down to the metal blade that was stuck in the root of a tree.

"Well, well," Lister said as the brothers marched towards him, glaring under heavy brows. "I guess I get to have wolves for dessert after all."

Shadowolf and Darcwulf growled together and attacked. Their swords flung through the air and drove Lister back, but the Saneth leaned back and picked up fallen weapons until he had four crude swords in his hands.

The two were relentless as they continued to assault the beast. Shadowolf managed to pierce Lister's hip, but Lister threw out his hand and the back of it neatly hit his face, the side of the orc sword narrowly missing his throat.

Darcwulf made a sweep to its legs, but Lister deftly lifted the thick, left leg and dropped it on the flaming sword, kicking Darcwulf back with the other. As Darcwulf's hand left the hilt, the blade returned to metal.

Shadowolf was about to retaliate when a winged creature jumped onto Lister's back and bit into its neck. He stared transfixed at the stony, crumbled face of Dren. The gargoyle was hit off but his wings lifted him up again and he dropped down to attack once more.

Ruben-Willow passed through Lister's chest while the gargoyle distracted him. Shadowolf looked up at the Saneth, pushing the sword deeper, waiting for him to die. Lister grunted out blood and then dropped an arm on Shadowolf sword. Ruben-Willow snapped in two and the ruby hilt clattered to the floor.

Shadowolf unsheathed his dagger, not succumbing to the shock that was rising in the pit of his stomach. He lodged the dagger into the sternum. Lister stumbled slightly, but let his arm fall again to break the dagger.

Lister leered over him, still with four swords in his arms. Darcwulf looked anxiously at the serpent blade beneath his feet, hoping it wouldn't meet the same fate as Ruben-Willow.

Two swords passed through Lister's back out of his ribs. Dren groaned aloud as he pushed it deeper. Shadowolf watched as Lister was near toppling, but wouldn't give in. He strode up to Lister, who swayed and looked down at him.

In a last futile attempt, Lister raised his four arms to attack. The broken blade and dagger vanished from Lister's chest and appeared whole in Shadowolf's hands. Lister had a second upon which to reveal the shock in his face before Shadowolf crossed his blades through Lister's neck.

"You need to show me how to bond with my sword," Darcwulf said, before picking up the serpent blade.

"I thought we lost you," Shadowolf addressed Dren, who was flapping his wounded wings.

"Luckily Sonersaat's attack wasn't fatal," he replied, but Shadowolf could see his face cracked where the damage had been done.

"The Lapis Pin?" Darcwulf asked.

"Lost," Dren said mournfully.

"Well, Masara will just have to make a new one," Shadowolf

said, and turned to look at the battle on the hill.

Knowing his brother, Darcwulf caught the closest horse's reins and mounted. Shadowolf waited on Mandy. The two rode, making a wide berth around Eldor, Chenesia, Genewiu and Ursula. The group saw the two with Dren flying above them and shouted for them to stop.

But Shadowolf was determined to be as close to Le'Mar as possible in case Masara lost. He didn't want Le'Mar to get away, even in a weakened state. The war had to end now.

A change in humidity and a lighting of the eastern horizon made him realise it was almost morning. With incredulity he realised that they had fought through the morning to sunrise. After a flash of speed beside him caught his eye, Shadowolf saw Ursula running.

"What are you going to do?" she asked, her tone pitched in fear.

"Await the outcome of the fight," he said. They cleared the broken perimeter of the Den and slowed on the rise of the hill. Masara and Le'Mar were on the peak of the hill. Genewiu landed beside Ursula with Chenesia and Eldor followed on his white pegasus.

The power between them was tremendous. They released balls of elements at each other, either to be smacked aside or held within palms. Occasionally they resorted to using their fists but it inevitably returned to fighting with the elements.

Masara waved his arm in a wide arc and a wave of water and spirit rose from the grass. Le'Mar ran into the froth and hit his fist through it. Shards of ice and fire soared towards the old saint, who caught them and turned them into flaming swords.

The soft, midnight blue horizon was becoming light, but from where Shadowolf stood it accentuated the red and yellow lights and auras surrounding the combatants that were so palpable any non-elemental could have seen it.

They ran in fury at each other again and locked fingers. Power surged through their shoulders and arms and Shadowolf could see lightning pass upon their broken skins. Le'Mar's face was contorted in fury, drenched with sweat, but he was fighting hard. Masara's elbows bent as he tried to withhold his younger brother's power.

In a sudden move, Masara's released the inner power he had been reserving and kicked at Le'Mar's abdomen. The white power travelled through his legs and sent the dark lord sliding through the sand, building a mound of grass behind his ankles.

Le'Mar bent and tensed his arms. The ground shook beneath him and two forms rose from the sand. The two stone centaurs shook their bodies free of the soot of the earth and charged at Masara. Masara dropped his hands and clicked his fingers.

In response, two fire lions rose. The beasts met in the centre and fought, but in the end the lions devoured the centaurs and returned to the ground.

Le'Mar started circling Masara, watching him carefully, trying to find his weakness. Shadowolf moved power to his eyes and studied them.

Masara had weakened and was not faring well, his fading health catching up with him. Le'Mar, however, seemed stronger than ever, the red evil within him seemingly at its peak.

"Do you really think you will win?" Le'Mar asked snidely.

"I believe whatever transpires between us this night," Masara replied, "that Bontu has a greater plan."

"Your Bontu," he spat, "was he there when you murdered my father?"

"Your father had to be stopped," Masara said, and then coughed. "Just as you do."

"You cannot stop me," Le'Mar replied. "Not even Shadowolf can stop me."

"Shadowolf will become the *Sadgi*," Masara said, turning to keep his eyes locked on the still circling dark lord.

"You fool!" Le'Mar laughed and let all pretence fall. "You blind idiot!"

Masara watched coldly at his brother, waiting for whatever revelation Le'Mar was about to reveal.

"There are three parts to the prophecy," Le'Mar continued. "When did you think the *Sadgi* Prophecy would be fulfilled?"

Masara listened and suddenly he realised what Le'Mar was telling him.

"Shadowolf might have fulfilled the Windfarer and DragonRider prophecies, but did you think I was going to wait until he was ready to challenge me for the last!"

Masara ran up, the fear written on his brow, but Le'Mar finally released the power he had been hiding from everyone. Masara flew and tumbled across the hills as the power hit him, not stopping until there wasn't one part of his body not covered in grass and blood.

Le'Mar looked awesome and terrifying at the same time. The earth rose around him in a swirling blanket of power. Fire coursed through each sand molecule, while the wind spurred it on with its ferocity. In the remaining gaps between the elements, water rose in a cyclone of intense energy.

Shadowolf shifted his head on the place he had fallen, while the others recovered around him. Shedaaij had reached his side and she looked down at him calling his name. But all he could hear was the thunderous rumbling of the elements on the top of the hill.

Le'Mar started walking towards Masara, who was lying as still as a doll at the end of the slope. Shadowolf remembered Nelnar, and leaned on his elbows to look at the scene. A mound of earth formed into a step before Le'Mar's feet and by the time he had climbed it, a higher step had formed behind it. The earth continued to rise, providing him a stairway in Masara's direction.

Shadowolf became wind and moved instantaneously to Masara's side. He lifted the old man's face onto his lap and cleared his face of debris. Shadowolf could not stop himself nor understand why, but tears crawled out of the corners of his eye as the man looked up at him.

"Will you heed the words of a dying fool?" Masara asked.

"I will always heed your words," Shadowolf responded, sensing that the mounds of stairs were almost upon them.

"You must let Bontu reign in your heart, Shado," Masara said, "if you are to become the true *Sadgi*. Evil cannot bring you to such power. Evil corrupts itself before it corrupts others."

"What has this to do with me?" Shadowolf said, realising that the stairs has stopped right beside him, rising high into the air.

"Le'Mar can never be the *Sadgi*, unless he repents to Bontu of his doings," Masara said, and coughed. His eyes went translucent and he murmured, "Take care of Ursula…"

The man's head rolled to the side as he gave up his spirit. Shadowolf shuddered as he felt Masara's spirit move through him towards the heavens, his final home.

A wisp of wind broke behind him and Elgoth bent down to

examine his father. He looked up and saw the spirit of his father leave the world, but behind his ghost the dark silhouette of Le'Mar grinned down.

The dark lord grasped his flame-embossed staff firmly and tapped it three times on the top-most step. A great gush of foul wind swept up from the sand and rose up passed Elgoth and Shadowolf and somehow managed to move the spirit of Masara in Le'Mar's direction.

Shadowolf gasped in horror and Elgoth exclaimed as Masara's spirit entered Le'Mar's staff. The black staff glowed and became a glossy blue. Shadowolf was sure he could hear the soft cries and moans of Masara emanating from the rod.

It seemed that Elgoth was too stunned to react. Shadowolf, however, rose up in the wind with an untempered fury. Without thinking he prepared his arm to attack, but when he cleared the step, Le'Mar grabbed him by his arm and neck and threw him down the stairs.

"Leave my brother alone!" Darcwulf cried, but Le'Mar wrapped his ugly free hand around Darcwulf's throat. The fire of Darcwulf's body extinguished as he dangled in the air.

"Brother of Shadowolf," Le'Mar said, and looked down at his own brother's dead body next to Elgoth, "how fitting. Yes. You will do well."

Darcwulf shook uncontrollably as power entered him. Memories flashed through his mind, and the evil contained within Le'Mar joined his veins and his spirit. The serpent sword dangling in his hand turned from sterling silver to ruby red.

Shadowolf stood up slowly and watched as the dark lord lowered Darcwulf to his feet. Darcwulf looked deeply into Le'Mar's eyes and then nodded, his bald head shimmering in the light of the sky blue horizon. When Darcwulf looked at his brother, it was red, burning irises that glared down filled with the pure evil of Le'Mar's soul.

Darcwulf became fire, but the sword remained red steel. He flew from the top step after Shadowolf. Shadowolf became wind and fled to Lard's Den.

Elgoth and Eldor reacted at the same time and rose into the air to meet Le'Mar. It seemed that Le'Mar was communicating with someone as the two met him, for he stepped back in confusion and focused his eyes again.

"You two are just as much fools as he was," Le'Mar said and held his staff ready for the attack. Eldor and Elgoth ignored him and struck.

Heula watched as the figure walked from behind the first step of the stairs. Her heart pounded harder, knowing that the war had just taken another turn for the worse.

"Do you know her?" Shedaaij said, turning from her observation of the wind and fire spirits to the new figure by the stairs.

"Yes, don't you remember?" Heula said. "It's Maerlesa."

"Oh no," Shedaaij said silently, dropping her daggers lamely to the ground in protest.

The witch watched them all from the mound, and a different kind of evil simmered into the air. A heat wave broke around the witch's silhouette as her voice carried over the Den. It was a sickly sweet voice that spoke the spell, and from the Den's land a hole started to form.

The hole grew larger and the smell of brimstone lifted into the air. The pit was cragged with rocks on the inside and an amber glow burned from its depths.

Shedaaij shuddered as she saw the demons rise. They crawled out of the rock, some flying into the air, and made their ways to nearby corpses. One by one they found a host until every elemental, Crethan, Clan member and creature of the dark lord was filled with the evil being.

The dead bodies moved and stirred, groaning in pain and misery. She watched as Rennick rose with his sword and Sny-Ten got up from the border of the Den. In fear, she looked around for Nelnar's body, but she couldn't see it anywhere.

The land was filled with the armies again, but this time they were all under the command of Maerlesa. Heula left Shedaaij's side and made her way up to the witch, her mind reeling with the spells she would use.

"Leave the forest!!" Ursula ran through the Den, shouting to anyone who was not of the undead. Theroy and Treville stopped in their tracks and started shouting for the remaining Horlorn fighters to leave. Maren-Ti similarly commanded the Vale of Tigers soldiers and dwarves to leave.

But they soon realised that the feat was easier said than done. Skeletal remains rose to block their paths out of the Den, and the undead corpses of their former allies glinted with lust to kill.

Elgoth fell off the stairs when Le'Mar struck him with an arc of fire, but he used the wind to bring him up again. Eldor shot power from his staff, but with Masara's soul trapped in Le'Mar's rod Eldor was no longer a match for Le'Mar.

Shadowolf landed on the ground and waited for Darcwulf to materialise.

"Darc," he said when his brother landed. "Don't let him control you."

Darcwulf proceeded to step forward, fire crawling on his skin and blazing out of his eyes.

"Please," Shadowolf pleaded. "I don't want to fight you."

The red of his eyes brightened and he attacked. Shadowolf barely unsheathed his blades in time to block the force and became wind again. Darcwulf attacked to kill, while Shadowolf only defended. He wondered if this was what Masara had felt when he fought Le'Mar, not wanting to kill him.

Shadowolf flew away and headed for a hillock. He turned, assuming Darcwulf had followed but he was wrong. Darcwulf stood where he had left him, his arms cradled in a ball by his left hip, gathering an orb of power.

Darcwulf threw the fire orb in Shadowolf's direction. It soared over the earth, scorching the leaves and twigs. Shadowolf braced himself, waiting for the moment of impact, vaguely wondering what would happen if he tried to hit it aside.

Darcwulf teleported behind Shadowolf and kicked him in the back. Shadowolf went soaring in the direction of the flaming ball heading his way. He knew, even if he had thought of becoming wind, that their velocities were too great to avoid each other and that he would now meet his death.

He raised his hand as the light of the orb blinded him, waiting for the searing heat to kill him, when something slammed his body away. He was bouncing up and down, and dropping his arms he saw that Mandy had shoved him onto her back. He looked back to see that Darcwulf had narrowly escaped his own ball. Mandy toppled to the ground as the orb hit the hillock and the earth shook.

Heula reached Maerlesa and flung out her arms. Sparks of fire erupted, but Maerlesa hit them aside. She murmured and then shouted the last words out loud as wisps of ice flew to Heula from her fingertips. Heula froze and shook, speaking inaudibly until her skin broke free of the ice from the heat of her veins.

Maerlesa cackled and shouted, and crows appeared behind her and rushed to attack Heula. Heula spoke a spell in return, and tears of lava rose from the ground to meet them, but they were too many. Crows scratched at her eyes, pinning her to the ground.

She spoke out loud and waved her arms, causing the crows to turn into minute dragons the size of fairies. They turned from her and flew at Maerlesa who stared in shock. She cried out and waved her arm and an arc of wind battered into them and they broke into sprays of dust.

Maerlesa was the first to act, and the dust sank onto Heula's skin and became thick, black leeches. They drank from her skin, sticking to her with fervour. She tried pulling them off, attempting a spell but exclaiming in pain in between.

Maerlesa walked up to her, a gleeful expression of victory upon her face. Her teeth poked out from her curled lips and her eyes shone with the pallor of death. Heula looked up at her for a moment and thought Maerlesa had bit her own lip, but realised that blood was streaming from the corners of her mouth.

The leeches on Heula died and fell to the side. Nolraldun removed the dagger from Maerlesa and moved like a snake onto her back and slit her throat. The stunned expression did not leave her face as she fell to the ground.

"Thanks, Nolraldun," Heula said, looking back at the undead in the forest. "It's a pity her death won't affect the demons she summoned. They no longer fall under her spell."

Dren killed another undead and then threw his sword through Rennick's head. The former Clan member fell to the ground. As he looked down, he saw his shadow on the ground. A larger shadow with four arms blackened his own out and Dren twisted around to face the undead, headless Lister.

The demon inside Lister's body grasped him around the throat and picked him up high. Dren's wings flapped wildly trying to break free, but there was strength greater than Lister's arms holding him captive.

"You fight bravely, gargoyle," the multi-voiced demon said from where Lister's head should have been. "But you seem to have forgotten something."

"What…is…that?" Dren gulped, gripping the large hand around his neck with both of his.

"Have you worn the Lapis Pin for so long that you have forgotten your curse?"

The demon turned Dren's head so that he could see the hill. The sun was rising around the mound of stairs, with Le'Mar, Elgoth and Eldor's shapes dancing at the top as they fought.

Dren's eyes opened in alarm as he realised his mistake. The sun touched his skin, but he let go of Lister's hand in defeat. As the sun caressed his skin, he solidified to pure stone. Lister smashed his two lower fists through his body, and Dren crumbled to the ground.

Shadowolf narrowly dodged Darcwulf's blow, and twisted to meet a river of red power flowing from his palms. He thrust his heels into the earth and held his hands out against it, sliding slowly back as Darcwulf's force pushed him.

Shadowolf stared up into Darcwulf's fiery eyes, baring his teeth and tensing his arms. In a fluid movement, he pulled the power, twisted his arms around and threw it back like a winding snake at Darcwulf's neck.

Darcwulf recoiled, trying to catch his power before it struck him but he failed. The river hit him in the chest and he flew back against a pile of timber. His back broke through the wood, scattering it around him until the fire and power subsided from his body.

Darcwulf leaned up to look for Shadowolf, but he wasn't around. The Den was filled with the fleeing elves and humans, not including the hordes of demons possessing the dead.

Le'Mar smacked his staff into Elgoth and the saint's son hit his head on the step and fell off the side to the earth below. Eldor attacked, but Le'Mar grinned and hit him with both ends of his rod and used fire to burn the elf's face. Before Eldor could react, as fast as he was, Le'Mar had kicked him off the top-most step towards the spot that Masara had died.

The wind stirred behind the dark lord, and he turned to look down his flight of earthly steps. The wind swirled like a dune in a desert until Shadowolf's form became solid. Shedaaij ran towards the stairs, followed in a short distance by Fransiska and Sorceress.

Shadowolf walked up the stairs, calming his nerves and lowering his power.

"Finally," Le'Mar grunted and walked down to meet him. Their silhouettes were marked by the sun that had completely topped the hill and shone on the devastation of Lard's Den. Shadowolf could feel the demons stirring. The sun seemed to unsettle them, although not harming them in any way.

"It seems like you are going to have a mutiny on your hands," Shadowolf murmured, not taking his eyes off the dark lord.

"They will remain as long as I command them," Le'Mar replied. "But I do not need them anymore."

Shadowolf allowed his eyes to peer from the corners of his lids and he could see the grotesque forms leaving the corpses of his former allies and creeping back down into the brimstone pit in the forest.

"Your time is up, Shadowolf," the dark lord leered, holding his staff tightly. "I have saved this moment for you."

When they finally met, Le'Mar one mound above him, Shadowolf anchored his feet on the step.

"And what is that, exactly?" he asked. He breathed slowly and calmed his body completely. His power drew down to the deepest depths of his soul, and Le'Mar frowned.

"I know you have power," Le'Mar said. "No need to hide it."

"Maybe I could say the same to you," Shadowolf attempted.

"Shadowolf the Windfarer, the wonderful *Enodhim*," Le'Mar said with the deepest disgust in his voice. "I hope there was satisfaction in killing Mercius."

"He wasn't much of a champion," he replied calmly.

"Shadowolf the DragonRider, the awesome *Wisoum*," Le'Mar continued, "taking out Sonersaat, whom I had been training and developing since your disappearance two years ago."

"Are you keeping a record?"

"What next, dear brave hero? I sensed the powers within you before you lowered them: *Enodhim, KariemsaPh, Goudlem,*

Merlandsi. Did you think that even after the trials you would become a *Sadgi* so soon? Not even Masara, after centuries, reached that feat."

Shadowolf readied his mind to release the power of the elements waiting within his soul, for the moment he could finally challenge the might of Le'Mar.

"Would you like to see what a Sagdi can do?" the dark lord said, nodding his head as if answering for Shadowolf. "Would you like to see what it is like to BE A GOD!!!"

Le'Mar's staff changed. Leaves and twigs were born upon the ancient wood, but Shadowolf could see it was not natural. There were sick shades of red and purple on the branches, ending in the maroon of the leaves.

"If I wanted a garden, I would have asked my mother," Shadowolf said sarcastically.

The earth started to tremble. Cracks formed on the surface of the ground below that split and opened up into crevasses. Bodies fell down the cracks and the escaping refugees struggled not to join them. From between the gaping holes, mounds rose to form small, crude mountains that rumbled passed the stairs.

Shadowolf looked down and saw Fransiska and Sorceress almost fall to their deaths. Sorceress grabbed Fransiska's wrist and closed her eyes. They both vanished.

"SHADO!" he heard Shedaaij call. The Merlani had attempted to reach him, and had fallen down one of the steps. Shadowolf looked at her and threw his arm out. The wind twisted into a hurricane over her and the forest vanished from her sight.

She looked around the room and ran for the door. When she opened it, she saw the courtyard of Degron Castle in Avalion.

"NOOO!!!!" she screamed in anger, running for the War Council tower. It took her several minutes and the sound of battle outside the broken walls of Avalion plucked at the strings of her nerves. When she ran into the tower, she looked through the smashed elvin window towards the elvin forest, ignoring the dying armies in Avalion. She couldn't see them, and she fell to her knees in anguish.

When the rumbling subsided to a slow tremor, Shadowolf saw a portal at the Pool of Radiance open. The last survivors were entering it, with Eldor ushering them through. He saw the white coat of Ursula, and she looked back once at him in sadness before proceeding through the portal.

"I see your friends have abandoned you," Le'Mar said.

"I don't need them to get in my way when I kill you," Shadowolf replied coldly, staring up into the dark lord's handsome face.

"Arrogant fool," Le'Mar said softly and sighed.

The staff stirred. Shadowolf looked at it and saw violet water spring from between the leaves and branches. It dripped onto the floor and coursed through the wood of the staff into Le'Mar's arm.

The sky cracked and thundered. The earth rumbled again as, this time, fountains broke from the crevices and spurted into the air. Clouds formed within seconds and rain cascaded down upon the earth. Shadowolf heard a loud crashing behind him.

The ocean to the south was breaking hard against the beaches. Gigantic waves smashed against the land once known as Iceland, and suddenly Shadowolf feared that Avalion was also being drowned by the tsunami.

"Do you still doubt my power?" Le'Mar said in front of him.

The rain stormed down upon him. Le'Mar pulled his free arm back and thrust it towards Shadowolf. The rain built into a solid form and broke against him, sending him hurtling back a few steps.

Shadowolf spun in the air and changed his body into water. He travelled up the spraying liquid from Le'Mar's palm until he was standing on the step below him again, the water passing through him, the evil within it stinging his nerves.

He needed one good strike. As Le'Mar lowered his arms, the earth still trembling below them, the rain incessantly battering the stairs and the oceans breaking to the south, Shadowolf knew he only needed one good strike to stop Le'Mar from continuing.

But thoughts of impeding the dark lord vanished as the staff transformed again. Fire erupted around the leaves and rivers on the staff and surrounded it with its heat. Almost in unison, fire broke from several of the pits in the forest not occupied by lakes or fountains. Trees that had been splintered in Lard's Den were consumed by the hungry flames.

Le'Mar tensed his arms and the power around his body increased. Shadowolf feared what this meant and released his energy, rising to attack. In answer, the dark lord swung his rod and Shadowolf was once again sent flying backwards to the lower mounds.

Shadowolf flipped over and landed on his feet. He shot up, running up the steps, when he saw large balls of flames falling from the skies. Within the flames were hard rocks that hit the forest and formed large craters of smouldering ash.

Shadowolf jumped off the stairs as a fiery meteor just missed him. He flew up on the wind to the dark lord, determined more than ever to stop him.

"And now, your favourite," Le'Mar murmured when he was in earshot, "my dear *Enodhim*."

Shadowolf's body jerked in the air as the wind stopped. The air pulled his arms out and he was trapped. Shadowolf strained his body, trying to use his spirit to wrench the wind back. All he succeeded in doing was contort his face in anger.

"Your time has come, my dear boy."

Le'Mar waved his staff that was flaring with the powers of wind, fire, earth and water. Shadowolf's body was thrown back by a wind that was filled with an essence of evil. The power stung his flesh and soul as he fell from the air. Lightning streaked through the sky and hit his body. He shook and shivered, the water drowning his face in tears of agony.

He waited for his death. Beneath his falling body he could hear the pits of lava waiting for him. The brimstone travelled up to his nose. He wanted to change into fire, but the tainted elements would no longer listen to his command.

A swish of wind and suddenly he was no longer falling. His weak, limp body fell once again upon the back of a horse, but when he opened his eyes he didn't see the black that belonged to Mandy. Instead, he looked up at a white equine face with a small horn upon its head.

"ELGOTH!" a voice shouted between the flowing lava, the raging storm and the thunderous lightning. Chenesia and Genewiu were flying ahead with a white portal beside them.

Shadowolf shifted his weight on Elgoth's back, but he was too weak to sit up. He looked at the stairs and saw Le'Mar watching them and then raise his arms. Lightning broke around them, while meteors broke from the sky again. Elgoth dodged and swerved, narrowly missing being hit.

Shadowolf's gaze fell upon the land below them and saw a solitary figure running to keep up with them. Mandy was striding across the broken earth, leaping over large chasms. The horse's red eyes glowed, her fervour burning upon her black coat that seemed to reflect the lava's glow.

With the last of his strength, he aimed his palm at Mandy. The wind twisted at his final command and the mare vanished from the grounds. Shadowolf aimed his palm at the portal and Mandy reappeared still running. The mare passed through the portal.

Shadowolf fainted. Elgoth swerved again to miss a lightning bolt, a welt forming along his side, and crossed the portal. Chenesia and Genewiu flew through last and the portal closed.

Le'Mar stared at the place they had vanished and lowered his powers. The staff dimmed and returned to its normal state. The earth calmed and the waters returned to the ocean. The rain stopped and the clouds dissipated.

Le'Mar closed his eyes and teleported to his castle above the Alcove of Light. He strode magnificently to his throne chair and sat down, staring out his curved window onto Celenic Earth.

Behind him, a man walked in holding his staff, his sword dangling on his hip. He walked up beside the dark lord and placed his free hand on the neck of the chair.

"It is done, my lord," Darcwulf said. "How else may I serve you?"

***

Nighthale cut another Dra-hu'Mar down, his arm aching and throbbing from the fatigue of battle. He mustered a little more strength to drive his blade into another, when something odd caught his attention.

The remaining Dra-hu'Mar, orcs and Froths were running away from Avalion. They moved until they were a certain distance from the city, between Avalion and Bontu's Wrath, and waited.

In any other situation, Nighthale would have sent his men to hunt them down and kill the last of them. But as he looked around he could see the other three lords were just as weak as he. Jasnon, Lowle, and Malkius all stood holding their weapons breathing heavily. Their faces and bodies were marred by the stains of battle.

The walls of Avalion were on their last threads. Even the inner walls that had separated the villages were crumbling to the ground, covering the houses in dust and stone.

A chill entered Nighthale's spine and, as he turned to face the dark lord's army, he saw a thick, black fog approaching from the direction of the Alcove of Light. It blew through the dark creatures, and the army disappeared.

The fog continued to pass through them. It rolled over Avalion and where it touched the fallen walls the stones also vanished. Angelicus's light flickered and vanished.

Eventually, when Nighthale's sight became accustomed to the fog, he saw that neither walls nor stone separated the villages any more. From beneath the city he could look straight up at Degron Castle.

Yet the castles of the lords and the houses still stood. The people appeared from their houses and taverns and peered glumly through the dark fog.

After a few moments of collecting his thoughts, it seemed to Nighthale that the fog had lifted and that the sun had penetrated through it. But he could still feel the evil in the fog and the chill and knew it must still be there.

A voice broke through the land. It echoed through the fog and everyone sat and stood still to grasp every word.

"It is over. I will no longer attack your homes and villages. You will now live in freedom and peace under my reign.

"As for the fog, it will remain upon your land as a testament to my grace. Your elemental privileges have been stripped from you. If anyone should try and use their abilities, I will personally have you committed to death. No longer will there be any need for war or battles. You will live in peace under my reign."

***

The wind stirred and the leaves rustled. The sparkling white snow rolled over the grass against the trees of the land. The mountains loomed imposingly over the bowl valley.

And towards the ancient forest of snow trotted the soft, padded footsteps of the white-specked wolf...

XXX...XXX...XXX...XXX...XXX

ANNEXURE A
HOW THE APOSTROPHETIC
PRONOUNS DEVELOPED

Through many centuries the elegance of our language has advanced, based on the standard of the humans. The language during the original Falgoth Age was mostly based on the elvin lore. Bentley, when he was awakened on the shores of the River of Light and was led to the elvin forest located west of the river, was nurtured in their ways.

Many centuries later, after the fall and separation from the elves, Masara developed runes. Runes were an adaptation of the elvin scripture, but simplified to assist those that forgotten the ancient ways. The Masaran Age brought many changes to the accepted norm of living. Some of them were welcomed, yet he still applied strict rules to the use of the elements, and condemned anything that aspired against Bontu.

This was one of the reasons for the fatal battle that ensued between Masara and T'Mar.

At the Age of Celene, a new system developed to adapt to the ever-changing civilisation. Insignia's assigned to the 'shai' syllable were reduced, as the 'shai' pronouns started becoming popular amongst the people. In the end, it was widely accepted that the apostrophe would serve as the 'shai' syllable.

Therefore, names such as Marsshainar and Teshaimar were reduced to Mars'Nar and T'Mar. The rules for the use of the apostrophe, the reduction of vowels and the capitalisation of consonants are the key focuses of this chapter...

- The Asbec Study of Celenas: Its influence on modernism
                    Part B: The Evolved Language
Chapter 6: The Integrated Pronoun
By Farnerd Malerus

ANNEXURE B
NOTE ON THE MASARAN PHENOMENON

Ringos is a small planet, although how small no one is sure. Its natural orbit in the solar system is around the central sun known as Creotos, as is the earth's. The only problem with the orbit of Ringos is that it differs from year to year, called the four cycles.

No one knows how far into the universe the planet orbits till it returns, but the known factor is that the sun is its central core of gravity. I have read a scholar make note in his thesis that perhaps the planet only has once cycle, and that the cycle takes four earth years to reach us. If that were so, several conclusions could be reached:

1.   That the orbit of Ringos takes the planet out to the far reaches of not only the solar system, but also the galaxy. A period of four years to return to earth is rather astronomical, but not impossible if the distance were attainable.

2.   That the sun's gravity is extremely powerful to allow the planet to travel so far and not release it into the unknown universe. If this were so, how could man possibly survive such a force on a planet so close to the source of power?

3.   That, because the planet circles earth and is thrown back into the system before it reaches the sun, it could be concluded that either:

a)   The earth interferes with the orbit of Ringos, in which case it cancels out point 2, the power of the sun's gravity;

b)   The earth itself is the planet's central core. In this case, it does seem strange that the planet only return to its core in fours years, and veers off into the universe. It would then have to be concluded further that the earth itself has an astronomical gravitational force and should in essence itself be a sun or dwarf star. This last point is however considered the most preposterous, as it creates a loophole, justifying once again the sun's immense power to orbit another sun in its presence. The solar system, in theory, should collapse upon itself.

Through the centuries, one possibility has survived the raptures of time, and this theory has been aptly supported by the sages of our world, including Masara. And that is the theory of Penoplus, better known in the last century as the Masaran Phenomenon.

The theory goes as follows, in the words of Masara:

Ringos orbits around the sun in four cycles. Its first orbit carries the planet far away from earth in a wide arc. On the second and third cycles, however, the planet closes in on ours and by the fourth its trajectory carries it towards earth. It does not collide with the earth, but its path is close enough for the earth's gravity to slow down its journey around the sun.

It takes forty-five days before it breaks our tardy gravity. During this period, the following takes place:

-       *The earth's rotation on its axis decreases. This causes the sun to travel from the eastern horizon to the western horizon for a prolonged period. It takes seventy-two hours, or three days, before it finally sets.*

-       *Sothos, earth's only moon, increases its orbital time. After the sun's setting on the third day, it takes the moon forty-two days to journey from east to west. The sun does not appear on the horizon during that time.*

-       *Due to Ringos's position relative to the earth, the planet is the only source of light and minimal heat during the moon's reign. After Sothos rises, it takes an hour before the first sign of Ringos. It travels for three hours in the sky, from the north travelling south to its peak in the sky, and then to the west where it sets. This erratic occurence has a time-lapse of three hours again between the setting in the west to the rising again in the north. The tug of gravity between the sun and Ringos is clear here. This pattern of rising and setting continues for the entire period that Sothos rules the sky.*

-       *Half-way across the sky, on day twenty-two of moon's reign in the sky, Ringos and Sothos align, and an eclipse occurs. But for the remaining days, Ringos slowly reclines into its familiar path, and on the forty-fifth night, the moon sets and earth's system returns to normal for the next four years.*

This is indeed a phenomenon.

- Presentation to the Orion Counsel
By Philgarn Asmuth.

GLOSARRY 1
LIST OF CHARACTERS

The Original Shadow Clan

Shadowolf Degron (Elemental): son of Nighthale and Karla; fulfilled the prophecy of the Windfarer and was taken to Asgorna the Dragon King's world for two years.

Darcwulf (Fire Elemental): left on the doorstep of Nighthale's room as a baby. Soul-brother to Shadowolf.

Nelnar: Shadowolf's faithful "pet" wolf.

Shedaaij (Earth Elemental): a Merlani; a warrior sent to assist Shadowolf on land with the war.

Angelicus (Spirit Elemental): Former fiancé of Darcwulf.

Skywolf Saphin (Water Elemental): daughter of Malkius Saphin. Met Shadowolf through Darcwulf.

Angelia (Water Elemental): Asbec College student; met Shadowolf through Harmony; moved home to Costen at start of war and then joined Shadow Clan.

Sny-Ten, Gwyn and **Lastgorn** (Weapon masters): Friends of Shadowolf through Darcwulf.

Dren (Gargoyle): Captured Shadowolf in Eldor's Dungeon, mistaking him for Mercius. Shadowolf obtained the Lapis Pins (see Glossary 2) for Dren.

Shadowwe, Scarlette, Sorceress, Rennick, Trevor & **Tinonte** (The Orion): Special group of warriors known as the "Hand of the Orion". Belong to a secretive wolf tribe.

Additions to the Shadow Clan

Fransiska (Water Elemental): one of the trio of girls with Skywolf and Angelia that resides in Costen.

Ursula (Unicorn): She had warned Shadowolf about the power node and informed him to meet Asgorna.

Malanite: Old man found wandering in Meëntis, claiming his village had been destroyed.

Heula (Witch): One of three witches that attacked Shadowolf in Plastinon, but then assisted him.

Trimistus / Lord Danaka (Saneth): He once served Mercius, but seeing Shadowolf's bravery he had a change of heart. Le'Mar had him exiled to death, but he plunged off a waterfall and escaped.

Madison, **Trish**, **Dayna-wolf**, **Teristé**, **Markors**, **Mino'Nelar**, & **Midnite** (Crethans): Saved by Shadowolf when their Creth-Demon was killed and the bondage of servitude removed.

Millon and **Kentaur** (Centaurs): Escorted the Clan to the Butcher of Philagis.

Nolraldun (Novice Assassin): Sent by the Semhum Kateth to find Trimistus and kill him as per Le'Mar's orders.

The War Council of New Avalion

Nighthale Degron (Wind Elemental): Lord of Avalion, Degron Core, and father of Shadowolf; adopted father of Darcwulf.

Franklin and **Nowles**: Personal friends and advisors to Nighthale.

Malkius Saphin: Lord of Costen, Saphin Vale, and father of Skywolf, Darna and Claire.

Sjedwolf Watre (Earth Elemental): Lord of Hasner, Watre Hills.

Jasnon Lowle: Lord of Iceland, Lowle Village, after the downfall and murder of Abutja Blue.

The Orion (vacant): was represented by Shadowwe, but he was called by the Clan. Amon Harhondsa was killed and Lucian declined the position.

Lucian Par'Mar (Wind Elemental): former member of the Sandrihelin of Mercius; former Wind Professor of Asbec College; advisor to the Council. He intends searching for uPendus.

Elgoth (Saint): the son of Masara sent by his father to assist the Council in their meetings and report back to him.

Eldor's Forest

Eldor (Elf): High King of the elves and former tutor of Masara.

Lesan (Elf): Prince of Eldor's Forest and son of Eldor; personal friend of Chenesia.

Masara (Saint): Centuries-old man who followed the path of Bontu and learned the lore of the elves. Fought in the Battle of T'Mar's Scourge and was victorious. Taken by the elves to the Far Isles to recover health, but returned to the Forest to assist in the war.

The Vale of Tigers

Chenesia: Princess of the Vale and daughter of Maren-Ti and Larnesia; captured by Le'Mar when she sought elfin protection from Eldor.

Genewiu (Pegasus): another captive in Chenesia's dungeons.

Hargon (Master Dwarf): Custodian of the Sanctuary of Jin-Tai and personal guardian of Chenesia.

Maren-Ti: Lord of the Vale of Tigers and custodian of the Heart of Tigers (see Glossary 1).

Gallon (Master Dwarf): King of the dwarves residing in the Dwarf Mountains, and advisor and friend of Maren-Ti.

Simnab (Crethan): Met Lucian and Chenesia in Carmel.

Nucial: a strange broken pedlar that claims he is escaping Le'Mar.

Horlorn's Gate

Treville: Lord of Horlorn's Gate.

Lanel, Mourna and **Harmony**: former AegleDaele students of Asbec College and Shadowolf's best friends.

Theroy: former Feniseraat student of Asbec College, and acquaintance of Shadowolf.

Nashela: former AegleDaele student that had a crush on Shadowolf; her home and family in Shenama were destroyed by Mercius and McCaniban.

The Dark Lord's Army

Le'Mar (Elemental): The dark lord; son of T'Mar and vowed enemy of Celenic Earth.

Sonersaat (DragonRider): Chosen by Le'Mar to fulfil the DragonRider Prophecy and initiate the War of the Dragons.

McCaniban: A general in Le'Mar's army that destroyed Shenama and Los'Temenar (Morkom Falls) and set a camp in both.

Maerlesa and **Nestef** (Witches): With Heula, they were ordered to destroy Plastinon and make sure the ghost village remained cursed. They are also responsible for raising the undead and demons in the army.

Kraakis (Centaur): The Butcher of Philagis; Lord of the Centaurs.

Lister and **Ru-Maak** (Saneths): The two remaining Kings of the Knight. Ma'Kanak was killed by Nellice and Trimistus left Le'Mar's army.

Blosom (mer-aVampeyeric demon-queen): Was a mermaid of *Marsandil* before her change; Mercius's aVampeyeric lover after the change; almost killed Shadowolf at Asbec Lake and still regrets not doing so.

Sona Nelma (Earth Elemental): a former Sandrihelin of Mercius; former Earth professor of Asbec College; Lanel spotted her meeting with the Sandrihelin in the college, but after the school closed, she was never heard of again.

Roaming Characters

Asgorna (Dragon): Dragon King, and bound to Shadowolf.

Maneto (Dragon): Dragon challenging for position of Dragon King, and bound to Sonersaat.

Mynisna (Dragon): Dragon in Asgorna's army, bound to Trimistus.

Nellice (aVampeyer): served under Mercius, but killed Ma'Kanak the Saneth in defiance. Now roams freely serving no one.

Danto & **Mallice** (aVampyere): Served under Mercius, but joined Nellice in the aVampeyeric rebellion.

Lellian (Mer-King): The destined ruler of the Mer-Kindgom, with a powerful trident to fight against the sirens. Resides in *Avalendil* beneath Avalion.

James (Merman): One of the mermen encountered by Shadowolf who fights alongside Lellian.

Reference Characters

Bentley: The first man to walk the earth.

Celene (Water Elemental): A woman whose influence was so great that she changed many of the systems that were founded by the ancients; her power created the Mists of Celene. The elves handed her a bow with the essence of the Mists contained within.

Mannius Saphin (Elemental Weapons Engineer): Skywolf's cousin that imbued Ruben-Willow (see Glossary 1) with the ability to adapt to the sword-bearer's powers.

Fornoren and **Masnen** (Gargoyles): Comrades of Dren in safe-guarding Eldor's Dungeons. Joined Shadowolf in an effort to obtain the Lapis Pins, but became stone when Mercius emitted solar energy and orcs loosed arrows into their statue bodies.

Hurticule (Merman): Ruler of *Marsandil* before it was attacked by aVampyere and Lellian became mer-king. He joined Lellian in defending Sea's Reach from sirens and died on a demon-queen's trident.

T'Mar (Elemental): father of Le'Mar. He was killed during a battle with Masara known as the Battle of T'Mar's Scourge decades ago. Le'Mar witnessed the murder and now seeks vengeance.

Mercius (aVampeyeric Windfarer): The servant of Le'Mar that was chosen to lead his armies with McCaniban and fulfil the Windfarer Prophecy; died when Shadowolf kicked him into the *Sadgi* power node.

Jorran, Lolan and **Moman** (Froth Huns): three, blue-flamed skull creatures that Shadowolf defeated after failing to save Iceland from Mercius's attack.

Ma'Kanak (Cannibal Saneth): one of the four Kings of the Knight. Was killed when Nellice the aVampeyer jumped from the shadows, bit him and drove his sword into him.

Kelsey Hodgsen and Malferus Ar'Mar (Elementals): two of the former Sandrihelin of Mercius; former Water and Fire professors of Asbec College; were killed by Asgorna after Shadowolf passed out during the last battle with them.

Abutja Blue: Predecessor of Jasnon Lowle as Lord of Iceland; was betrayed by an Amethyst pendant of Le'Mar into believing that there was no war and was murdered by purorcs when the spell was lifted and Iceland was destroyed.

Morkom Lenarsa: former Lord of Los'Temenar (Morkom Falls);
Commissioned by the War Council of Avalion to unite the northern
villages into a War Council and stand against McCaniban together. The
message arrived too late and Los'Temenar was lost to McCaniban and
renamed Morkom Falls. Morkom's dead body was revived into a
Crethan and renamed Midnite.

GLOSARRY 2
WEAPONS, ARTEFACTS AND
CREATURES

Weapons

Ruben-Willow (Sword): two-edged sword ending in pointed tip, with rubies encrusted in the wooden hilt, a Lapis Pin within the steel and amethyst fused within the base of the blade. Name derived from the willow and ruby hilt. Shadowolf obtained it during his first orc battle in Shenama.

Ruben-Willow (Dagger): single-edged blade ending in a barbed tip, with a serrated back. Forms part of the mystery of Ruben-Willow and is obtained by Shadowolf in Dwarf Mountains.

Serpent Fire: single-edged, curved sword that ends in a two-tongued fork and has a soft, green hue that turns red when used with fire. Obtained by Darcwulf in Dwarf Mountains.

The Blue Falchion: single-edged, curved sword with blue-hued blade and sky-blue hilt. Belongs to Lastgorn.

Axehorn Reaper: double-edged axe twice the size of a large, dwarven axe, with a sling attached to the handle. Given as a gift to Sny-Ten by the dwarves.

Scarlet Orion: single-edged, curved Orion blade with maroon sheen and blood-like crusts on blunt back of sword. Belongs to Scarlette.

Artefacts

The Lapis Pins – cylindrical in shape and clear as quartz; magical gems created by Masara to enable gargoyles to walk in the light of the sun without turning to stone. The three known ones belonged to Dren, Fornoren and Masnen.

Rose Pendants – in shape of open rose and ruby red; amulets created by Masara and given to the Mer-Kindgom to enable human visitors to breathe under fresh and salt water in the absence of the mermaid's kiss. The one given to Shadowolf mystically fused to his sternum and activates whenever submerged in water.

The Amulet of Larna Thorn – a silver, dragon amulet. It consists of a circle, with two dragons rising in the centre and entwining their bodies to the top where they face each other. It is used to summon the Dragon King.

Butterfly Pendant – in shape of butterfly and made of many small gems; it is the discarded horn of Ursula transformed into a pendant for safe keeping.

Heart of Tigers – diamond-shaped ruby-coloured gem the size of a large fist. Created by the ancient elves as the key to the elvin forest; entrusted to the Vale of Tigers as guardians of the Heart.

Creatures

Assassin: a stealthy, efficient mercenary hired to kill a target for a price by any means necessary.

aVampeyer: pale, black-robed creature relatively close to being human, except that it is dead. It sucks on the blood of the living to survive, with razor sharp teeth to pierce the skin of its victims. Has adversity to sunlight. Once part of Le'Mar's army, their allegiance is currently unknown.

Centaur: has the body of a horse, and the abdomen and upper body of a human. The centaur kings have horns attached to their heads as a sign of their superiority.

Creth-Demon: a beast with a wolf head and human body; torso usually uncovered and a loose cloth around waist. It holds a golden sceptre that is used to transform cursed humans into Crethan wolves. Part of Le'Mar's army.

Crethan / -thine: a human cursed by the bite of a Creth-Demon; whenever a Creth-Demon is nearby, they transform against their will into a deformed wolf that does the bidding of the Creth-Demon. Part of Le'Mar's army when summoned by the Demon.

Demon: Hideous, ethereal beast of the underworld with the sole purpose of destroying every good in the world. Has the ability to take many shapes and possess other creatures, thereby giving them supernatural abilities. Part of Le'Mar's army when summoned from the underworld.

Demon-Queen: A mer-queen that rules over a group of sirens, with a dark trident of her own. Has snakes twisting from her hair and four arms attached to her body that ends in a twin mer-tail. Part of Le'Mar's army attacking the Mer-Kindgom.

Dra-hu'Mar: Looks like a human, and has characteristic blond hair and green eyes. Has the ability to transform his bow into a sword and vice versa. Part of Le'Mar's army.

Dragon: Great, reptilian beast with sharp fangs, ferocious talons and enormous wings; has the ability to breathe fire from its lungs and can bond with a single human in extremely unique circumstances, but usually only when a bargain is struck. They reside in Bentley Strip in temples linking to their home worlds.

Dwarf: A short, stocky human with large beard and usually an axe for a weapon. They are masters of dwarven lore and architectural engineering. They reside in Dwarf Mountains and are the guardians of the Vale of Tigers.

Elemental: A human or creature with the ability to summon one or more of the four elements, whether in form or essence. Uses power of the spirit to master the elements.

Elementël: A being composed of one or more of the four elements of nature. Has no allegiance and can be summoned by an Elemental.

Elf: One of the ancient creatures that were on the world when it was created; pointed ears and green-shaded skin, with the elder elves deep green in colour. Adept at any weapon, but specialise in staff and bow. They are masters of the elvin lore and servants of Bontu; they reside in the Far Isles and Eldor's Forest.

Fairdievell: a species of fairy known for their variety of light and colour and mostly for their power. This species resides in the Fairiwell, a haven provided by the elves in tunnels beneath Eldor's Forest.

Firestrom: mountainous fire elementël that hovers off the ground; has four heads upon its fiery body – lion, shark, gorilla and horse. Can separate into four elementëls, with a central core keeping them together.

Fletchling: small, blue creature similar to a fairy but three times the size and with bat-like wings and sharp fangs. Part of Le'Mar's army.

Fretling: human-size version of the Fletchling, but part of an experimentation where aVampeyeric blood has been mutated with theirs. Unfortunately the curse of the sun came with the blood. Part of Le'Mar's army.

Froth Hun: a beast with a skeletal head engulfed in blue flames. Carries a two-handed sword the length of a man and rides a black mare with dark pits for eyes and ghostly torn mane and tail. Part of Le'Mar's army.

Ma-Wreth: large beast, towering twice a man's height with large, oak-like arms that move faster than its weight should permit. These lightning-fast arms are mostly used to break down walls and defences. Part of Le'Mar's army.

Merlani: Of human and mer-conception, usually man and mermaid. Can transform tail to human legs at will.

Merman / -maid: has the body of a human, but its legs are replaced by a scaly tail and lives in rivers, lakes or oceans. Ruled by a mer-king who possesses a three-pronged trident as a weapon of power.

Orc: a foul creature with dark, grey skin and putrid smell. Those whose blood are untainted by any other are referred to as "purorcs". Where a human has been crossed with an orc through the dark lord's cruel experiments they are referred to as "hurorcs".

Pegasus: mythical horse with large wings and special powers for combat. Located in a mythical land called uPendus.

Saint: Servant, sage and fighter of Bontu, the one true God. Uses the powers given to him by Bontu to defend the innocent and defeat evil.

Saneth: also known as Kings of the Knight. It is a leader from a remote planet used to command the troops of Le'Mar when conquering a new world. The four Saneths brought to Celenic Earth were Lister, Ru-Maak, Ma'Kanak and Trimistus.

Siren: a ghostly apparition or being that can take many physical forms and can travel on air, land or sea; known for its tendency to seduce men in order to kill them, and lures them by beauty and song. Often mistaken for a mermaid when in the form of a water-siren and can be killed when in physical form. Ruled by a Demon-Queen with a dark trident.

Undead: the corpses and skeletons of the dead reanimated, usually through possession by demons but can be reanimated without them.

Unicorn: mythical horse with a power sack embedded beneath a single, pointed horn that protrudes from the horse's forehead. Has many powers, including the ability to fly.

Witch: woman with dark powers, using them to thwart their enemies and known for their ability to summon and vanquish the undead and demons.

THE WINDFARER
Book 1 of the epic fantasy series
The Celenic Earth Chronicles

CELENIC EARTH: A WORLD OF MIGHT, MAGIC AND MYSTICAL CREATURES

A shadow lurks over the earth, as foul creatures attack the villages. The leader of hurorcs and purorcs commands them to attack the southern tribes, and is captured. But Mercius, once known as the Windfarer, finally breaks free after years of imprisonment and sets his sight upon the Asbec College of Elements where an ancient power is rumoured to be hidden.

Shadowolf is in his last year of studies at the Asbec College of Elements when word of the escape spreads. Strange things happen and he becomes entwined in a world of mystery and murder, using the power of the elements to survive. And as war erupts, Shadowolf returns home and does everything in his ability to protect the five southern wolf tribes. For his effort he merely frustrates Mercius's plans, but significantly learns that Mercius is subservient to a dark lord; someone more powerful, known as Le'Mar.

Between the protection of his family, the loyalty of the Shadow Clan and the new-found love of his life, can he pull himself away to stop Mercius from reaching the potent power node? For neither the elves nor the dwarves can stop him should he gain the power he seeks. Even the dark lord seems troubled.

The Masaran Phenomenon approaches, and the "Prophecy of the Windfarer" is upon them.

REVIEWS AND PRAISE

"Jooste's imagination has depth of both scale and scope, with parallels between this imaginary world and the real world, characterised by an interesting contrast between the industrialised evil forces and the 'natural' forces of good..."

THE SADGI
Book 3 of the epic fantasy series
The Celenic Earth Chronicles

LE'MAR THE OMNIPOTENT, THE OMNIPRESENT, THE
OMNISCIENT…..

The Battle for Eldor's Forest cost the world not only the elvin forest, but
also every chance they had of standing up against the dark lord. The
Southern Wolf tribes live defenseless in New Avalion, their walls shaken
to the ground and the art of the elements forbidden. The mer-Kingdom
was defeated in *Avalendil*, with no knowledge of where the survivors
reside. And the elves have left for the Far Isles, leaving the ancient forest to
the rule of Le'Mar's new servant, Darcwulf.

And all across the land lies Le'Mar's fog, his ever-present window to all
that is happening on the land. The people of the earth have lived in relative
peace in the two year's since Shadowolf's victory over Sonersaat the
DragonRider, a victory that had almost cost him his life when he
challenged Le'Mar thereafter. With no knowledge of where the hero
escaped to and under the watchful gaze of Le'Mar and Darcwulf, the earth
makes no move to retaliate against the dark lord.

It is to such circumstances that Shadowolf returns with powerful allies at
his side. Determined to take back the world from Le'Mar's clutches, he
begins his quest for four powerful artefacts encrusted with the tomes of
time. Entwined in this quest is his personal mission to find and reclaim
those he loves and lost. Yet, the greatest undertaking he faces is to
convince the world to fight for their freedom. This time, Shadowolf is
taking the war to Le'Mar.

The Masaran Phenomenon approaches again, and the "Prophecy of the
Sadgi" is upon them…

REVIEWS AND PRAISE
"If you are looking for an epic, sweeping expanse fantasy book to read,
then this is it. Congratulations Shaun Jooste for entering the world of print
in the fantasy genre with a tale that will be picked up again and again just
so I can immerse myself into his richly described world that is Celenic
Earth."

SILENT HILL: BETRAYAL

SILENT HILL HAS MORE THAN ONCE CANVAS, PAINTED BY THE
TAINT OF YOUR SINS.
CONSIDER THIS YOUR PERSONAL HELL

Trevor wakes up from another nightmare of Silent Hill just before getting a
call that the police are after him following the apparent suicide of his wife,
Caroline. He barely escapes with his lover Kathy and best friend Jay
Nixon, the police force hot on their tail on the dark highway. During the
pursuit, a mist covers the road and a strange man with a metallic object on
his head causes them to crash on the outskirts of Silent Hill.

When Trevor awakens, he finds himself alone at the scene of the accident
with no knowledge of where the others are. His search for them not only
reveals that the town is haunted with terrifying creatures, but is also
tainted with clues of Caroline's presence. As his struggle through the misty
town leads him closer to Kathy's whereabouts, Trevor learns the truth of
Caroline's death and the link to her brother's murder. And with this
knowledge, he discovers that everyone that had a part to play in her
misery has been brought together to Silent Hill to account for their sins.

In the midst of the pain and the blood stands Caroline's mysterious
guardian with the metallic stained pyramid on his head... and he is ready
to exact justice for their betrayal...

REVIEWS AND PRAISE

"I love this version of Silent Hill, the twists and build up, I almost expect to
see some terrifying creature around every corner. Two words,
HORRIFICALLY STUPENDOUS"